The
Philosopher's
Apprentice

Also by James Morrow

This Is the Way the World Ends
Only Begotten Daughter
Towing Jehovah
Blameless in Abaddon
The Eternal Footman
The Last Witchfinder

The
Philosopher's
Apprentice

James Morrow

Weidenfeld & Nicolson
LONDON

First published in Great Britain in 2007
by Weidenfeld & Nicolson

1 3 5 7 9 10 8 6 4 2

A CIP catalogue record for this book
is available from the British Library

ISBN- 978 0 297 85343 5 (HDBK)
ISBN- 978 0 297 85344 2 (TPB)

Typeset by Input Data Services Ltd, Frome

Printed in Great Britain by Clays Ltd, St Ives plc

Weidenfeld & Nicolson

An imprint of the Orion Publishing Group
Orion House, 5 Upper St Martin's Lane, London WC2H 9EA
An Hachette Livre UK company

To my grandson,
William Alexander Morrow,
this story of generation, procreation,
and talking iguanas

Vain is the word of a philosopher
by whom no suffering is cured.

Epicurus (341–270 BCE)

CONTENTS

PART ONE

The Sisters Sabacthani

CHAPTER 1

This begins with a butterfly. The insect in question, a monarch, was flitting along a strand of morning glories threaded through the fence outside my first-floor apartment window, systematically dipping its proboscis into the powder-blue cones. It was a warm, fecund morning in August, and I was twenty-seven years old. Contemplating the *Danaus plexippus* through a gash in my screen door, I was utterly mesmerised, transfixed by the creature's ethereal antennae and magnificent orange wings limned by black stripes as bold and stark as the leading in a stained-glass window. How numinous it must have appeared to a lesser insect: a cricket's epiphany.

Inevitably Lao-Tsu's famous riddle crossed my mind – 'Am I a man dreaming he is a butterfly, or a butterfly dreaming he is a man?' – and I performed a thought experiment, mentally trading places with the monarch. I don't know whether the butterfly enjoyed being an impoverished philosophy student with a particular interest in ethics, but my lepidopterous condition delighted me. The sun warmed my wings, the nectar sated my hunger, and the perfume gratified my olfactory organs, located in, of all places, my feet.

The telephone rang: a representative from my bank, recommending that I go further into debt. I slammed down the receiver and attempted to reenter my reverie, but it had evaporated. No matter. The butterfly had served its purpose. Thanks to that fragile creature, I'd finally acquired the hook on which to hang my doctoral dissertation. Mason Ambrose, embryonic ethicist, would write about the imperatives entailed in humankind's connection to *Danaus plexippus*, and to insects in general, and to everything else in the world boasting wings, legs, tentacles, talons, tusks, claws, scales, feathers, fins, fur or flesh. With a rush of joy, I realised that this Darwinist stance would appeal neither to secular Marxists, for whom moral lessons lay exclusively within history's brute curriculum, nor to evangelical Christians, for whom a naturalist ethics was a contradiction in terms, nor to middle-class mystics, who detested any argument smacking of biological determinism. A philosophical position that could simultaneously antagonise the collectivist left, the God-besotted right, and the Aquarian fringe must, I decided, have a lot going for it.

'I've even thought of a title,' I told my long-suffering advisor, Tracy Blasko, as we shared a pitcher of sangria in the Pettifog Café that afternoon.

'That's half the battle,' Tracy said. In recent months she'd begun to despair that I would ever find what she called, not unfairly, 'a topic sufficiently pretentious to hold your interest during the writing phase'.

'I want to call it "Towards a Materialist Deontology",' I said.

'Sounds like a goddamn doctoral dissertation,' Tracy replied, unsheathing her wickedest grin. She had a round, melodic face whose softness belied her gristly intellect. When the renowned deconstructionist Benoît Tourneur had visited our campus earlier in that year, Tracy alone had summoned the gumption to dismantle, publicly and definitively, his ingenious apologia for Heidegger's Nazi affiliations. 'Whatever you call it,' she added, looking me in the eye, 'the topic is eminently worth wrestling to the ground.'

'Will the committee agree?' I said, all aglow.

She nodded. 'I'll call in a few favours. Congratulations, Mason. You've cracked the first nut – the fruitcake won't be far behind. Shall we order another pitcher?'

'Love to, but I'm late for a class.' I rose abruptly, kissed her on each cheek, and explained that in prelude to my Darwinian explorations I was auditing Ben Glockman's legendary Biology 412, *Monkey Business: Sexuoeconomic Transactions in African Primate Communities.*

'One more thing,' Tracy said as I started out of the café. 'You should call it "Ethics from the Earth".'

*

4

For the next two years I taught English at Watertown High School by day and wrote 'Ethics from the Earth' by night, labouring to convert my status at Hawthorne University from ABD – which at most schools stood for 'All But Dissertation', though Tracy preferred 'Aristotle Be Damned' – to genuine Doctor of Philosophy, and so it was that raisin by raisin, currant by currant, the fruitcake took form until 382 manuscript pages lay in my hard drive. And then disaster struck.

Tracy Blasko, dear Tracy who was half in love with me and I with her, went to pieces, checking herself into the Boston Psychiatric Center for clinical depression and alcoholism. The task of shepherding me through the final revisions fell to the innocuous Carol Eberling, a glum Hegelian who boasted none of Tracy's acid humour or affection for audacity. But for me the real catastrophe – and I'm afraid this is how graduate students construct these matters – was that the person selected to round out my committee was certain to cause me trouble. The nemesis in question was the celebrated postrationalist theologian Felix Pielmeister, newly arrived from Notre Dame.

There are certain coordinates on this planet, spatial and temporal, where one is well advised to avoid antagonising the locals. The Lower East Side of Manhattan at three o'clock in the morning, for example, or the philosophy department of a major university any day of the week. I never found out how Felix Pielmeister came to visit my website. This scholar, who'd delivered the Gifford Lectures, published eighteen books, and routinely communed with Saint Augustine's shade – why would such a man waste his time picking through the dregs and dross of cyberspace? I suppose he was slumming it one day, ordering his search engine to display all reviews of his newest book, an anti-Darwinist screed called *The Algorithms of Immortality*, and suddenly, *voilà*: the blistering review I'd composed to amuse myself during the gestation of 'Ethics from the Earth'.

It was Dr Eberling who alerted me to Pielmeister's displeasure. 'He's livid, you know,' she said. 'Really, Mason, you ought to send him an apology.'

'I will not eat humble pie,' I replied. 'Nor any other confection that Pielmeister would put on my platter.'

What most infuriated the Augustinian, I suspected, was not my essay's sarcastic tone, savage rhetoric, or unkind cuts. My sin was that I'd caught him in a logical error. Pielmeister's argument reduced to an assertion that the admitted incompleteness of the evolutionary model (paradigm A) meant that divine creationism (paradigm B) must be the case. In other words, he was telling his readers that *not A* equals *B*, a lapse in rationality of a sort normally granted only to incoming freshmen and ageing department heads.

It is a particularly bad idea to make academic enemies when the school in question is Hawthorne. At the turn of the millennium our eccentric president, Gaylord Boynton, since retired, inaugurated a tradition that endures to this day: dissertation defences staged in a large auditorium and open to the general campus community. Boynton believed that such a practice would increase both the quality of the dissertations and the intellectual vigilance of the sponsoring faculty. Did this in fact occur? Hard to say. I know only that the innovation makes the average Hawthorne PhD candidate feel less like he's explicating a thesis in early twenty-first-century Boston than answering a charge of necromancy in late seventeenth-century Salem.

So there I was, striding through the foyer of Schneider Auditorium in prelude to mounting the stage and holding forth on my 'Ethics' while several dozen students and professors stared at me and salivated. Perhaps a heated argument would break out, complete with red faces and projectile epithets. Maybe Dr Pielmeister would ask a question so devastating that the candidate would faint clean away. Conceivably the event would turn physical, the professors assailing each other with half-eaten doughnuts. You never knew.

My abdomen spasmed. My bowels went slack. I gritted my teeth, decorated my face with a grin, and entered the arena.

My passion for philosophy traces to an unlikely source. When I was ten years old, a subversive babysitter allowed me to stay up till midnight watching *The Egyptian* on American Movie Classics. This 1954 Cinemascope spectacle stars stolid Edmund Purdom as Sinuhe, an abandoned infant who rises to become the most famous healer of his generation, physician to the pharaoh Akhenaton. It's not a very good movie, being overlong, ponderous, and badly acted. I love it to this day.

Early in *The Egyptian*, Sinuhe's adoptive father, a master of the trepanner's art, opens up a patient's skull. 'Look, this tiny splinter of bone is pressing on the brain,' the old man tells his son. 'When I remove it, he will speak again, and walk, and live.'

Young Sinuhe asks, 'Why, Father? Why?'

'No one knows.'

Cut to our hero, still a boy, walking beside the ancient world's most philosophical river, meditating on the mystery of it all. 'From the beginning I kept to myself,' Sinuhe tells us in voice-over. 'I used to wander alone on the banks of the Nile, until the day came when I was ready to enter the School of Life.'

Cut to civilisation's would-be elite prostrating themselves before a basalt idol, among them Sinuhe, now a handsome adolescent.

'In the School of Life were trained the chosen young men of Egypt, her future scientists and philosophers, statesmen and generals,' Sinuhe continues. 'All the learning of Egypt lay in the keeping of the gods. For ten years I served them in the school, that I might earn the right to call myself a physician. I learned to bend my body to them, but that was all. My mind still asked a question, "Why?"'

From the moment I saw Edmund Purdom feigning piety in that Egyptian academy, I was hooked. The inquiring and defiant mind thriving within a begrudgingly reverent posture – it all made sense. Bow before Isis and Horus and Thoth, perhaps even believe in them, but give them no sovereignty over your thoughts. That was the way to be in the world. Sign me up. Call me Sinuhe.

At Villanova I took every undergraduate philosophy course I could squeeze into my schedule, and soon I'd set my sights on the doctoral programme at Hawthorne. Late in my senior year I went through a crisis of doubt when my provisional girlfriend, a willowy physics major named Morgan Piziks, informed me at the end of our fourth date that anybody seriously interested in the question 'Why?' should look not to philosophy but to the physical sciences – to cosmology, quantum mechanics, molecular biology, and the periodic table of the elements.

My mind went blank. Try as I might, I could contrive no riposte.

I felt instinctively that Morgan's claim enjoyed the nontrivial virtue of being true. What could I say? What counterblast was possible? By what conceivable stratagem might I send her worldview tumbling down when I couldn't even get her to sleep with me?

A few weeks later I chanced upon a quote from Wittgenstein that renewed my faith in philosophy. 'At the basis of our contemporary picture of the universe lies the illusion that the so-called laws of nature are the explanations of natural phenomena.' Today that assertion strikes me as glib at best, but at the time it saved my sanity. Science could merely describe a phenomenon; it could never tell us the purpose of that phenomenon. The seminal question 'Why?' still sat squarely within philosophy's domain. So I continued to think of myself as the post-Aristotelian Sinuhe, exploring the banks of the Nile, wandering and wondering and idly tossing stones into the water.

A long table, draped in white, and five folding chairs occupied the centre of the Schneider Auditorium stage, as if the audience was about to endure an avant-garde play in which the characters spent two hours sitting down, standing up and doing other minimalist things. Clutching a fresh printout of 'Ethics from the Earth' to my breast, I trod across the boards, assumed my place at the table, and locked my anxious gaze on a plate of frosted doughnuts.

My committee entered from the wings, each member carrying a copy of my dissertation. One by one they shook my hand, beginning with Dr Eberling, who wore the pessimistic countenance of a deer at the outset of the hunting season. Then came Desmond Girard, last of the Medieval Scholastics, stocky, grim, reportedly in possession of a steel-trap mind, though these days he baited it not for bear but for the occasional logical positivist who found his way to Hawthorne. Next to greet me was Joseph Schwendeman, our Nietzschean department chair, radiating his usual air of exultant nihilism. And finally I stood face-to-face with Pielmeister, a hulking, densely bearded figure who looked prepared to defend his views via whatever forum might present itself, from philosophical colloquium to pie-eating contest.

A palpable hush settled over the auditorium as the committee, seated now, passed a carafe of water around and filled their tumblers. Dr Girard asked if I, too, would like some water. I accepted his offer, lest I appear diffident on a day I was expected to exhibit tough-mindedness.

Dr Eberling said, 'Mr Ambrose, please begin by telling us what you feel you've accomplished in "Ethics from the Earth".'

'Be happy to,' I said, cringing to hear such a dumb, folksy locution escape my lips, then launched into my well-rehearsed précis. The fact that humankind now finds itself in a post-Darwinian epistemological condition, I explained, need not trouble us from an ethical perspective. Indeed, by problematising our tendency to view ourselves as creatures apart − God's Chosen Species, discontinuous with the rest of Nature − the evolutionary paradigm obliges us to address the assorted evils, from over-population to climate disruption to the destruction of habitats, that we have visited upon this, our only planet. Through a Darwinian deontology we might at last come to know the true character of our sins, a catalogue of transgressions not against heaven but against the earth and its life forms.

Throughout the auditorium there arose mutterings of approval mingled with bursts of applause, a smattering of jeers, and several sustained moans.

'Mr Ambrose, are you saying that your naturalist ethics supplants the other moral systems surveyed in these pages?' Dr Girard removed his glasses and rubbed his aquiline nose. 'Are you telling us to forget about Platonism, Aristotelianism, Stoicism, Epicureanism, Thomism, Kantianism, and Utilitarianism?'

Although I was prepared in principle for Girard's question, a nugget of dread congealed in my stomach. I took a slow breath, swallowed a mouthful of now tepid water, and assumed a swaggering smile that immediately degenerated into a grimace. For the next ten minutes I spouted convoluted and uniformly incoherent sentences, many turning to vapour before their subjects could enjoy intimacy with their verbs. Phrase by awkward phrase, I endeavoured to explain why the admitted materialism underlying my dissertation was perfectly in step with the parade of ethical discourse that had tramped through human history from the ancient Greeks to the early Christians to the twentieth-century Rawlsians.

The audience grew restless. They'd come for blood, not dialectic. Only in my concluding remarks did I manage to articulate a reasonably feisty thought.

'Rather than eclipsing Kantianism or Utilitarianism,' I said, 'Darwinian deontology adds yet another pigment to the palette of moral philosophy.'

At this juncture Felix Pielmeister slammed his copy of my 'Ethics' on the table – violently, righteously, as if crushing a cockroach. From his throat came a sound somewhere between a wild boar enjoying a good joke and an orgasm.

'As I'm sure you're aware, Mr Ambrose,' Pielmeister said, 'postrationalist thought is not *ipso facto* at odds with the arguments of Charles Darwin. And yet I find that these fulminations of yours carry the reader far beyond the theory of natural selection, depositing him in a place devoid of all hope, meaning, and teleology. Is that in fact your position? Is transcendence an illusion? Is God dead?'

Excited murmurings wafted through the hall. This was why our audience had got up at nine o'clock on a Saturday morning – to watch state-of-the-art Augustinian theology stomp Mason Ambrose into the dirt.

'It depends on what you mean by transcendence,' I said.

'I believe you know what I mean by transcendence,' Pielmeister replied.

'Honestly, sir, I can't unpack your question.'

'Stop temporising, Mason,' Dr Schwendeman said.

I fixed on the uneaten doughnuts. A solitary fly hovered above the pile, wondering what it had done to merit such sugary grace. My dilemma was elegant in its simplicity. I needed merely to assert that evolutionary biology, like the other physical sciences, had nothing to say about God, and I was home free. I had only to insist that I had no fundamental quarrel with either Jesus Christ or Felix Pielmeister, and I could pick up my union card.

With an impertinent flourish I seized the carafe and filled my tumbler to the brim. I sipped. The fluid that entered my mouth, however, was not Hawthorne tap water but some metaphysical beverage drawn from the Nile by Sinuhe himself. It tasted sweet. I savoured the sensation, then took another swallow. Why did I want to be a Doctor of Philosophy anyway? Would I jump through any conceivable hoop to join that dubious fellowship whose attention I had momentarily claimed? What quantity of self-respect was I willing to lose in acquiring this most conventional of prizes?

'I believe I can best answer Dr Pielmeister's question with a few questions of my own,' I said at last. 'They all begin with Sinuhe's favourite word, "why".'

'Sinuhe?' Dr Girard said. 'You mean from *The Egyptian*?'

'Correct,' I said.

'That's not a very good movie,' Dr Girard said.

'The book was better,' Dr Schwendeman said.

'Why,' I asked, 'do our postrationalist theologians, Dr Pielmeister among them, expect us to prostrate ourselves before a deity who, by the Darwinian insight he claims to endorse, stands exposed as a kind of cosmic dilettante—'

'That is not the language of philosophy,' interrupted Pielmeister, wagging his finger.

'—a kind of cosmic dilettante, idly coaxing plants and animals into existence only to have them go extinct through the very environmental conditions he provided for them?'

Delicate but palpable vibrations filled the stuffy air of the Schneider Auditorium. The attendees shifted in their seats, delighted that the gladiator had mysteriously elected to insert his head directly into the lion's mouth. My committee was likewise astir, wondering what sort of demon had possessed this outwardly rational candidate.

'Why,' I continued, 'was Dr Pielmeister's presumably competent God unable to produce the contemporary biosphere through any process other than the systematic creation and equally systematic obliteration of countless species?'

Nervous laughter emerged here and there throughout the audience.

'And why,' I persisted, 'would this same divine serial killer have begun his career spending thirteen billion years fashioning quadrillions of needless galaxies before finally starting on his pet project: singling out a minor planet in an obscure precinct of the Milky Way and seeding it with vain bipedal vertebrates condemned to wait indefinitely for the deity in question to reveal himself?'

'Mason, this isn't going anywhere,' Carol Eberling asserted.

'Right you are,' I said. 'The show is over. I would rather teach front-end alignment at an auto mechanics school in Framingham than continue to cast my lot with higher education. And so, with all humility and a deep appreciation for the effort you've expended in reading my dissertation, I withdraw my candidacy.'

'Mason, no,' Dr Eberling said through gritted teeth.

'That's a terrible idea,' said Dr Girard.

'Most Nietzschean,' said Dr Schwendeman.

'Withdrawal accepted,' said Dr Pielmeister.

'Go back to your offices, good professors,' I concluded. 'Pick up your pay checks. See who's reviewed your latest book in *The Journal of Astonishingly Articulate Academic Discourse*. But from this moment on, Sinuhe is his own man.'

I rose and, stepping towards the footlights, dipped my head in a theatrical bow. The audience members clapped, booed, hissed, and cheered. As I rushed down the aisle and into the foyer, a young man drew abreast of me and asked if I wanted to star in his student film about Sigmund Freud's first sexual encounter. I gave him my email address, then hurried into the street.

Every college campus has its beer hall, its rathskeller, its underground den of inconsequential iniquity, someplace where philosophy majors can huddle in the corners hashing over eros and mortality while the athletes sit at the bar discussing fucking and sudden-death overtime. At Hawthorne this favoured hangout was the Shepherd's Pie, a convivial grotto where, according to rumour, H. P. Lovecraft had composed what is probably his worst piece of fiction, 'Herbert West – Reanimator', though the theory is dubious at best, as that hidebound recluse rarely left Providence.

I skipped dinner and headed straight for the Pie, where I ordered a pitcher of Guinness, then sidled towards my favourite alcove, the very niche in which I'd once got my fellow PhD candidate Matthew Forstchen, a card-carrying pragmatist, to admit the logical flaw in William James's assertion that refusing to believe something is in itself a kind of faith. (Do I have faith that the moon is not made of green cheese? Must I experience a divine revelation before rejecting Ouija boards?) Although my intention was to celebrate my escape from academe, I could not summon the requisite jollity. My position at Watertown High was about to evaporate, and since I wasn't remotely qualified to teach front-end alignment, I would soon be staring privation in the face. Returning to my parents in Philadelphia wasn't an option, as the law of self-preservation required me to distance myself from the slow-motion train wreck of their marriage, nor could I imagine moving in with my sister Gwen, who was barely surviving through a combination of waitressing and off-Broadway acting gigs and didn't need a grumpy unemployed little brother in her life.

I was also enduring the emotional aftermath of my meltdown in Schneider. Holding forth on the stage, I'd imagined I was participating in a venerable heroic tradition – the individual versus the system – but now I simply felt like a screw-up. I vowed to send apologetic emails to Eberling, Schwendeman, Girard, and perhaps even Pielmeister. Tracy Blasko also deserved a letter, a real one, the kind that reposes on paper and arrives in an envelope. I would thank her for tolerating my eccentricities during the past five years, then attempt to explain why I'd jumped ship.

'Mind if I join you?' a sonorous voice inquired.

I looked up. My visitor was an owlish black man in his late forties, with a salt-and-pepper beard and eyes as dark and soft as plums.

'I'm not in a very good mood,' I told him. 'Have a seat.'

We shook hands.

'Dawson Wilcox, Palaeontology Department,' he said. 'Your notoriety precedes you. Mason Ambrose, late of the Philosophy Department, author of a quirky dissertation called "Ethics from the Earth".' On the nearest empty chair he deposited a leather satchel, brown and scuffed and also bulging, as if perhaps it contained a fossil mandible. 'May I buy you a beer?'

I gestured toward my pitcher of stout. 'I'm fixed for the evening. Here's a question for you, Dr Wilcox. Does this pitcher truly hold four beers, or merely hold four potential beers, each awaiting the reification that will occur upon being poured?'

Wilcox gave me a blank look. 'No wonder philosophers can't get funding.'

I filled my glass with stout. An ivory wave of foam frothed over the rim and cascaded on to the table. 'Will you help me get to the bottom of this? The pitcher I mean, not the ontological mystery.'

Wilcox fetched a second glass from the bar, along with a bowl of miniature pretzels. I poured him a beer, grabbed a pretzel, and took a gulp of Guinness.

'I followed you here from Schneider,' my drinking companion said. 'Let me congratulate you on what was perhaps the liveliest dissertation defence in Hawthorne's history.'

'Self-destruction is always entertaining,' I said, munching.

'I'm here to offer you a job.'

'I've never even played with plastic dinosaurs.'

'Oh, no, not in my department, though I appreciate the kind words you put in for Mr Darwin this afternoon.'

'Let me guess. You decided to become a palaeontologist when you fell madly in love with *Tyrannosaurus rex* in fourth grade.'

Wilcox issued a cryptic laugh and downed some Guinness, embroidering his upper lip with a second moustache. 'Ever hear of Isla de Sangre?'

'Blood Island?'

'Ringed by a rare species of red coral,' he replied, nodding. 'The coccyx of the Florida Keys, so far south it nudges the Tropic of Cancer. The owner's a former colleague of mine, Edwina Sabacthani, a molecular geneticist. Eccentric, capricious, smart as God – the sort of person who'll show up on the last day of an academic conference, sniff out whoever's been a particularly pompous boor all week, and start hinting that she noticed a major methodological flaw in his latest published results.'

I drained my glass. The Guinness started doing what it was designed to do. 'Three cheers for academic conferences,' I said. The one time I'd delivered a paper at a conference, 'The Geist in the Machine', a précis of my master's thesis on Schelling, I didn't meet any minds of Edwina Sabacthani's calibre, but I was memorably seduced by a tenured Utilitarian from Princeton named Frédérique Wintrebert, who said she'd become aroused by my use of the word 'praxis'.

'Here's the deal,' Wilcox said. 'Edwina wants me to find a tutor for her teenage daughter. I think you're our man.'

'I'm a neo-Darwinian atheist, Dr Wilcox. The average American mother would rather fill the position with Humbert Humbert.'

'It's not your Darwinism that caught my attention,' Wilcox said. 'What impressed me was your rambling but nonetheless astute overview of Western ethics. I've never met the young woman in question, but apparently she has a handicap. In Edwina's words, Londa Sabacthani "lacks a moral centre". We propose that you give her one.'

I poured myself a second glass. 'Maybe I should print up a business card: "Mason Ambrose. Failed Philosopher. Superegos Installed While You Wait."'

'This is a sad and serious case,' Wilcox said in a mildly reproving tone.

I gulped some stout and picked up a pretzel, orienting it so the parabolas suggested laudable breasts. 'There's a whole science to pretzels. 'Mathematicians can plot the twists and curves. Wittgenstein would not be impressed. Actually, I don't think anything impressed Wittgenstein, with the possible exception of Wittgenstein.'

'The position pays one hundred thousand dollars for the first year. After that, you and Edwina can negotiate.'

I sucked on the pretzel, enjoying the sensation of the salt crystals copulating with my taste buds. One hundred thousand dollars? Pielmeister probably made more than a hundred thousand a year, but certainly not per *student*.

'You have to realise, this is an extremely difficult decision for me. I'm broke. I'm about to lose my job. I just threw away my future. And yet, sir – and yet you have the audacity to imagine I would accept a small fortune for taking an undemanding sinecure in a tropical paradise.'

Wilcox patted his battered satchel. 'I have the paperwork with me.'

'I think I should meet this girl before I sign anything.'

'A sensible precaution, but Edwina and sensible precautions haven't been on speaking terms in years.' Wilcox unzipped his satchel, rooted around, and pulled out a file folder labelled 'Sabacthani'. 'I'm afraid you must either accept the job right now, or send me off in search of another ethicist.'

'One hundred thousand dollars? No fine print?'

15

'None required – the bold print is outrageous enough. Edwina expects you to drop everything, fly to Key West on Friday, and be prepared to give Londa her first lesson at ten o'clock on Monday morning. On my way over here I made your plane reservations, and my graduate assistant will sublet your apartment and forward your mail. Don't worry about your worldly possessions. We'll crate everything up and ship it to you.'

'No moral centre,' I said. 'What could that possibly mean?'

Wilcox shrugged, then set the contract on the table, taking care to avoid the liquid rings stamped by our glasses. 'Your liaison in Key West will be Edwina's colleague, Vincent Charnock, another geneticist. Maybe he can answer your questions.'

I retrieved a ballpoint pen from my jacket and clicked the cartridge into place. 'One hundred thousand?'

'Plus room, board, and travel expenses.' Wilcox ate a pretzel. 'By the way, it was third grade, and it was the ankylosaur ...'

CHAPTER 2

In a characteristic display of procrastination I put off packing till the last minute. As dawn's embryonic light suffused my apartment, I jammed the normal necessities into my suitcase – toothbrush, electric razor, underwear, yellowed Penguin paperbacks – then topped off the jumble with a bound copy of my dissertation. I pulled on my Kierkegaard T-shirt, hurried out the door, and by the grace of Isis, Thoth, and public transportation caught the 8.20 a.m. flight, wafting from staid and predictable Boston to the exotic metropolis of Miami.

I found my way to the airport's ghetto and boarded a shuttle plane, its seats designed to accommodate hobbits but not a six-foot-one beanpole like me. Forty minutes later I touched down in the city of Key West on the island of the same name. As arranged, Edwina Sabacthani's colleague, Vincent Charnock, was waiting at the terminal, clutching a white cardboard rectangle on which he'd carefully misspelled my name with a red felt-tip marker: MASON AMBROWSE. A rotund man with thinning hair and eyes set so far back I wondered if he might be legally blind, Dr Charnock displayed a sardonic smirk that evidently never left his face, while the rest of his countenance suggested a waxen Charles Laughton following a breakdown in the air-conditioning system at Madame Tussaud's.

So long had I lived in the hermetically sealed world of graduate students, where the daily demands of subsistence teaching and posturing for professors make extroverts of us all, that I was not prepared for Dr Charnock's aloof demeanour. As we followed the usual protocols – locating the luggage carousel, retrieving my suitcase, hiring a taxi – my companion remained as taciturn as a tortoise, answering my questions in clipped phrases and uninformative grunts. Did he know my prospective pupil? Yes, he did. Had he ever observed her behave in an antisocial fashion? Yes, he had. Would he like to tell me about those episodes? No, he wouldn't. Was he glad I'd accepted the position as Londa's tutor? He wasn't sure.

Our destination proved to be a dreary marina on Krill Drive, where a silver-moustached Cuban expatriate waited to facilitate the next leg of our journey. The plan called for Captain López to ferry us to the island in his thirty-foot cabin cruiser, which he normally chartered to weekend fishing parties of paunchy CEOs in search of their inner Hemingway. We weighed anchor at one o'clock. The weather was wretched, the sort of chilly fine-grained precipitation that quickly seeps from skin to ligament to bone, so Charnock and I retreated below decks to quarters stinking of kelp and bluefish.

Our passage to the Tropic of Cancer took nearly four hours, during which interval the rain stopped, so that the thickly forested hills of Isla de Sangre presented themselves clearly, dipping and rising like the spine of a sea serpent. We navigated the Bahía de Flores and landed at a ramshackle wooden dock, tying up between a derelict trawler and a battered sailboat. As we disembarked, Charnock deigned to initiate a conversation, explaining that the geography of Blood Island was in a class of its own, 'part Florida swamp, part Mexican rainforest', and that in recent months he and Edwina had 'succeeded in making the local flora and fauna more congruent with our personal tastes'.

'I hope God wasn't offended by the implied criticism,' I said.

Charnock frowned and informed me that he'd arranged for Edwina's staff to prepare a meal and leave it for our consumption. He hoped I liked seafood.

During our long wordless walk through the jungle I pondered the psychic dislocations inherent in the advent of jetliners. Ten hours earlier I'd been packing my suitcase amid the chatter of the neighbourhood children skipping off to school, and now here I was in the tropics, swatting mosquitoes, sweating profusely, and contemplating hundreds of spotted green lizards as they skittered along the tree trunks. I felt not so much like a traveller as a man on whom an operation called travel had been performed. What would modernity bring next? Might a day soon arrive when I would go to bed as Mason Ambrose and, courtesy of some brave new technology, wake up as someone else?

A half-hour's hike brought us within sight of Charnock's house, a weathered A-frame adjacent to the complex of Quonset huts in which he conducted his experiments. 'Five years ago, I was just another molecular geneticist, collaborating with fools and grovelling for funds,' he told me. 'Whatever impression Dr Sabacthani makes on you tomorrow, remember that she's a person of vision. She's not afraid to ask the big questions, or to have me try to answer them. Why only four bases in a DNA molecule? Why only twenty amino acids in our proteins? What might the world look like if nature had used a larger set of building blocks? Ever wonder about that, Ambrose?'

'Guess I'm not a person of vision.'

Although its isosceles façade suggested a cramped interior, the A-frame proved spacious, complete with a screened back porch bisected by a hammock – the guest room, Charnock explained. The windows held not glass but mosquito netting, and as the gauzy fabric filtered the setting sun, I briefly fancied myself a moth trapped inside a Chinese lantern. As promised, dinner was waiting inside for us. The servants were nowhere to be seen, which made me feel a bit like Goldilocks about to partake of her illicit porridge, through my unease soon vanished through the agency of a warm Dos Equis.

Resting on a bed of saffron rice and surrounded by slices of fried mango, the two indigenous spiny lobsters looked delectable, but their anatomy disturbed me. This species had never evolved the fighting claws that characterise its northern cousin, and yet our entrées boasted pincers as large as tin snips. Noting my perplexed expression, Charnock said, 'After nine hundred trials I managed to endow a Caribbean spiny lobster with a Maine lobster's claws.'

'Impressive,' I said.

'Thank you.'

I smiled and said, 'Of course, I'd be more impressed if you'd taken an ordinary Caribbean starfish and turned it into a Jewish one.'

'Jewish?'

'With six points.'

'Biology is not a joke, Mr Ambrose.'

We finished our dinner in silence, leaving behind two vacant lobster shells and seven empty beer bottles. Outside the house a thousand insects sang and sawed in wondrous harmony. Wrapped in the beer's muzzy embrace, I shuffled to the porch and climbed into the hammock. For the next hour I read my paperback of Walker Percy's *The Message in the Bottle*, wondering whether Londa Sabacthani might be suffering from what Percy called 'the loss of the creature', the alienation that modern man has inflicted on himself by ceding the world's most valuable things – its natural wonders, artistic marvels, erotic energies, and common sense – to dubious cults of expertise. I extinguished the Coleman lantern and closed my eyes. Half awake and half asleep, I entertained many strange fancies, eventually imagining that Charnock had experimented on me. In this reverie my hands had become leopard paws, my nose was a boar's snout, and my gums had sprouted two-inch fangs. When I went to the bathroom later that night to void the residual beer, I made a point of looking in the mirror.

Beyond his wizardry with DNA, Charnock was evidently a competent cook, for I awoke to find him preparing two complex omelettes stuffed with cheese, peppers, onions, and morsels of shrimp. The meal passed without conversation. It was not yet eight o'clock and already I was sweating. I drank two glasses of ice water. Fragrances drifted in from the jungle: sweet gardenias, dulcet hibiscus, silken magnolias. The previous night's insect musicians had returned to their burrows, and the island now belonged to the birds, filling the air with territorial caws and arpeggios.

Shortly after breakfast a Jeep pulled up outside Charnock's A-frame, driven by a raffish safari-jacketed Latino with a drooping black moustache and olive skin, a pith helmet crowning his head. He introduced himself as Javier Cotrino, Dr Sabacthani's personal assistant, despatched to chauffeur me to her mansion. For the next twenty minutes, Javier and I lurched and bounced along an unpaved road, descending into a valley flush with rhododendrons and bougainvillea, until at last we came to a high chain-link fence surmounted by spirals of barbed wire. We drove beneath a raised crossing gate, then continued past acacia groves and cypress stands towards the rising sun.

The mansion in question – Faustino, Javier called it – was straight out of the antebellum American South, complete with square columns and great tufts of Spanish moss drooping from the roof. As we climbed the steps to the veranda, Javier warned me that Dr Sabacthani had slept badly the previous night, and I must not take her exhaustion for haughtiness. We passed through the front door, its central panel carved with a bas-relief Aztec god who took pride in being unappeasable, then proceeded to a geodesic dome where hurricane-proof glass triangles served to shield a private jungle from the ravages of Gulf storms. Ferns, vines, and orchids flourished everywhere. Fumes compounded of humus and nectar filled my nostrils. At the centre of all this Darwinian commotion the naked roots of an immense mangrove tree emerged from a saltwater pond. Beneath the tree, dressed in a white lace gown and reading an issue of the *American Journal of Human Genetics*, a woman of perhaps forty sat in a wicker chair, its fan-shaped back spreading behind her like Botticelli's shell giving birth to Venus.

'Every Saturday morning,' Javier told me, 'you'll find two beautiful and fascinating creatures in our conservatory – my friend Dr Sabacthani, and this queen of the trees, Proserpine.'

'The mangrove has a name?' I asked.

'A Christian name only,' the woman replied in a sandpaper voice. Her face was a disconcerting conjunction of high-cheeked beauty and humourless ambition, as if Katharine Hepburn in her prime had been cast as Catherine de Medici. 'The experiment was not sufficiently successful for me to admit Proserpine to the Sabacthani family.' She flipped a pair of gold-framed polarised lenses into place over her glasses, then set her book atop a wheeled cart holding a coffee urn, its shiny convex surface elongating Proserpine's reflection. 'Forgive me for not rising to greet you, Mason, but I've not been well lately, and etiquette would only aggravate my condition. Call me Edwina. May I offer you some coffee?'

'The food of philosophers,' I said, though a better case could be made for beer.

Javier gestured me into a second fanback chair and, approaching the urn, released an ebony stream into a mug bearing the Odradek Pharmaceuticals logo. He passed me my coffee, filled a second Odradek mug for Edwina, and made an inconspicuous exit.

'Tell me, Mason, is sin something that Anglo-American philosophers worry about these days' – Edwina rested a bony hand on the mangrove's nearest root – 'or do you leave that to your Continental colleagues?'

'Sin?'

'No sooner had Dr Charnock and I given Proserpine a rudimentary brain than it became clear that we had sinned.'

'A brain?'

'It's gone now, most of it. Her first words—'

'Words?'

'We also gave her a tongue, a larynx, primitive lungs, and a crude circulatory system. Her first words were: "Put me out of my misery." Not what we expected to hear. What do you suppose she meant?'

'Are you testing me?'

Edwina smiled.

'Perhaps you'd created some kind of basket case.' I sipped my beverage. It had a heady chocolate flavour, as if Charnock had induced a coffee bush to have sex with a cacao plant. 'A being with an inherent desire to move its body through space but lacking the means to do so.'

'Good,' Edwina said, acclaiming my answer with a clap of her hands. 'Dawson did not overestimate you. I told Dr Charnock we had no choice but to amputate Proserpine's consciousness. Mercy demanded it. He said such an operation would amount to physician-assisted suicide, a practice he has always found repellent, so I took up a scalpel and performed the procedure myself. There's a lesson in all this, a parable for the neural-network community as they go about imposing self-awareness on their computers. To

pour a free-floating intellect into a machine is to risk making ...
you know.'

'A tormented Dr Johnson,' I mused, 'eternally eager to kick a
stone and thus give Berkeley's idealism the boot. But he can find
no stone in his universe, nor a leg with which to kick it.'

'Well said.'

Just then a mild tremor passed through the mangrove's limbs
and roots. Edwina and I exchanged glances.

'You didn't imagine that,' she said. 'I couldn't excise the entire
nervous system without causing death. And so, several times a
day, Proserpine shudders.'

Curious, I rose and picked my away across the saltwater pond,
one stepping stone at a time, then leaned towards the mangrove's
trunk. I froze. A chuffing reached my ears, low and coarse, like
the sound of a passing steamboat. Counterpointing Proserpine's
breaths was a second cadence: the thump of the sap pulsing
through her xylem.

'She's breathing,' I said. 'Her heart is beating.'

'Vestigial reflexes,' Edwina said. 'She's no longer sentient, I
promise you.'

For a moment I considered reneging on my contract and going
back to Boston. Yes, I needed the money, but did I really want to
spend a year among people who routinely fashioned mutant
lobsters and breathing trees and God knew what other sorts of
biological surrealism?

'"No growth of moor or coppice,"' Edwina quoted as I returned
to my seat, '"No heather-flower or vine / But bloomless buds of
poppies / Green grapes of Proserpine."' She extended her arm and
plucked one of the mangrove's many fruits, a small green sphere.
'The world has never met with my approval.'

'You're an idealist,' I said.

'Or a cynic.'

'The same thing.'

It was a glib answer, and we both knew it. Although her
polarised lenses mitigated Edwina's scowl, I still felt its impact.

'In any event,' she said, 'from the moment of my daughter's
birth I contrived to give her a sheltered existence, educating her
entirely at home. Her father would not have assented, but he died

before she was born: pancreatic cancer, a banal end for a remarkable man.' She took my hand and pressed the strange fruit into my palm. 'Javier calls them "rococonuts". Charnock prefers the term "mummy kumquats" – "mumquats" – for they can make the consumer imagine he's immortal. Be careful where you eat your mumquat, Mason.'

'Thanks for the warning,' I said, nesting the fruit in my shirt pocket.

Edwina raised her hand in a half-hearted attempt to conceal a yawn. 'By the age of six Londa was an expert swimmer. On the morning of her seventeenth birthday, however, she dived into a lagoon and struck her head on a rock. Javier fished her out before she could drown. The blow didn't kill her, but the resultant memory loss remains one of the severest in the annals of amnesia.' She swallowed some coffee. 'Gradually it became clear that Londa's childhood recollections weren't the only casualty – she'd also lost her ability to distinguish right from wrong. Depravity is not a diagnosis one makes lightly, but the evidence seems unequivocal.'

For the next fifteen minutes Edwina expounded upon the sorry condition of Londa's conscience. In recent weeks the feral adolescent had set fire to the rug in the east parlour, stolen cash from Javier's wallet, smashed the chinaware on the dining-room floor, thrown rocks through the windows of Dr Charnock's lab, eaten mumquats against her mother's orders – the list went on and on.

'In undertaking Londa's cure, you have one great asset,' Edwina said. 'She has retained her ability to pick up any book and absorb its contents at an astonishing speed, a genetic endowment from her maternal grandfather. By devouring most of the Faustino library, she has succeeded in reorienting herself to Western civilisation and its cultural norms. As for reality per se, she prefers to account for it in reference to the capricious Yahweh of pre-rabbinical Judaism. Not the deity I'd have picked for her, but probably better than no deity at all, given her present stage of development.'

A disturbing image flitted through my imagination. I was in Sinuhe's surgical theatre, Londa lying before me on an operating table. I had scrolled her scalp away from her skull, sawed off her cranium, and exposed her brain to daylight. Now all that remained was for me to take up my knife and inscribe the Ten Commandments on to her cerebral cortex.

'I'll be honest, Edwina. I'm hesitant to intervene so radically in another person's psyche.'

'Oh, but Londa wants you to intervene.'

Just then Proserpine, for no apparent reason, began to quaver, her exposed roots vibrating like the strings of an immense lyre.

'You're certain the tree has no awareness?' I asked, brushing the nearest branch.

'A complete void,' Edwina said. 'No qualia whatsoever. If I thought she was still suffering, I would uproot her immediately, much as I would miss her fruit and companionship. My daughter wants you to intervene, Mason. More than you can possibly imagine.'

Javier reappeared, now dressed in a blue silk kimono. Taking Edwina's hand, he guided her free of the chair and for an instant the two of them seemed to be dancing. I wondered whether Javier's duties might include appeasing Edwina's libido, though I doubted he would relish these carnal obligations, not if she were as quixotic in bed as she was in conversation.

The three of us followed the labyrinth of shrubs and bushes to a frosted-glass door that Javier slid back to reveal a courtyard tiled with ceramic hexagons and girded on all sides by great ropey masses of jungle. A fishpond lay at the centre of the patio, complete with a school of golden carp flashing through the shallow water like pennies sparkling in a fountain. Edwina led me to a round table swathed in white linen and arrayed with porcelain bowls from which rose fragrant twists of steam. Sliding into the nearest chair, I saw that we'd be lunching on calamari stew, and I wondered whether, before turning them over to the Faustino kitchen, Charnock had given the little squids fins or wings or some other capricious enhancement.

'The Chardonnay or the Merlot?' Javier asked Edwina as she assumed her chair.

'Our guest will decide,' she replied, presenting me with a blank stare. 'Though personally I believe it's barbaric to consume red wine with seafood.'

'The Chardonnay is fine,' I said, inhaling the perfume of the rhododendrons.

'Londa will have the usual,' Edwina told Javier.

As Javier passed through the patio doorway, a ginger cat with a flat churlish face escaped from the conservatory, scurried across the tiles, and leaped into Edwina's lap.

'In making your diagnosis,' she said, gesturing towards a path through the jungle, 'you must not hesitate to risk her annoyance. If we spare her feelings, she'll never get well.'

Branches rustled, vines swayed, a macaw took flight, and the jungle disgorged a young woman of commanding height and abundant auburn hair, flipping through a volume of the *Encyclopaedia Britannica* as if hunting up a favourite recipe in a cookbook. Was she in fact reading the thing so quickly? Comprehending it? She did not so much enter the patio as alight upon it, such was the fluidity of her tread. Bronzed by the tropical sun, her arms extended from a white cotton blouse, her legs from khaki shorts. Her cheek and jaw muscles seemed atrophied, giving her a vacuous, uninhabited expression, but her eyes were as large and green as mumquats, and her lips had matured into an appealing pout. To cure this young woman's malaise, I realised, would be to awaken a face of great beauty.

Edwina grasped her daughter's free hand, pressing it between her palms. 'Darling, meet Mason Ambrose. He has flown over a thousand miles to help us with our difficulties.'

'Hello, Londa,' I said.

She set her encyclopaedia on the table and, extending her arm, gave me a surprisingly vital handshake. 'I am pleased to meet you, Mr Ambrose,' she said. Her voice had a hollow, ethereal timbre, as if she were speaking from the bottom of a well.

The instant Londa slid into her chair, Javier reappeared pushing a tea trolley on which rested the Chardonnay and a carafe containing a mysterious brown fluid. He filled Edwina's goblet and my own with wine while Londa received the unknown offering.

'Iced tea?' I asked.

'Coca-Cola,' Londa said. 'At one time its promoters favoured the slogan, "Coke is it", an assertion I find ontologically incoherent. Will there be pecan pie for dessert, Mother?'

'Naturally.' Edwina brushed Londa's forearm. 'Some people would say that by indulging my daughter I inflate her ego, but here at Faustino we have little use for received wisdom.'

We proceeded to eat our stew, the silence growing increasingly conspicuous. I doubt that Edwina consumed more than four mouthfuls, though the wine occasioned no such prudence, and she eagerly drank three full glasses.

'The *Kama Sutra* catalogues seventy arts of graciousness,' Londa said abruptly, staring at her half-empty bowl. 'In 1859 the French daredevil Charles Blondin crossed Niagara Falls on a tightrope. The phylum *Schizophyta* comprises two thousand species of bacteria. Cyrus the Great, Persia's brilliant warrior and statesman, conquered Babylon in 500 BC.'

'That's very interesting,' I said.

'According to Sumerian mythology, the universe was fashioned out of the primeval sea and divided into heaven and earth by Enlil, god of air and storms. All igneous rocks begin as magma. In 1972 the American swimmer Mark Spitz won seven gold medals at the summer Olympics in Munich. The carrion-eating caracara bird has sharp hooks on its beak for tearing open animal hide.'

Feeling suffocated by this congestion of facts, I decided to begin my evaluation, using the closest thing Western philosophy has to a sacred text, Plato's *Republic*. In Book One, Cephalus defines 'justice' as speaking the truth and paying one's debts. Socrates refutes this notion by suggesting it would be wrong to repay certain debts – for example, to return a borrowed axe to its mentally imbalanced owner.

I lifted a morsel of calamari to my mouth, chewed the rubbery tissue, and said, 'Londa, may I ask you a question? I would like you to imagine that a woman named Alice has borrowed an axe from her friend Jerome so she can chop a dead limb off her beech tree. When Jerome comes to reclaim his axe, he's obviously very agitated—'

'You mean he's like me?'

'Like you?'

'Insane.'

'We're not insane,' Edwina said.

'Alice becomes afraid that Jerome may use the axe to kill

someone,' I said. 'So here's my question. Should Alice give it back?'

Londa closed her eyes. 'In 1088 the Patzinak Turks settled between the Danube and the Balkans. The talking drum of Nigeria's Yoruba people has strings that, when squeezed, can produce notes ranging over an octave or more.'

'Please try to cooperate, dear,' Edwina said.

'The question has no answer,' Londa snapped.

'Many philosophers would say that the question has a very good answer,' I countered.

'It doesn't,' Londa insisted. 'Dilemma, noun, a situation in which a person must choose between two undesirable alternatives.'

I glanced towards the nearest hibiscus. A swarm of butterflies was moving among the blossoms with rapid stitching motions. I fixed on Londa and said, 'May I ask you a second question?'

'Another fucking dilemma?'

Edwina winced. 'Londa, darling, we do not say "fucking" at lunch.'

Having failed to get anywhere with Socrates' axe, I decided to try Lawrence Kohlberg's variation on Jean Valjean stealing the loaf of bread.

'Once upon a time in Europe,' I said, 'a man was near death due to bone cancer. The doctors thought a particular drug might save him, a radium extract that Fritz, the local pharmacist, had recently discovered. Although Fritz paid only one hundred Deutsch-marks for each specimen of raw radium – enough to prepare one ampoule for hypodermic injection – he priced the dose at a thousand marks. The sick man's wife, Helga, went to everyone she knew to borrow the money, but in the end she could scrape together only four hundred Marks. Desperate now, Helga begged Fritz to either lower his price or let her pay the remaining six hundred marks in instalments. But the pharmacist said, "No, I discovered the extract, and I'm going to profit from it." That very night, Helga broke into Fritz's store and stole an ampoule of the drug. Now, Londa, here's the problem. Did Helga do the right thing?'

Her eyes narrowed to a squint. 'Why would you ask me a question like that?'

'It's just a game,' I said.

'It's a stupid game! You're trying to trick me! You're trying to make me even crazier than I am!'

Edwina said, 'Sweetheart, we're not being fair to our teacher.'

A howl erupted from deep within Londa's coltish frame, and the next thing I knew she'd tilted her bowl ninety degrees, sending the remainder of her stew slopping across the table. She bolted from her chair and, kneeling beside the fishpond, dipped the empty bowl into the water like a ladle. In a matter of seconds she'd made a helpless carp her prisoner.

'Londa, no!' Edwina screamed, startling her misanthropic cat, who bailed out and disappeared down the jungle path. 'The fish did nothing to deserve that!'

'Titanium is the ninth most abundant element!' Londa wailed. 'In 1962 Francis Crick, Maurice Wilkins, and James Watson received the Nobel Prize in Physiology!'

Still on her knees, she upended the bowl, dumping both the captive fish and its liquid habitat on to the patio. Somehow the creature flipped from its left side to its abdomen, dorsal fin up. Inspired by its success, the carp next attempted to navigate the tiles in a pathetic mockery of swimming. It got nowhere, mired by friction and the malign indifference of the carp gods.

'The rules of the ancient Chinese game of Liu Po have been lost to history! The bubonic plague of the 1340s killed nearly one-third of Europe's population!'

'Put the fish back!' Edwina shouted.

I leaped from my chair, seized the valiant carp, and heaved it into the pond.

'In 1900 the Cake Walk became the most fashionable dance in the United States!'

Crouching beside Londa, I set my fingertips beneath her chin and lifted her head until our gazes met. Her nostrils quivered. Her lips grew taut. Her eyes looked as hard and dry as ball bearings. Never had I seen such anguish in another human face, and so it was that as the warblers sang merrily and the tanagers trilled with joy, I vowed to Isis and Horus and most especially to myself that somehow, some way, I would teach my sad and sorry pupil how to weep.

After Londa took leave of us, loping into the jungle with the fretful gait of a gazelle who'd lingered too long at the lions' watering hole, Edwina rose and approached the pond. She stared into its depths, counting the local population.

'Apparently this was her first carp attack,' she said. 'Give me your verdict, Mason. As a professional ethicist, would you say Londa is a full-blown sociopath?'

'I don't know,' I said. 'I'm not a professional ethicist. In my opinion, nobody is.'

'Cruelty to animals is a strong predictor of future criminality,' Edwina said. 'Most serial killers started out torturing their pets.'

We drank a final glass of wine, then talked about my contract. Once it was clear that I understood the terms – beginning on Monday, I would tutor Londa every weekday morning over the next ten months, two hours per session – the conversation turned to my living accommodation. Although Dr Charnock would be happy to offer me his hospitality, Edwina explained, I would instead occupy a cottage on the very lagoon where Londa had fractured her skull. I was about to contradict this assessment, noting that Charnock did not seem like a person who cherished guests – I doubted he felt comfortable hosting himself, much less intruders from the mainland – when Javier returned waving a cashier's check for twenty-five thousand dollars and explained that I could expect an identical payment every three months. I decided that I would order myself a laptop and also start sending regular grants from the Ambrose Arts Foundation to my sister Delia in New York, so she could spend more time attending auditions and less time waiting tables.

As dusk came to Isla de Sangre, Javier dropped me off at Charnock's A-frame. The biologist was nowhere to be seen. Perhaps he was in his laboratory, concocting our Jewish starfish. Beguiled by the sound of the surf, I pulled off my shoes and socks and walked down to the beach. The tide was going out. Again and again the sea threw itself upon the shore and glided away, losing ground with each cycle, a liquid Sisyphus.

'"Pale beds of blowing rushes,"' I muttered, '"Where no leaf blooms or blushes / Save this whereout she crushes / For dead men deadly wine."'

I took the mumquat from my shirt pocket, then knelt beside a rockpool and washed the skin clean. Rising, I popped the fruit into my mouth. The flesh fell away from the pit and melted into a thick sweet syrup that rolled across my tongue and caressed my gullet with its viscous warmth. I wrapped my tongue around the stippled stone and spat it out.

Barefoot, I waded into the surf, and as the mumquat took charge of my mind, I looked up and saw that Orion and Canis Major had left their dark niches and were now romping together across the sky. As the hunter and his dog gambolled through the celestial meadow, my monarch butterfly fluttered into view, and behind this regal creature flew ten thousand more, their wings beating so vigorously I could feel the wind against my cheeks. Soon every heavenly body above Isla de Sangre had transmuted into a radiant insect, flitting and floating, pollinating the night with countless new stars, and for the moment I was master of them all, an omnipotent being, a god who answered only to himself.

CHAPTER 3

Plato had his Republic, Francis Bacon his New Atlantis, Candide his El Dorado, and I had my private cottage in the jungle, an easy walk from Edwina's estate. Among the amenities of this pocket Utopia, two delighted me in particular: a sturdy wooden deck overlooking the algae-coated expanse of Laguna Zafira, and a home-entertainment centre complete with a CD collection featuring the sorts of orchestral music that would incline even the most stringent interstellar cultural commission to rank Earth a civilised planet. On the night before I was scheduled to give my pupil her first lesson, I settled into the chaise longue, uncapped a beer, and made ready to let Ralph Vaughan Williams liberate me from the prison of my skin.

Although 'Sinfonia Antarctica' sounded as sublime as ever, its pleasures were insufficient to keep me from brooding. Who was this lost young woman whose broken moral compass I was expected to repair? Would I need to teach Londa Sabacthani every ethical principle since 'Don't eat of the tree', or merely help her recover certain previously assimilated rules that the amnesia had obscured? How might I follow in the footsteps of Sinuhe's father, finding and extracting the secret splinter that had paralysed her conscience?

'Sinfonia Antarctica' yielded to 'The Lark Ascending', a composition through which Williams, during my worst bout of junior-year depression at Villanova, had single-handedly persuaded me that the world was not in fact a festering cesspool of such primordial meaninglessness that even suicide would seem like a gesture of assent. I drank one beer per movement, falling asleep in my chair.

Shortly before dawn, I awoke to find my bladder distended and, less predictably, my mind ablaze with a bright idea. What Londa needed, I decided, was to participate directly and viscerally in the sorts of ethical dilemmas devised by Plato and Kohlberg. Instead of simply pondering morality with her intellect, she must perform morality with her hands and feet and larynx. To wit, I would turn the Riddle of the Borrowed Axe and the Fable of the Stolen Radium into drama improvisations, placing my student at the centre of both crises.

Somewhere in the void, the spirit of John Dewey, America's greatest philosopher and a tireless champion of learning by doing, looked down on Laguna Zafira and smiled.

Later that morning I jogged to the manor, flying past a dozen languid iguanas sunning themselves along the forest trail. As I mounted the steps to the veranda, Edwina came gliding towards me, her chronically disaffected cat curled around her neck like a yoke. The beast hissed at me. I hissed back. Edwina explained that her daughter's rehabilitation would occur amidst the estate's vast book collection, then guided me down the hall, through a set of French doors and into the library. Scanning my new classroom, I felt a surge of optimism: the ranks of handsome hardbacks, the globe as big as a wrecking ball, the pair of corpulent armchairs by the hearth – it all seemed conducive to moral discourse of the highest order.

The one anomalous feature was a department-store dummy, its tawny plastic flesh dressed in the incised breastplate, morion helmet, and leather hip boots of a Spanish conquistador. Armed with sword and musket, this vigilant agent of the Inquisition stood guard beside the philosophy section, as if charged with making sure nobody checked out a work by David Hume, Baruch Spinoza, Bertrand Russell, or any other heretic.

'We call him Alonso,' Edwina said. 'He came with the mansion. Javier likes to make up stories about him. Apparently it was Alonso who convinced Ponce de León to quit the governorship of Puerto Rico and seek the fabled island of Bimini and its legendary Fountain of Youth. In 1514 Ponce and Alonso discovered a great land mass, which they called *Pascua Florida*, Flowery Easter, because it was Easter Sunday.'

Before Edwina could continue her breezy narrative, Londa floated into the room wearing white shorts and a red polo shirt. Her mother and I wished her good morning. Ignoring us, she approached the hearth and flopped into an armchair.

'Ponce and Alonso then embarked on a series of exploits,' Edwina said, 'conquering the Florida Indians, quelling Taíno rebellions back in Puerto Rico, and making pathetic attempts to circumnavigate their newfound island, not realising it was a peninsula.' She drew me to her side and continued in a whisper. 'I would say you've succeeded with Londa when she can see the irony in a gang of adventurers seeking eternal youth while leaving corpses wherever they go.'

Edwina slipped out of the room, closing the French doors behind her. I settled into the vacant armchair and faced the dormant fireplace – a peculiar installation here in the tropics, as incongruous as a pinball machine in a funeral parlour.

'Mother doesn't know jack shit about Ponce de León,' Londa said abruptly. 'He discovered Florida in 1513, not 1514.'

'I'm sure you're right,' I said.

'It's in the fucking *Encyclopaedia Britannica*. And he never massacred the Indians. They kicked his Castilian ass.'

'I'm sure they did. Ready for your lesson?'

'No.'

'This morning we're going to try something called a theatre game. You and I will play roles, like the actors and actresses you see on television.'

'Mother doesn't like me to watch television, but I do it anyway. The comedians make me laugh. So do the soap operas and the tornados and the children who've fallen down mine shafts.'

'Do you remember the story of Alice and Jerome and the borrowed axe?'

Londa tugged absently at her auburn hair. 'How could I forget?'

'I'll take the part of Jerome,' I told her, 'and you'll be Alice.'

'Alice Walker is best known for *The Colour Purple*, published in 1982. Mother tells me you're from Boston.'

'Correct. Shall we start the game?'

34

'Boston is the capital of Massachusetts.' From her skirt pocket she retrieved a matchbook and a blue pack of Dunhill cigarettes. 'During the Boston Tea Party, the colonists dumped three hundred and forty-two crates of cargo into the harbour.'

'Londa, are you listening?'

'Our planet has a solid inner core, a molten outer core, a warm rocky mantle, and a thin cool crust. On 17 December 1903, the Wright Brothers made four flights in their propeller-driven glider.'

'Londa, I need your attention.'

With a flick of her wrist she prompted a single cigarette to emerge from the pack. 'The filter tip goes in my mouth.' She wrapped her lips around the cigarette and slid it free. 'The other end receives the match. I'm seventeen years old, and I have many skills. I can bake a cake, unclog a drain, and build a castle out of sand.'

'Does your mother let you smoke?'

'Yeah, but she's not too fucking wild about it.' She struck a match, lit her Dunhill, and launched into a deft impersonation of Edwina. '"Sweetheart, we know that tobacco is bad for our health."' She removed the cigarette and coughed. 'I'm afraid Mother's opinions don't carry a whole lot of weight in my book. Neither do yours, as a matter of fact.'

I stared at a fire poker, standing in its rack like an arrow in a quiver. During a post-war meeting of the Moral Science Club at King's College, Wittgenstein had reportedly brandished such an implement in Karl Popper's face when the latter refused to admit there were no genuine philosophical problems, only linguistic puzzles. My urge to threaten Londa in a similar manner just then was not negligible.

'You're suffering from a serious dysfunction,' I told her. 'It behoves you to cooperate.'

'I'm well aware of my serious dysfunction. Know something else, Socrates? I'm just as fucking moral as you. Rule one, thou shalt have no other fucking gods before me. Rule seven, thou shalt not commit fucking adultery. I can recite all ten. Can you?'

'Your mother tells me you set fire to a rug. You've thrown rocks through Dr Charnock's windows. That doesn't sound like moral behaviour to me.'

'Me neither.'

'On Saturday you almost killed a fish for no reason.'

'If you're worried I might break your windows, I promise I won't.' She parked the cigarette in her mouth and stretched out her arm, poking the flesh with her thumb. 'It's so strange being wrapped in this stuff.' The cigarette bobbed up and down as she spoke. 'Epidermis, dermis, fascia. I'm always leaking. Blood, sweat, saliva, mucus.'

'But never tears.'

Our eyes met. Her irises were two different shades of green. She seemed about to waft out yet another datum but instead offered a faltering smile and a snort of begrudging assent.

I climbed free of the armchair and, taking Londa's hand, led her to a mahogany reading table, where I seized a convenient duster, a bouquet of white feathers sprouting from the handle. 'Let's imagine this is the axe.' I waved the duster in Londa's face. 'Good morning, Alice,' I began in a smarmy voice. 'How lovely to see you today.'

Five seconds elapsed. Ten. Fifteen. Londa took a long drag on her cigarette, then flicked the ember into an inverted crab shell.

'Say something, Londa.'

'The age of once-living matter can be determined by measuring its radioactive carbon-14.'

'Say something Alice would say. You're Alice, remember?'

'In 1959 Los Angeles defeated Chicago to win the World Series.'

'Londa, say the following: "Good morning, Jerome. Thank you for bringing me your axe."'

'You're not Jerome,' she noted, blowing smoke through her nostrils. 'You're Mason Ambrose. A Mason jar has a wide mouth and an airtight screw top.'

'"Good morning, Jerome." Say it, Londa.'

'The Freemasons are known for their charitable work and secret rites.'

'Say it.'

'Why the fuck should I?'

'Because I'm the teacher, and you're the pupil. "Good morning, Jerome."'

Londa closed her eyes. She grunted and gritted her teeth. 'Good morning, *Jerome*.' She sounded like a microchip. 'Thank you for bringing me your axe. This is bullshit, Mason.'

'Happy to oblige, Alice. I sharpened the blade this morning – but I forget why you want to borrow it.'

'I forget too.'

'Perhaps you intend to remove a dead limb from a beech tree?'

'A beech tree, sure, whatever you say, except this is the fucking tropics, and there aren't any fucking beech trees.'

'How sad. There are plenty of beech trees back in Boston.'

'Boston cream pie has chocolate icing on top and a custard filling between the layers.'

'True enough, but you're wrong about the Boston Tea Party. Three hundred and forty-*one* crates went into the water, not three hundred and forty-two.'

'No, three hundred and forty-two.'

'Sorry. Not true.'

Londa cringed and sucked in a deep breath. 'The *Encyclopaedia Britannica* says so.'

'An ancestor of mine was there, Londa. He counted the crates. The encyclopaedia is in error.'

Her body contracted as if she were a passenger on a plummeting elevator. 'You're lying!'

'Books are often in error.'

'Like holy fuck they are!'

'Three hundred and forty-one,' I insisted.

'Forty-two!'

'Forty-one!'

Londa drifted towards Alonso and, tugging on his boot cuff, dropped her cigarette butt into the cavity. I dogged her steps, the duster tucked under my arm. She sprawled across a russet leather couch, rolled on to her back, and pulled her hair over her face like a veil.

'Was this a favourite beech tree of yours?' I asked, joining her on the couch. Her sandals brushed my thigh.

For an entire minute she made no sound, then at last she swept the hair from her eyes and muttered, 'You want me to pretend I'm Alice, is that it?'

'Uh-huh.'

'Would you like to hear my poem? "The French say *merde*. We say turd."'

I stroked the back of her hand. 'You know, Alice, I'd bet money that we're talking about one of your *favourite* beech trees.'

A pensive frown furrowed her brow, and she assumed a sitting position, scratching her bare ankle with the opposite toenail. 'When I was a little girl in Vermont,' she said, slowly, precisely, 'my father suspended ... an old tyre ... from the lowest branch. I spent many a goddamn joyful hour swinging back and forth.'

'Then you must do everything you can to save the tree's life.' I set the feather duster in her palm and wrapped her fingers around the handle. 'However, I expect you to return my axe when I need it again. Can you promise me that?'

'Sure thing,' she grumbled.

'The instant I ask for my axe back, you'll give it to me.'

'I fucking heard you the first time. I'll guard your fucking axe with my fucking life.'

Not a breakthrough, exactly. And yet my spirits rose. I could see the photon at the end of the tunnel. 'Londa, you're doing great. I would even venture to say you're having fun.'

'Fun? Right, Socrates. Fun on a bun.' She waved the feather duster about like a pom-pom. 'This is slightly less boring than I expected.'

'You have a talent for improvisation.'

'Let's just get it the fuck over with.'

'Scene two,' I said quickly. 'One week later. Jerome has come back for his axe.' Seeking to make the game as engagingly lurid as possible, I bared my teeth and presented Londa with the fierce burning gaze of Edward Hyde transfixing a barmaid. 'I need my axe, Alice,' I snarled, 'and I need it *now*!'

My savagery seemed to gratify her. 'Thundering fuck, Jerome, you look upset!' she yelled, flourishing the duster in my face.

'My wife and I had a dreadful argument last night. With any luck I'll catch her by surprise.'

'Holy shit, are you saying you intend to *kill* your wife? In Exodus chapter twenty, God says it's wrong to kill!'

'It's also wrong to break a promise. You said you'd return the axe when I needed it. Now keep your side of the bargain.'

38

Revelling in the crude melodrama of it all, Londa marched to the nearest window, threw open the shutters, and hurled the duster into the jungle.

'Straight to the bottom of the sea!'

'Our friendship is over, Alice!'

She pivoted towards me, her grin as wide as a slice of melon, then released a high whistled C-note and hugged herself with palpable delight.

'Curtain,' I said, dipping my head in a gesture of admiration. 'Congratulations, Londa. You've just saved a human life.'

'Fun on a bun,' she said again in a tone that, if not exactly amicable, was nevertheless a full octave of sarcasm lower than last time.

'I'm going to reward you by ending the lesson right now. Class dismissed. See you tomorrow morning.'

'Will we be doing another fucking theatre game?'

'That was my plan, yes.'

'Will it be more interesting than this Alice and Jerome shit?'

'I think you'll like it.'

'I was planning to play hooky,' she said, lighting a second cigarette, 'but maybe I'll show up after all.'

Although it was Edmund Purdom's wooden portrayal of *The Egyptian* that inspired me to study philosophy, the sensibility that underlay 'Ethics from the Earth' was shaped no less by my father's unmarried and oddball sister Clara, who lived with us until, shortly after my twelfth birthday, an ambulance took her besieged body to a Germantown hospice from whose benevolent chemical embrace she would never return. Aunt Clara was certainly no devotee of evolutionary theory – she believed wholeheartedly in the genial Creator-God of middle-class Methodist revelation – and yet for me her awed appreciation of the world's unglamorous species, its humble finches and homely toads and mundane chipmunks, was in the very best Darwinian tradition. Were I to paint the woman's portrait, I would depict her standing in our backyard, offering a squirrel peanuts with one hand and holding a birdfeeder aloft with the other.

Her passing was an event on which I needn't dwell. I shall

merely report that, as Londa and I pursued our second lesson, an improvisation based on Kohlberg's Fable of the Stolen Radium, wrenching memories of Aunt Clara's ill-advised radiation treatments inevitably rushed back. Yet I persisted, imagining that this eccentric Saint Francis was looking down from on high and blessing my attempt to give my pupil a robust naturalist ethics. Londa took the part of Helga Eschbach, the woman whose husband was dying of bone cancer. I cast myself as Jürgen Hammerschmidt, the police inspector who apprehends her after she breaks into Fritz's pharmacy and steals the radium extract. An empty Perrier bottle served for an ampoule of the vital drug.

'What's going on here?' I demanded.

Londa puffed on her cigarette and clutched the green bottle to her chest. 'My name is Helga Eschbach, and my husband has a malignant tumour. Radium therapy might cure him.'

'Well, Frau Eschbach, it appears I've caught a thief.'

'Put me in jail – I don't care.' She hunched protectively over the bottle. 'But first let me take this ampoule to my husband and give him an injection.'

'My duty is to uphold the law, not to facilitate the transportation of stolen goods.' I snatched the Perrier bottle away and, grabbing Londa's arm, escorted her across the library towards the local prison.

'But the pharmacist pays only one hundred Deutschmarks for each specimen of raw radium!' she protested. 'He charges a thousand for the extract!'

Halting beside the conquistador, I absently took his sword by the hilt and pulled it several inches clear of the scabbard. 'A thousand marks?' I said. 'A tenfold profit?'

'A thousand fucking marks,' she said, twisting free of my grip.

'How terribly unfair.'

'I pawned my wedding ring, sold our furniture, begged money from friends. It wasn't enough.'

'I must say, Frau Eschbach, I admire your effort.'

'I love my husband,' Londa said.

I let the blade slide back into place. 'Even if the pharmacist charged only five hundred marks, he would still be engaged in an immoral activity.'

'But not an illegal one?'

'Alas, no,' I said. 'Whereas you are engaged in an illegal activity—'

'But not an immoral activity.' Londa took a drag and flashed a triumphant smile.

'On the contrary, Frau Eschbach. What you're doing is—'

'It's pretty goddamn moral, isn't it?'

I returned the Perrier bottle to Londa's grasp. 'Here. Give your husband the treatment. I never saw you tonight, and you never saw me – understood?'

'Understood.'

'Herr Eschbach is fortunate to have such a wife.'

She stubbed out her cigarette on the conquistador's breastplate, then dropped the butt down the barrel of his musket. 'Tell me your name.'

'Hammerschmidt,' I said.

'I shall not forget your charity, Inspector Hammerschmidt.'

'In certain contexts, Frau Eschbach, the sacredness of love counts for more than the sanctity of law.'

'Why, Inspector – you're a fucking philosopher.'

Much to Londa's satisfaction, I laughed spontaneously. 'Take your curtain call, dear.' Stepping out of character, I gave her a tentative avuncular hug. 'Soak up the applause. Catch the bouquets. Great job.'

Londa took my hand, led me into the biography alcove, and stamped my cheek with a moist kiss. 'I'll never forget Herr Hammerschmidt's charity, and I'll never forget *your* charity either,' she told me, pursing her lips. 'I hope you'll always be my teacher, Mason, even after I get my conscience back.'

A borrowed axe, a beech tree, an ampoule of radium extract. Three physical objects that had played a crucial role in my efforts to rehabilitate Londa, each with a unique essence, its axeness, treeness, ampoulerity. But as Jean-Paul Sartre reminds us, in the case of human beings this metaphysic is reversed: a person's existence precedes his essence – he is a subject among objects. The danger, says Sartre, following Heidegger, is that the person will 'fall' into the world of objects, becoming ever after the prisoner

41

of arbitrary strictures masquerading as universal principles. And so it was that I resolved to give Londa a taste of Sartrean existential freedom, confronting her with a dilemma beyond the competence of any canon.

The conundrum was one that Sartre himself devised, concerning a student whose elder brother has died in the German offensive of 1940. The student resolves to join the Free French and help defeat the Nazi beasts who killed his brother, but his invalid mother wants him to stay at home. He is her only consolation, and she can't adequately care for herself.

To minimise the strain on Londa's imagination, I decided that the embittered student should be female, and I cast Edwina as the mother. Though preoccupied with packing – in twenty-four hours she would join Charnock for a week-long artificial-intelligence conference in Chicago, where they would implore the neural-network community not to make basket cases of their computers – Edwina gladly took the part, and in a matter of minutes the two actors had fully immersed themselves in the bedevilling scenario.

'*S'il te plaît, Madeleine* – reconsider,' Edwina gasped. 'We've already lost your brother. I couldn't bear to lose you as well.'

'Claude would want me to avenge his death,' Londa said.

'Claude would want you to look after me,' Edwina insisted.

'If I stay here, I'll spend every waking minute thinking of the Resistance.' Londa grimaced. 'On the other hand, if I join the Resistance, I'll spend every waking minute thinking of you.'

'Exactly my point,' Edwina said. 'Stay with me.'

'But, oh, *Maman*, consider the implications of driving the Germans out of France! Thousands of mothers, not just you, *thousands* will get to spend their dotages with sons and daughters who might otherwise have fallen into the Nazis' clutches!'

Edwina cupped her palms around Londa's shoulders, drawing the child so close that their noses practically touched. 'Dearest Madeleine, how can you sacrifice my happiness to this futile business of sniping at Nazis? How can you make a bargain like that?'

'I can make such a bargain because ...'

'Yes?'

'Because ...'

'I'm listening.'

A tremulous moan broke from Londa's throat. She lurched away, rushing towards the conquistador. 'Shit, Mason, you're doing it again! You're trying to drive me crazy!'

'Londa, that assertion gained nothing from the word "shit",' Edwina said.

'My head's spinning,' Londa said. 'I need ...'

'A rule?' I suggested. 'A binding principle? An eleventh commandment?'

Gasping like the carp she'd almost murdered, Londa slumped against Alonso.

'The anti-malarial drug quinine comes from the cinchona tree! In Riemann geometry, a curved line is the shortest path between two points!'

'There *are* no rules for dealing with a dilemma like this,' I said.

'An adult human skeleton contains two hundred and six bones!' 'Galaxies can be categorised as elliptical or spiral! Joyce Kilmer wrote "Trees"!'

'Instead of applying a rule, you need to engage all your powers of moral reasoning.'

'I *hate* this fucking lesson!'

Approaching Londa, I took her right hand and massaged the palm as if to heal a Christly stigma. She heaved a sigh, then relaxed.

'Let's call it quits for today, OK?' I said.

'Good idea.' She inhaled audibly, filtering the stuffy air through her clenched teeth. 'Best fucking idea I've heard all morning.'

I retrieved my backpack from the reading table, zipped it open, and pulled out 'Ethics from the Earth'. 'For your homework tonight, please read chapter four and write a thousand-word essay giving your personal reaction to the Stoics' worldview.'

'Well *that* certainly doesn't sound like much fun.'

'It's not supposed to be fun.'

'Haven't you read the goddamn US Constitution, Mason? Cruel and unusual punishments are forbidden.'

Edwina said, 'Londa, sweetheart, we do not stoop to sarcasm during our lessons.'

Snatching the book away, Londa announced that she intended to prepare herself 'a depraved lunch full of saturated fats and refined sugar', then exited the room with the punctuated jumps of a nine-year-old playing hopscotch.

Edwina and I locked gazes, and I saw that Londa's mismatched green irises were a legacy from her mother. She laid her delicate fingers against my cheek like a psychic healer performing a root canal procedure.

'She's doing awfully well, wouldn't you say?' Edwina ventured.

'I see progress,' I replied, trying not to sound too satisfied with myself. How many real philosophers, I wondered, the kind with PhDs, could have brought Londa so far so fast?

'She knew why Madeleine felt compelled to fight the Nazis, but she understood the mother's feelings too. Before you came here, Londa couldn't empathise with anybody except herself. "Progress" is an understatement. I'd say she's practically cured.'

The longer I stayed on Isla de Sangre, this tropical Eden with its squawking birds, squalling monkeys and murmuring surf, the more certain I became that my years in academia had wrought a serious imbalance in my mental ecosystem. Thanks to Hawthorne University, a kind of Aristotelian kudzu had taken root in my skull, choking out the more dynamic blooms and covering the whole terrain with a creeping carpet of rationality. It was high time for me to reclaim my natural right to entertain whimsical notions and formulate indefensible ideas.

I resolved to spend Wednesday afternoon trekking around the island, admitting to my consciousness every species of thought, no matter how grandiose. If so moved by Lady Philosophy, I would prove once and for all that humans possess *a priori* knowledge, devise an airtight case against *a priori* knowledge, and pronounce so pompously on the mystery of Being that every Heideggerian within earshot would reach for his gun. This strange quest, with its aim not of spiritual enlightenment but of intellectual decadence, began immediately after lunch. I donned my hiking clothes – the crate containing my earthly possessions had arrived from Boston the previous evening – stuffed my backpack with three bottles of Evian and a half-dozen Power Bars, and set off for the beach, humming my favourite melodic idea from 'The Lark Ascending'.

According to Charnock, the island had the general shape of a human kidney, and my intention was to circumnavigate the cortex before the stars came out. At first my journey proved congenial, and I continued humming 'The Lark Ascending' while negotiating a range of dunes that separated the verdant rainforest from the placid Bahía de Flores. The sky was the deep blue of unoxygenated blood, the air redolent of dahlias and orchids. Shells of every variety – conch, clam, oyster, scallop, mussel, snail – covered the sand like cobblestones, and soon I fancied that I was strolling the streets of eighteenth-century Königsberg, following in Kant's footsteps as he explained why the physico-theological argument for God's existence did not yield a transcendent Creator, merely a cosmic Architect at the mercy of available materials.

By the time I'd travelled perhaps three miles, I was no longer a happy hiker. Rivulets of sweat trickled down my scalp, making my brow itch and my eyes sting. Mosquitoes whined in my ears like defective hearing aids. Worst of all, an impediment now presented itself: a sheer sandstone bluff heaving out of the rainforest and jutting into the bay. For an instant I considered making an about-face and returning to my cottage with its mosquito netting and cold beer, but instead some dormant sense of adventure awoke within me, and I strode into the jungle, the sound of the surf falling away by degrees, from boom to growl to grainy whisper.

Several miles inland I was astonished to behold the bluff merge with a soaring concrete wall, not quite massive enough to confine a giant prehistoric gorilla, but of sufficient height to thwart human traffic, its moss-cloaked bulk continuing south into the jungle before dissolving into mist and shadow. Equally surprising was the taut string rising from behind the wall to join a silken kite – a golden phoenix with a flaming red tail – lodged in a kapok tree. I stopped in my tracks. Sobs filled the air. A child was crying. Of all the explanations now flitting through my brain I quickly discarded my initial, admittedly far-fetched hypothesis – the child was a prisoner and had launched the kite to signal for help – and settled on the obvious: distress over a lost toy.

Although athletically incompetent as a youngster, doltish at everything from softball to pitching pennies, I was always a serious

45

tree climber. Confidently I shed my pack and, on the third attempt, leaped high enough to grab a limb. I hoisted myself into the kapok and mounted the branches until one golden wing was within my grasp. I unhooked the kite, untangled the string and, descending several branches, inched forward until my feet dangled above the forbidden domain.

A slender little girl stared up at me, her heart-shaped face luminous with gratitude. Over a blue dress she wore a pink pinafore daubed with tomboy blotches of mud and moss, and she clutched a wooden spindle around which was coiled the surplus kite string.

'I believe you lost this,' I told my beaming admirer, lowering the toy into her outstretched arms.

'Thank you *so* much!'

She held the kite against her body like a shield, the vertical axis extending all the way to her forehead. I moved to the bottommost branch and, after hanging briefly like a sloth, unhooked my legs, relaxed my grip, and dropped to the ground. No sooner had I recovered my balance than a large and lithe Dobermann pinscher appeared from out of nowhere, his amber eyes glowing as he patiently awaited the child's command to extract the intruder's throat.

'My name's Donya,' she said, stroking her guardian's broad rocky skull. 'And this is Omar.' The dog had been spared the modifications to which breeders commonly subjected his kind – docked tail, ears forced erect by scar tissue – but Omar looked scary enough without them. 'What's your name?'

'Mason,' I said, cautiously extending my hand, palm down, towards the Dobermann. 'Hi there, Omar.' The dog sniffed my fleshy offering, then issued a semantically complex snort. Evidently I was not to be trusted entirely, but at least I'd followed the proper protocol.

Surveying my surroundings, I saw that Donya's intention to launch her kite that afternoon was not unreasonable, for we were standing on a windswept scrubland broken only by distant ranks of cypress trees and the occasional lone acacia. To have a successful kite-flying experience here, you needed merely to avoid the concrete wall and the forest beyond.

'I'm five years old, and I'm having a tea party with Charles and Henry and Deedee,' Donya said, starting away. 'Would you like to come, too?'

'Sure.'

Crossing the scrub, Donya at my side, I looked in all directions, hoping to spot an adult. Apparently the child was playing unsupervised. What sort of dumb-ass irresponsible parents would abandon their preschooler to the perils of an island wilderness? Was Omar really equal to any threat that might arise?

My hostess guided me towards a banyan tree as vast and sprawling as its Indian cousins, the naked roots arcing from trunk to earth like ropes supporting a circus tent. Cradled within its branches was a clapboard cottage, white with yellow shutters, scaled to Donya's proportions. The child deposited her kite at the base of the trunk, told her dog she'd be back soon, and directed me up a zigzagging wooden staircase to the porch, where the other guests awaited. Donya made the introductions. Charles was a velveteen giraffe boasting red fur covered with yellow polka-dots, Henry a stuffed koala bear dressed in a *Come to Queensland* T-shirt, and Deedee a plush chimpanzee whose right paw grasped a real banana.

Stooping, I entered Donya's diminutive domain. The raw materials of a tea party – four white china cups and saucers, a small silver pot, a stack of peanut-butter sandwiches, a plate holding chocolate-chip cookies and vanilla wafers – lay on a table adorned with Ernest Shepard's classic drawing of Christopher Robin descending the stairs dragging Edward Bear behind him, bump, bump, bump. Donya brought Charles, Henry, and Deedee in from the porch, propping them up in their little cane chairs, then installed herself at the head of the table. Given the frailty of the chairs, sitting was not an option for me, so I crouched in the corner.

'Might I infer you're here on vacation – or are you a local resident?' In my efforts to avoid condescending to children, I commonly burden them with my most tortured diction, but Donya understood me nevertheless.

'I live here,' she said, offering me a cherubic smile. Freckles decorated her cheeks like sprinkles of cinnamon.

'With your mother and father?'

47

'Just my mother. I don't have a father. Henry and Brock visit every day.' Donya took the silver pot, poured out a measure of red liquid, and set the teacup before her stuffed chimp. 'The other Henry, I mean, Henry Cushing, not Henry Koala.'

'Is Henry Cushing a person?'

'Of *course* he's a person. He gives me my lessons. Brock does too.'

How strange to think I wasn't the only tutor on Isla de Sangre. I wondered how many of us there were, and whether we all worked for Edwina.

While my hostess filled two more teacups, passing one to Henry Koala, keeping the other for herself, I increased my crouch ten degrees and peered out of the window. A grand and garish edifice met my gaze, a kind of ancient Spanish villa secluded by cypresses, each tower capped by a conical roof. Thick swarthy vines crisscrossed the dark stone walls like twine securing a brown-paper package.

'Tell me your full name,' I said. 'Is it Donya Jones maybe? Donya Smith?'

'Donya Sabacthani.' Puckering her lips, my hostess whistled 'Pop Goes the Weasel' as she filled the remaining teacup and held it out to me.

'Shouldn't this be for Charles?' I asked, staring into Donya's eyes. Her irises, like Edwina's and Londa's, were two different shades of green.

'Giraffes don't like Hawaiian Punch.'

'Donya, do you know your mother's first name? Does she call herself something like Judy or Carol or Edwina?'

'I call her Mommy. She's the best mommy in the whole world. She built the wall just for me.'

'Could her name be Edwina?'

'I don't know, but I can show you her picture!'

Donya reached under the table and obtained a blue lacquered music box. She lifted the lid, unleashing a tinny rendition of 'Lara's Theme' from *Doctor Zhivago*. The green velvet interior held several pieces of costume jewellery, a compact mirror, and a snapshot of Edwina wearing a grin as artificial as a paper carnation.

'My mother's very pretty, isn't she?' Donya said.

'Very pretty,' I echoed. In a rainy-day, Blanche DuBois sort of way. 'I'm a friend of hers.'

'Are you a molecular geneticist too?'

'No, I'm a teacher, like Henry and Brock. My student is your sister Londa. She's seventeen years old.'

'I don't have a sister Londa. Mommy says I'm a lonely child.'

'An *only* child?'

'That's what I meant. *Only* children are lucky. They get their mommies all to themselves. What makes you think I have a sister?'

I took my first swallow of Hawaiian Punch. It tasted vaguely like watered-down mumquat nectar. Something extremely odd was happening on this end of the archipelago. If the March Hare suddenly appeared at the present festivity, I would not be entirely surprised.

'My student's name is Londa Sabacthani,' I said.

'Well, she can call herself that if she wants to, but that doesn't mean she's allowed to be my sister.' Donya picked up the snack plate and addressed the chimp. 'Would you like a cookie, Deedee?'

I affected a falsetto and dubbed in Deedee's voice. 'I would *love* a cookie.'

'What kind?'

'Vanilla wafer.'

My hostess served her chimp a vanilla wafer and said, 'I invited Mommy to the party, but she's in Chicago this week.'

'I know,' I said. 'An artificial-intelligence conference.'

'That's right. She's teaching people to be nice to their computers.'

I sipped more punch. Why hadn't Edwina told me about this second child? Why had she bisected the island? Why did her daughters need separate estates? I wondered whether the woman in the photograph might actually be Edwina's twin sister, likewise a molecular geneticist, and likewise attending a neural-network conference in Chicago – a fanciful theory, but not unimaginable.

I drained my Hawaiian Punch. 'Donya, I have to say something. This is important. If you ask me, a five-year-old girl should not be out flying a kite by herself.'

'Mommy says that as long as I stay inside the wall, nothing bad will ever happen to me.'

'I believe that an adult should be watching over you at all times.'

Donya gestured towards the rear window. 'Henry's looking at me right now.'

My opinion of parenting standards at Donya's villa improved considerably as my gaze alighted on the highest tower. A bulky human figure, backlit by the descending sun, scrutinised the scrub through a brass telescope. The instrument seemed to be focused directly on me. I wondered if it was powerful enough to show Henry my perplexed expression.

'Would you like to know the name of my house?' Donya asked. 'My real house, I mean, not my tree house. It's Casa de los Huesos. That means the House of Bones.'

'What sorts of things do Henry and Brock teach you?'

She bit into Deedee's vanilla wafer. 'You ask a lot of questions, Mason. It's getting on my nerves.'

'That's not a very nice thing to say, Donya.'

Instantly her brow and cheeks turned red, and I braced myself for a squall of tears. Instead she took a deep breath. 'I'm ... I'm sorry.'

'I accept your apology.'

'I'm so sorry.'

'It's all right.'

'I say bad things like that because I don't have my rectitude yet.'

'Rectitude. That's an awfully big word.'

'Like the time I smashed Mommy's cell phone and said I didn't, and that other time when I threw Chen Lee's watch into the bay, and once I dug up all of Mommy's hyacinths. Henry and Brock are teaching me the three Rs. Reading, writing, and rectitude.'

'I see.'

'After I get my rectitude, I won't dig up any more hyacinths. Are you teaching Londa her rectitude, too?'

'That's one way to put it.'

Over the next half-hour I consumed three additional cups of punch, two peanut-butter sandwiches, and four cookies like nobody's grandmother used to make: discs of impossibly moist cake studded with scrumptious chunks of chocolate. When not eating, Donya and I played Candyland, sang nursery rhymes, and discussed whether Christopher Robin might have found a more considerate way of transporting Winnie-the-Pooh downstairs. It would be a better world, I decided, if tree-house tea parties occurred more frequently.

At four o'clock Donya announced that Henry and Brock expected her to be home soon, so we descended to the scrub. Omar sniffed my knees, thighs, and ankles, deciding I'd acquired no unacceptable aromas since his previous inspection. Donya made me promise to visit her again. I scrambled back into the kapok tree. As I returned to the jungle and retrieved my pack, I wondered whether Edwina, by applying her considerable monetary and material resources to Donya's domain, had indeed made it a completely safe haven. Quite possibly I was living on the wrong side of the concrete wall, and if I moved into Casa de los Huesos nothing bad would ever happen to me.

CHAPTER 4

A particularly baroque product of Charnock's genetic-engineering skills greeted me when I entered the library the next morning: a winged and feathered iguana boasting the same talent for uncomprehending repetition found in parrots and post-structuralists. The creature was perched on Londa's shoulder, swathed in her luxurious hair, his forked tongue flicking wildly as he peeked out from behind her tresses.

'Does he have a name?' I asked.

'Quetzie,' Londa replied, feeding the iguana a handful of dried ants. Her bright yellow sundress gave her the appearance of a gendered banana. 'After Quetzalcoatl, the Aztec feathered serpent god.'

'Quetzie is a handsome devil,' the iguana said. His plumage was indeed astonishing, a red-and-gold raiment flowing behind him like an emperor's robe.

'Quite so,' I told him.

'Quetzie is a handsome devil,' he said again.

'Indeed.'

'Quetzie is a handsome devil.'

'There's no disputing it.'

'Quetzie is a handsome devil.'

'That will do,' Londa said, and Quetzie apparently understood her – at any rate, he dropped the subject.

'I'd like to see your homework,' I said.

Londa sighed and rubbed up against the conquistador's breastplate like a housecat alerting its owner to the menace of an empty food dish. 'Your chapter on the Stoics – I'm not sure how to put this – it simply *amazed* me. My pathetic essay doesn't even *begin* to convey what it's like to meet a mind like yours.'

'Chapter four isn't about my ideas. It's about the Stoics' ideas.'

Quetzie hopped from Londa's shoulder to the conquistador's helmet. 'Mason is a genius,' the iguana announced from his new perch.

I furrowed my brow and groaned. 'Did you *teach* him that dubious proposition,' I asked Londa, 'or is it merely something he overheard?'

She smiled coyly, then approached a massive writing desk, ornately carved with flowering creepers – I imagined some mad Caribbean poet at work there, scribbling the national epic of Isla de Sangre, a phantasmagoria of mutant lobsters, sentient mangroves, talking iguanas, and greedy conquistadors – and retrieved a printout from the top drawer. Retracing her steps, she transferred Quetzie back to her shoulder and presented me with an essay entitled 'In Praise of Adversity'.

'While you were slaving away on this, I had something of an adventure,' I told her. 'I was hiking along the beach and suddenly found myself facing a high concrete wall. Do you know about it?'

She pursed her lips and shook her head.

'Evidently it runs far into the jungle. I climbed over—'

'I thought it was high.'

'I used a tree. I climbed over, and you'll never guess what I discovered.'

'The Fountain of Youth?'

'A large house – as big as Faustino, bigger even, a villa.'

'How strange.'

'A little girl lives there. She calls herself Donya. Is that name familiar to you?'

'I don't think so. Donya?'

'That's right.'

'Since I hit my head' – Londa gulped loudly, as if swallowing a horse pill – 'I've forgotten so many things.'

'Is it possible you have a little sister?'

'Named Donya?'

'Yes.'

She blinked in slow motion. 'Mother says I'm an only child. What makes you think this Donya person is my sister?'

Londa's morality teacher now proceeded to lie to her. 'A wild hunch. I shouldn't have mentioned it.'

'Shit, I hate it when the amnesia takes somebody else away from me. I goddamn fucking *hate* it.'

'For what it's worth, I believe you've never met the child in question.'

'Know something, Socrates? I'm not enjoying this conversation one little bit.'

'Mason is a genius,' the iguana said.

'Shut the fuck up,' Londa said.

Quetzie took flight and landed atop the globe, perching on the North Pole like a gigantic vulture about to devour the rotting carcass of planet Earth. I apologised to Londa for introducing such a painful topic, promised never to do so again, then suggested that while I negotiated 'In Praise of Adversity' she should amuse herself with a book of her own choosing. She ambled to the fiction collection, plucking out *Pride and Prejudice*, and we sat down together at the reading table.

I was barely into Londa's essay before realising that she was uncommonly skilled at articulating her thoughts on paper: not a complete surprise, given the many acres of text she'd soaked up of late – though, God knows, my Watertown High students had rarely made the leap from reading lucid prose to writing it. Her last paragraph struck me as downright eloquent.

Above all, the Stoics sought wisdom, a condition that I myself hope to achieve after I stop wrecking and burning things. While I can't claim to understand this philosophy, despite Mason's dazzling overview, I imagine there must be great rewards in living one's life by Stoic principles. Am I equal to the challenge? There's only one way to find out.

During the ten minutes I spent with her essay, Londa reached the midpoint of *Pride and Prejudice*.

'You're a good writer,' I told her.

'You think so?' she gushed. 'How good?'

'Very good. Excellent, really.'

'I'm not as good as this woman,' she said, tapping her novel. 'Jane Austen makes me believe that Elizabeth Bennet is fucking alive.'

'A pithy tribute, Londa, but how about curbing the profanity?'

'OK. Jane Austen *doesn't* make me believe that Elizabeth Bennet is fucking alive.'

I rolled my eyes and snorted. 'You clearly got a lot out of chapter four. But there's one small problem. From these pages it almost sounds as if you intend to *become* a Stoic.'

'Of course I do.'

'Stoicism died out fifteen centuries ago.'

'Quetzie is a handsome devil,' the iguana said.

'As a matter of fact, the experiment has already started,' Londa said with a disconcerting grin. 'Yesterday at lunch I had a smaller piece of pecan pie than usual, and I passed up the scoop of vanilla ice cream entirely. It's like I said in my essay: "Just as Nature abhors a vacuum, a Stoic abhors satiety." What's more, as you may have noticed, I've stopped smoking.'

'But not swearing.'

'I'm working on it.'

'And how long do you plan to pursue this project?'

'Long as I can. The hardest part will be to stop masturbating.'

'I see.'

'I'm rather well informed about sex,' she told me, as if I'd said she wasn't. 'I've read all the books. *Fanny Hill. Justine. Lady Chatterley's Lover.* I know there's a positive side to fucking, but on the whole it's messy and dangerous, don't you think?'

I swiped my tongue across the roof of my mouth, as if to detach a popcorn husk. 'Messy. Dangerous. Yes.'

'A person could get a venereal disease.'

'This is true.'

'Do you have a girlfriend, Mason?'

'Not right now.'

'What about in the past?'

'Several girlfriends. Your essay is marvellous.'

'Did you fuck them?'

'We're drifting away from the topic.'

She snickered and said, 'Stoicism: putting pleasure in its place. The Stoics believed that in bearing pain without complaint a mortal might transcend the mundane world and enter the eternal matrix of divine thought – so that's part of my experiment too.'

'What is?'

'Pain.'

'I don't understand.'

'Pain is part of my experiment.'

Several harsh and foreign chemicals flooded my stomach. 'Pain has nothing to teach you, Londa.'

'Not according to chapter four.'

'The Stoics did not deliberately hurt themselves.'

'I intend to build on their work.'

The chemicals roiled around, interacting with the native acids. 'Listen to me, Londa. You will not, under any circumstances, you will *not* hurt yourself.'

'Last night I snuffed out a candle with my hand.'

She held up her left palm. A shudder of alarm passed through me. At the juncture of her head line and fate line, the very spot I'd massaged twenty-four hours earlier, lay a stark white blister.

'Fuck,' I said, frightened and confused, but mostly angry.

'A useful word, huh?'

'I don't believe this.'

'I whimpered a bit, but I didn't shriek. I also did stuff with a rose thorn.' She extended her right thumb. An angry red welt was blooming beneath the nail.

'Christ, Londa, I think it's infected!'

'It hurts like hell.' She sounded pleased. 'Later today I'm going to sit in the conservatory and push a sewing needle through my tongue and open my heart to the divine matrix.'

I clasped Londa's shoulders and shook her, emphatically, as if I might dislodge her fantasies as I would a quarter stolen by a vending machine. 'You will *not* push a needle through your tongue! Not today or any other day! You have to promise me that!'

'This is really important to you, isn't it, Mason?'

'Promise me.'

'All right, if that's what you want, I promise.' She approached the world-eating iguana and gently stroked his tail feathers. 'But I don't see how I'm supposed to be cured if I can't take my goddamn lessons seriously.'

We passed the rest of the morning in a heated and unhappy conversation, in the course of which I tried to convince her that a person could comprehend a moral principle without becoming obligated to act on it. After a two-hour debate, Londa finally conceded that self-mutilation was not essential to the pursuit of ethics, but her words sprang more from acquiescence than assent. Before our next meeting, I told her, she must reread chapter four, searching for the nuances she'd missed the first time around, the better to benefit from our upcoming role-playing exercise.

I did not so much leave Faustino that afternoon as flee it, seeking the buoyant company of Donya and the serenity of her tree house. Jogging frantically along the beach, I vowed to begin Friday's lesson by inspecting Londa's tongue and every other part of her that lent itself to scrutiny. If I saw the slightest evidence of violence, I would probably conclude that I was out of my depth, return to Boston, and send Edwina an email advising her to replace me with some fuck-the-Enlightenment Lyotard disciple from Vassar.

By the time I reached the concrete wall, a storm had broken over Blood Island, not quite a hurricane but still fearsome, with lashing winds and sheets of rain, so I was not surprised, after scaling the rampart and surveying the banyan tree, to find Donya's little cottage empty. I proceeded to the villa. The doorknocker was a brass quoit fixed in the jaws of the same Aztec god who decorated the portal to Faustino. I banged the ring emphatically, thereby setting Donya's Dobermann to barking.

'Omar, be quiet!' came a man's voice, chirping through the loudspeaker above my head.

'It's Mason Ambrose. I'm a friend of Donya's.'

'Your reputation precedes you.'

The door swung back to reveal the frenzied dog, bouncing up

57

and down, bellowing madly in a fit of canine hysterics. Holding Omar's collar was a portly middle-aged man who introduced himself as Henry Cushing. His beard was white, his face sunburned, his manner genial: a Santa Claus for adults, I mused, bringing tax refunds and nonaddictive hallucinogens to good grown-ups everywhere.

At last recognising my scent, Omar grew calm.

'When I saw Donya escorting you to the tree house, my impulse was to run over and check you out,' Henry said. 'But she and Omar obviously found you acceptable' – he released the dog's collar – 'and they're both excellent judges of character.'

'She charmed me off my feet.' I staggered into the foyer, the rain spouting from the sleeves of my anorak to form puddles on the stone floor.

'Preschool children,' Henry said, 'they're one of the better things in the world – wouldn't you agree? – Like red wine and *New Yorker* cartoons and Christina Rossetti. "When I am dead, my dearest, / Sing no sad songs for me; / Plant thou no roses at my head, / Nor shady cypress tree."'

I peeled off my soggy jacket and hung it on the coat rack. 'You left out George Gershwin.'

'Don't tell Brock. He'd never forgive me.'

'My lips are sealed.'

'"Be the green grass above me / With showers and dewdrops wet; / And if thou wilt, remember, / And if thou wilt, forget."'

Omar returned to his post, settling down on the rug before the door. Henry led me into a Gothic parlour, its fluted pillars ascending to a vaulted ceiling, its stained-glass windows thrusting heavenward like rectangles who'd found Jesus. Dressed in an oilcloth smock and gripping a paintbrush, Donya stood before an artist's easel, staring at a half-finished watercolour of Deedee the chimpanzee. Her subject sat two feet away on a Windsor chair, self-possessed as only a professional model or a stuffed animal could be.

'Donya, look who's here,' Henry said.

'Mason!' She dashed across the room and threw her arms around me as if I were Edward Bear himself. 'I'm so glad to see you! I told Henry and Brock all about our tea party!'

'The social event of the season,' I said.

'Look what Brock's building for me!'

She led me to the far corner, where a man in his early forties, handsome as Dorian Gray, was methodically adding tiny trees to a miniature amusement park spread across a plywood platform. This raucous and frenetic marvel, as lovingly detailed as the Lionel O-gauge electric train set I'd inherited from my grandfather, featured a Ferris wheel, a six-horse carousel rotating to the tune of 'The Washington Post March', and a rollercoaster subjecting a dozen diminutive passengers to its scale-model vicissitudes. As I gaped in appreciation, the tree planter introduced himself as Brock Hawes, 'the sensitive half of the relationship, Henry being in charge of dental appointments and tax returns'.

'Donya, will you excuse us, darling?' Henry said. 'The adults need to talk.'

'I want to stay here,' Donya said.

'Sorry, tomato,' Henry said.

'You can't *make* me go.'

'Donya ...'

'If you try to make me go, I'll tell Mommy you were mean to me, and I'll do other stuff, with matches maybe, or scissors.'

'Know what, Donya?' Brock said. 'I'll bet you a million dollars there's something yummy in the fridge, second shelf down on the right.'

'You can't *make* me do anything. What's in the fridge?'

'I forget exactly,' Brock said, 'but there's some major yumminess involved, I promise you.'

Donya pirouetted towards the kitchen, moving so gracefully that I wondered if Henry and Brock's curriculum might include ballet lessons. Omar, stretching, rose from his rug and followed his mistress out of the room.

'The person who hired you – she claims to be Donya's mother, right?' I asked.

'Edwina Sabacthani,' Henry said, nodding.

'Edwina,' I muttered. So much for my theory that Donya's mother was Edwina's twin sister. 'I'm working for her too.'

'We know,' Brock said. 'Donya told us.'

'Are you by any chance a connoisseur of children's television?'

59

Henry asked. '*Professor Oolong's Oompah-pah Zoo?*'

I shook my head.

'For six years running I was Professor Oolong on Nickelodeon, but then the ratings went south, and I became plain old Henry Cushing, unemployed actor. This job was a gift from heaven. Edwina's nephew used to enjoy my antics every Saturday morning, and that was recommendation enough.'

'I was hired to tutor an adolescent named Londa,' I said.

'Londa Sabacthani,' said Brock. 'Seventeen years old. Donya's got a fabulous memory. She showed you a photograph of her mother.'

'Who looks exactly like Londa's mother,' I said. 'Apparently our students are sisters – half-sisters at least.'

'Are you merely tutoring Londa,' Brock asked, 'or would it be more accurate to say you're rehabilitating her?'

'Rehabilitating, yes,' I said. 'A diving accident resulting in cerebral trauma. The symptoms include severe amnesia plus—'

'Let me guess,' Henry said. 'Alienation, anomie, and sociopathic behaviour.'

I frowned and nodded.

'In other words, Londa woke up without a conscience,' Brock said. 'Donya has the same deficit.'

'No rectitude, is how she puts it. Strange coincidence.'

'I don't think it's a *coincidence* at all,' Henry said. 'It appears that Edwina has been playing games with our heads, and her children's heads, too, maybe even her own head.'

'Did Donya have a diving accident?' I asked.

'Supposedly she fell off her bicycle,' Brock said.

'Londa has inherited her maternal grandfather's gift for speed reading,' I informed my new friends. 'And Donya?'

Henry hummed in corroboration. 'Yesterday she got through *Heidi* in fifteen minutes. This morning she devoured *The Secret Garden* in ten.'

'Did Edwina ever mention a second daughter?' I asked.

Henry and Brock shook their heads in unison.

'When I had tea with Donya, she told me she's an only child. Londa believes the same about herself. Evidently Edwina makes a point of it.'

'Curiouser and curiouser,' Henry said.

For the next half-hour we attempted to construct a rational explanation for the bizarre domestic arrangements on Isla de Sangre, but far from dissolving the mystery we only deepened it. Our employer's nomadism had us especially confused. Just as I'd assumed that Edwina resided exclusively with Londa at the mouldering estate called Faustino, so did Henry and Brock believe she was permanently ensconced with Donya at Casa de los Huesos.

'Apparently she spends much of her time on the move, a peculiar lifestyle for a person allegedly in poor health.' Henry flipped back the top of the carousel and removed the mini-CD. 'Proposition, Mason. While the cat's away in Chicago, why don't we mice spend Saturday afternoon exploring the island?' Receiving my nod, he smiled, then inserted a disc labelled 'Being for the Benefit of Mr Kite' into the carousel. 'I can't speak for you or Brock, but I won't rest until I've figured out precisely how many daughters Edwina has, and why the hell the children aren't supposed to know about each other.'

During the interval since my last encounter with the mutant iguana, a new sentence had coalesced in his cold-blooded brain. When I walked into the library on Friday morning, Quetzie stared at me from his perch atop the conquistador's helmet and proclaimed, 'All you need is love.'

'That's a matter of some controversy,' I said.

'All you need is love,' he insisted.

Just then Londa stepped into the room, dressed distractingly in blue denim cutoffs and an orange halter top, clutching her copy of 'Ethics from the Earth'. As she approached Quetzie, he hopped from the conquistador to her head, thus adorning her in an Aztec princess's feathered crown.

'Stick out your tongue,' I instructed her.

'I didn't mutilate it.'

'All you need is love,' the iguana said.

'Stick out your tongue,' I repeated.

Londa stuck out her tongue. It looked entirely healthy.

'Show me your hands,' I demanded.

She did as instructed. The inflamed skin beneath her thumbnail seemed to be healing, likewise the blister on her palm, and I saw no evidence that she'd manually snuffed another candle. I inspected her shoulders. No aberrations. I glanced at her knees and calves. The skin seemed intact.

'I'm still a Stoic,' she explained, 'but from now on I won't behave like one, since it makes you so fucking unhappy, though your fellow educator Jean Piaget believes that a developing child constructs her world through action.'

'Your teacher this morning is Mason Ambrose, not Jean Piaget. Did you reread chapter four?'

'Twice.'

'Mason is a genius,' Quetzie said.

'Here's the set-up,' I said. 'Pretend you're an artist living in a contemporary version of the Stoics' fabled City of Zeus. Your name is Sybil Bright, and you believe that personal integrity is the highest virtue.'

'Let me get this straight,' Londa said. 'I'm allowed to *play* at Stoicism, but I'm not allowed to practise it.'

'What you're not allowed to do is burn your palm or puncture your thumb or any such crap,' I said curtly. 'A man named Alvarez has come to your studio. He works for a bank. Ready?'

'Whatever you say.'

I rapped my knuckles on the reading table to simulate Mr Alvarez knocking on Sybil Bright's door.

'Could I have a minute of your time, young woman?'

Londa pulled a colourfully packaged piece of bubble gum from her hip pocket. 'My newest vice,' she said, unwrapping the pink lozenge. 'It helps me overcome the urge for a cig.'

I cleared my throat. 'Could I have a minute of your time?' I said again.

She shrugged and popped the gum into her mouth. 'Would you like to buy a painting?'

I pantomimed a banker entering Sybil's studio. 'Casper Alvarez of the Seaboard Bank and Trust Company. I'm here to offer you a credit card. No annual fee, a stunning five-point-eight per cent APR, and you get to accumulate $150,000 in debt before we bat an eye, assuming you keep up the minimum monthly payments.'

'I don't need a credit card.'

'Sure you do.'

'Why?'

'To buy things.'

'What things?'

'A recreational vehicle, a snowmobile, a sailboat, a home theatre.'

'Will they make me a better person?' she asked.

'They won't make you better,' I said, 'but they'll afford you countless hours of enjoyment.'

'We Stoics distrust enjoyment. My life is a quest for divine wisdom.'

'Don't be self-righteous, Sybil. When you experience intimations of the divine, this gives you a rush of satisfaction.'

'True enough, but it's the wisdom I value, not the rush.'

A crackerjack retort, I thought. Perhaps I was a better teacher than I knew.

Our conversation went on for another twenty minutes, during which interval Mr Alvarez failed to make Sybil stray even one centimetre from her personal code with its imperatives of integrity, forbearance, and openness to epiphany.

'Curtain,' I said, resting an affirming hand on Londa's bare shoulder. 'You were terrific.'

'Was I?'

'Absolutely sensational. For Monday's class, I want you to study the next chapter, all about Epicurus, then write out a two-page conversation between an Epicurean and an anti-Epicurean.'

She set her hand atop mine, pressing down until I felt the bone beneath. 'The Epicureans believed pleasure was a virtue, didn't they?'

'True enough,' I said, retrieving my hand.

'You won't allow me to experiment with pain. Am I supposed to run screaming from pleasure too?'

'Depends on what you mean by pleasure. An Epicurean would be the first to argue that hedonism is both degrading and dangerous.'

Londa blew a bubble that looked like a pink cantaloupe. She let it pop, returned the strands to her mouth, and smiled. 'I've got the whole fucking weekend ahead of me. There's no telling *what* I might do.'

On Saturday morning I filled my backpack with Power Bars and cranberry juice, then hiked to Casa de los Huesos, where I found everyone assembled on the lawn for croquet – Donya, her tutors, plus a rangy Asian man and a ruddy, zaftig woman, whom Henry introduced respectively as Chen Lee, 'a cook with Szechwan credentials', and Rosita Corona, 'a gardener with a green thumb on each hand'. Omar sat on his haunches just beyond the midfield stake, ready to referee. Donya offered me the blue-striped mallet – me, the washout at soccer, badminton, volleyball, kick-the-can, and every other athletic activity save tree climbing. I told her I'd rather watch.

The game was barely ten minutes under way when I realised that the four adults were arranging for Donya to win. They deliberately missed wickets, allowed her to retake bobbled shots, and declined to roquet her ball even when that was the only rational tactic. I wondered how this pathetic charade was supposed to enhance her moral education. Did Henry and Brock really believe that a sham victory would help give Donya a superego?

When at last the contest reached its predictable conclusion, Donya the winner and still champion, Henry shouldered his own backpack, bulging with food, and announced that he and I were about to go rambling around the island in imitation of Robinson Crusoe.

'I want to come, too!' Donya shouted.

'Sorry, cupcake,' Henry said.

Storm clouds gathered above the child's head. She screwed her features into a cameo of disgust and hurled her croquet mallet on to the grass. 'You never let me do *anything*!'

'Guess what, pumpkin?' Brock said, strolling nonchalantly up to Donya. 'A special package came yesterday.'

'What special package?' she demanded shrilly. 'What was in it?'

'*Indoor* voice, Donya,' Brock admonished her, '*indoor* voice.'

'But we're outdoors.'

'Let's say we go open that special package,' Brock suggested, stooping into a leapfrog position. Donya jumped on to his shoulders, swinging her legs around his neck. He rose, grasped her ankles, and started towards the villa. 'I think it might be the bumper cars for our amusement park.'

'Giddyup!' Donya cried. 'Giddyup! Giddyup!'

As I followed Henry across the croquet lawn, he informed me that the narrative of Robinson Crusoe was very much on his mind these days. He'd recently hit on a concept for a children's show, 'Uncle Rumpus's Magic Island', centred on a castaway who spends his days combing the beach for whatever flotsam and jetsam might help him survive. Being part of a larger artefact, each piece of junk he finds proves perplexing – a table leg, bicycle chain, umbrella frame, clock face – and so Rumpus enlists his young viewers in interpreting these various treasures, thus presumably increasing their powers of inference.

'I think the Nickelodeon people will go ape,' he said. 'I just need to show them a couple of spec scripts.'

Breaching the rainforest, we headed south along the wall, the ground beneath our feet dissolving in muck and marsh, the air thickening with bird cries and peppery swarms of gnats. The farther inland we ventured, the more Isla de Sangre revealed itself as a world of great beauty and abiding strangeness. We gobbled Power Bars under the watchful eyes of an alligator clan whose title to the surrounding swamp we were not about to dispute, drank cranberry juice by an amber waterfall cascading down a series of ridges like ale spilling from an ogre's keg, and consumed our lunch – red grapes and beef jerky – near a quicksand bog ringed by astonishing conical blossoms as large and golden as French horns.

'Do you always let Donya cheat at croquet?' I asked, eating the last grape.

'The first time we played, she lost and became instantly hysterical,' Henry replied. 'She ran into the kitchen screaming, "I'm no good! I'm no good!" If Chen hadn't intervened, she would've cut off her little finger with a bread knife.'

'Jesus.'

'She's a far more troubled child than she appears. For the immediate future, we're rigging the game in her favour.'

'On the day I first met Londa, she tried to kill a carp,' I said, commiserating. I approached the nearest blossom and inhaled its perfume, a heady scent suggesting peanut butter mixed with mumquat nectar. 'We've spent the past week acting out ethical dilemmas. I think it's helping.'

Henry joined me by the flower, savouring its fragrance. 'Oddly enough, the therapy that seems to work for Donya is moralistic TV programmes.'

'You mean like *Professor Oolong's Oompah-pah Zoo?*'

'Professor Oolong rarely addressed matters of right and wrong. We started her out on *Mr Rogers' Neighbourhood*, and we've just added that family-values superhero thing from the Jubilation Channel, *The Kindness Crusaders*. They're grinding the usual salvation axe, of course, but the ratio of ethical signal to evangelical noise is much better than you'd expect. Be gentle, be generous, think of someone besides yourself – who can argue with that?'

'And you've seen progress?'

Henry raised his eyebrows and dipped his head. 'Before the month is out, I believe that Donya will come to us and say, "I know you've been letting me win at croquet, and I want you to stop."'

We resumed our trek, eventually reaching the island's ragged, craggy spine. Here the wall met a second such concrete barrier, angling off abruptly to the right, the juncture reinforced by a gritty sandstone pillar. Henry suggested that we had 'nothing to gain by staying inside the box', and I agreed. It took us only a minute to locate an overhanging kapok limb. We availed ourselves of this natural bridge – despite his bulk, my companion was quite agile – crossed over the rampart without mishap, and dropped safely to the ground.

The pillar, we now saw, lay at the hub of three discrete walls. Supplementing the familiar north-to-south barrier were two others, one running south-west along the ridge, its twin coursing south-east into the forest, both stretching past the limits of our vision but seemingly destined for the sea – an arrangement that evidently divided Isla de Sangre into three equal regions. Henry and I proceeded due south, improvising a downward path through a dense and fecund wedge of jungle.

By mid-afternoon the forest had turned to scrub, and then a ribbon of gravel appeared, perpendicular to our path. Naturally we were inclined to follow this unexpected road – it might teach us something important about the island, and its pursuit was unlikely to involve alligators or quicksand – but we decided it was only an enticement, built by Edwina to lure her more inquisitive employees away from places she didn't want them to see. We crossed the road and continued our journey, descending towards a line of cypress trees, and in time the guttural wash of the incoming tide reached our ears.

Beyond the cypress windbreak another surprise awaited us: a Spanish fortress lying in ruins like a sandcastle demolished by a wave. Only the central keep remained, emerging from a rocky spit surrounded by a turbulent green bay. The longer I stared at the looming tower, the more ominous it seemed – a twin to Kafka's castle, perhaps, or a nuclear-tipped missile. Stoicism was an admirable philosophy, and Epicureanism had much to recommend it, but no Greek school would ever equip Londa to comprehend and critique the bombs and rockets of modernity. We must advance to the Enlightenment as soon as possible.

Having come so far without misadventure, Henry and I blithely decided to inspect the woebegone stronghold. We approached slowly, moving among lone acacias and solitary boulders, until at last we reached sea level. A gazebo appeared before us, a bamboo construction as large as a village bandstand, its funnel-shaped roof shading two human figures, one slender and birdlike, the other squat and sluggish.

Anger rushed through me like a hit of grappa. Edwina had lied to us. She and Charnock were not in Chicago any more than Henry and I were in Istanbul.

'Rubbish,' my employer was saying. 'Pure twaddle.' She stepped towards the gazebo bench, on which rested a glass container the size and shape of a fire hydrant. 'You need a vacation, that's all.'

Henry and I ducked behind the nearest acacia.

'This isn't fatigue,' Charnock said.

'Who's the troll?' Henry whispered.

'Biologist named Charnock,' I replied. 'Operates a genetic-

67

engineering lab near Faustino. Highly strung, irritable, probably a little nuts.'

'Coming soon to a theatre near you,' Henry muttered, '*The Mad Doctor of Blood Island*.'

'Indeed.'

'That's a real movie.'

'I don't doubt it.'

Scrutinising the glass object, I realised it was a huge beaker to which various devices – pump, compressor, oxygen tank – had been fitted, presumably to sustain whatever creature inhabited the foggy interior.

'I'm experiencing – what should I call it? – a crisis of conscience,' Charnock said. 'During this past month I've extinguished forty-three embryos.'

'Naturally you heard their pathetic little screams.' Edwina made no effort to purge the scorn from her voice.

'Some screams are silent,' Charnock said.

'Since you so enjoy crying crocodile tears over dead embryos, perhaps you should join a community of likeminded mourners,' Edwina said. 'The Roman Catholic Church, for example, or the Republican Party.'

'I was hoping we might have a serious discussion.'

Edwina offered no response but instead sat down beside the beaker and contemplated its misty reaches. 'You do such beautiful work,' she said at last, her tone now free of sarcasm, almost reverent, in fact. 'The painter has his pigments, the sculptor his stone, and you have your medium, too.'

'My medium,' Charnock said. 'Bald egotism wedded to rampant ambition and galloping self-deception.' He settled his gelatinous frame on to the bench and heaved a sigh. 'Maybe you're right. Maybe I need a vacation.'

'Then take one, for Christ's sake.' Edwina gestured towards the tower. 'We can bring everything to fruition as early as – when? Tomorrow afternoon?'

'God rested on Sunday. I intend to do the same.'

'Monday night?'

Charnock grunted in assent.

'And then we'll send you to the Bahamas,' Edwina said.

'I would prefer Hawaii.'

'Excellent choice. You'll have a splendid time. I can picture you on Waikiki Beach, drinking mai tais and diddling the native girls.'

'I thought I might get around to reading *War and Peace*,' Charnock said.

At that instant the vapour in the beaker lifted, and I saw a sleek fishlike something immersed in a translucent fluid. Briefly Charnock and Edwina contemplated the creature, and then the fog rolled in again.

'She'll be the best of the lot,' Charnock said.

'Did you hear the man, Yolly?' Edwina said. 'You're the best. And don't worry about living up to your potential. There are people around here who will do that for you.'

Needless to say – a phrase that any language-obsessed, word-bewitched, Wittgenstein-haunted philosopher like myself uses only with great reluctance – Edwina's duplicity was the principal topic of conversation as Henry and I made our way back to Casa de los Huesos. At first he sought to explain away her presence in the gazebo. Perhaps the artificial-intelligence conference had been cancelled. Maybe Edwina and Charnock had given their presentation and flown directly home. But the tension in Henry's voice suggested that he, too, felt betrayed, and by the time we reached the sandstone pillar he was imagining how we might deceive Edwina in kind.

'Come Monday night, when she and Charnock do whatever the hell it is they plan to do, I'm going to be there, hiding in the shadows,' he said. 'Might I persuade you to join me?'

I responded at once, without consulting the more prudent and self-protective areas of my brain: 'You bet, Uncle Rumpus, I'm your man.'

On Monday morning I left the cottage promptly at nine-thirty and headed for Faustino with the aim of tutoring Londa in Epicureanism. Suddenly, with an almost predatory pounce, she burst from the jungle and stationed herself directly in my path. Her attire was as minimalist as a knock-knock joke: a yellow spandex tube top revealing regions of skin both tanned and untanned (apparently she favoured one-piece bathing suits), plus pink flip-flops and a white towel slung around her waist like a sarong.

'Hardly the proper outfit for a philosophy lesson,' I admonished her. 'You'll have plenty of time to go swimming this afternoon. Right now your business is chapter five.'

'You asked me to make up a conversation between an Epicurean and an anti-Epicurean.' She opened her shoulder bag and removed a manuscript of perhaps a dozen pages. 'Before I knew it, I'd written a one-act play.'

'*Mazel tov*,' I said mordantly. 'Now go change into something that bespeaks the life of the mind. I'll read your play in the meantime.'

'I call it "Coral Idolatry",' she persisted, depositing the pages in my hands. 'I've given you the part of Thales, a fictional Greek Epicurean. I'm playing Sythia, a sea nymph seeking to fulfil her destiny. The setting is my secret beach. Follow me.'

Although Londa's interpretation of the assignment struck me as too clever by half, I decided that such creativity should be encouraged, so I allowed her to lead me along a path I'd never taken before. In time the trees and bushes yielded to dunes as white as refined sugar, a pristine canvas that the incoming tide painted in agreeable shades of beige and brown. A quarter-mile out to sea a mound of crimson coral rose from the reef like a buoy, and the instant Londa told me the formation's name, the Red Witch, I knew exactly what she meant, for it resembled a crone wearing a conical hat.

'Don't worry, I'm not about to bore you with a thousand facts about witches,' Londa said.

Spontaneously I removed my socks and sandals, allowing my toes to savour the sand. Directly before us lay a piece of driftwood that suggested the horned head of a Cretan bull. Londa instructed me to sit between the prongs and wait for the curtain to rise. I declined, explaining that the sun was too hot for a pale philosopher from Boston, and if I stayed out here much longer I'd be broiled alive. Londa responded by retrieving a bottle of sunscreen from her bag and spraying my arms.

'Close your eyes,' she demanded.

I did so. A vivid bloodscape filled my field of vision. Londa lacquered my brow, jaw, nose, and neck, rubbing the cream into my pores with her fingertips.

'Your cue occurs halfway down the page,' she said. 'Will the man I see before me grant my wish?'

She unhitched the towel from her waist, letting it drop in a heap on to the sand. Her bikini bottom matched her top in colour and audacity. She headed towards the Red Witch, wading into the sea until it reached her hips. She took a breath and disappeared. Evidently her diving accident had not left her with an indiscriminate fear of water. I sat on the driftwood and glanced at the script. The setting was the Greek island called Sérifos. According to the stage directions, the undine Sythia would now abandon her home beneath the waves and approach Thales as he relaxed on the shore thinking rarefied Epicurean thoughts.

'Action!' I called in Londa's direction.

Slowly, elegantly, she rose from her aquatic abode, the foam spilling from her hair, cascading down her tube top, trickling along her thighs. She strode towards me through the surf, each step an emphatic splash.

'An undine lives with one purpose in her heart,' she declaimed, as that was indeed Sythia's first line. 'She seeks a mortal who will love her, betroth her, and lavish his body upon her, for in this manner alone might she acquire a soul.' Gaining the beach, she took a dozen steps forward and stood over Thales, dripping sea-water on to his script.

'Two hundred days have I followed the submarine currents, seeking the legendary Isle of Sérifos, whose pleasure-loving hedonists never hesitate to avail themselves of succulent nymphs and willing sylphs. Could it be that my search has finally ended? Might the man I see before me grant my wish?'

'Forgive me for gaping, but I'm astonished to find myself a mere stone's throw from a creature of your kind,' I said. 'Until now I've observed undines only from afar. Whenever I take ship, I stand on the deck and stare out to sea, hoping to glimpse a nymph sporting with the dolphins.'

'My name is Sythia. Are you a hedonist?'

'Call me Thales, disciple of Epicurus.'

'Epicurus? Then I must surmise that for you the essence of pleasure is the removal of pain.'

'True, fair Sythia. Once pain is gone, pleasure admits of variation but not of increase. I'm equally at odds with the self-indulgent hedonists and the life-denying Stoics. An Epicurean pursues the quiet virtues: friendship, conversation, tranquillity.'

'So for you the nubility of an undine is no more pleasurable than the nobility of an idea?'

'Quite so.'

'Could you direct me to the nearest hedonist?'

'Alas, there are none on this isle.'

'I'd heard that Sérifos is swarming with profligates.'

'You were misinformed.'

It was at this point that I had the good sense to skim the next three pages, and what I encountered was so appalling I had no choice but to shut down the production on the spot.

'Well, Londa,' I said, lurching free of the driftwood and stepping out of character, 'you certainly know your Epicureans. I especially enjoyed your wordplay: nubility, nobility. Wonderful. For your next assignment, I'd like you to—'

'We haven't finished.'

'I glanced ahead,' I told her. 'The script requires you to kiss me on the lips.'

'No, the script requires Sythia to kiss Thales on the lips. And for Thales to kiss her back. Before you know it they're following their pagan impulses.'

'Only last Thursday you described that sort of behaviour as messy and dangerous. An Epicurean eschews all pleasures that have potentially painful consequences. Bacchanals, binges, fornication.'

'But that's what makes the play *interesting*,' Londa insisted, running a hooked finger along her thighs to remove the furls in her bikini bottom. Her nipples had moulded the yellow spandex into lemon drops of such magnificence they would have confounded any passing postmodernist bearing theories of gender as a social construction. 'Thales is torn in two. He can't decide between his desire for the undine and his loyalty to Epicureanism.'

'Your assignment for tomorrow is to read my chapter on

Aristotle's *Nicomachean Ethics*,' I said. 'We'll sit in the library and discuss it wearing street clothes.'

'Of course, after Sythia and Thales have their roll in the clover, he realises that pleasure *does* come in degrees.' Londa took hold of her beach towel, spreading it across the sand as if fitting a sheet to a mattress. 'And once Thales realises that Epicureanism is flawed, he no longer hesitates to bend its rules.'

This was not an unprecedented situation. Such circumstances had arisen before. Young teacher, moonstruck student, sufficient privacy.

'I'm not going to kiss you,' I said.

'When you give me a conscience,' she replied, setting her rump on the towel, 'I'll become a completely honest person, won't I?'

'No one's completely honest.'

'But it's an ideal worth striving for, right?'

'Indeed.'

'Do you want to kiss me, Mason? Tell me honestly.'

Saying nothing, I resumed my driftwood seat and pulled my socks back on without bothering to shake out the sand. I restored my sandals, the straps and buckles vibrating in my hands. Londa stayed on her towel, smiling broadly, and arranged herself in a lotus position.

'The Aristotle chapter is one of my better efforts,' I said. 'Study it thoroughly.'

'Don't you want to fuck me?' she asked.

'Pay particular attention to the notion that virtue consists in avoiding extremes. When Aristotle speaks of the optimum response to a stimulus, he's not endorsing mediocrity. He's celebrating harmony.'

'Mother is still in Chicago. Dr Charnock never comes here. We could fuck until our eyes fell out, and nobody would know.'

My stomach seemed to break free of its moorings and collide with my heart. An erotic lava gushed through my veins. 'This sunscreen isn't working very well,' I said, starting into the jungle. 'I'm getting burned.'

'What did you think of my play?' she called after me.

'B-plus at the very least, perhaps an A-minus!' I shouted over my shoulder, running towards my cottage as fast as my conscience could carry me.

A simple concrete wall, an unremarkable rampart of sand and cement – but as Henry and I followed its southerly course that evening, our path lit by moonbeams and the glow of our Coleman lanterns, I felt as if the thing had replicated itself, again and again, so that we were negotiating a maze as complex as the one Daedalus had designed to confine the Minotaur. I suspected that Edwina and Charnock counted Daedalus among their heroes, for he was arguably the world's first genetic engineer, having supervised the synthesis of a beast as chimeric and unnatural as Proserpine. If I'd correctly interpreted the conversation in the gazebo, tonight Henry and I would witness the birth of a biological contrivance called Yolly, though I could not imagine whether its lineage would be piscean, reptilian, amphibian, mammalian or some profane amalgam of all four.

'Londa tried to seduce me this morning,' I said as we approached the sandstone pillar.

'Tell me more,' Henry said. 'I'll try to keep an open mind.'

'There's nothing more to tell, I'm happy to say. I ran away before things got out of hand.'

'A wise policy. Stick to it.'

We vaulted the wall, advanced to the scrub and, fearful of encountering some armed sentry with a damaged superego, jogged all the way to the cypress windbreak. By the time we reached sea level the heavens were rumbling with the kettledrum cadence of a thunderstorm. Moments later the deluge arrived. We took refuge in the gazebo long enough to catch our breath and shake off the rainwater. Staring through the downpour, I beheld a great trellis of lightning flash behind the Spanish fortress. The tower was dark but for the uppermost window, which emitted a luminous white shaft as bright as a lighthouse beacon.

We abandoned the gazebo, negotiated the ragged spit, and followed the span of a lowered drawbridge extending from the keep like an impertinent tongue. Although Henry had thought to bring along what he called his 'Official Professor Oolong Breaking and Entering Kit' – a satchel packed with a crowbar, a sledge-

74

hammer, and a coil of rope – it proved superfluous, for to breach the keep one needed merely to push open a squat wooden door that nobody had bothered to lock.

Cleaving to the shadows and shedding raindrops, we made our way along the perimeter of the great hall, a pristine and convivial space clearly intended for human habitation: new furniture, linen curtains, oriental carpets. We crept up the main staircase, a stone helix winding ever upward through the tower, until we gained the topmost landing, where a steel door presented itself. Henry twisted the knob. The door pivoted quietly on well-oiled hinges, and we slipped unnoticed into the room beyond, hiding behind a free-standing glass cabinet jammed with glittering surgical instruments, perhaps including the very scalpel Edwina had used to rid Pro-serpine of her brain.

The laboratory proper was a sunken affair harshly illuminated by halogen lamps and dominated by a worktable on which rested the mysterious beaker with its retrofitted pump, compressor, and oxygen tank. Dressed in black rubber aprons and neoprene gloves, Edwina and Dr Charnock peered into the vessel's mouth. I stifled a gasp. Sitting amid the whorls of mist was a human foetus – eyes closed, lips sealed with silver tape, body immersed in a clear fluid. A newborn? Doubtful, for it could not yet breathe on its own, or so I surmised from the pair of delicate plastic tubes connecting the nostrils to the air supply.

At the far end of the worktable rose a steel gantry culminating in a pulley from which hung a nylon cord that, before reaching the beaker, split into two strands that looped around the foetus's upper arms, giving the creature the appearance of a Christmas-pageant angel bound for the rafters of a church. No sooner had I absorbed this weird tableau than Edwina approached the gantry and began cranking the winch, slowly, carefully, clockwise, rav-elling up the cord and lifting the foetus from its amniotic bath. I glanced at the ceiling. An array of plasma computer monitors lined the dome, each screen displaying a sea of shivering grey static. The foetus continued its ascent, the beaker fluid trickling from its miniature fingers and toes.

Now Edwina pivoted the gantry, so that the foetus travelled horizontally across the laboratory until it dangled above the sealed hatch of a tarnished metallic chamber that, with its spherical shape, riveted plates, and bellyband of portholes, suggested nothing so much as an antique diving bell. Charnock locked his gaze on four glass tanks stacked like aquariums in a pet store, each holding a vivid liquid – gold, crimson, violet, turquoise – and connected to the diving bell via a mesh of translucent corrugated hoses. Approaching a console bristling with valves and regulators, he proceeded to turn the handles in tiny increments, thus controlling the force and generosity with which the tanks delivered their contents to the rivetted sphere. In less than fifteen minutes the chamber had acquired a dark seething soup in which millions of bubbles cavorted like fireflies speckling a summer night.

Charnock threw a lever on the console, causing the chamber hatch to groan and creak and finally flip back like a cranium yielding to Sinuhe's fingers. Coils of steam rose from the vat, plus a nauseating fragrance redolent of burning hair. A burst of lightning filled the laboratory with a sudden radiance, turning the suspended foetus as white as a christening gown. An instant later the thunder boomed.

Edwina worked the gantry winch, anticlockwise this time, and the foetus began its descent, soon disappearing into the broth, oxygen tubes trailing behind it like filaments from a silkworm. Henry and I fixed on the nearest porthole, peering into the milky fluid in the hope of learning the creature's fate. Briefly I entertained the darkest of notions – the scientists were dissolving the nascent baby in a caustic fluid, sacrificing it to some god to whom only Daedalus and Edwina and Charnock prayed – but then I realised that a different phenomenon was unfolding. The foetus was growing, its flesh and bones pressing outward in an image that evoked a set of Russian nested dolls being packed safely away, each hollow soul subsumed by its descendants.

For a full hour, the foetus continued to undergo its hyperbolic maturation, steadily progressing from the tender flesh of infancy to the pliant lines of childhood to the supple contours of pre-adolescence.

'Finished!' Charnock cried.

Henry and I exchanged bewildered glances. In recent years I'd beheld Max Crippen's sculpture of the Crucifixion rendered

76

entirely in Lego, Valerio Caparelli's Norman Rockwell-style painting of God inseminating the Virgin Mary on their first date, and Leonard Steele's rock opera set in the Vatican's luxury suite for retired paedophile priests, but what Edwina and Charnock had achieved was sacrilege of a wholly different order: blasphemy beyond the meaning of the word.

Edwina rotated the winch. The girl rose from the diving bell, oscillating like a criminal on a gibbet, the dark fluid sluicing down her limbs, her flesh glistening under the halogen lamps.

Now came the final flourish, the last ingredient in the stew of her nativity. From a black box embedded in the dome a gleaming inverted bowl descended on a golden thread. Bristling with bright nubs and silvery nodes, the device resembled a motorcycle helmet customised by a schizophrenic bent on receiving messages from another galaxy. Even as the strange gear settled over the girl's damp hair, snugging against her cranium, the computer monitors flared into life, their static dissolving into frenetic montages. Trees, plants, flowers, insects, birds, fish, snakes, lizards, turtles, toads, rodents, and ruminants paraded across the screens – kind after kind, beast after beast – soon yielding to pots, pans, light bulbs, hammers, saws, hats, gloves, guns, eyeglasses, automobiles, and ten thousand other artefacts. Then came a cavalcade of kings, queens, emperors, empresses, caliphs, pharaohs, rajahs, shahs, dictators, prime ministers, and presidents, followed by mathematical signs denoting addition, subtraction, multiplication, division, ratios, percentages, and square roots. The child learned of shoes and ships and sealing wax, of cabbages and yet more kings, each input registering for a fraction of a second, like pips on playing cards being shuffled by a manic croupier.

Edwina and Charnock approached the diving bell and cast their gazes upward.

'Yolly, this is your mother,' Charnock said to the newborn pre-adolescent.

'Welcome to the world,' Lady Daedalus said, 'my dearest, sweetest darling.'

Yolly's lids flickered open. Her eyes, mismatched emeralds, glowed and pulsed in her skull like luminous moons orbiting her cerebrum. She raised one hand and tore the silver tape from her lips. She clucked her tongue and coughed, but it was only when she released a howl of fear, shock, and dismay that I grew certain of her lineage. The creature suspended before Henry and me was Londa's newborn sister, and Donya's sister too – bereft of ethics, barren in experience, and condemned to live whatever facsimile of a life Edwina had designed for her.

CHAPTER 5

Mantles aglow like luminous mumquats, our Coleman lanterns lit the way as Henry and I doubled back through the jungle, every leaf and branch dripping with the residue of the storm. The surrounding darkness colluded with my fevered imagination to populate Isla de Sangre with monsters, misbegotten beasts spawned by Edwina's ambition and Charnock's art. I saw a colony of shaggy primates, half-man, half-ape, sucking up water from the swamp. An immense spider spinning a web whose jagged geometry suggested a windshield bashed by a mailed fist. A python coiled around an acacia, its tubular body studded with a hundred eyeballs, so that not only could the creature see in all directions, it could see itself seeing in all directions.

Throughout our return to the island's saner shore, Henry and I discussed the conception, prenatal development, and artificial maturation of Yolly Sabacthani, trying without success to persuade ourselves that Londa and Donya had not arisen from the same unseemly science. We decided that in each case Edwina must have donated the essential ovum and we further hypothesised that once this egg had been fertilised by some Nobel laureate's sperm, she'd been unable or unwilling to gestate the subsequent zygote. A rational scenario. So far, so good. But why subject the embryo to that infernal diving bell when dozens of financially desperate women would gladly lease their natural reproductive apparatus to Edwina? And what did Lady Daedalus hope to accomplish by treating Yolly and her sisters – yes, it seemed logical to assume that Donya and Londa had been similarly accelerated – like hothouse orchids?

Without particularly meaning to, I ended up escorting Henry all the way to his beachfront bungalow, a stout breezeblock structure set on concrete piles as a defence against the ubiquitous hurricanes. The place was vibrant with paintings of the local monkeys, macaws, flamingoes, and toucans, each signed with Brock's filigreed initials, a soothing gallery that soon drove the ape-men and their brethren from my mind. The artist himself had fallen asleep in his armchair, snoring softly before an unfinished canvas of a cone-hatted wizard, bent with age and weary with wisdom, staring into a mirror and seeing his youthful self stare back – doubtless a gift for little Donya. Before parting company, Henry and I exchanged cell-phone numbers, agreeing that whoever first sighted Edwina would tell her what we'd witnessed and that therefore a candid con-versation among Lady Daedalus and her employees would be in order.

'I wonder, from now on will we bring some subtle prejudice to our dealings with Donya and Londa?' I asked.

Henry moaned knowingly. 'I'll get up each morning, and I'll tell myself that Donya is completely human, but then a sardonic voice will whisper in my ear, "What ugly epithet shall we invent for her today? Shall we call Donya a beaker freak?"'

'A vatling,' I suggested.

'Petri doll,' Henry said.

'Bouillababy.'

'Gumbo girl.'

'Tureen queen.'

'Shame on us,' Henry said.

'Shame on us,' I agreed.

Ten hours later, I entered the Faustino library in thrall to a despair whose utter Aristotelian reasonableness – only a fool or a madman would have reacted otherwise to the previous night's circus – did nothing to lessen its intensity, and so I felt especially grateful when Londa, standing crestfallen beside the conquistador, apologised for attempting to seduce me, calling her scheme 'sneaky and snaky'.

'Those are two good words for it,' I said.

'I guess I'm still basically crazy, huh, Mason?'

'Of course not. You're coming along fine. A few rough edges, but the prince of philosophers will smooth them off for you.'

'You *are* a prince, Mason.'

'I meant Aristotle.'

'Snakiness aside, I'd still like to know whether you find me attractive.'

'Aristotle is commonly regarded as antiquity's most brilliant mind. Let's try to find out why.'

'Sometimes I think I'm terribly ugly.'

'You're not ugly, Londa. Once you're in college, you'll have dozens of boyfriends.'

'None of them as interesting as my morality teacher.'

'Every time I read the *Nicomachean Ethics*, I find something new.'

We spent the rest of the lesson on the venerable Greek's doctrine of the mean – the virtuous man does not burden himself with inhibitions, nor does he permit his impulses to reign unchecked – and I must admit that this principle now struck me as superficial in the extreme, unlikely to have netted Aristotle a master's degree from Parsons, much less a PhD from Hawthorne. All through the lesson I pondered Henry's astute and disturbing question. Were we now fated to perceive our charges as not quite human? Like an alchemist's potion or a witch's brew Londa had evidently been made in a cauldron. Quite probably she could summon no pre-adolescent memories for the breathtakingly bizarre reason that she'd had no pre-adolescence. I still knew her as my pupil, my mentee, my eminently worthy mission – but now she was also my vatling.

On Wednesday we mulled over Aristotle's answer to a paradox first identified by Socrates. How can a human being know what is right and yet do what is wrong? But because neither of us found this puzzle compelling – it seemed a non-problem, really – we couldn't get excited by the solution: anger or desire may moment-arily compromise a person's philosophical commitment to virtue. The following day we wrestled with the great man's notion of justice, and within an hour we'd become so bored with the usual dreary Aristotelian dichotomies, universal justice versus particular justice, distributive justice versus rectificatory justice, household justice versus political justice, natural justice versus legal justice, that we turned our energies to teaching Quetzie the phrase 'Hedonism, anyone?' By the time Friday rolled around, Londa and I were heartily sick of Aristotle, and so instead of analysing his excruciating consideration of pleasure, complete with the usual paean to temperance, we sat down at the chessboard. During the first game Londa succumbed to my skill with the knight, inadvertently allowing me to fork her queen and her queen's rook. She learned from her mistake, however, and in game two I barely played her to a draw.

I passed all of Saturday morning lazing around the cottage, drinking too much coffee and reading too much Gadamer. At noon my cell phone rang. It was Henry, bearing the news that he'd just stumbled upon Edwina playing Liszt on the villa's Steinway. She'd stopped her performance long enough to announce that she and Dr Charnock had returned from Chicago the previous evening. 'No, you didn't,' Henry had insisted, then proceeded to explain how he knew this, and so Edwina had agreed to meet with him, Brock and myself three hours hence in the Faustino conservatory.

'I imagine she wasn't too thrilled to hear we'd witnessed Yolly's birth,' I said.

'She avoided the subject,' Henry said, 'but when she went back to playing Liszt, she switched from the Concerto in D to *Totentanz*. If music could kill, Mason, I'd be a dead man.'

Before we three unhappy tutors entered the conservatory that afternoon, I warned Henry and Brock about the sentient tree, lest Proserpine's unnerving habits distract them from the matter at hand. A wise precaution, for throughout our conversation with Edwina the mangrove's branches quavered, her lungs chuffed, and the sap throbbed audibly in her trunk.

Lady Daedalus occupied her customary wicker chair, the spiteful ginger cat socketed in her lap. The rest of us were accorded fanback furniture as well, so that our meeting resembled a gathering of wilting southern aristocrats in some particularly gaudy and best forgotten Tennessee Williams play.

'Had you not already established nourishing relationships with my daughters,' Edwina began, 'I would dismiss the three of you as spies and traitors.'

'Unless we quit first,' I noted.

'Your prerogative,' she said

'Our prerogative,' Henry agreed.

Edwina heaved a sigh, stroked her cat, and contemplated her anamorphic reflection in the silver coffee urn. As usual she had dressed elegantly, her white lace gown accessorised by a rope of lustrous pearls. 'Hear my confession,' she said at last. 'If you find my actions unconscionable' – whatever remorse her tone contained could not conceal the sarcasm – 'I'll put on sackcloth, stuff my mouth with ashes, and otherwise mortify myself.'

'We'd settle for severance pay,' Henry said.

She began by admitting that our pupils owed their existence less to sexual reproduction than to scientific contrivance. By repeatedly fusing her cumulus-cell DNA with anonymous denucleated donor eggs, nurturing the resulting zygotes in Petri dishes, transferring the surviving blastocysts to glass wombs, injecting the three most auspicious embryos with pituitary hormone, allowing them to reach foetushood and, finally, inserting each genetic twin into Dr Charnock's titanium chamber, his RXL-313 ontogenerator, its arcane broth carefully brewed to stimulate the child's glands, Edwina had brought Londa, Donya, and Yolly into the world.

'Names that, as you may have noticed, meld rather musically into "Yolonda",' she said.

By Edwina's account, Londa possessed the body of a woman in late adolescence, yet she'd been on the planet barely eight weeks. Although she appeared no younger than five years of age, Donya was only six weeks out of the vat. And while Yolly's growth had been accelerated until she'd come to resemble an eleven-year-old, she was in fact – as Henry and I knew all too well – a newborn.

The headgear through which the girls' brains had been flooded with facts was quite possibly the most complex machine–human interface on the planet. Its inventor, Vincent Charnock, had dubbed the thing a DUNCE cap: Data Upload for Normal Cognitive Efficacy. As Edwina proceeded to describe in detail the onto-generator and its concomitant DUNCE cap, I soon realised that her enthusiasm for this technology bordered on fetishism, and I found myself rejecting her claim that, alienation and anomie notwithstanding, Londa, Donya, and Yolly had all left the laboratory as whole and healthy persons. Even the lesions in her children's superegos gave Edwina no genuine pause. After all, this pathology could evidently be circumvented by a competent professional – Yolly's tutor, a female psychologist from Baltimore named Jordan Frazier, would arrive before the week was out – and so there was little reason to doubt that her progeny would enjoy normal and happy lives.

'And has your sick little enterprise run its course,' Henry asked, 'or are you building up to a lacrosse team?'

'Yolly is the last,' Edwina said. 'From your long faces and low comedy, gentlemen, I surmise that you find my project unsavoury.'

The three of us nodded in unison.

'Unsavoury, unseemly, and self-centred,' Henry said.

'Your children aren't the only ones around here with an ethics problem,' Brock noted.

'Question, Edwina,' I said. 'When you told me Londa's father died of pancreatic cancer, was that a total falsehood, or did you in fact once have a husband?'

'For ten years I was married to a plastic surgeon named Francis Ulmer,' Edwina replied. 'Our union was without issue. At last report he'd moved his practice to New York City and committed himself to helping Park Avenue matrons stay off the mortality track.' She took a long sip of mumquat-enhanced coffee. 'If only you could comprehend the depth of a woman's need to have children. But such empathy is probably beyond the male imagination.'

'No, Edwina,' I said, cheeks burning with anger, 'I can empathise just fine. What I can't grasp is a woman bringing three duplicates of herself into the world without their consent.'

'We all come into the world without our consent,' she noted.

Henry issued an indignant snort. 'As *babies*, Edwina, as *babies*, not as ethically impaired doppelgängers who've been told they're amnesiacs. I can respect your desire for children, but I can hardly condone the way you've denied Donya her infancy, Yolly her childhood and Londa her pre-adolescence.'

'You've stolen *years* from the lives of those girls,' Brock added.

Edwina raised a hand to her collar, nervously sliding her fingers along the pearls. 'True enough,' she said, slowly and without emotion. 'But it happens that I shall never have the luxury of watching a child of mine pursue a conventional developmental path. In a year I shall be dead, give or take two months. I might even die before Christmas.'

Decades after Edwina's abrupt announcement, I still remember how it stunned and disoriented and – yes – infuriated me. The woman was terminally ill. Most lamentable. The pale priest had her on his radar. What a shame. And yet her attempt to redeem her imminent oblivion through this genomic jamboree seemed utterly deranged to me: narcissism promoted to a psychosis.

'My disease is so rare the haematologists need three Latin words to name it,' she continued. 'Gradually but relentlessly, my blood is turning to water. Happily for Yolonda, the etiology is not genetic but traces to certain toxins I encountered during my years at Odradek Pharmaceuticals.'

'How sad that you have such a knack for bending nature to your will,' I said, 'and yet you can't cure yourself.' A cruel remark, but sparing Edwina's feelings was not my top priority just then.

'The irony is not lost on me,' Edwina said. 'But at least, thanks to Yolonda, I'll get to experience the totality of motherhood before I die.'

Against my expectations, she now became buoyant. In the months that remained to her, Edwina said, eyes sparkling, fingers dancing as if scurrying along her piano keyboard, she would know the pleasures of nurturing a preschooler. She would likewise experience the delights of amusing, and being amused by, a pre-adolescent, even as she tackled the challenging but rewarding business of ushering a young woman into adulthood.

'And then, when the end comes, I shall have my daughters to comfort me.'

'Who will comfort *them*?' Brock asked, curling his lip.

Edwina suddenly turned defensive, haughtily asserting that she'd 'put more thought into Yolonda's future' than we could possibly imagine. The patents she held on various genetically engineered seeds, foodstuffs, and antivirus drugs were 'worth several fortunes', and each sister would inherit a sum sufficient for her to hire

85

whatever caregivers, teachers, and legal advocates she might require.

'If you would like to remain on the island after my death and continue to instruct your charges, that can be arranged,' she told us. 'But please don't begrudge me the satisfactions that the coming year promises to bring.'

Before the month was out, we now learned, as soon as Yolly had acquired a rudimentary conscience, Edwina would throw herself into the project, alternately imparting maternal wisdom to the children and lavishing them with love. During any given week, she would circulate among the three domains – Faustino, Casa de los Huesos, and the renovated Spanish fortress on the Bahía de Matecumba – according each daughter at least two days of her undivided attention. She hoped we would allow the girls to continue ascribing their memory gaps to amnesia, and she entreated us to keep them ignorant of one another, so that their energies and affections would stay focused on their mother.

Their *mother*. Edwina kept using that word. This woman was no more a mother than her pearls were her father's eyes.

'So that is my story, gentlemen,' she said. 'And now it's your turn to hold forth. Go ahead. Be honest. What do you think of me?'

Without hesitation I said, 'I think you're the woman Nietzsche would've wanted for a mother. The *Übermom*.'

'I shall take that as a compliment,' Edwina said. 'And what is your opinion, Henry? Do you find anything in my project beyond Nietzschean bravado?'

'Here's my promise to you, Edwina,' he replied. 'Once Yolly has grown up and moved out of her tower by the sea, I'm going to hire a mob of peasants with torches to wreck your damn laboratory.'

'I'll be leading the attack,' Brock said, 'and by the time we've finished with Charnock's ontogenerator, it won't be good for making a bowl of popcorn, much less a human being.'

'Are you saying you wish to resign?' Edwina asked.

'I would *love* to resign,' Brock replied. 'But that wouldn't be fair to Donya.'

'I feel more loyalty to this mangrove than I do to you,' Henry said. 'I won't desert my post, though, not until Donya's cured.'

'What about you, Mason?' Edwina asked. 'Can Londa count on your continued tutelage, or do you plan to walk out the door?'

I reached towards Proserpine's nearest branch, curling my fingers around the pulsing bark. Could Londa count on me? An excellent question. The best question I'd heard all day.

'I must say that Brock's reasoning makes sense to me,' I began. 'He and Henry have an obligation to Donya, and they intend to honour it. And I can easily imagine Yolly's tutor hearing the whole story and still deciding to go ahead with it. But my case – that is, Londa's case – is rather different.'

I plucked a mumquat and inhaled the consoling scent. Londa, I explained, had entered the world burdened with the flesh and physiology of a seventeen-year-old, and yet, before I took her under my wing, her psyche had been a blank slate – a literal blank slate, not John Locke's hypothetical *tabula rasa*. And it was still largely a blank slate. Apart from our role-playing exercises, she'd had absolutely no experience of confronting ethical dilemmas or making moral choices.

'Don't you see the evil in this, Edwina? Chronological age, seventeen. Deontological age, zero. Don't you see the disconnect? You didn't hire me to shape Londa's soul – you hired me to *make* her soul. What right does a mere mortal have to do that?'

'A scintillating distinction, Mason, but you haven't answered my question,' Edwina said. 'Are you going to walk out the door or not?'

Call it my sin, dear reader. My fall from grace, my plunge into presumption, my seduction by pride. Whatever its name, I did not walk out the door that afternoon. Instead this mere mortal fixed Edwina with an incandescent eye and said, 'If I don't finish my work with Londa, you'll simply hire another philosopher, somebody who doesn't know Epicurus from ipecac.'

'Good decision,' Edwina said.

'God help me,' I said.

During the remainder of this fractious gathering, we three teachers struck a bargain with our woefully ill and possibly insane employer. Professional ethics, we insisted, forbade us to sit back and watch her deceive yet another member of our fellowship. We fully intended to give Jordan Frazier of Baltimore a complete account of Yolly's genesis, making it clear that, for better or worse, she would not merely be tutoring the girl but crafting her moral essence, and if Edwina contradicted us on any point, we would gleefully tell the children that they each had two sisters – three, counting Edwina. For our part, we would allow Londa and Donya to continue believing they were amnesiacs bereft of siblings, and we would prevail upon Jordan to nurture the same illusion in Yolly.

My colleagues persuaded me to spend the rest of the afternoon in their bungalow, sampling beers from various Miami micro-breweries and attending what Henry called 'the first official meeting of the faculty of Hubris Academy'. I wasn't sure whose hubris he was referring to, ours or Edwina's, but the name fitted in either case. As our colloquy progressed, we gradually convinced ourselves to adopt a more generous attitude towards Lady Daedalus's scheming, something between acquiescence and acceptance. After all, both Londa and Donya seemed fairly well adjusted, and Yolly was probably equally sound of mind and body. True, Edwina meant to exploit them, but it so happened that this exploitation looked a great deal like love.

'I'm afraid our efforts to help the children may prove even trickier than we imagine,' I confessed, sipping my coconut ale.

'I don't want to hear this,' Henry said.

'Martin Heidegger,' I said.

'Heidegger was a Nazi,' Brock said.

'A Nazi, a nitpicker, and the worst sort of pedant, but I still have to respect his concept of *Geworfenheit*,' I said.

'Sounds like a character out of the Brothers Grimm,' Henry noted, sampling his mango lager. '"Geworfenheit and the Enchanted Lederhosen".'

'*Geworfenheit*, thrownness, the paramount fact of the human condition,' I said. 'Every person is hurled into a world, a culture, a set of immediate circumstances not of his own choosing. The authentic life is a quest to comprehend one's status as a mortal *Dasein*, a self-conscious subject, a creature for whom the riddle of situated existence – being here, inhabiting the given – is a central problem, if not *the* central problem.'

'I don't know what the fuck you're talking about,' Henry said irritably, an attitude I attributed to his enthusiastic beer consumption.

'But if the average person is *thrown* into the world,' I continued, 'then Edwina's offspring have been *shot* into the world, like a circus performer being blasted out of a cannon. For most of us, pondering the mystery of *Dasein* leads to anxiety. For Londa and Donya and Yolly – well, I shudder to imagine what they might be facing down the road. Exponential despair. Angst to the nth. But there's reason for hope. According to Heidegger, a *Dasein* can ameliorate its encounter with nothingness by adopting a nurturing attitude towards other beings.'

'And according to me, a *Dasein* can ameliorate its encounter with nothingness by not reading Heidegger,' Henry said.

'I'm feeling pretty anxious myself right now, but it has nothing to do with my thrownness,' Brock said, taking a long swallow of velvet cream porter. 'I keep thinking about that DUNCE cap thing. I'm jealous of it.'

'You're jealous of a machine?' Henry said.

'It got to Donya before we did,' Brock explained, 'filling her brain with whatever crap Edwina and Charnock thought she'd need to survive. I know this sounds strange, but I feel like *I* should've been Donya's first tutor, not that damn headgear. I want to go to Edwina and say, "The next time you ask Henry and me to forge somebody's soul, invite us in sooner, and leave technology out of it."'

'I'll tell you what's got *me* rattled,' Henry said. 'It's not that Edwina decided to make three copies of herself. It's that she insists on collapsing them into a single person.'

'*E pluribus unum*,' Brock said, nodding.

'Exactly,' I replied.

Sunday afternoon found me searching through the Faustino library, looking for whatever works by Heidegger might be in residence. I'd decided that the more deeply I plumbed his notions of *Dasein* and *Geworfenheit*, the more effective I might be in treating Londa's nascent despair. I didn't expect to come across *Being and Time*, that Mount Everest of philosophy tomes, but the collection did boast *What Is Metaphysics?*, sandwiched alphabetically between Hegel's *Aesthetics* and Husserl's *Logical Investigations*. I abducted the book from beneath the conquistador's vigilant gaze, returned to my cottage, and dived in.

My initial perusal of *What Is Metaphysics?* yielded no insights into Londa's situation, but my efforts were nevertheless rewarded. 'Only because the Nothing is revealed in the very basis of our *Dasein* is it possible for the utter strangeness of what-is to dawn on us. Only when the strangeness of what-is forces itself upon us does it awaken and invite our wonder. Only because of wonder, that is to say, the revelation of the Nothing, does the "Why?" spring to our lips.' Where else but in Heidegger could a person find such exhilarating obscurity? This wasn't the Food Channel. This wasn't *Chicken Soup for the Credulous*. This wasn't Jesus on a stick. This was philosophy, by God, red in tooth and claw, Sinuhe wandering the banks of the Nile, asking the great 'Why?' question until Isis and Horus and even wise Thoth himself were sick of hearing it.

A frenzied pounding interrupted my idyll. Reluctantly I abandoned my Heidegger and stumbled to the door. My visitor was Edwina, breathlessly announcing that Londa was in trouble.

'An ark full of assholes has run aground in the cove,' she elaborated. 'They're driving her crazy. She could use our help.'

'Huh?'

'Get dressed.'

As always, I bristled at the *Übermom*'s presumptuous manner, but if Londa indeed needed me, then my obligation was clear. I slipped into my khakis and They Might Be Giants T-shirt, then joined Edwina as, huffing and puffing, she made her way down to the Bahía de Flores.

Our three intruders, beefy men in Bermuda shorts and strident Hawaiian shirts, had recently enjoyed a picnic supper on the dunes, or so I guessed from the smouldering fire and the trail of trash and paper plates streaked with grease strewn between the campsite and their beached dinghy. In the middle of the bay a sleek fibreglass cabin cruiser, the *Phyllis II* according to her stern, lay jammed against the red coral reef. Not only had the intruders despoiled the beach, they were also polluting the water. A profane halo of full-spectrum, iridescent petroleum surrounded the yacht's hull, spreading outwards like the rainbow through which Satan had sealed his covenant with Exxon in Genesis 9:13.

Londa was wandering around the picnic site, methodically picking up the trash and placing it in a burlap sack. The intruders showed no inclination to assist her, being content to play Frisbee in the gathering dusk, killing time while waiting for the rising tide to free their yacht.

Upon spotting her mother and me, Londa halted her bagging operation and strode towards us wearing an expression of supreme dismay.

'This is a private island, not a public dump,' Edwina informed the nearest sailor, a bearish man with a Hapsburg jaw. 'Kindly dispose of your crap.'

The yachtsman raised his hand, nonchalantly intercepted the Frisbee in mid-flight, and offered Edwina a deferential nod. 'Of course, ma'am, you're absolutely right.' To judge from his headgear, a captain's cap embroidered with an anchor, he was the skipper of the *Phyllis II*. 'If there's one thing I respect, it's private property.'

'I'm not surprised to hear that,' Edwina said drily.

'Ralph Gittikac, CEO of Gittikac's Getaway Adventures,' the captain said, as if we were dying to know how assholes earned their living these days. 'That's my brother Brandon with the major sunburn.'

'And I'm Mike the Spike,' said the third intruder, his neck hung with gold chains, 'king of the investment brokers.'

'Well, I'm Edwina Sabacthani, queen of Isla de Sangre.'

'Queen, huh?' The captain set the Frisbee spinning on his index finger and shouted to his friends. 'You heard Her Majesty! Hop to it! In five minutes I want this beach looking as tidy as Buckingham Palace!'

Resentful grunts arose from the other two Frisbee players, but they proceeded to obey their captain's orders. While brother Brandon held Londa's burlap sack wide open, Mike the Spike combed the beach, gathering up armloads of debris and dumping them into the cluttered cavity.

'Your Majesty's resemblance to this exquisite creature' – Ralph tipped his cap towards Londa – 'tells me I'm in the presence of a mother and her daughter.'

'Quite so,' said Edwina, ever eager to cultivate her favourite falsehood.

'And the way you rammed your boat into the reef tells me *I'm* in the presence of a piss-poor pilot,' I said. 'Your ineptitude has caused an oil spill.'

Mike the Spike halted his beachcombing long enough to say, 'No, sirree, she's been dripping like that ever since we left Sugarloaf Key. We'll try to fix the leak later.'

'You'll *try* to fix it?' Edwina said, aghast.

'With all due respect, ma'am, oil spills aren't the unmitigated disaster certain Marxoid squid-kissers make them out to be,' Mike replied. 'Aquatic bacteria gobble the stuff right down. I'm giving you basic biology here.'

'You're giving us basic horse manure,' I said.

Ralph shot me a poisonous glance. 'Who *is* this person?' he asked Edwina. 'Your court jester?'

'My daughter's tutor. His speciality is moral philosophy. Let me suggest that you hire him yourself.'

'He's absolutely brilliant,' Londa said, her first comment of the afternoon.

'Ma'am, I can see we've caused you grief,' Ralph said, bowing before Edwina, 'for which I'm truly sorry, so let me make it up to you.' From his wallet he retrieved a business card, pressing it into her palm. 'Just send me an email mentioning you're the feisty lady with the private island and the lovely daughter, and I'll see to it your whole family and all its philosophy tutors receive a special gift – like, say, first-class tickets on the *Titanic Redux* when she steams out of Southampton in maybe ten years from now.'

'Ralph knows how to think big,' brother Brandon noted.

'You're building a new *Titanic*?' I said, at once intrigued and appalled.

'Project *Titanic* Ascendant,' Ralph said, beaming. 'We're recreating the grand old Ship of Dreams down to her last frigging rivet, keel to crow's nest, poop to prow.' He pointed in the general direction of Greenland. 'There's a whole raft of demons out there, Your Majesty – all those imps and devils who haunted the North Atlantic on the fateful night of 15 April 1912. We're going to exorcise the lot of them, and then, presto chango, the way will be clear again for the sort of entrepreneurial derring-do that gave birth to the first *Titanic*. Brandon here knows the Latin word for it. What's that word of yours, Brandon?'

'Catharsis,' Brandon said.

'Catharsis,' Ralph said. 'Our plan is to take the whole catastrophe and give it a by-God catharsis.'

'The word is Greek,' I noted.

'I've never heard a more arrogant idea in my life,' Edwina said.

'I have,' I said, casting a cold eye on my employer. She bristled and frowned.

'There are lots of ways of being arrogant, ma'am,' Ralph said. 'Some people would say it's arrogant to practise extortion on our country's most creative sector and call it progressive taxation. Some people would say it's arrogant to pay single mothers for spreading their legs.'

Before Ralph could further develop this subtle line of thought, the metallic shriek of a Klaxon horn echoed across the bay. The captain pivoted towards the *Phyllis II*, frantically waving his arms. 'We hear you, Billy!'

'Looks like we're afloat,' said Mike.

'Don't you worry about the leak,' Brandon told Edwina. 'The bugs'll take care of it. Gobble, gobble, gobble.'

Moving with the confident swagger of the congenitally privileged, our visitors loaded their trash into the dinghy, scrambled aboard, and rowed towards the damaged reef.

As the three sailors climbed into their vessel, Londa made her second remark of the day. '*Phyllis II*,' she said, pointing towards the yacht. 'I guess that means they're – you know, Phyllistines!'

'Very witty, sweetheart,' said Edwina.

'A clever name,' I said. 'But let's remember' – I touched Londa's forearm – 'it's easier to label our enemies than to forgive them, and easier to forgive them than to love them.'

'Love our enemies?' Londa said. 'We haven't done that lesson yet, have we, Mason?'

'I've been saving the worst for last.'

The following morning we continued our voyage through 'Ethics from the Earth'. Had Londa and I dropped anchor at the next scheduled port-of-call – chapter seven, 'From Parable to Parousia' – we would have ended up exploring that vast moral continent first reconnoitred by the same Jesus Christ who'd exhorted us to love our enemies. But I sensed that she was not yet ready for such heady terrain, so we sailed on, circumnavigating the Dark Ages, cruising past the medieval era, and skirting the Renaissance, until at last we disembarked in the Enlightenment, subject of chapter twelve, 'From Revelation to Reason'.

My pupil was profoundly impressed by Immanuel Kant's notion of the 'categorical imperative' – doing the right thing because it was right – versus the 'hypothetical imperative' – doing the right thing to get what you want. Indeed, Herr Kant's discovery was in her words 'the perfect way to keep Ralph Gittikac and his fellow Phyllistines from getting the upper hand.' But she balked at Kant's claim that the 'moral law within' amounted to a proof of God's existence.

'Do you prefer some other proof of God's existence?' I asked.

'I guess you haven't heard the news,' she replied. 'I'm going to stop believing in God.'

'You're going to *stop*?'

'If it's all the same to you.'

'It's all the same to me, but it's hardly the same to most people. The leap into disbelief is not a step one takes lightly. It will put you at odds with the rest of the world.'

'I'm already at odds with the rest of the world.' She picked up my dissertation, squeezing it tightly against her chest. 'I know the God hypothesis has its partisans, but what a *boring* idea. Where did the universe come from? He did it. How do we account for rivers and rocks and ring-tailed lemurs? He made them. Ho-hum.'

'You've been reading ahead.'

She smiled coyly. 'Your chapter on Darwin took my breath away.'

I studied my reflection in the conquistador's breastplate. Darwin had taken Londa's breath away, even as her mother and Vincent Charnock were busy taking Darwin's breath away. The bright metal showed me the convex shape of things to come, a future in which humankind, tired of being mere *Homo sapiens sapiens* and enamoured of the RXL-313, had elected to plunge headlong into a perilous age of cottage eugenics and do-it-yourself evolution. At the mirror's glittering centre stood the forbidding figure of Charnock, leaning over his titanium cauldron and pulling out confection after confection, each a slippery wet neonate stronger and swifter and smarter than the last.

A terrible pounding arose in my skull. Nausea unfurled its cold quivering wings in my stomach.

'You look sick,' Londa said, joining me by the conquistador.

'Hedonism, anyone?' Quetzie said.

'*Homo sapiens sapiens sapiens sapiens*,' I said.

'If you'd like to go home and take a nap,' Londa said, 'that'd be all right with me.'

I was tempted to accept her offer, but instead we continued our conversation. With admirable coherence and startling confidence she argued that the Kantian 'moral law within' by no means implied the existence of a benign, omnipotent deity who spent his waking hours supervising human affairs. The God who'd planted a conscience in his creatures might instead be the *deus absconditus* of Enlightenment scepticism, winding up the universe like a clock, going home for lunch and never coming back.

On Tuesday we left God on his Enlightenment lunch break and took up the next topic in my book. Chapter thirteen, 'The Square Root of Happiness', featured my attempt to explicate Utilitarianism, that imperially pragmatic – indeed, mathematical – system devised by Jeremy Bentham in his quest for an ethics unencumbered by values, ideals, or other soggy sentiments. It soon became apparent that Londa had grasped neither my critique of Bentham nor the refinements in Utilitarianism wrought by John Stuart Mill and G. E. Moore, but as we parted company, she agreed to revisit the chapter and prepare a paper or project proving that she'd wrestled chapter thirteen to the ground.

Although Londa was twenty minutes late for class the next

morning, she arrived bearing the promised demonstration: the prototype of Largesse, a Monopoly-like game of her own design, complete with tokens, chits, chance cards, a spinner, and a posterboard rectangle on which she'd drawn the continent of Benthamia. Largesse could be enjoyed by two, three, or four players, each of whom assumed the role of a benevolent dictator ruling his own nation-state of nine million citizens. During any given round, the participant made a well-informed and charitable decision that he believed would promote the famous Utilitarian goal of 'the greatest good for the greatest number'. A typical winning ratio: 8,999,985 happy citizens, fifteen unhappy citizens. Another normally successful combination: 8,999,990 happy citizens, ten unhappy citizens. Any monarch who could ultimately claim 8,999,999 happy citizens and one unhappy citizen automatically won the game.

'Haven't you left out an important possibility?'

'Nine million happy citizens on the nose?' Londa replied.

'Indeed.'

'Ah, but you see, in the universe of Largesse, there must always be at least one innocent victim. You might say that's the whole point.'

We traded sly grins. Londa continued to summarise the rules. As the game progressed, each Largesse player-dictator acquired a hand of cards that specified exactly what those subjects identified as 'unhappy' were enduring. There was no way to escape these distressing narratives: a mother lacking the wherewithal to have her son treated for leukaemia; a starving alcoholic living in a cardboard box under a bridge; a slave with an iron manacle around his neck and an overseer's whip on his back; a five-year-old girl whose parents had locked her in a freezing woodshed and were feeding her nothing but sawdust and dogshit. Londa had written one hundred and thirty such scenarios.

'So, Mason, do I understand your critique of Bentham, or don't I?' she asked.

'I think you understand it better than I do.'

'Hedonism, anyone?' Quetzie said.

'I got the freezing child from Dostoyevsky,' Londa said.

It occurred to me that, ruthless and unprincipled as the universe of Largesse might be, Edwina Sabacthani had failed to attain even that impoverished plane of morality. The greatest good for the greatest number? Edwina's demented dream had required for its realisation four genetically identical sisters of four different ages, and yet she'd sought the greatest good for only one of those – herself. As any serious Utilitarian would tell her, it simply didn't compute.

CHAPTER 6

On Saturday afternoon Henry appeared at Laguna Zafira driving the most pathetic automobile I'd ever seen this side of a junkyard, its engine clattering like a garbage disposal devouring loose change. Evidently it had once been a Volvo. Brock lounged in the back seat, reading the *Key Largo Times*. The miserable vehicle, Henry informed me, was on loan from Edwina, and I immediately recalled an observation once made by my sociology professor at Villanova: in America, the transcendently wealthy – a population to which Edwina clearly belonged – didn't give a damn what sort of broken-down cars they drove.

'You might say our new recruit is on loan from Edwina too,' Henry said, indicating his passenger, a slender, fortyish woman with sculpted features and café-au-lait skin. She flashed me a warm croissant of a smile. Henry elaborated that he and Edwina had been waiting on the pier when Captain López's cabin cruiser had sailed into the Bahía de Flores two hours earlier. Before Jordan Frazier could disembark, Henry had reminded Edwina that no serious discussion would occur between Edwina and Yolly's prospective tutor until the latter had spoken with us. Edwina had then accused Henry of blackmail, and Henry had replied that blackmail was a very good word for it.

I welcomed Jordan to my humble cottage, supplied everyone with Mexican beer and Nyonnaise olives, then led the way to the rear deck with its expansive view of the lagoon. The air was stifling and muggy, as if the entire island were suffering from a low-grade fever. Two chubby green frogs responded to our intrusion by croaking indignantly and jumping into the water.

The more Jordan spoke about herself, the more obvious it

became that Edwina could hardly have picked a better mentor for Yolly. A Montreal-born educator with a Master's in child development, Jordan had been variously employed as a guidance counsellor at a middle school in Alexandria, a riding instructor at a day-camp in Silver Spring and the associate editor of a classy but short-lived 'parenting skills' magazine called *Wonderkids*. She hoped one day to acquire a PhD in 'knowledge building', a discipline that 'doesn't quite exist yet', but whose founding father was her intellectual hero and fellow Canadian, Dr Carl Bereiter, from whom she'd learned that 'whatever the human mind is, it's not a container'.

For the next hour Henry and Brock unspooled the story of Yolly Sabacthani: her passionless conception, mechanised maturation, *tabula rasa* conscience. Throughout the presentation I scrutinised Jordan's ever-shifting expressions. To judge from her gaping mouth and furrowed brow, the chances of her joining our dubious company lay somewhere between abysmal and non-existent.

'So there you have it,' Henry said, squeezing Jordan's hand. '*Nancy Drew and the Secret of Blood Island*. What do you think, lovely lady?'

'What do I *think*?' Jordan said, narrowing her eyes. 'I think your Dr Sabacthani is a lunatic.'

'You'll get no argument from me,' Brock said.

'I also think I should take the first boat home,' Jordan said.

'We've all had the same impulse,' Henry said.

'Hubris Academy, where angels fear to teach,' I said.

'But I *still* wish we could talk you into staying,' Brock said.

'No way,' she said.

'None at all?' I said.

'None.' Jordan grinned obliquely. 'However, there's a distinct possibility that *I* can talk me into staying.'

I laughed and said, 'You seem like a very persuasive person.'

'I'll bet you could convince Vlad the Impaler to take up knitting,' Brock said.

'Point one, you seem like my kind of oddballs,' Jordan said. 'Point two, the city girl is enchanted by her tropical surroundings. Point three, if I were to back out now, Edwina would probably replace me with a total incompetent.'

'An utter doofus,' Henry added.

'A complete chowderhead,' Brock said.

'Yolly deserves better,' I said.

'OK, gentlemen, deal me in. I'll take the whole damn package. The health plan, the stock options.' Jordan sighed expansively. 'The responsibility.'

'What about the duplicity?' I said.

'For the time being, I'll take that, too. Yolly's an amnesiac? Sure, Mom. She doesn't have any sisters? Fine, Edwina, if that's how you want it.'

'You won't regret this,' Henry said. 'Or, rather, you *will* regret it, but you'll be among friends when the pain starts.'

'It would appear that Edwina's invented a brand new sin,' Jordan said, nodding. 'God's still trying to figure out a name for it.'

'She insists that any woman with the right technological resources would have done the same thing in her place,' I said. 'Being men, Henry, Brock and I can't understand her urge to experience motherhood.'

A sceptical grunt escaped Jordan's lips. 'In my opinion women don't need to be mothers any more than they need to be trapeze artists.' She cracked the knuckles of her graceful hands. 'So what sort of curriculum do we use around here?'

For the remainder of the afternoon, as the setting sun turned the lagoon into an immense bowl of gazpacho, we described the lessons that had proved effective so far: Kohlbergian drama improvisations for Londa, a steady diet of *Mr Rogers' Neighbourhood* and *The Kindness Crusaders* for Donya. Jordan said that she would probably amalgamate the two strategies, Yolly being 'old enough to do role-playing exercises without getting bored, and young enough to watch *The Kindness Crusaders* without becoming embarrassed', though she intended to point out that the series was basically 'just another opiate of the bourgeoisie'.

'I'd like to see Edwina's face when she realises you've turned her daughter not only into a moral agent but a moral *Marxist* agent,' Henry said.

Jordan smirked and launched an olive pit into the lagoon. 'Unless I'm mistaken, Yolly is about to become obsessed with horses. It's practically a stage on Piaget's developmental profile.

Do you suppose Edwina might be willing to buy Yolly a horse?'

'If I know Edwina, she'll buy Yolly a *herd*,' Henry replied.

'A toast,' Brock said, raising his Dos Equis high. 'To the beautiful children of Isla de Sangre.'

'To the bewildered faculty of Hubris Academy,' Henry said.

'To trapeze artists,' I said.

Our four bottles came together in a benign collision. The glassy clatter echoed across the lagoon and decayed into the dusk.

The most dramatic scene in *The Egyptian* occurs when Sinuhe, recently returned from his self-imposed exile among the Hittites and now enjoying a lucrative private practice in Thebes, is sought out by his old nemesis, the Babylonian courtesan Nefer, whose machinations once prompted him to lose his ideals and betray his adoptive parents. Formerly wealthy, glamorous, and proud, Nefer now creeps through the city like a vision of death, veiled and shrouded. Upon finding Sinuhe, she opens her robe and bares one breast. He confirms her self-diagnosis – cancer – and proposes to excise the malignancy. 'I can save your life,' the physician tells his old enemy, 'but I can't restore your beauty,' though the expression on Sinuhe's face suggests that her condition is terminal. As you might imagine, this moment had a profound impact on my pre-teen sensibility. I was terrified by the gnawing tumour, appalled by the paradox of a breast that wasn't beautiful, and moved by the dignity with which the doomed Nefer accepted her fate.

In the weeks that followed Edwina's revelations in the conservatory, I gradually, and with mixed emotions, came to see her as a contemporary equivalent of Nefer. Edwina, too, was under sentence of death, yet she maintained her regal bearing. Her devotion to her daughters – and, yes, we'd all acquiesced in that misnomer, daughters – was absolute. Every Monday and Thursday, Lady Daedalus travelled to the Spanish fortress, Torre de la Carne, where Yolly was now in residence, and favoured the newborn eleven-year-old with unqualified adoration. On Tuesdays and Saturdays, it was Donya's turn. Wednesdays and Fridays belonged to Londa, which meant I was now seeing my pupil only three mornings a week, though given the robust condition of her soul, the moral compass she'd acquired by withholding borrowed axes, stealing cancer drugs, and embracing Immanuel Kant, I didn't regard the abridgement of our studies with alarm. As for Sundays, Edwina had wisely set this day aside for whichever girl seemed most in need of her – normally little Donya, of course, though sometimes the inchoate Yolly received the extra session, as did our moody adolescent.

Sundays also proved the ideal time for the Hubris Academy faculty to meet and trade notes, usually on my deck, occasionally on the terrace of Jordan's beach house or the screened porch of Henry and Brock's bungalow. Donya had made substantive progress of late, even to the point of insisting, as Henry had predicted she might, that the grown-ups stop rigging the croquet games. As for Yolly, after some inevitable experimentation – smashing windows, mutilating furniture, plundering Jordan's wallet, learning how to make 'fuck' function as every part of speech – she now possessed a flourishing conscience. A person would never have known she was playing ethical catch-up. In short, it seemed that everyone's superego was developing normally, and so far the children's *Geworfenheit* had not plunged them into a nihilistic vortex or sent them wandering through Dante's dark wood. Instead of dwelling on deontology, we tutors were now free to discuss the topic that most interested us, our employer's ostensibly praiseworthy campaign to give her daughters every blessing within her power.

By Henry's report, Edwina was having little difficulty connecting with Donya, who always articulated her desire of the moment loudly and unambiguously – cupcake, cookie, bedtime story – subsequently showering a delectable affection on whoever took the trouble to make her wish come true. Under Donya's guidance, Edwina had become an expert teller of folktales, a skilful flyer of kites, and a welcome guest at tea parties. After a few failed attempts, Edwina had even projected herself into the rarefied world of Donya's miniature amusement park, learning how to make tiny plastic heroes outwit their pocket-sized enemies, who were forever plotting to derail the roller-coaster and other such deviltry.

Yolly, meanwhile, was entering the stage at which many parents would like to arrest their daughters' growth, that interval between ten and twelve when sophistication has not yet allied itself with cynicism. True to Jordan's prediction, Yolly had become enamoured of all things equine, though she was equally enthusiastic about cultivating orchids, reading dopey fantasy novels, and taking music lessons from an itinerant teacher – Pandora Duval, formerly a flautist with the Baroque Ensemble in Seattle, now an alcoholic with the Hog's Breath Saloon in Key West. Edwina responded to Yolly's horse obsession not only by giving her dozens of horse books, horse knick-knacks, and horse DVDs, everything from the smarmy *My Friend Flicka* to the splendid *Black Stallion*, but also – as we knew she would – by presenting the child with a living, breathing exemplar of the species, a Chincoteague pony. Thanks to Jordan, Yolly learned to saddle and mount the spirited Oyster in a matter of hours, ride him in a matter of days, and ride him skilfully before the month was out.

With the aid of a digital camera, Jordan recorded her pupil's growth in a series of beautifully composed snapshots, periodically displaying them to the rest of the faculty via her laptop. Each image bore a pithy caption: 'A Whiff of Heaven' (Yolly smelling an orchid); 'Goodness, How Delicious' (Yolly eating a mango); 'Morning Swim' (Yolly and Edwina floating on their backs in the Bahía de Matecumba); 'Racing the Wind' (Yolly on her pony); 'Vivaldi's Spring' (Yolly playing her flute); 'Sun Worshippers of Blood Island' (Yolly and Edwina napping on the beach, dressed in identical green spandex bathing suits); 'Harvesting the Tide' (Yolly and Edwina standing on the point, surrounded by a plume of surf). Far from occasioning anxiety, the child's thrownness had evidently made her a connoisseur of every imaginable sensory delight. I could only hope that her devotion to the pleasure principle did not portend a disastrous encounter with Dr Heidegger's nothingness.

'Whatever you're doing with that child, it's obviously working,' I told Jordan.

Not surprisingly, it was with her eldest daughter that Edwina had the most trouble connecting. Like the rest of the civilised world's seventeen-year-olds, Londa had recently discovered that her prime nurturing parent was not, in fact, a brilliant and omnicompetent demiurge who could do no wrong, but just another dreary adult. And like the rest of the civilised world's seventeen-year-olds, she had grown infinitely indignant at this discovery.

Edwina, to her credit, refused to be daunted by the billowing black thundercloud that hovered perpetually above Londa's head, and in time Londa came to realise that she could have drawn a far worse parent in the great *Geworfenheit* lottery. By Londa's admission, their regular Wednesday and Friday luncheons boasted a reasonable facsimile of rapport enhanced by occasional flashes of candour. Particularly gratifying to Londa was her mother's willingness to give her a plenary sex education. It was one thing to read about such bewildering matters as menstrual cramps, yeast infections, the G-spot, birth-control pills, STDs, and condoms, and quite another to receive such information from a blood relation who loved you without condition.

Being older, cannier, and better informed than her sisters, Londa did not for a minute imagine that she was living a remotely normal existence on Isla de Sangre. Although Edwina had denied Londa the Internet, she did permit her to receive *Up!*, a lurid and almost comically materialistic magazine targeted at female adolescents, every issue of which implicitly informed Londa that the gap between Faustino and the outside world was very large indeed. Above all, *Up!* bespoke a civilisation filled to bursting with hip clothing, mesmerising jewellery, alchemical cosmetics, and innocuously transgressive music, and before long Londa had developed a keen interest in the loot that the Western industrialised nation-states and their Asian equivalents had to offer. Every sane young woman wanted her share of the goods, wanted it desperately, and so Londa, always eager to have her mental health corroborated, decided that she must, simply must, become a consumer.

Edwina satisfied her daughter's yearning for conventional treasures in the simplest manner imaginable, by having them delivered to the door. Sweaters, jeans, boots, sneakers, lipstick, fingernail polish, eyeliner, perfume, lotions, bracelets, necklaces, and CDs started appearing at Faustino like gifts left by elves in a Hans Christian Andersen story. Day and night, the halls of the mansion reverberated with the apocalyptic chords of Shoot the Works, Distressed Leather, Et Tu Brute, and other bands that specialised in commodified nihilism. Wherever Londa went, the cloying aroma of her *parfum du jour* trailed behind her, her bracelets clanking and jangling like a nightwatchman's keys.

In her maternal wisdom, the *Übermom* understood that without a social context this cavalcade of artefacts would afford Londa only limited amusement. Edwina solved this problem – brilliantly, I must say – through the clever expedient of turning Faustino into a residential haven for Florida adolescents in need of summer employment. The job-seekers variously arrived by catamaran, houseboat, trawler, yacht, and cabin cruiser, and with the exception of a female heroin addict from Coral Gables and a wild-eyed Key Largo lad hooked on *Grave Robbers II*, a stupefyingly violent computer game, Edwina hired them all. There was lanky Julio, who promised Edwina that by summer's end he would single-handedly build a stone wall circumscribing the patio; meticulous Brittany, who contracted with Edwina to reorganise the library; industrious Nick, who undertook to repair the dock on the Bahía de Flores; cheerful Charlotte, who assumed the role of Javier's girl Friday; ethereal Shana, who agreed to cultivate the manor's flower gardens; and a brooding fellow named Armand, who apprenticed himself to Charnock. The Mad Doctor of Blood Island had just returned from Honolulu, skin tanned, misanthropy intact, and was now spending his days catching geckos and iguanas for some experiment the purpose of which I preferred not to know.

And then there was Gavin Ackerman. There had to be a Gavin Ackerman: the handsome, muscular, nincompoop drummer in Savage Rabbit, a high-school garage band that had recently released its fourth home-brew CD, *Spur of the Moment*. Although Edwina had ostensibly engaged Gavin to repair gutters and pick figs, it was obvious that his real function was to develop a requited crush on Londa. From Edwina's viewpoint, this was a win–win situation. If her daughter neglected to fall in love with Gavin, then Edwina would have occasion to praise Londa, extolling her for not allowing mere hunkiness to inspire her admiration. Should Gavin greet Londa's apathy with passion, Edwina could then play the wise mentor, advising her daughter on how to let a suitor down gently. In the event that it was Londa who became smitten while Gavin remained unmoved, Edwina would be right there by her daughter's side, recounting the time that she, too, had nearly died of a broken heart. Finally, scenario number four: Romeo and Juliet in the Florida Keys, savouring the joys of puppy love and goatish lust.

Naturally Edwina would monitor the relationship through every twist and turn, sharing vicariously in Londa's happiness and commiserating with her when September arrived and Gavin had to return to the mainland.

For better or worse, the two youngsters and their hormones performed as anticipated, and it soon became impossible to run into Londa without simultaneously encountering Gavin. They held hands constantly, necked conspicuously, and bragged about each other to anyone who would listen. The figs that Gavin had been engaged to pick remained on their trees, though I came to suspect that, as the torrid Florida days rolled by and the sultry tropical nights elapsed, swain and maid were reaping their own succulent harvest.

So complete was Londa's infatuation that, at least once per tutorial, the topic would shift from the conundrum of justice – we were devoting the summer to my chapter on John Rawls – to the protocols of desire. Londa wanted to know exactly what went on in men's minds, and whether their seeming enslavement to their penises made them despise women without knowing it. I addressed her confusion as best I could, explicating various theories that indeed posited an unconscious male *animus* towards the female, though at some point in each disquisition I insisted that we return to Professor Rawls and his ingenious idea that a truly just society would be founded behind a 'veil of ignorance', each architect totally unaware of where in the socio-economic hierarchy he might end up. The fact was, however, that I found these digressions therapeutic. By tuning in to Londa's romantic life, listening patiently as she waxed rhapsodic over Gavin's scorched-earth politics and off-the-shelf alienation, I convinced myself that she was really just another bubbleheaded *Up!* subscriber, and this conclusion proved crucial to my feeling that, on the whole, all things considered, certain indications to the contrary, I was not madly in love with her.

Thanks to the benign hedonism of Faustino's youthful work corps, the estate soon came to resemble a beach-party movie from the mid-1960s. On the dunes of Isla de Sangre our imported teenagers staged barbecues, dance marathons, and sandcastle competitions. It occurred to me that, like the vast majority of Western adolescents, they believed themselves immortal, though I myself had no difficulty picturing their various appointments in Samarra. Occasionally, prompted by self-pity combined with too much beer, I would wander down to the bay and superimpose my depression on their rites, beholding limber zombies tossing horseshoes, agile corpses riding surfboards, and frisky cadavers burying each other in the sand. *Beach Blanket Geworfenheit.*

While Londa was the putative hostess of these celebrations, Edwina did most of the planning and supervising, and during the festivities my student and her boyfriend stayed noticeably aloof. As 'Medusa's Mirror' or 'Redneck Serenade' or some similarly dance-friendly Distressed Leather hit poured from the boom box, and the teens shook, rattled, and rolled accordingly, Londa and Gavin would linger in the shadows, sparking everyone's annoyance through this seeming assertion of a superior sensibility.

A curious situation. Now that Londa finally had a social life, she apparently didn't want it – unless, of course, the vacuous Gavin satisfied her need for companionship. When I apprised my fellow teachers of this paradox, Jordan revealed that, every time she proposed to ferry her own prepubescent stepsister from Tampa to Torre de la Carne, Yolly replied that she wouldn't have any idea how to entertain such a visitor, nor did she want to learn. Henry told a similar story about Donya. On numerous occasions he'd announced that he would happily fly to Houston, collect both his nieces, and bring them back to Casa de los Huesos. Invariably Donya had responded that she wanted as her playmates only Edwina, Henry, Brock, her dog, and 'that man called Mason who talks so funny'.

'The loneliness of a vatling must be dreadful,' Brock said.

'They aren't just stuck on an island – they're marooned in their skulls,' Jordan said.

'Perhaps,' Henry said, 'they are waiting for each other.'

While Edwina had done a reasonable job of scripting her eldest daughter's adolescence, she'd evidently failed to anticipate the most obvious crisis of all. At some point in the courtship, the boy was certain to ask Londa about her past – and what was she supposed to do then? Change the subject? Perhaps Edwina actually imagined Londa telling Gavin she was an amnesiac, in which case someone would have to inform Lady Daedalus that the average teenage girl would rather spend eighteen hours a day manicuring a golf course with nail scissors than risk being thought a clueless, vapid, brain-damaged dork.

It happened that Londa herself had not only foreseen this problem, she'd also attempted a solution. Upon realising that these days her every waking thought invariably circled back to Gavin, she went rooting through her mother's desk, found a blank leather-bound journal, and spent the next six hours inventing a life for herself. She titled her project 'The Book of Londa', and upon its completion she talked me into taking it home for the weekend.

'The Book of Londa' told of a seven-year-old girl, born and raised in Boston, whose mother, the stellar molecular geneticist Edwina Sabacthani, had one day vanished without a trace. The father of this hypothetical Londa – the equally hypothetical David Sabacthani, a writer of bestselling murder mysteries – soon decided that his beloved Edwina was gone for good. He arranged for his wife to be declared legally dead, then married his most ardent fan, a disturbed dental hygienist named Gretchen Caldwell.

The fictionalised Londa's fortunes now went from bad to worse. Two days after her eighth birthday, her father died in a sailing accident off Cape Cod. When Gretchen Sabacthani née Caldwell undertook to raise Londa single-handedly, the woman's latent depravity emerged from the swamp that was her soul. With a nod to the sadistic parents who figured in Largesse, her Utilitarian board game, Londa imagined Gretchen feeding her stepdaughter worms and dirt, beating her with a bicycle chain, and locking her in the basement for weeks at a time.

This monstrous state of affairs persisted for five years, until one glorious day when Edwina managed to escape from her abductors, an anarchist cabal that had been forcing her to design biological weapons in the Canary Islands. Arriving home, Edwina lost no time in deposing her dead husband's wife, bonding with Londa once more, and assisting the CIA in tracking down the anarchists, after which mother and daughter fled to Isla de Sangre to start a new life together.

'The Book of Londa' did not end there, however. Years later, Gretchen was kidnapped by a mysterious woman called the

Crimson Kantian – a swashbuckling vigilante, masked and cloaked like Zorro – and was taken to a secret grotto on the southern shore of Isla de Sangre. After threatening Gretchen with a thumbscrew and menacing her with a torture rack, the Crimson Kantian abruptly switched strategies and introduced her prisoner not only to the categorical imperative, but also to Stoic self-denial, Epicurean self-restraint, and Rawlsian fairness. These mandatory tutorials took hold, and Gretchen eventually became a model citizen who dedicated her remaining years to organising food schemes and running soup kitchens.

'So what do you think of my life?' Londa asked me, shortly after the start of Monday's lesson. I had just given her the fundamental Rawlsian thought problem: specify the limits – to both wealth and privation – that you would impose on an embryonic human community, knowing that you yourself could be cast into any of the circumstances you allow, from the lowest to the highest.

'You want my honest reaction?' I replied.

'Uh-huh.'

'Gavin won't buy any of it.'

'The ending *is* rather fanciful,' she said in an abashed tone.

'I won't mince words, Londa. The ending is ridiculous.'

'Perhaps the Crimson Kantian shouldn't wear a mask.'

'I meant psychologically ridiculous. This Gretchen character wouldn't mend her ways just from hearing about Stoicism or Epicureanism.'

'But isn't that what happened to me?'

I exhaled wearily and returned the journal. 'I don't know *what* happened to you, Londa.' Our gazes met. Her mismatched green eyes had never looked lovelier. 'I wish I did, but I don't.'

We proceeded to give her a more credible childhood, one spent largely on Isla de Sangre under her widowed mother's tender care, with occasional trips to the mainland. From 'The Book of Londa' we took only the idea of a father who'd died while sailing. For the balance of her manufactured memories we cracked the spine of my own life and rifled through its bland but credible anecdotes. Romping with a German shepherd named Kip, collecting postcards from around the world, falling under the spell of *The Little Prince*, staging amateur fireworks displays for my cousins on the Fourth of July, improvising a stink bomb using the antique but functional Gilbert chemistry set I'd acquired at a flea market – it all entered Londa's trove of non-existent recollections.

'Gavin was especially impressed with the fireworks,' she told me later that week. 'He wants me to add skyrockets to the Savage Rabbit concerts.'

'Skyrockets? That's insane.'

'The outdoor concerts. I told him I'd forgotten all that stuff, but my tutor could probably help out.'

'Tell him your tutor has forgotten too.'

'There's a cut on *Spur of the Moment* called "My Country, Right or Wrong". A satire on mindless Phyllistine patriotism.'

'How subversive.'

'Did you know that the man who wrote "The Star-Spangled Banner" was related to Roger Taney, the Supreme Court Justice responsible for the Dred Scott decision? Pretty astonishing, huh? Francis Scott Key goes all gushy about the land of the free and the home of the brave, and forty-three years later his brother-in-law rules that black people belong to an inferior biological order. All Gavin wants is a bunch of computer-launched rockets turning into flaming pinwheels when the lead vocalist sings about the racists' red glare.'

'I wouldn't know where to begin. Perhaps you should suggest to your boyfriend that good music doesn't require pyrotechnics.'

It was at this juncture in our uneasy conversation that Londa issued the first negative remark I'd ever heard her make about Gavin. 'Listen to any Savage Rabbit CD,' she told me, a wry smile curling her lips, 'and you'll decide that they need the goddamn Chicago fire.'

Although 'The Book of Londa' was in theory a moot text, its preposterous thumbscrew-wielding vigilante at best peripheral to our work, the wretched thing continued to trouble me. Why had she cultivated in these pages so dark an alter ego, this Crimson Kantian nearly as cruel as the stepmother she'd sought to rehabilitate? Could it be that Londa had merely learned to *mimic* a Stoic love of integrity, an Epicurean taste for virtue, an Enlightenment sense of duty, and a Rawlsian commitment to fairness? At the end of the day was she still the ambulatory moral vacuum with whom Edwina had first presented me?

From these unhappy thoughts flowed my fateful decision to transport Londa and myself to ancient Judea, circa AD 30. Our itinerary had us following the rising terrain as it resolved into that Jerusalem Mount made immortal by the Gospel According to Saint Matthew. Continuing upward, we reached the summit and met the prince of paradox himself, delivering his famously counterintuitive sermon.

Londa's first reading of the Beatitudes and their surrounding text left her utterly perplexed, and so she decided that, having previously benefited from role-playing exercises, we should apply this same approach to Christian ethics. We began by re-enacting the story of the Good Samaritan, Londa portraying the title character while I sprawled across the floor as the robbed and beaten wayfarer. She ministered to my imaginary wounds with surpassing kindness. The following morning I repeatedly panto-mimed the action of slapping Londa's cheek. After every such assault she confounded her assailant by inviting him to strike again. Later that week we staged the famous story of the vengeful mob chasing after the woman taken in adultery. Our teenage librarian Brittany played the slattern, I was the mob's leader, and Londa became the Nazarene. I can still hear her saying, in her sensual husky voice, 'Let him among you who is without sin cast the first stone.'

Picture two freight trains meeting in a head-on collision, or a tornado corkscrewing through a trailer park, hurtling gas grills and crates of Budweiser every which way, and you will understand the impact that Londa's repeated readings of the Sermon on the Mount had on her psyche. In retrospect it all seems inevitable. Here was a young woman whose encounter with Stoicism had inspired her to burn her palm; the Beatitudes were bound to loosen a few screws as well. But what really got under Londa's skin, I soon learned, was not the Messiah's sermon per se but the discontinuity between its sublime directives and the ignominious course of Western history, a spectacle that, the more we thought about it, struck Londa and me as largely a fancy-dress *danse macabre – Titus Andronicus* on a hemispheric and ultimately global scale – though I hastened to point out that the chronicles of other civilisations were likewise awash in blood. What had gone wrong? she wanted to know. When and why had the teachings of Jesus Christ become an optional component of Christianity?

'I'm not the right person to answer that question,' I said. 'Try an anthropologist, or maybe a religious-studies professor.'

'You know what the world needs, Mason?' she asked. 'It needs a Second Coming.'

'I'd say one was quite enough.'

'Not of Christ. Of Christianity. I'm going to make it happen.'

'That's not a very good idea.'

'Well, *somebody* has to arrange for the merciful and the meek and the peacemakers to take over. The Phyllistines can't remain in charge for ever.'

'May I be frank, my dear?' I said, rolling my eyes. 'You don't want to become a Christian. You want Christianity to become *you*. That way madness lies.'

On certain days my pupil's hungering and thirsting after righteousness seemed so intense that I half-expected her to flagellate herself, put on a hair shirt, or walk barefoot on broken glass. She settled for a less florid saintliness, however, persuading Javier to become an organ donor, Dr Charnock to join Amnesty International, her morality teacher to send his parents a smarmy email ('You sacrificed so much for my benefit . . .'), and Edwina to write a million-dollar check to the Heifer Project, a non-denominational Christian foundation providing domestic animals for families in impoverished countries. Poor Gavin Ackerman, he didn't stand a chance. He thought he'd been blessed with a dreamy and eccentric but eminently desirable girlfriend, and suddenly he had a wacko hyperventilating Joan of Arc on his hands. The situation came to boiling point when Gavin mentioned that his mother used to drag him to Lutheran services in Orlando. From that moment on, there was no stopping Londa. She simply *had* to know whether he'd taken the Beatitudes to heart.

'I asked him to imagine that Savage Rabbit had become an overnight sensation,' she told me. 'Would he be willing to give his newfound fortune to the poor, after which we'd run off together and start an AIDS hospice in Nigeria? You'll never guess what he said. He said that if he *kept* his money, we'd find it a lot easier to start an AIDS hospice in Nigeria.'

'I can follow his logic,' I admitted.

'Then I told him to imagine he'd turned Savage Rabbit into a success only by making enemies. Might he see his way clear to loving those enemies instead of hating them?'

'A provocative question,' I said, suppressing a smirk. 'What did he say?'

'He said I was getting on his nerves, and he didn't know how he felt about me any more, and then he confessed he was thinking of dating Brittany, which I said was fine by me, but I would appreciate it if he didn't fuck her in the same places we'd used, and he said he would fuck her wherever he felt like, and then we got into a big fight, and then we broke up.'

'I'm sorry, Londa.'

'Don't be. He's really a very immature person.'

At Londa's request we spent the rest of the morning talking about Jesus's cryptic concept of the Kingdom, and whether it was earthly or ethereal, but my thoughts kept drifting to the schism between Londa and Gavin. This was perhaps not the first time the Sermon on the Mount had wrecked an adolescent romance, but I was disturbed by the vehemence with which she'd forced the issue. Love me, love my Beatitudes. The Crimson Kantian had much to answer for, but this new version of Londa, this *belle dame avec trop de merci*, this Purple Pietist, was hardly an improvement. The sooner we left first-century Judaea, fleeing across the Mediterranean like the *Trois Maries* of Provençal legend, the better.

For the rest of the summer Londa and Gavin engaged in an elaborate dance of mutual avoidance, until the time came for our youthful roustabouts to scramble aboard their vessels and sail home. The kids had acquitted themselves well. A sturdy sandstone wall now encircled the patio, a magnificent new dock jutted into the Bahía de Flores, the Dewey decimal system had wrought its rationality upon our previously chaotic library, and the manor gardens boasted a vitality that would have sent Edwina's beloved Swinburne retreating pell-mell into his gaunt and glamorous wasteland. Being a romantic at heart, I imagined a last-minute rap-prochement between Londa and Gavin, but when I asked her about his departure she reported, with magisterial indifference, that he'd sailed off without even saying goodbye.

As September came to Isla de Sangre, Londa and I took a much-needed imaginary cruise to the Galápagos Islands and thence into the heart of Darwinism. Just as I'd hoped, the core chapters of my 'Ethics', with their argument that a universal and robust morality lay dormant in the theory of natural selection, seemed to bring Londa to her senses. Whenever we talked about our planet's vast ecological tapestry with its innumerable species pursuing their interconnected existences, and how the Phyllistine megamachine with its insatiable appetite for forests and wetlands and other fragile habitats was tearing that tapestry to pieces, she would occasionally spice the conversation with a Beatitude or two, but she had evidently abandoned, or at least postponed, her ambition to supervise the Second Coming of Christianity. Just as the Crimson Kantian had deferred to the Purple Pietist, so the Purple Pietist was now yielding to a thoughtful and humble Scarlet Darwinist.

'I think I'm almost cured,' she told me. 'I feel like a lizard who's had his tail cut off, but now the thing's growing back. I'm ashamed of the person I used to be. Setting fires. Killing fish. The old Londa makes me want to puke.'

'We're *all* ashamed of the person we used to be,' I said.

As for Donya and Yolly, their tutors were convinced that both girls had finally conquered the void to which their ontogenerated flesh was heir. For a while Henry and Brock considered celebrating Donya's breakthrough by giving her some objective correlative of a conscience, a statuette of a Kindness Crusader perhaps, or a heart-shaped clock like the one Professor Marvel awarded to the Tin Man. Jordan likewise imagined presenting her pupil with a trophy, and Brock our resident artist soon hit upon a concept we liked: a Lucite slab in which was suspended a burnished blue sphere representing the human soul. But in the end my colleagues decided that any such material prize would trivialise their students' accomplishment.

Despite our apparent success in providing each Sister Sabacthani with a moral compass, Jordan argued that we still had work to do. In her view we were now obliged to give our charges what educators of her epistemological persuasion called 'conceptual artefacts', so that the ultimate fruit of each girl's DUNCE cap programming and subsequent consumption of book after book after book would be 'a mind enlivened by knowledge, as opposed to a brain anaesthetised by data'. It all made sense to the rest of us, and so we four Hubris Academy tutors set about enriching the curriculum. Our lesson plans boasted a theatricality that I believe fell short of gimmickry. To give Donya an experience in cartography, Brock buried a box filled with costume jewellery behind Casa de los Huesos, drew a pirate map on a crumpled sheet of coffee-stained paper, and cheered his pupil on as she moved, chart in one hand, spade in the other, from the patio to an oleander bush to a garden gnome and finally to the rock beneath which the treasure lay. To introduce a unit on astronomy, Jordan had Yolly study the night sky, thread the stars into novel constellations, and then invent her own myths accounting for these sparkling beasts and glimmering gods. To help Londa grasp the poetry of mathematics, I invited her to recapitulate the steps, so elegant, so exquisite, by which Euclid had proved the Pythagorean theorem.

'He didn't need algebra at all,' I noted as we bent over my diagrams. 'Look, he brings it off entirely with geometry. His stroke of genius was to frame the right triangle with three perfect squares, so that the proof becomes a matter of—'

'A matter of showing that the big square is the same size as the two smaller squares combined!'

'Shazam!'

So Hubris Academy was a lively place, with nearly every lesson occasioning an intellectual epiphany, a Eureka moment, a flash of rational revelation. We were all taken aback, therefore, when a malaise descended upon the Sisters Sabacthani, a condition that had them nodding off in class and moving about the island with the lethargic gait of deep-sea divers shuffling along the ocean floor. By monitoring the girls' sleeping habits we soon cleared up the mystery. In the middle of the night Londa would rise from her bed, wander down to the Bahía de Flores, and spend hours staring at the rollers as they crashed against the rocks. Yolly's nocturnal anxiety prompted her to saddle up Oyster and go galloping through the surf like a banshee making his latest house call. Even little Donya's nights were plagued. At the godforsaken hour of 4 a.m., she would suddenly awake, thrashing and writhing and tearing the sheets until she escaped the clawed and scaly clutches of her phantasm.

Upon learning of her daughters' insomnia, Edwina decided to give Yolly and Londa sleeping remedies from her personal store, a therapy that proved generally effective, though Jordan complained that Edwina was treating the symptoms and not the cause. The *Übermom*'s approach to Donya's disquiet was less mechanistic. She installed an extra bed in the child's room, so that at the earliest sign of distress whoever was on duty – Henry, Brock, Chen Lee, or Edwina herself – could hug Donya reassuringly and tell her, over and over, that she wasn't really sinking in quicksand or fleeing from hornets or climbing the branches of a burning tree.

In theorising about the children's demons, Brock seized upon Henry's remark of the previous summer – 'Perhaps they are waiting for each other' – and speculated that each girl had somehow intuited the existence of her doppelgängers. These nebulous presences, these intimations of a second self, and a third after that, were haunting our charges night and day. My own theory was that *Geworfenheit* had started catching up with the girls. The least elaborate and, as it turned out, most accurate explanation came from Jordan, who noted that Edwina's failing health was no longer something she could hide. Her death was now encoded all over her body, and the children had deciphered the woeful text.

Oddly enough, it was little Donya who first put her terror into words, taking Henry and Brock aside and describing her mother's skin, whose mottled brown surface she compared to the peel of an overripe banana. Her tutors told her the analogy was astute, but said no more. Yolly spoke up next, mentioning with feigned casualness that Edwina seemed to have trouble breathing. Jordan admitted that she'd observed the same phenomenon. Only Londa remained silent about her mother's symptoms, exhibiting instead a preoccupation with death in the abstract. This development would not have surprised Heidegger. The more clearly the *Dasein* recognises its thrownness, the more intense its encounter with nothingness.

'Which alternative is worse, I wonder?' she said. 'To deny death and thus risk never being wholly alive, or to face oblivion squarely and risk becoming paralysed by dread?'

'Nobody knows,' I said. 'It's ambiguous.'

'If I ever get to be God,' she said, unleashing the grin of the person who'd invented Largesse, 'my first act will be to make ambiguity illegal.'

Much to the faculty's dismay, Edwina declined to be honest with her daughters, answering with weasel words and outright lies their questions about her blotchy skin, sunken eyes, and chronic exhaustion. Usually she told the girls that she looked haggard merely because she'd been working too hard. Sometimes she mentioned an experimental drug guaranteed to restore her vitality. I could not exactly accuse Edwina of being in denial – privately she still spoke freely of her disease, noble Nefer baring her breast to Sinuhe – but by leaving to us the task of preparing the children for her death, she confirmed my suspicion that this whole Byzantine scenario was being performed solely to appease her voracious egotism, and the children's ultimate welfare be damned.

'My mother's dying, isn't she?' Londa said abruptly as we sat down to discuss Social Darwinism, Mengelism, and other dark chapters in the Galapágos saga. 'Tell me the truth.'

'She's dying. Yes. I'm sorry.'

'I knew it. Fuck. Will she die soon?'

I squeezed her hand between my palms. 'Sooner rather than later. I'm so sorry.'

'When I was in love with Gavin, I used to have horrible dreams.' With her free hand Londa wiped away her tears. 'Once we went swimming, and he drowned in the bay. Another time Alonso shot him with his musket, and the next thing I knew, Gavin was lying in a coffin.' Approaching the conquistador, she grasped the hilt of his sword. 'I crouched over him, trying to push his eyes open with one of his drumsticks, but they were frozen shut.' Abruptly she pulled the sword from its scabbard, sending a harsh clang through the air like the resonance of a diabolical tuning fork. She held the weapon upright, its blade corroded with rust and tinged with dubious battle. 'I would say that my life is underpopulated, wouldn't you? Gavin's gone. My father's gone. Mother's dying. I'm not a happy person, Mason. You'll always be my friend, won't you?'

'Of course.'

'Maybe some day I'll learn how to use a sword,' she said, sheathing the weapon. 'A woman should be ready to take the offensive at a moment's notice.'

CHAPTER 7

On the first day of spring Edwina staged a birthday party for Donya at Casa de los Huesos. The child was now ostensibly seven. I didn't doubt that she'd been winched from the vat on that date, and giving her advent the name 'birthday' was by no means the most dishonest game Edwina had ever played with the English language, but the whole affair still struck me as pathetic and false.

All the guests brought gifts. Chen Lee gave Donya a pair of cuckoo clocks, suggesting that she mount them on opposite sides of her room, so that once an hour the birds would enter into a spirited conversation with each other. Dr Charnock presented her with one of his biological contrivances, a colony of twelve seahorses from whose customised bodies sprouted delicate membranous wings. My own contribution was a new addition to Donya's stuffed-animal collection, Septimus Squid, whom I'd crafted from odds and ends found around Faustino: a silk pillow for the body, discarded vacuum-cleaner hoses for the tentacles, tennis balls for eyes. But the most extravagant offering came from Henry and Brock – the Stargazer Deluxe, a portable planetarium they'd obtained two months earlier during a trip to Orlando. You inflated the plastic dome with a bicycle pump, thereby creating a cavity large enough for the projector and several amateur astronomers. After everyone had squeezed inside, you threw the switch, then watched in awe as dozens of constellations materialised on the walls.

It may have been Donya's party, but it was Edwina's celebration. The *Übermom* was everywhere at once that afternoon, distributing conical hats and novelty noisemakers, supervising rounds of Pin the Horn on the Unicorn, leading the guests in a rousing chorus of 'Happy Birthday to You', and serving the chocolate cake she'd meticulously baked and frosted. From start to finish the event delighted Donya, though occasionally I saw her cast a worried eye on her mother's forearms, the blue veins rising from Edwina's skin like earthworms dispossessed by a rainstorm.

In the name of physical fitness and metaphysical prowess – I was still taking every opportunity to weed my brain of its Aristotelian dandelions – I had jogged to Casa de los Huesos. But being bloated with chocolate cake and cherry-vanilla ice cream, I was now disinclined to repeat the regimen, and so I gladly accepted Charnock's offer of a lift home in his Land Rover.

'I would like your perspective on a philosophical problem,' he said as the villa's silhouette receded in the rearview mirror.

'What sort of philosophical problem?' I asked, cringing. While I was always eager to dally with Lady Philosophy, Charnock was among the last people with whom I could imagine having a substantive discussion about Plato's cave or Heidegger's abyss.

'Ethical.'

My cringe entered the realm of contortion. 'I see.'

'I'm impressed by how much you've helped Londa,' Charnock said. 'Being the oldest of the three, she was doubtless the hardest to civilise.'

'Civilising her was a walk in the park. The challenge will be to decivilise her, so she can function in the real world.'

A soft rain descended on the Land Rover and the surrounding scrub. Charnock activated the wipers, thus compounding the visibility problem by smearing grime across the windshield.

'Am I a murderer, Ambrose?' he asked abruptly. 'Do I have blood on my hands?'

'I don't follow you,' I said, though in fact his conversation with Edwina in the gazebo had already alerted me to his protective attitude towards microscopic beings.

Among the steps required to satisfy Edwina's 'unfathomable passion', he explained, 'her unhealthy need to create iterations of herself', was a technique he found repulsive. Yolly's advent had entailed the sacrifice of forty-three embryos. Donya had come into the world at the cost of sixty-eight. Behind Londa lay ninety-seven cancelled lives. 'Placed in the RXL-313, any one of those creatures would've become a person. Naturally we always had a reason for throwing it away. Spina bifida, dysfunctional heart, malformed kidneys. But in seven cases – I remember them all – in seven cases Edwina asked me to discard the thing merely because she didn't feel right about it. "This one isn't my daughter. This one won't do."'

I fiddled absently with the favour I'd borne away from Donya's party, a hooter capped with a coiled paper tube. 'I can imagine Edwina saying that.'

'So why did I obey her? When it came to our mutant mangrove, I refused to do the dirty work – I made Edwina extract the cerebrum on her own – but with those embryos I lost my bearings. I dumped them into the Bahía de Matecumba and let the salt water destroy them.'

The road from Casa de los Huesos now brought us to the soaring façade of the island's south-west wall, its spiky iron gate padlocked shut so that Donya's life would never accidentally spill into Yolly's. Charnock had the key, and thus we passed without incident into the principality of Torre de la Carne.

'I'm afraid Western philosophy can't answer your question,' I said. 'Aristotle never told us what basket to put our eggs in. Is a zygote a human being, an insensate speck, or something else? For once in his life, he neglected to categorise something.'

'I can feel the blood coagulating on my fingertips,' Charnock said.

A mile beyond the gate the road split, one branch running south-east towards the Spanish fortress, the other becoming the east-west gravel strip that Henry and I had encountered during our explorations. Had Charnock and I followed the lower fork, we might have seen Yolly and her Chincoteague pony, but we logically took the alternative, heading for the wall demarking Londa's domain.

'Western philosophy can't help you,' I told Charnock, 'but maybe I can. I think you're being too hard on yourself. It's all very well to become an anti-abortionist and spend every waking hour fetishising foetuses, but those seven discarded embryos belong to a different class altogether.'

'Let's not call them fetishists,' he admonished me. 'Let's not stoop to caricature.'

I blushed profusely, a crimson chagrin made even redder by my anger at Charnock. Yes, I'd maligned the embryophiles, unfairly for all I knew, but I hated being scolded about it by this creepy curmudgeon. 'My point is that when most people speak of the rights of the unborn, they're simply expressing a hope that every existing pregnancy will come to term. They don't mean that all conceivable souls must immediately achieve *Dasein*. Otherwise, their motto would be, "Fuck now."'

Charnock laughed – probably not for the first time in his life, though I couldn't be sure. '"Fuck now." Not a slogan you're likely to find on Father O'Malley's rear bumper.'

I placed the hooter to my lips and blew a festive toot. 'If Father O'Malley came upon the plans for your RXL-313, would he set about building one of his own, so he could pass his evenings manufacturing children in his basement? I think not. Most likely he'd burn the blueprints on the spot.'

'A beaker is not a uterine wall,' Charnock said haughtily. 'An ontogenerator is not a womb. I knew that before we began this conversation.' He lifted his hand and studied the pudgy digits. 'No solvent can remove this stain. Not soap, not turpentine, not sulphuric acid.'

I offered him a commiserating grunt, saying I was sorry that I hadn't relieved his guilt.

'I didn't expect you would.' He restored his tainted hand to the steering wheel. 'Nevertheless, I found our exchange fruitful. Having heard your incoherent thoughts on embryos, I realise what I should do with my life. Edwina has – what? – two months to live. After she passes away, I'll shut down my laboratory, forsake molecular genetics, and devote myself to a different domain.'

'Sounds like a plan.'

'The spiritual realm.'

'Ah, yes, the spiritual realm.' In those days 'spiritual' was my least favourite word. It still is.

Charnock tightened his grip on the wheel, his fingers turning white. '"This one isn't my daughter. This one won't do." Seven different times she said it, and then she gave me the beaker, and I made my decision, the vat or the bay? In each case I would first swish the fluid around and watch the embryo swimming in its little universe. I'm not sure whether I believe in God, but I know I no longer believe in biology.'

Edwina decided to accomplish her dying where she'd done so much of her living – in the Faustino conservatory with its damp air and Mesozoic fragrances. Somehow Javier had manoeuvred her bed, a wide trolley hedged with satin pillows, through the labyrinth of ferns and vines, bringing it to rest alongside Proserpine's salt pond. This Eve was going to stand her ground and die in the Garden, prostrate before the Tree of Knowledge.

There were to be no votive candles for Edwina, no smoking censers or hovering priests. Two male nurses from Miami, solemn Hector and jovial Sebastian, supervised the requisite technology – an array that included a cardiac monitor, a liquid-nutrient drip, and a computerised morphine dispenser, this last machine deployed to guarantee that in the end she could elect to trade lucidity for lack of pain. With their immaculate white jackets and equally immaculate trousers, Hector and Sebastian looked less like medical personnel than stewards on a cruise ship – and the conservatory had indeed become such a vessel, the sleek and seaworthy *Lady Daedalus*, bearing Edwina to that distant keep where even the wealthiest woman is beyond the reach of ransom.

Not surprisingly, the *Übermom* had written an endgame scenario that would enable her to continue regarding Donya, Londa, and Yolly as a single individual occupying three distinct space–time domains. The plan called for each child to pay her mother a separate farewell visit, so Edwina would feel that she was experiencing a succession of adieus from the same daughter. Only after she was dead might we teachers escort our pupils out of the conservatory, introduce them to one another, and help them to weather the hurricane of cognitive dissonance that was certain to follow.

While Henry, Brock, and I all thought it was a bad idea for Donya to attend Edwina's passing, Jordan took the opposite view. She did not recommend that Donya be present when Edwina actually drew her last breath, but she insisted that the child join the vigil, lest she pass the rest of her life vaguely anticipating her mother's return. A logical argument, and it soon gained everyone's assent, though it seemed to me that if we didn't whisk Donya away in time, she might spend that same life trying to forget her mother's death throes.

Shortly after dawn on the first Friday in June, as golden spokes of sunlight filled the eastern sky, and the toucans and parrots loudly proclaimed the acoustic borders of their territories, Javier telephoned to say that, within the hour, Henry, Brock, and Donya would arrive at Faustino and proceed to the geodesic dome. Londa and I, meanwhile, should go to the library, where we must wait until summoned, even as Jordan and Yolly bided their time in the drawing room.

Twenty minutes later, Londa and I settled into the russet leather couch before the ancient-history collection, her head pressed against my shoulder in a posture recalling one of Jordan's best digital photos: Oyster nuzzling Yolly, captioned: 'I Love You, Now How about Some Oats?' Evidently aware that something was amiss, Quetzie fluttered around the room in erratic ellipses. A soft staccato wheezing rose from deep within Londa's frame, a kind of anticipatory dirge. Part of me wanted to reveal that her mother's death might not be the most disorienting of the day's events, but having kept my promise to Edwina all these months, I wasn't about to break it now.

The morose Hector appeared and announced that Edwina required a sponge bath, after which she would receive her beloved daughter, 'sponge bath' no doubt being a coded term for Donya's visit to the deathbed. There was little conviction in the man's voice – I hoped he was better at nursing than at mendacity – but Londa seemed to accept his story. As Hector slipped out of the library, Quetzie landed on the conquistador's helmet and squawked out his newest sentence, '*Cogito ergo sum*,' which Londa had taught him the previous month by way of commemorating, as she'd put it, 'the first anniversary of that fateful meeting between a Boston philosopher and a crazy Florida girl without a conscience'.

A cry of grief slashed through the glutinous air. I knew its source immediately. Little Donya's scream contained a greater measure of cosmic despair than I thought a seven-year-old's soul could hold.

'That sounded like a child,' Londa said.

'It did,' I muttered. 'It was,' I added.

'What child?' demanded Londa. 'Do you know her?'

A second cry penetrated the library.

Now that Donya had revealed herself to Londa, should I continue cleaving to the script? Given this turn of events, Edwina's charade was surely beyond salvation.

'I've eaten cookies in her tree house.'

'Who is she?'

A third shriek. The iguana, frightened, hopped from the conquistador to Londa's shoulder. Without a moment's hesitation she strode through the French doors and scanned the hallway. '*Cogito ergo sum*,' Quetzie repeated with inimitable reptilian dismay.

'Remember the day I theorised that you might have a sister named Donya?' I said, drawing abreast of Londa. 'In point of fact the person making those sounds—'

'She's my *sister*?'

'Your sister Donya.'

'I don't understand.'

I took Londa's hand and guided her towards the conservatory, all the while attempting to explicate the strange procreative ecology of Isla de Sangre. A Petri dish instead of a marriage bed. A beaker instead of a womb. A catalyst instead of a childhood. Amnesia that wasn't amnesia but something far stranger. Three genetically identical sisters – and a fourth, progenitor sister bent on representing herself as the first three girls' mother.

'You're not making much sense,' Londa said.

Donya's next scream inspired us to break into a run. Quetzie abandoned Londa's shoulder but stayed with us, gliding directly above his mistress's head. We rounded the corner and veered into the conservatory. Edwina lay on her back, wrapped in a green smock and sleeping soundly. Donya, sobbing and quivering, had flung herself across her mother's chest. Henry stood over his pupil, a guardian tree as faithful and protective as Proserpine.

Our arrival prompted Donya to lift her head and glance towards the doorway. Tears stained her cheeks and her eyes were as red as radishes.

'Hello, sweetheart,' I said.

'Mason . . .' Donya stepped towards me, then changed her mind and, retreating, hugged her mother more tightly than before, a shipwreck survivor clinging to a floating spar.

The two nurses fidgeted near the cardiac monitor, a noisy black box the size of a microwave oven, its cathode-ray tube displaying a dancing sine wave, its sound chip bleeping in high-pitched counterpoint to Edwina's heartbeats. Brock leaned against the sentient mangrove like Ulysses bound to the mainmast of his ship. Upon noticing Proserpine, Quetzie judged her an ideal perch and soared to the highest branch.

I rushed to Donya's side, and in tandem Henry and I looped our arms around her quavering body until she stopped crying.

'Mommy's not going to get better,' she gasped. 'Not ever.'

'I know,' I said.

'Isn't that *terrible*?'

'It's terrible.'

Donya jabbed an accusing finger towards Londa. 'Who are you?'

'This woman's daughter.'

As Londa set her hand on Edwina's shoulder, the patient opened her eyes, then rotated her head far enough to determine that the worst had happened: her youngest daughter and her oldest were occupying the same spatiotemporal location, and they looked conspicuously like two different people.

'No, she's *my* mommy,' Donya protested. 'She's mine.'

'We're sisters,' Londa told Donya.

'It's true, Donya,' Henry said.

'No, that's wrong,' Donya said. 'I don't want a sister.'

At last Edwina spoke, her voice bloodless and faraway. 'You must stop this, dear child. Stop coming apart.'

Now Yolly raced into the conservatory, doubtless drawn by Donya's cries, and behind her came an equally bewildered Jordan. I'd not seen the middle Sister Sabacthani since her nativity. Sharp, bright, and skilfully composed as they were, Jordan's snapshots hadn't done Yolly justice. She was a glorious child with radiant skin and shining eyes, her hair as vibrant as a crown of laurels.

'Are you the person Jordan says you are?' Yolly asked, pointing at Londa. 'Are you my sister?'

'Probably.'

'Londa, right?'

'Right.'

'I'm Yolly, and I don't like *any* of this.'

'Me neither,' Londa replied.

'Me neither,' Donya echoed.

'My teacher says I'm really thirteen months old,' Yolly said.

'Mine says I've been around just two years,' Londa said.

Yolly circumnavigated the bed, entering Edwina's field of vision. 'My wonderful mother.'

'You're not supposed to be here yet.' Edwina sounded like a lost ghost asking directions to a seance.

'But I *want* to be here,' Yolly said.

Edwina closed her eyes, and for a few moments the air was free of human voices. The only sounds were the caws of jungle birds and the bleeping of the cardiac monitor.

Stretching an arm towards Donya, Yolly ran her palm through the child's hair. I imagined she brought a similarly unqualified affection to the act of stroking Oyster's mane.

'Little sister?' Yolly said.

'I'm *not* your sister.' Donya began to weep again.

'Donya, it's great having a big sister, and now you've got two,' Henry said.

Tears trickled down Donya's cheeks like raindrops on a window-pane. 'But who's going to take care of me?'

'I will,' Henry said. 'Brock will.'

'You bet,' Brock said.

'And I'll take care of you too,' Yolly added.

Donya's sobs grew softer. The monitor kept bleeping. Edwina opened her eyes.

'This is not acceptable behaviour, Yolonda,' she said in a thick whisper. 'I forbid you to break apart.'

'Mommy, can't we have just one more tea party?' Donya said.

This proved too much for Yolly, who started weeping as prolifically as her little sister. She wrapped her arms around herself, then slumped against the IV dispenser, whimpering, her face hatched by tears.

'I was a good mother, wasn't I?' Edwina said to no daughter in particular.

'You're the best mommy in the *whole world*!' Donya exclaimed.

Yolly uncurled one arm and pulled her sleeve across her nose and mouth. 'Thank you for everything, Mother,' she said, staggering towards the trolley. She kissed Edwina's pale thin lips. 'Thank you for Jordan and Oyster and the flute lessons. I'm the luckiest girl alive.'

'Mommeee!' wailed Donya.

Londa now shifted her gaze from her doomed mother to her bemused morality teacher. We locked eyes. She glowered. 'Damn it, Mason, you should've *told* me about this! You *liar*!'

I grimaced but remained silent.

'Londa, your mother needs a kind word from you,' Jordan said.

'You're a liar too!' Londa wailed, lurching towards Jordan. 'You made Yolly think I didn't exist!' She extended her index finger, aiming it first at Henry, then Brock. 'And you two did the same thing to Donya! But I *do* exist!'

I wanted to tell Londa there were five liars in the room, not four, most conspicuously the patient on the bed, but I simply said, 'Jordan is right. You owe your mother something. Blessed are the comforters.'

There is no such Beatitude, and Londa knew it, but rather than correcting me, she stepped towards Edwina and grasped her limp hand. 'I love you, Mother. Whatever this crazy thing is you've done, I love you.'

I assumed that Edwina would now smile. I expected her to acquire a seraphic face, aglow with peace and maternal fulfilment, but instead an arcane, almost preternatural force seized her body. Her teeth chattered. Her lips quivered. Her limbs trembled so violently I feared her ligaments might rip free of her bones.

Without exchanging a word, the tutors moved to shelter their charges from Edwina's terminal spasms. Henry took one of Donya's hands, Brock the other, and together they propelled her towards the patio. Jordan approached the bed, curled an arm around Yolly's shoulder, and escorted her behind the cardiac monitor.

Londa did not resist when I set my palm against the small of her back and guided her into Proserpine's fecund shade.

'Stop splitting!' Edwina suddenly cried. 'Stay together!'

Donya released a shrill moan.

'Quetzie is a handsome devil!' squawked the iguana.

'Together!' Edwina demanded.

The cardiac monitor played a few final, reassuring bleeps, and then the cadence disintegrated into random chitters.

'*Cogito ergo sum*,' Quetzie averred, but his insight was lost on Edwina, who had entered a realm where cogitation does not occur.

Although the two nurses had proved only marginally useful during Edwina's final days, they certainly earned their salaries after she had gone. Seizing upon a hidden potential of the IV dispenser, Hector and Sebastian filled Edwina's veins with a small quantity of embalming fluid, just enough to counter the spoilage threatened by the Florida heat. They ordered a steel casket, signed the death certificate, and ran interference with a health inspector from Key West who'd long ago deduced that biological events on Isla de Sangre rarely fell within the norm. They even interred the body, digging a grave at the axis of Edwina's empire, in the shadow of the sandstone pillar where the three concrete walls converged.

Shortly before the funeral, Londa composed an epitaph, which Brock, master of all media, succeeded in etching on to a bronze tablet the size of a sandwich board. After everyone had assembled by Edwina's resting place – children, tutors, chefs, servants, groundskeepers – we propped the tablet against the burial mound, so that the grave acquired a door: a brazen gate opening on to the Nothing, much as the ontogenerator was a portal into *Dasein*.

In Loving Memory of

EDWINA SABACTHANI

Servant of Science

Seeker of Wisdom

Eternal Protector of
Three Devoted Daughters

Donya read the words aloud, slowly, haltingly, then began to cry, partly from her frustration over not understanding them, partly from her realisation that those same words, comprehended, would have broken her heart. Henry deftly led her away from the knot of mourners towards a commodious clearing ringed by ferns. From his backpack he withdrew a bag of figs, a bunch of bananas, and a flask of Hawaiian Punch, immediately convening a jungle picnic for Donya and himself, leaving the rest of us to continue the ceremony on our own.

For the next hour we eulogised Edwina with anecdotes. Brock described her touching attempts to enter the universe of Donya's miniature amusement park. Javier praised Edwina's financial generosity, most especially her insistence on paying for his father's bypass surgery. Chen Lee recalled the time he'd carelessly allowed thirty pounds of fish to go bad, and how his boss had unhesitatingly absolved him. Charnock offered his opinion that Edwina's brief but productive career with GenoText, Inc. would eventually lead to effective germline therapies for cystic fibrosis and muscular dystrophy. Yolly spoke of how she and her mother had wept openly during *The Black Stallion*. Londa noted that her mother was 'always there when I needed her', then added, under her breath, 'as long as I needed her on Wednesdays and Fridays'. Paralysed by ambivalence, Jordan and I said nothing.

Later that week two attorneys from the classy Miami law firm of Acosta, Rambal and Salazar descended upon the island. While their ostensible intention was to apprise the girls of certain postmortem arrangements, it was obvious that Rex Fermoyle and Martha Carrington were primarily looking to score slices of the walloping financial pie Edwina had left behind. Watching them sift through their late client's private papers, I thought of that proud corps of airport dogs employed to detect heroin, explosives, and illegal foodstuffs, though Fermoyle and Carrington's speciality was sniffing out neglected stock options, government bonds, and life-insurance policies.

When it came to the legal dimensions of her death, Edwina had obviously been willing to regard Yolonda as three distinct entities, for Fermoyle and Carrington began their presentation by noting that each girl had inherited her own billion-dollar trust fund.

Moreover, by scrutinising every twig and burl of the Sabacthani family tree, Edwina had located three blood relations willing to become the girls' legal guardians, though in her prescience she'd also included a provision whereby we tutors might also take custody of our charges. For Londa, Edwina had found a dullard first cousin whose life revolved around his marginally profitable hotel in Milwaukee; for Yolly, a dotty female second cousin who turned her Baltimore mansion into a Poe-themed haunted house every Halloween; for Donya, a gifted great aunt still employed as a cellist by the Pittsburgh Symphony Orchestra. I was not surprised when Henry and Brock announced their intention to adopt Donya, nor was I taken aback when Jordan said she would make Yolly her ward, for despite her protestations concerning motherhood and trapeze artists, it was obvious that Yolly's advent had simultaneously diagnosed and treated a void in Jordan's life. I myself did not address the guardianship issue that day, but the following morning I confided to Fermoyle that I'd be just as happy to let the Milwaukee hotel manager worry about Londa for a while, even as I admitted that this decision was unlikely to free me of her clinging charisma.

In the months following the funeral, the Sisters Sabacthani came remarkably close to fulfilling their mother's dream of a unified Yolonda. They laughed together, cried together, ate, slept, gossiped, sang, danced and – once Jordan had imported a mare named Guinevere for Londa and a Welsh pony named Crackers for Donya – rode across the scrub together. And of course they also drove one another batty, for only a sister has that special talent for breaking your last bottle of perfume, spilling juice on your best sweater, dropping your curling iron into a sink full of soapy water, losing your favourite Distressed Leather CD, borrowing your bicycle and then blowing out the tires, and cutting you to pieces by criticising your taste in music or clothes or movies.

But such lapses were rare. On balance the children were as companionable as littermates, as compatible as Dumas's musketeers, with Londa and Yolly entering into an amicable rivalry over who could be the better big sister. They nursed Donya through an episode of chickenpox and an encounter with a poison sumac plant, presented her with abridged versions of Londa's colourful answers to Yolly's incessant questions about sex, and despite their own sorrow ministered diligently to Donya's grief, suggesting that she and Edwina might one day be reunited in some transcendent realm, though they declined to call it heaven, paradise, or any name implying geographic actuality.

It was Jordan's idea for the sisters to explore the upper reaches of Torre de la Carne, a domain that, prior to Edwina's death, Yolly had been forbidden to visit as strictly as Bluebeard's new bride had been barred from the room in which her pickled predecessors hung. Jordan invited the other tutors along, Charnock to boot, and so we were a party of eight who ascended the tower that afternoon, following the spiral staircase ever upwards.

Stepping into the laboratory, I inhaled a gulp of mummified air and immediately began to cough. Dust covered everything – ontogenerator, control console, enzyme tanks, DUNCE cap – like a stratum of newly fallen snow. The spiders had been industrious in Edwina's absence, so that the place suggested the atelier of an artist who was forever modelling avant-garde suspension bridges. Londa went instinctively to the great riveted sphere that had functioned as her placenta, cradle, and playpen. She selected a porthole and peered inside, and soon Yolly and Donya did the same, so that the sisters formed a tableau that evoked memories of my favourite New England Aquarium poster: three children standing before a fish tank, faces aglow with curiosity.

Charnock now improvised a lecture concerning the rarefied procedure by which he'd taken five hundred anonymous donor eggs, stripped away their DNA, and injected each hollowed-out oocyte with cumulus cells harvested from Edwina's ovaries. A subtle electric jolt was sufficient to transform the majority of these chimerical zygotes into blastocysts, scores of which survived to become full-blown embryos. With consummate care Edwina and Charnock had nurtured each nascent life, and in three particular cases the experiment had yielded auspicious specimens: the budding Londa, the blossoming Donya, and the burgeoning Yolly, all of whom were allowed to enter foetushood. The biologist exuded an understandable pride while describing the hormone shots he'd given each sister shortly before her transfer to the RXL-313, explaining how these injections had interacted with the vat's enzymes to radically accelerate the child's maturation.

Throughout Charnock's lecture I studied the sisters' faces, soon concluding that nobody was remotely interested in what he had to say, and I realised that if they were to truly comprehend their situation – their passionless conceptions, ultramarine infancies, lateral kinship with Edwina – they must spend some time alone in this place. When I suggested in a cheery but emphatic tone that 'our young charges would probably like a few moments of privacy', the girls all released spontaneous sighs of relief.

Ten years later, when Londa and I were no longer tutor and pupil but partners in a considerably more convoluted relationship, she told me what had happened that afternoon once the adults left the laboratory. By fiddling with the knobs on the control console, the girls had managed to flip back the hatch on the ontogenerator. Without a single word passing among them, they had removed their clothing, climbed the exterior rungs, and – heedless of the amniotic residue clinging to the inside surfaces – descended into the chamber. The sharp scent of the titanium was oddly soothing. For well over an hour the girls had huddled in the dark, talking and then not talking, fused like Siamese triplets, arms linked, hip against hip, until it was apparent they'd made peace with the late Edwina Sabacthani in her many guises – mother, sister, progenitor, confidante, nemesis – and so they returned to the outside world, laughing and joking and eager for a swim in the Bahía de Matecumba.

Dozens of American universities would have been pleased to count Londa among their first-year students, but she would consider only her mother's alma mater. She intended to follow in Edwina's footsteps, pursuing her undergraduate studies at Johns Hopkins, obtaining a PhD in molecular biology from that same institution, and subsequently joining the cutting edge of medical research. My vatling was determined to master and improve upon the existing techniques for delivering healthy genes to patients who'd drawn losing tickets in the great DNA sweepstakes – bone-marrow infusions, liver resections, domesticated retroviruses, artificial chromosomes – and perhaps invent a few such vehicles as well.

But unlike her mother, Londa assured me, she would never succumb to the allure of self-replication.

Initially the Hopkins admissions committee raised a collective eyebrow at Londa's inability to produce anything resembling a high-school transcript. They weren't sure whether to believe her claim that she'd read her way through the largest private library in the Florida Keys, likewise her curious assertion that she'd received 'a rigorous education in ontology from an independent scholar whose unpublished thesis, 'Ethics from the Earth', will one day set philosophy on its ear'. But then they noted her stratospheric SAT scores, her sterling performance on the Biology and Mathematics Achievement Tests, and her cheque for one year's tuition in advance, and their scepticism evaporated like alcohol in a Petri dish.

It turned out that Yolly, too, would be leaving on Labor Day. Jordan had accepted a job running the Human Development Department at Merrimack Academy, a private school in Haverhill, Massachusetts, and she'd lost no time arranging for her ward to join the freshman class. One campus visit was enough to persuade Yolly that she'd be happy at Merrimack. It had an equestrian programme, after all, including a stable that Oyster would find congenial, not to mention an orchestra, a state-of-the-art computer lab, a theatre modelled on the Globe, and a low teacher-student ratio. When I first heard of Yolly's imminent departure, my instincts told me she was making a mistake, for the middle Sister Sabacthani had thus far failed to concoct a convincing personal history, a plausible 'Book of Yolly', and I worried that the other Merrimack students, realising they had a naïf in their midst, would torment her mercilessly. I ran this troubling prediction past Jordan, and against my expectations she managed to allay my fears with a single cogent remark.

'Yolly's practically my *daughter*, for Christ's sake,' she said. 'I'll be looking out for her twenty-four hours a day, which is a better deal than most kids get from their parents.'

As for Donya, both Henry and Brock wanted to continue educating her on the island, though they admitted to enjoying little objectivity in the matter, as neither could imagine a better place for pursuing his pet passion – in Henry's case, a cycle of speculative scripts for 'Uncle Rumpus's Magic Island', in Brock's case, a magnum opus: ten huge canvases that would ultimately form a 360-degree cyclorama of Isla de Sangre refracted through his surrealist's sensibility. It was Jordan who settled the question, arguing that several more years of idyllic isolation would do Donya more good than harm. Sometime around her sixteenth birthday she should be given the same choice as Yolly – another season in Eden, pumpkin, or a leap into the larger world?

On the same day that Yolly received her acceptance letter from Merrimack, Javier informed me that Vincent Charnock, having completed his last experiment and removed his equipment from the Quonset-hut complex, was no longer in residence. Shortly after sunrise, the father of ontogeneration had strolled down to the Bahía de Flores, boarded Captain López's cabin cruiser, and left for Key West without telling a soul. I was hardly surprised. Charnock had got what he wanted from me – corroboration of his suspicion that philosophers couldn't think straight about embryos – and he obviously had nothing more to say to the Sisters Sabacthani.

'Now that Edwina and Dr Charnock have gone, I can do a forbidden thing,' Javier told me one night as we savoured Cuba libres on my deck. 'I speak now of our poor, miserable Proserpine.'

'Let me guess,' I said. 'You're going to gobble down a dozen rococonuts and mud-wrestle an alligator.'

Smiling, he sipped rum and shook his head. 'I want to end her suffering. Edwina wouldn't allow it – she always said Proserpine can't feel anything – and Dr Charnock, he was just as stubborn, but for different reasons. Whatever Proserpine's quality of life, he said, we have got no right to commit euthanasia.'

'So you're going to uproot her?'

'The tree will bless us for it.'

Two days later Javier gathered together Henry, Brock, Londa, and myself, fed us a hearty lunch of calamari in the Faustino dining hall, and guided us into the conservatory. We stripped Proserpine of her fruits. The harvest fitted into two hundred king-size Ziploc bags, which we stored in the manor's largest freezer. Having never known the unique inebriation afforded by mumquat nectar, Henry and Brock briefly considered sharing a rococonut, but they decided to abstain, knowing that the day's task would require a clear head and steady hands.

We returned to the conservatory and, after three hours of hard labour with picks and shovels, extracted Proserpine from her brackish habitat. As we carried the mangrove to the Quonset huts, her breathing became softer, her heartbeats slower, her trembling imperceptible. Charnock's research laboratory was even larger than his workshop atop Torre de la Carne, but Proserpine's roots and branches still jammed the place to its corrugated walls. Under Londa's direction we inserted the tubers into buckets of morphine and, once convinced that the tree was insensate, incised her trunk with a chain saw and got to work. Our efforts continued from mid-afternoon till dusk, but at last all traces of Edwina's interventions were gone, every chunk of lung, scrap of heart, and curd of neural tissue.

Shortly after dark, we hauled the vegetable cadaver down to the beach, stopping near the site of Ralph Gittikac's prodigal picnic. A full moon rose over the Bahía de Flores, painting the waters with streaks of such silvery beauty as to suggest some benevolent inverse of an oil slick. We filled the mangrove's dredged trunk with kerosene, then set it on fire. For nearly an hour the five of us stood on the shore, chatting idly as sparks swarmed around the flaming tree. Javier was the first to leave, saying he needed to work on his résumé. Henry and Brock departed next, explaining that Chen had done more than his share of babysitting that day.

Dressed in ragged chinos and a white T-shirt, Londa looked exquisite by firelight. The flames bronzed her cheeks and burnished her brow. She told me that earlier in the week she and Yolly had brought Donya to this very spot. The three girls had baked clams and played Frisbee, and when the stars came out, they'd sprawled on the beach and wriggled their toes in the sand, 'playing footsie with the planet'. Thanks to her Stargazer Deluxe, Donya had quickly identified Orion, the Pleiades, the Big Dipper, and a half-dozen other constellations. Seeking to stimulate her youngest sister's sense of wonder while expanding her other sister's intellect, Londa had speculated aloud that the night sky was an illusion – a projected vista of bright bodies and black voids generated by an immense planetarium located on Platonia, an invisible world in orbit between Earth and Venus.

'I trust your siblings were amused,' I said.

She answered with characteristic Sabacthani solemnity. 'They giggled idiotically. Humour was not my intention. I wanted them to imagine that Platonia and the Platonians really exist.'

'Sisters can be so annoying.'

'You call us sisters, which is more or less correct – but I'll bet our teachers call us something else behind our backs. Be honest, Socrates. Are we kettle kittens? Bisque bitches?'

'Vatlings, actually.'

'Vatlings?' Londa laughed, pleased with herself. She'd smoked us out. 'Very funny. What else?'

'Beaker freaks, gumbo girls, and tureen queens.'

'Any more?'

'Well, yes.'

'What?'

'Bouillababies and Petri dolls. That's all.'

'I like gumbo girls best.'

'Me, too.'

She hooked her thumbs through the belt loops of her chinos. 'Mr Fermoyle tells me you don't want to be my guardian.'

'I wouldn't put it that way.'

'You stuck me with some goofball cousin. I don't mind, really – not as long as you'll keep on being my auxiliary conscience.' She gestured towards Sagittarius, as if signalling the centaur to release his arrow. 'Hey, Mason, you want to hear something interesting about the Platonians' projection? It isn't just a sky map. It's also a blueprint.'

'A blueprint,' I repeated with manufactured enthusiasm.

'A blueprint for a city.'

'A city. Right.'

'See how it shines? Street lamps, lighted windows, mooring beacons for zeppelins, all glittering like Donya's seahorses.'

'I love those seahorses. They're all I know of God.'

'The Platonians fully intend to build it one day, a perfect city, a haven for the misbegotten.'

'The misbegotten deserve no less,' I said drily.

'Once the Platonians get an idea in their heads, there's no stopping them.'

'Be careful, Londa. Even Jesus failed to bring heaven to earth.'

'Jesus didn't have a trust fund.' She lifted a stone from the beach and tossed it into the fire, breeding a new generation of sparks. 'For a while I was committed to the name "Zeus City", in honour of the Stoics' Utopia, but then I decided "Themisopolis" was a better choice, you know, after the goddess with the sword and the blindfold and the balance scales.'

'I applaud your ambition.'

'Don't patronise me.'

'The last thing on my mind.'

'Themisopolis, the City of Justice. And with the help of my auxiliary conscience, I'm going to make it happen.'

'Your auxiliary conscience has other plans,' I said. True enough: I was planning to have nothing to do with Themisopolis.

'You'll miss all the fun,' she said.

'Fun on a bun,' I said.

A vibration passed through my bones, as if I were the late Proserpine enduring a vestigial fit. When Londa installed herself as monarch over her trust-fund Utopia, which of her personae would be ascendant? Even if the benign Scarlet Darwinist proved dominant at first, the Crimson Kantian and the Purple Pietist might be lurking in the shadows, waiting to seize power.

'Question, my dear,' I said. 'What will happen when the Platonians switch off their planetarium?'

'Isn't it obvious? The heavens will vanish, every last star, and then we'll finally see what lies beyond. It promises to be impossibly magnificent and utterly incomprehensible.'

'That's the difference between you and me, Londa. I don't want to be there when the stars blink out.'

'Whereas I would try to get a front-row seat.'

She took two steps forward, kissed me squarely on the lips and, pivoting abruptly like a weathervane in a gale, melted into the night.

'Your gumbo girl will build a city!' she called out of the darkness.

'You don't believe her, but she'll do it! The Phyllistines will curse every brick and the downtrodden will cheer!'

I shifted my eyes from Londa's retreating form to the flaming tree and then to the bright speckled dome. For a full minute I stood on the beach and studied the luminous City of Justice. Slowly, one by one, the lamps, windows, and mooring beacons floated free and transmuted into stars again, so I lowered my gaze and turned from the sea and walked into the forest.

PART TWO

Londa Unbound

CHAPTER 8

No, ladies and gentlemen, I did not unscrew her skullcap, insert her brain into its white vault, and knit her medulla to her spinal cord: someone else performed that operation. Still, I was her creator. I did not take gouts of dripping tissue in my hands and sculpt them around her bones, feeding the scraps to the dog who ate God's homework. She was nevertheless my creature. I did not install her beating heart in its thoracic cavity, lodge her eyeballs in their sockets, or tap her teeth into place with a steel mallet tempered in the Pierian spring. And yet, I am responsible for what she became.

Yes, ladies and gentlemen, my detractors speak the truth. For nearly ten years following my departure from the Florida Keys, I pretended to the outside world that I'd played no part in the construction of Londa Sabacthani's increasingly conspicuous soul. Every time her press secretary, the indefatigable Pauline Chilton, despatched yet another reporter to my abode, eager to hear about the Isla de Sangre curriculum and maybe learn what made Londa tick, I would tell the invader that, while I had indeed served briefly as Dr Sabacthani's private tutor in certain abstruse deontological matters, my influence on her ethical development had been negligible.

I am still haunted by the case of Emily Seldes, who tearfully begged me to grant her an hour of my time lest she lose her job at the *Hartford Courant*. When I turned her down, Miss Seldes proceeded to fabricate and publish a story, 'Sabacthani's Mentor Recalls His "Moral Prodigy"', subsequently receiving the boot and descending into clinical depression when the article was exposed as a fraud. An unfortunate episode, but I was immune to regret in those days. Nor could I be moved by avarice. The producers of *The Roscoe Fisher Show* offered me $15,000 for a ten-minute interview. I told them I would appear on the condition that we talked about nothing but Heidegger's concept of *Dasein*. The powers behind *Cordelia Drake Live* raised the stakes to $20,000. I responded that I was ill disposed to revisit a closed chapter in my life, but I'd be pleased to tell Cordelia's viewers why Darwinian materialism offers a more exalted view of humankind than the Book of Genesis.

Londa herself had no better luck getting my attention. I recycled her letters unopened, erased her phone messages without listening to them, slammed doors in the face of her envoys, and deleted her emails with alacrity. Subject: Mason, I Need You. Subject: Calling All Consciences. Subject: Please, Socrates. Subject: Win a Free Trip to Themisopolis. Subject: Desperately Seeking Superego. Subject: Gumbo Girl on the Verge of a Nervous Breakdown. Subject: For God's Sake. Subject: I'm Not Kidding. Subject: Jesus Christ! Subject: Fuck You!

What sense was there in my self-imposed exile? By what lights would a reasonable man dissent from the Sabacthani miracle? Who but the crustiest curmudgeon would disdain the omnibenevolent community that Londa and Yolly had seeded in the wild environs of Bel Air, Maryland? Who but the sourest sophist would gainsay the splendid projects administered within the walls of that Susquehanna River Utopia? One thinks immediately of the Mary Wollstonecraft Fund, providing contraceptives and small-business loans to women in underdeveloped countries, not to mention the Susan B. Anthony Trust, running to earth the architects of various international prostitution rings – sexual slavery, the sisters called it with a characteristic contempt for euphemism – as well as the Elizabeth Cady Stanton Foundation, tirelessly lobbying against the user-friendly fascism, feel-good theocracy, and creeping Phyllistinism that dominated the American political landscape. O come, all ye faithful. Come ye to Themisopolis. Come and behold the Institute for Advanced Biological Investigations, dedicated to eradicating female cancers. Tour the Vision Syndicate and chat with its idealistic engineers, all determined to inaugurate a post-carbon age in which fossil-fuelled automobiles will have gone the way of telegrams and pterodactyls. Drop by the Artemis Clinic, offering free medical services, including abortions, to pregnant women. Visit Arcadia House, sheltering hundreds of runaway wives, battered girlfriends, pregnant teenagers, abused children and unadoptable orphans.

But you see, ladies and gentlemen, despite Londa's munificence, or maybe because of it, there was never a moment when she did not seem monstrous in my eyes: beauty and beast in a single skin. In short, the woman frightened me. She scared me to death. Whenever I started to compose an email to my vatling, images of her stigmata flooded my brain – the scar on her palm, the thorn under her thumbnail – and I shut down the computer. Each time I picked up the phone to call her, the vindictive Crimson Kantian from 'The Book of Londa' rose in my imagination, and I returned the handset to its cradle, knowing that, for the sake of my sanity, and perhaps hers as well, I must continue to banish her from my life.

And so it happens that these pages contain a dearth of inside information concerning Londa's ascent from biology major to celebrity saint. You will find nothing here to supplement the standard narrative – how a beautiful and brilliant molecular geneticist from Johns Hopkins one day burst upon the clinical-research scene, perfecting a therapeutic technique whereby specially designed patches of healthy DNA were knitted into the chromosomes of patients suffering from malign mutations; how this same prodigy ultimately turned her back on avant-garde chimeraplasty and announced that she intended to pursue an even grander agenda; how she then joined forces with her younger sister, Yolly, her personal manager, Dagmar Röhrig, and her eternal inspiration, the Good Samaritan, to bring a substantial tract of paradise to earth, in time earning the sobriquet Dame Quixote. If you want to learn about the Golden Age of Themisopolis, rent the PBS documentary *She Walked Among Us*. Read Sandra Granger's surprise bestseller *Weltanschauung Woman*. Hunt out back issues of that old Marvel Comics series *The League of Londa*, the first of which currently commands a $350 minimum bid on eBay. Collect the trading cards. Play the board game. Fondle the action figure.

So extreme was my wariness that it extended even to Londa's youngest sister back on the island. Every time Donya invited me to Casa de los Huesos, I invented a pretext for staying put – poor health, low spirits, a deadline for delivering of a new revision of 'Ethics from the Earth' to a prospective publisher – though I did agree to exchange emails and Christmas cards with her. When Omar the Dobermann went to the Elysium of Endless Bones at the ripe old age of fifteen, I composed a five-stanza elegy, 'I Just Got a Postcard from My Dog', that, as Henry put it, 'helped us move our favourite little girl from mourning to remembrance'.

By Donya's account, all was well on Isla de Sangre. Henry had written a half-dozen scripts for 'Uncle Rumpus's Magic Island', 'and they're really, really funny', she assured me. Brock's emerging surrealist cyclorama 'makes you feel like your eyeballs have fallen out and gone rolling around on a pool table', which I took to be a recommendation. As for Donya herself, while her handcrafted conscience was probably no less extravagant than Londa's or Yolly's, her messages betrayed little of the unbounded swash-bucklery that had made her older sisters the decade's most beloved and most vilified women. When not marking the Bahía de Flores with signs imploring passing yachtsmen to keep their refuse out of the water, she was busy protecting newly laid sea-turtle eggs from predatory egrets and petitioning the federal government to designate the island a National Wildlife Refuge. I imagined that Donya might one day redirect these pastoral passions, scaling her ambitions upwards from her local ecosystem to planet Earth, but for the moment she seemed happy to circumscribe her dreams.

Had I been utterly determined to keep Londa from crossing my path, of course, I could have moved as far from Maryland as possible, to San Francisco maybe, or even London. But instead I returned to Boston – to my old haunts, in fact, Hawthorne University and its environs. My goal was not to engage in further tussles with Felix Pielmeister, nor was it to resurrect my PhD candidacy. What drove me there was my craving for philosophical discourse, the desire that Sinuhe's riverside ruminations had sparked in me at such an impressionable age. I needed to hear sentences ornamented with 'categorical imperative', 'Cartesian dualism', 'Hegelian idealism', and 'the encounter with nothingness' the way a believing Sabacthanite craved the latest issue of *The League of Londa*.

My bright idea was to open a second-hand-book store, an amenity to be found nowhere within a six-block radius of the campus. A solid nugget of $100,000 remained from my Isla de Sangre salary, and this proved sufficient for me to attract a business partner, easy-going Dexter Padula, a member of that ubiquitous academic breed, the professional graduate student, forever revising his dissertation and eyeing external reality like a nursing infant struggling to imagine life beyond the tit. Dexter stood out from his fellows on four counts. He was not on antidepressants, he knew how to groom himself, he had a plan for finishing his thesis – 'Overlapping Intersubjectivities in *The Canterbury Tales*' – before the year was up, and he'd inherited a bundle from his father, though apparently the bundle would have been bigger had Dexter decided to become a lawyer instead of a Chaucerian. In a matter of weeks we'd secured a two-year lease on 1,924 square feet of the Pequot Building, an easy and picturesque walk from campus, and we'd also acquired the private libraries of four bibliophiles whose ability to enjoy their collections had been compromised by, respectively, illness, impoverishment, blindness and death. After these acquisitions, we still had sufficient funds for several part-time employees and a hand-carved sign reading PIECES OF MIND: USED BOOKS, FRESH COFFEE, LIVELY CONVERSATION.

Neither Dexter nor I knew the first thing about running a small business. We were entrepreneurs the way Abbott and Costello were watercolourists. And so naturally it came to pass that Pieces of Mind was a hands-down, thumbs-up, flat-out success. Was it possible that those Egyptian gods to whom Sinuhe had declined to defer – regal Isis, valiant Horus, wise Thoth, and the rest – were not only real but sending their smiles our way? I liked to think so, though when we did the maths it appeared that the decisive factor was not divine intervention but the espresso machine at the back of the store.

We'd been in business barely three months when another stroke of luck augmented my bank account. After collecting a dozen rejection letters, I somehow persuaded Bellerophon Books to publish an abridged version of 'Ethics from the Earth'. Defying expectations, my opinionated opus soon earned out its $1000 advance, and then the biannual royalties began to arrive. Sometimes the payments would be as much as $200, enough for two weeks' worth of cream, sugar, and toilet paper.

Although we were thriving in the material realm, my grander vision for Pieces of Mind never came to pass. My dream was that, while Daphne, Forrest and our other student employees attended to the tedious tasks – shelving the merchandise, working the cash register, posting selected inventory on the Internet – I would sashay through the coffee bar, inviting myself into whatever fascinating discussions caught my ear. A foolish notion. A delusion on stilts. For one thing, the owner of a second-hand-book store does not sashay. He runs around putting out fires – the irate customer, the overdue phone bill, the crashed computer, the housewife from Chelsea who's just shown up expecting a hundred dollars for her worthless box of Reader's Digest Condensed Books. Furthermore, even if I'd had time to mingle, I wouldn't have enjoyed it, for what emerged from my customers' mouths was not so much conversation as a litany of complaint. The undergraduates lamented the high price of textbooks and the equally outrageous fact that they were expected to read them. The graduate students bemoaned their small stipends and large workloads. The professors apportioned their spleen among the graduate students, the administrators, and one another. Indeed, during the store's entire lifespan, I never encountered a single spontaneous seminar concerning Foucault or Derrida, though I learned more than I wanted to about tenure. Sad to say, the one time I heard the delectable question 'How, then, should we live?' within the walls of Pieces of Mind, the speaker turned out to be Felix Pielmeister. I instantly made an about-face and retreated to the children's section.

If my little haven was no agora, there were compensations nonetheless. It became my habit, after closing up for the evening, to pour myself a glass of Cabernet Sauvignon, sprawl on the couch, and think, taking incalculable delight in what I'd wrought, this bibliographic cornucopia, this box seat in God's brain. Then, too, there was the happy fact that managing a bookstore is a terrific way to meet women. Fair are the daughters of men, and fairest are those who read. Is there any creature more desirable than a

damsel in intellectual distress? I see you're a Joseph Heller aficionado – allow me to argue that *Something Happened* is a greater
achievement than *Catch-22*. No, we don't have *A Prayer for Owen
Meany*, but in my opinion *The Cider House Rules* is a much better
novel.

Throughout this period, Pieces of Mind netted me dozens of
dates and several unexpected seductions. I suffered three broken
hearts and inflicted as many in turn. Then one day the woman of
my dreams walked into the store, and my life changed for ever.

Like Dante catching his fateful glimpse of Beatrice, I first spied
her from afar – or, rather, from above. I was standing on the
stepladder, shelving a near-mint collection of Heinlein juveniles in
the topmost loft of our science fiction and fantasy section, when
a female voice called out from the precincts of J. R. R. Tolkien
below.

'Excuse me. I'm looking for a hardcover *Faerie Queene*. Is there
such a thing?'

I glanced downwards, and my eyes met the face of a goddess
with generous lips, endearing dimples, and the sort of large
intelligent eyes behind which, if I was any sort of judge, elegant
thoughts were routinely entertained.

'It's not with the poetry,' she continued, 'and I tried literature
too, so maybe somebody shelved it with your wizards and elves?'

As luck would have it, two days earlier a retiring professor of
British Literature had dropped off a complete run of those lavishly
illustrated, out-of-print marvels known as the Erlanger House
Classics, including a slipcased edition of *The Faerie Queene*, so I
could assess their condition and make him an offer. 'There's a
rare three-volume set on the premises, but I haven't priced it yet,'
I told my adorable Spenserian, then carelessly followed up with a
question that a retailer must never, under any circumstances, ask
a customer. 'How much are you willing to pay?'

'Anything,' she said. 'Three hundred dollars.'

Assuming it was in good shape, I would happily have given the
good professor $400 for his *Faerie Queene*, which would probably
fetch $700 on the Internet. 'You can have it for two hundred and
fifty,' I told her. 'Meet me at the cash register.'

Leaving my heart aloft, I descended to earth and floated into the back room, where I unsheathed all three volumes and leafed through them in search of underlinings and dog ears. The books seemed free of blemishes. I considered lowering the price to $200, then decided that if my goddess ever found out what this edition was really worth, she would think me an idiot.

'We don't get many Spenserians in here,' I said, approaching the sales counter.

'I'm sure,' she replied.

As if Isis and Horus hadn't already done enough for me, the object of my infatuation wrote the store a personal cheque with her address on it, and thus I learned not only her name, Natalie Novak, but also her whereabouts.

I probed, I pried, I snooped, I sleuthed, and by the end of the month the salient facts were mine. An ABD in the English Department, Natalie divided her time between writing her dissertation, something about the function of Providence in Emily Brontë, and teaching a panoply of courses ranging from Elizabethan Tragedy to the Twentieth-Century Novel. On agreeable spring days she was not embarrassed to escort her Victorian Poetry class down to the Charles River and recite 'The Lady of Shalott' aloud, while the students imagined the hapless maiden drifting past on her funeral barge. But the surest route to Natalie's heart doubtless lay in Spenser's Faerie Land, and so I undertook a journey to that extravagant realm.

For six full weeks I immersed myself in the epic, keeping company with its valiant knights, foul witches, beautiful shepherdesses, lustful giants, virtuous adventurers, and depraved magicians. I accomplished this feat even though *The Faerie Queene* suffers from the defect of not being very good, or such was my reaction to its stone-obvious moralising and in-your-face allegory. It wasn't easy working up an affection for this god-awful masterpiece, but somehow I suspended my revulsion long enough to start appreciating its positive aspects: the occasional neat plot twist, the intermittent linguistic felicity. 'Sleep after toil, port after stormy seas, / Ease after war, death after life does greatly please.' A fine couplet, no question. 'Her angel's face / As the great eye of heaven shined bright, / And made a sunshine in the shady place.' Well done, sir. 'Her birth was of the womb of morning dew.' I had no idea what that meant, but I liked it.

One golden April afternoon I decided to bring my project to fruition. I left Dexter in charge of the store, rode my bike to the river, and hid behind a forsythia bush. Right on schedule Natalie appeared, her fifteen Shakespeare students trailing behind her like ducklings. For the next forty-five minutes she lectured on *Antony and Cleopatra*, arguing that it was at once the most cerebral and the most emotional of the tragedies. She fielded some questions, answered them astutely, then bade her ducklings scatter. Time for me to make my move.

'Hello again.' A good opening gambit, I felt. Precise, but non-threatening.

'Have we met?'

'I'm the guy who runs Pieces of Mind. I'll be honest, Natalie. When you bought that pricy *Faerie Queene*, I was so dazzled I lost the power of speech, and before I'd untied my tongue you were out the door. At long last, I told myself. At long last – a kindred spirit!'

'We're not communicating.'

'"Her birth was of the womb of morning dew." It doesn't get any better than that.'

'It doesn't?'

'I'll wager that, of all the people down by the river today, only you and I fully appreciate that astonishing moment when Duessa stands exposed as a filthy, scabby hag, not to mention Error showering the Red Cross Knight with her vomitus of books.'

'I really love your store.'

'Thank you.'

'I'm afraid I can't say the same for *The Faerie Queene*.'

'Come again?'

'To tell you the truth, I think Spenser is the most pompous twit ever to molest the English language. Sorry. Really. Art is so subjective.'

All my muscles contracted, a whole-body wince. 'I see,' I mumbled. 'So that's how it is.'

'I know the man has his partisans. He also has his virulent anti-Catholicism, his bigotry towards Saracens, his contempt for democracy, and his treacley notions of piety. But Pieces of Mind is a gift to our community. May I buy you a beer?'

'If you can't stand Spenser, why did you spend two hundred and fifty dollars on that Erlanger House edition?'

'A college-graduation present for my brother. Verbal filigree and ersatz medievalism never had a bigger fan. You and Jerry should get together.'

'What sorts of books *do* you like?'

'Lately I've been reading a lot of non-fiction, looking into the impact of science on philosophy. I just finished a thing called *Virtue from the Dirt*. No, that's not it. *Ethics from the Earth*, by somebody named Ambrose. I think he lives around here. Breathtaking book. Do you know it?'

Two days later Natalie moved out of her cramped, cluttered, second-floor apartment on Cummington Street and into my cramped, cluttered, third-floor apartment on Sherborn Street, and we joyfully set about our objective of living happily ever after. For the better part of a year, our relationship flourished. Having previously transformed Londa into the restless and obsessive Dame Quixote, I had no ambition to make any woman, vatling or otherwise, into a putatively better version of herself, and I willingly endured Natalie's habit of scrawling illegible messages on the kitchen calendar and stashing unpaid bills in her handbag. Natalie, for her part, announced that she would not battle my various defects – my illiterate understanding of laundry, my tendency to deface the bathroom sink with blobs of toothpaste – until I was her eager and unresentful ally. In short, we allowed one another to be terrible roommates, a forbearance that doubtless figured crucially in our becoming great friends.

But there was a serpent in the garden, a worm in the apple of our idyll. Natalie's symptoms were not particularly disturbing of themselves – intermittent pelvic pains, numbness in her legs and feet – though in this case they pointed to a serious condition: blood clots. Once the diagnosis was confirmed, we listened in dismay as a team of specialists argued not only for putting her on a regimen of Coumadin injections, but also for equipping her circulatory system with plastic screens designed to trap errant embolisms before they could lodge in her lungs. This plenary approach was no cure, as clots could easily form upstream from the Greenfield filters. It was better than doing nothing, however, and so despite her chariness towards orthodox medicine, Natalie submitted to the technique. There were no complications, and within a few weeks she was back at work, reciting Tennyson as the waters of the Charles lapped against the shore. Truth be told, she handled the situation much better than I, for whom this sword of Damocles seemed especially heavy, its thread singularly thin. Many were the nights I trolled cyberspace searching out the latest sonic, surgical, and pharmaceutical approaches to blood clots – once I even visited the website of Londa's avant-garde Institute for Advanced Biological Investigations – but I failed to unearth any breakthroughs.

Among the consequences of Natalie's romantic, vaguely Luddite worldview was a commitment to what she called 'pagan birth control', which boiled down to a combination of fertility charts, herbal contraceptives, and wishful thinking. I was sceptical but willing to gamble, especially since for Natalie the natural correlate of pagan birth control was pagan lovemaking. Under cover of night we shed our garments in woods and dells. We connected in sacred spaces, calling each a Bower of Bliss – for a couple of anti-Spenserians, we were peculiarly ready to appropriate his diction – most memorably the shallows of Walden Pond, the stacks of Widener Library, and those cryptic New Hampshire megaliths known as America's Stonehenge.

Despite our prophylactic intentions, we soon learned that one likely outcome of conjoining pagan birth control to pagan love-making is a pagan pregnancy.

'I *knew* this was going to happen!' I wailed when Natalie told me the news. 'I goddamn fucking *knew* it!'

'No birth-control method is foolproof,' she said.

'We didn't practise birth control. We practised superstition.'

'This is not your finest hour, Mason. You're behaving abominably.'

'I'm behaving abominably,' I agreed, and then I continued behaving abominably for the rest of the afternoon, accusing Natalie of 'self-delusion masquerading as shamanism' and 'flakiness posturing as subversion'. Natalie, to her credit, accepted delivery on none of these indictments. By sundown we were calm again, assuming demeanours more appropriate to our circumstances: two civilised adults facing questions for which neither civilisation nor adulthood furnished palatable answers.

As any good Darwinist will tell you, ontogeny does not recapitulate phylogeny: in noting the transient gill slits of a developing human foetus, one must avoid the temptation to regard the creature as an adult fish. And yet, as that same good Darwinist will tell you, there is something astonishing about a foetus's gills, for they resoundingly echo the corresponding features in an embryonic fish. And so it happened that as Natalie's pregnancy progressed, I found myself wondering whether the mite in her womb had embraced its piscean ancestry, and when it might take title to its reptilian estate. As long as the thing had not claimed its mammalian heritage, I could endorse whatever decision Natalie made.

Over the next three weeks we consulted a quartet of health professionals, and they were unanimous in their view that Natalie's pregnancy would aggravate the propensity of her blood to form rogue clots. 'The danger is serious but not grave,' said Dr Millard, her primary-care physician. The gynaecologist was equally unhelpful. 'If you elect to bring the foetus to term,' Dr Harris told Natalie, 'I'll do everything possible to keep you out of the danger zone.' Haematologist number one, Dr Protter, offered a more upbeat verdict – 'Although I can't make any promises, this impresses me as a low-level risk' – but her optimism was cancelled by the unequivocal gloom of haematologist number two. 'In your shoes,' Dr Shumkas informed us, 'I would terminate the pregnancy.'

The human mind, I learned that month, had not yet evolved sufficiently to wrap itself around this sort of issue. My thoughts were a stroboscopic muddle of flashes and voids, every second burst showing me a vignette from the life of my provisional son, my hypothetical daughter, a Donya Sabacthani version of childhood, abrim with tree houses and toy planetariums. Yet it was the interlaced images, the glimpses of mourners and pall-bearers, that stayed with me. Two days after our consultation with Dr Shumkas, I told Natalie I thought she should have an abortion.

'I don't want an abortion.'

'You want a baby then?'

'No.'

'What *do* you want?'

'I want the pregnancy to go away.'

At the end of the week we drove to Mass General and withdrew our contribution to posterity. It was the simplest of procedures, a routine out-patient dilation and curettage. My root canal had been more complicated. We decided not to ask about the gender of the extinguished foetus. On the way out of the hospital, we stopped by the pharmacy and obtained the prescribed antibiotics. We went home, split a bottle of Chianti, and crawled beneath the blankets, sobbing in each other's arms.

In the weeks following her D & C, Natalie grew increasingly sad, until it seemed she was in thrall to that wan and manipulative troglodyte from Book One, Canto IX, whom Spenser had with characteristic subtlety named Despair. Nothing helped. When I recommended that we get a cat, she reminded me about her allergies. When I proposed that we fly to the Bahamas for the weekend, she pointed to a stack of ungraded papers. When I suggested she might be a candidate for Prozac, she accused me of wanting her to be 'somebody else, anybody else, so long as she isn't Natalie Novak'. We had sex infrequently and indifferently, keeping further embryos at bay with the aid of condoms. Neither of us was surprised when I reverted to my old habit of staying in the store after hours, Mason the Gutenberg ascetic, immured by other people's wisdom.

With our relationship withering, our affection wilting, we did what any rational couple would do under the circumstances. We got married. The ceremony occurred at the home of Natalie's geeky medievalist brother Jerry. We decided that no depressing people could attend, which ruled out any of our parents and most of our relatives. Besides Jerry, our audience was limited to Dexter Padula, my sister Delia – then in the process of transplanting her non-existent acting career from New York to LA – and three of Natalie's friends: willowy Helen Vanderbilt, who'd recently published three chapbooks of unpublishable poetry, zaftig Margery

Kaplan, who'd gone to high school with Natalie and now raised basset hounds, and a lantern-jawed Henry James scholar named Abner Cassidy, Natalie's former lover and present advisor, to whom I took an instant liking despite his carnal knowledge of my bride.

'I am grateful to thee, Archimago,' she told me on our wedding night, Archimago being our favourite *Faerie Queene* character, a protean magician deployed by Spenser to symbolise variously hypocrisy, Satan, and the Pope. 'Not every man would put up with a melancholic Emily Brontë freak who can't finish her dissertation.'

'If 'twould please thee, Malecasta, I would fly to the moon and paint it the colour of thine eyes,' I replied, Malecasta being the mistress of Castle Joyous, the sensualist's paradise and a magnet for every letch and satyr in Faerie Land.

To consolidate her rising spirits, Natalie began to follow a regimen that, while it sounded like something out of a particularly vapid self-help book, actually seemed to work. I couldn't say whether her deliverance from Despair – 'His raw-bone cheeks through penury and pine / Were shrunk into his jaws, as he did never dine' – traced to her nightly doses of St John's wort, her twenty daily laps in the YMCA pool, the Tuesday night fiction-reading group she'd organised at the Caffeine Fiend, my jovial willingness to be the butt of her jokes, or a combination of all four remedies. In any event the ogre gradually loosened his grip and slunk back to his lair.

It was not long after Natalie's recovery that, courtesy of our subscription to the *Boston Globe*, Londa's name and photograph began to appear almost daily in our lives. Back then hardly a week went by without a Dame Quixote story seeing print, but this was front-page stuff – the revelations by the Reverend Enoch Anthem, founder and chairman of a postrationalist think tank called the Centre for Stable Families, about an outrageous scheme being hatched in that bastion of degenerate feminism, Themisopolis. Somehow Anthem had obtained an audio recording of a meeting between Londa's staff and the vice president of the Baudrillard Simulacrum Corporation, a Toulouse-based manufacturer of audio-animatronic robots. When the FBI decided that Reverend

Anthem's case against Londa was fundamentally preposterous, he took his complaint to the *Washington Post*, whereupon the tale proliferated like a bacterial culture, flourishing from coast to coast in a thousand cybernetic Petri dishes.

If Anthem's transcript of the Baudrillard session was to be believed, many ideas were entertained on that sweltering August afternoon, from the clever to the harebrained. In one particularly wild scenario, an enormous robotic replica of Abraham Lincoln, scaled to the ponderous proportions of the famous DC sculpture, would appear on the Capitol steps, screaming a challenge to the assembled representatives. 'Does any man amongst you cleave to an ideal higher than his own re-election?' An equally outlandish project had the Sisters Sabacthani smuggling some simian androids into the Primate House of the Washington Zoological Gardens. The next day's visitors would witness the New World monkeys lamenting the destruction of their relatives' jungle habitats, a crime readily traceable to American fast-food corporations bent on creating new grazing lands for beef cattle. But it was Operation Redneck, the most demented of the afternoon's brainstorms, that caught Enoch Anthem's attention. The plan called for the Baudrillard people to construct a score of android joggers indistinguishable from their flesh-and-blood prototypes, each decked out in a T-shirt endorsing reproductive rights, gay marriage, evolutionary biology, or some other institution of which Jesus Christ disapproved. Sooner or later a reactionary motorist, intoxicated by beer or piety or both, would run down one of these benighted athletes, a gesture that the motorist would not live to regret, for the robots were in fact bombs, wired to explode on impact.

A lardish man whose small head, bulbous frame, and anxious demeanour put me in mind of a bowling pin about to topple, Enoch Anthem spent the next three weeks attacking Operation Redneck through mass mailings, saturation blogging, and dozens of appearances on what Natalie called the 'revengelical' networks. He accused Londa of concocting 'a terrorist plot worthy of those who crucified our Lord', and by the pollsters' reckoning a majority of Americans agreed. The image of even the sleaziest yahoo being blown sky high did not sit well with Mr and Mrs John Q. Public.

Ever since Natalie had got me to admit that an atmosphere of sexual tension had characterised the classroom back on Isla de Sangre, she'd been vaguely jealous of Londa. But like almost every feminist in the Western world, Natalie also admired Dame Quixote, and she urged me to proclaim publicly that my former pupil would never implement anything as rash as Operation Redneck. I was within hours of phoning the *New York Times* when Pauline Chilton, that canny spin-mistress, announced that Dr Sabacthani would be holding a press conference 'for the purpose of answering Reverend Anthem's absurd accusations'. Once again, it seemed, Isis and Horus and Thoth had come to my rescue. For the immediate future, at least, I would be permitted to remain outside Londa's sphere.

Over a hundred journalists attended the event, which Natalie and I watched on television while consuming gourmet microwave pizza. Londa acquitted herself brilliantly, using the occasion not only to assail Enoch Anthem as 'a man who wouldn't recognise a joke if it walked into his house with a duck on its head', but also to remind her fellow Americans that 'the Themisopolis community has an impeccable record of eschewing violence in all its forms, which puts us one up on the Centre for Stable Families'. Before the week was out, the polls disclosed that Mr and Mrs John Q. Public had forgiven Dame Quixote her offensive fantasies.

'Londa was wrong about one thing,' I told Natalie. 'Operation Redneck may be pure whimsy, but there really *is* an ambulatory bomb inside the walls of Themisopolis.'

Natalie had heard me question Londa's sanity before, but she'd never found my arguments persuasive. 'How long till she detonates?'

'I'd give her three years at the most.'

On the evening of our first wedding anniversary I came home bearing a dozen roses, presenting them to a startled Natalie with a theatrical flourish and a facetious remark about the care and feeding of the Japanese beetles inhabiting the bouquet. Our eyes met. Natalie was ravishing even when embarrassed.

'Dear Abby,' I said, 'my wife forgot our wedding anniversary. Should I feel hurt by this role reversal, or should I laugh it off?'

Seeking to break the grip of the Spenserian monster Error, Natalie forced a smile, squeezed my hand, and invited me to dine with her at the Tasty Triffid, our favourite vegetarian restaurant. I accepted graciously. We made pagan love on the couch, then went out to eat. I spent the soup course joking about a hypothetical restaurant for total carnivores, the Bleeding Carrot, its menu featuring zucchini-flavoured sausage, chicken wings prepared to taste like broccoli, and cauliflower made from pork. My wife pretended to be amused. She owed me that.

Later, standing on the front stoop while Natalie rummaged through her handbag searching for her keys, I realised I might have forgotten to lock the store safe: hardly a crisis as the chances of a break-in were low. Still, I felt compelled to check. I told Natalie I'd be back in time for another roll in the bower, then dashed off.

My habitual commute took me along the asphalt path girding the south bank of the Charles, a pleasant twenty-minute stroll past willow trees and park benches. By day this promenade teemed with joggers, cyclists, mothers pushing strollers, and those good-hearted folk whom the ducks had conditioned to toss bread into the water, but by night it was normally deserted. Alone, I moved through the soft summer air, listening to the river lap the shore with the soft rhythmic gurgling of Error suckling her progeny.

My solitude did not last. Within minutes I became aware, subliminally at first, then with a disquieting certainty, of a stooped and sinister presence dogging my steps, flitting in and out of the shadows like an immense luna moth. An asthma victim, evidently, as every breath was an effort. Doubtless Boston had its share of compulsive stalkers and psychos, but why had this wheezing spectre picked *me*?

Keep moving, Mason. Left foot, right foot, left, right. I patted my jacket pockets, hoping I'd brought the cell phone. No such luck. The nearest police station occupied a location known to several thousand Bostonians, and perhaps God, but not to me. In my spinning brain a tactic materialised. If I sprinted to the store, I could probably put a locked door between the psycho and myself in a matter of minutes.

The stalker drew nearer, hyperventilating like an expectant

mother practising her Lamaze exercises. I broke into a run. Parked cars flew past, lighted windows, dark trees, until at last the store loomed up. The key vibrated in my hand. Somehow I jiggered it into the lock. Securing the door behind me, I flicked every switch within reach. The secular radiance of sodium vapour flowed forth. I drew a thick breath, my heart thumping in my ribcage as I wondered what to do next: call the cops, call Natalie, or arm myself with the claw hammer from the toolbox Dexter kept under the counter.

The hammer seemed the best option, and I was about to grab it when my nemesis hobbled into view, his silhouette filling the doorframe. 'Keep the door shut,' he insisted, his voice effortlessly penetrating the bullet-proof pane.

'What do you want?'

He ignored my question. 'When you let me in, it must be a free choice, no coercion, no threats.'

'Who are you?'

'Like that *other* free choice you made about me.'

'I've never met you.'

'This is true, Father. Acknowledge me when you're ready. I'm a patient foetus.'

My intestines tightened. Father? Foetus? What?

'Where are you from?' I asked the man who thought he was my son. 'Which institution? I can't help you, really. Only the doctors can help you.'

'Perhaps you and Mother would've named me Peter. Or Nigel. Marcus. Kelton. Call me John Snow. It would be much easier if you unlocked the door. John Snow and Mason Ambrose, talking face to face.'

Without knowing why, I did as the intruder requested. As he struggled across the threshold, I thought of the second Kohlbergian dilemma with which I'd presented Londa: Frau Eschbach breaking into the pharmacy to steal the radium extract.

Not until he'd reeled into the light did I realise that, far from being a conventional urban menace, this vagabond was fundamentally pathetic. He moved with the gait of an arthritic locust, his defective spine imprisoning him in a permanent cringe. His right arm hung limp as a bell-rope, while his left eye, unyoked from his nervous system, turned upward in perpetual contemplation of clouds and geese.

'You called me Father,' I said.

'Would you prefer Papa?'

A spasm of sorrow contorted John Snow's face, which was pocked and stippled like a golf ball. He wore torn Levis, a soiled beige windbreaker, and a scuffed baseball cap sporting the Red Sox logo. Shuffling forward, he fixed me with an expression mingling disdain with curiosity, and I saw to my horror that his bushy eyebrows and Roman nose corresponded to my own, while Natalie's genes accounted for his ample lips and dimpled cheeks.

'I am an immaculoid,' he continued. 'Pure as milk, clean as soap, spotless as the lamb. Maturational age, thirty years. Chronological age, twenty days.'

'Did Charnock send you? Dr Vincent Charnock?'

'An immaculoid, and yet you scraped me out of the world.'

I staggered towards a newly arrived shipment of Harvard Classics and slumped on to the box, all the bones and fibres of my *Dasein* trembling with perplexity. By what means had the degenerate behind this scheme obtained the residue of Natalie's D & C? Did he pay for the material, or simply steal it? No need for the whole foetus, of course. The tiniest scrap of tissue would have sufficed. A single healthy cell.

'All satisfaction is denied my kind,' John Snow said. 'We can smell the rose but never savour it. Taste the cherry but never relish it.'

A single cell. Next stop, the Petri dish, followed by the high-tech beaker, and then the ontogenerator.

'Never to enjoy the sun's warmth on my face – that's what you did to me.'

And finally the DUNCE cap. John Snow's creator was surely Charnock, using the RXL-313 to salve his guilt over sluicing away those seven viable embryos.

'Never the sweetness of an ice-cream cone.'

Or, if not Charnock, then ... Londa? Unthinkable, but not unimaginable.

My visitor collapsed on to a box of calculus texts and stared in fascination at his good hand. He leaned towards me. Strangely enough, my anxiety faded, supplanted by an unexpected affection. When John Snow moved to kiss me, I did not recoil.

'Does the name Londa Sabacthani mean anything to you?' I asked.

'Stainless as a saint.' He rose from the calculus books, fixing me with his mother's blue eyes.

'Was Londa your creator?'

'Innocent as rain.' He approached the entry and, in a surprisingly vigorous move for one so enfeebled, yanked open the door. 'Natalie Novak made me. Mason Ambrose made me.'

'Must you leave already?' I asked.

'Never the fragrance of a pine forest.'

'Are you going to visit Natalie?'

'Every child deserves a maternal caress, whether it gives him pleasure or not.'

'Will you see her *tonight*?'

'Not tonight, but soon. I intend to call her Mother. She won't like it. Never the song of a lark. Sleep well, Father. Happy wedding anniversary. You shouldn't have murdered me.'

John Snow slipped soundlessly into the night, closing the door behind him, and for a full ten minutes I simply sat on the Harvard Classics, my mind as blank as a newborn vatling's soul.

CHAPTER 9

Moved by the frustration her lustful son endures when the chaste and lovely Florimell declines his offer of rape, a malevolent woodland witch hatches a plan. She will present her jilted offspring with a simulated maiden, easily overwhelmed and eminently ravishable. Thus does the Byzantine plot of *The Faerie Queene* give birth to yet another strange creature, the False Florimell, an alchemical concoction on whom the witch has bestowed burning lamps for eyes, golden wire for hair, and an indwelling sprite 'to rule the carcass dead', the carcass in question being a fusion of painted wax and snow, a material the witch doubtless chose in sly mockery of the real Florimell's virginity.

Sly mockery was probably the last thing on the mind of whichever unbalanced biologist had fashioned my nocturnal visitor and named him John Snow. Most probably he wanted to convey his belief that this foetus, like all foetuses, was innocence incarnate, far closer to God's original intentions than those depraved *Homo sapiens sapiens* who'd actually inherited the Earth.

Against all odds, I remembered to check the safe – it was indeed locked – whereupon I left the store and sprinted pell-mell down Commonwealth Avenue. By jostling the pedestrians and ignoring a half-dozen *Don't Walk* signs, I reached our front stoop in under ten minutes. Natalie was silhouetted in the parlour window, the Sisyphus of Sherborn Street, jogging on her treadmill. I lurched through the front door, rushed across the marble foyer, and ascended the staircase two steps at a time. In my imagination a horrid tableau appeared: the immaculoid hovering over Natalie as she ran frantically in place, faster and faster, while John Snow remained at her side, spewing out accusations.

I burst into the parlour. Natalie threw the switch and the treadmill jerked to a halt.

'Welcome back,' she said, panting.

'Something happened tonight.'

'You look like you've seen a ghost.'

There was ultimately no way to talk about John Snow without upsetting Natalie, but I still decided to broach the subject obliquely. 'Do you remember the False Florimell? From *The Faerie Queene*? Sometimes called the Snowy Florimell?'

'What about her?'

'Here's the truth of it, darling. Somebody has made a live facsimile of our son.'

'What son?'

'You know what son. He calls himself John Snow.'

'You're not making much sense.'

'Our foetus has come back.'

'That's preposterous.'

'No. Technology.'

We spent the rest of the night in our claustrophobic kitchen, talking and drinking coffee, and by dawn Natalie had become convinced that someone had used the ontogenerator and its collateral DUNCE cap for a stupefyingly sick purpose. Caffeinated but exhausted, we shuffled into the bedroom. A leprous moon smirked through the window. Heavy traffic growled and squealed its way along Commonwealth Avenue. For a brief instant, John Snow floated before me, fixed to my subjective retina, offering a wistful grin.

'He intends to track you down,' I said. 'He wants to call you Mother.'

'And murderer?'

'Yes, but that's just the DUNCE cap talking. Believe it or not, I felt a certain tenderness towards him. Especially when he kissed my cheek.'

The last time Natalie and I had gone to bed sobbing in one another's arms, John Snow had been the cause. Tonight, the same desperate embrace, the same passage into sleep on a stream of tears, only now the occasion was not our foetus's death but his equally distressing resurrection. I vowed that if Londa was behind

164

this business, I would accept that long-standing invitation to appear on *Cordelia Drake Live* and tell the viewing public that my former pupil, though ostensibly a humanitarian, was not above dabbling in biological diabolism. If you want my opinion, Cordelia, Dr Sabacthani is insane.

I awoke at noon and composed an email to Londa, a message that would come either as a bolt from the blue or proof that her plot against me had worked. In a few terse sentences I told her about my bookstore, my marriage, my success in publishing *Ethics from the Earth*, and, finally, my foetus, calling his advent – for I wanted to think the best of her – 'a bit of news that will shock you'. I stressed the ambiguity of the situation, the strange combination of pathos and banality that characterised John Snow's speech, his unsettling aura of sadness leavened with menace. 'Might we get together soon and discuss this misbegotten beaker freak?' I clicked on Send and hoped for the best.

Later I went trolling for the Mad Doctor of Blood Island, feeding 'Vincent Charnock' into my search engine and, when that failed, 'ontogenerator'. Zero. Growing desperate, I hunted for web pages containing the words 'immaculoid' or 'John Snow' or 'Smell the rose but never savour it'. Zilch.

On Saturday night Natalie suffered her first visitation. She and Helen Vanderbilt, the self-appointed poet, were leaving a revival of *My Dinner with André* at the Coolidge Corner Cinema when a gaunt man shuffled out of the darkness, laid a hand on her shoulder, and introduced himself. Their conversation was brief but pointed. The immaculoid called her 'a ruthless exterminator of defenceless babies'. Natalie countered that carrying him to term might have killed her.

'Then there would have been no net loss of life,' he replied.

'Evidently there was an absolute gain,' Natalie said.

'I am not alive,' John Snow asserted.

As he slipped back into the shadows, Helen turned to Natalie and said, 'What the fuck?'

The creature kept his distance on Sunday, but then the haunting began in earnest. John Snow attended our every waking minute, sometimes through his physical presence, more often via our troubled thoughts and acid spasms of dread. Each ticking instant lay heavy with this parody of our son – John Snow and his malign purity, his unending devotion to our disquiet.

That summer, owing to the Catherine de Medici protocols by which the Hawthorne English Department operated, Natalie was obliged to shoulder a four-course load: Freshman Composition, British Renaissance Poetry, Greek Drama, and Arthurian Romance. Almost every time she entered the classroom, John Snow would be waiting in the far corner, slumped in a chair, tapping his fingernails on the retractable Formica writing board. He never participated in the discussions, though sometimes a non sequitur would escape his lips like a shout from a Tourette's victim. 'Booted into the abyss!' 'She praises humanists and murders humans!' 'Never to feel my heart soar when Perry Como sings "I Believe"!' Natalie told her undergraduates that John Snow was her highly medicated brother, recently delivered into her charge by a state mental institution.

When not harassing Natalie, the immaculoid would appear at the bookstore, gimping past the shelves, then flopping into an empty chair in the coffee bar. I allowed him to run up a tab. Most of the time he simply sat there, bathing his insensate tongue in a latte and reading a random selection from our science fiction and fantasy stock. Occasionally I had to endure his outbursts. 'Tossed away like an orange peel!' 'Deny the Devil his curette!' 'Impaled by my own parents!' Despite the discomfort he caused our customers, no one asked me to eject him. In those days many a homeless schizophrenic roamed the streets of Boston, and we shopkeepers were expected to supply these wretches with free coffee, shelter from the rain, and as much patience as we could muster.

On Tuesday and Thursday mornings, relatively tranquil periods at the store, I usually found time to speak with John Snow. Our encounters were unenlightening. He refused to tell me who had supervised his birth, how he supported himself, or where he spent his time when not hectoring his supposed parents. Only once did a question of mine catch him off guard, and he answered it with a frankness that I suspected would have displeased his maker.

'I can't help noticing you are not a well man,' I told him. 'Does an immaculoid have a normal life span?'

He shook his misshapen head and coughed. 'My days are numbered.'

'Do you anticipate living for five more years? One more year?'

'Soon my purpose will be complete.'

'What purpose? To drive me crazy? To make Natalie miserable?'

But the foetus had exhausted his reserves of candour. With the apparent aim of ending our conversation, he leaped from his chair and screamed, 'Masturbate I must, but each orgasm is duller than the last!'

The customers variously gasped, moaned, giggled, or pretended to be somewhere else.

'Ejaculation without elation! Can you imagine?'

On Sunday morning Londa finally answered my email. No greeting, no 'Dear Mason'. Just a single sarcastic sentence. 'When the gumbo girl was anxious to communicate with her old morality teacher, he hit Delete, and now she's supposed to roll out the fucking red carpet?'

My answer was simple. 'You owe me a civil reply, and you know it.'

She was back at her keyboard within the hour. 'I have many enemies, but Mason Ambrose isn't one of them.' She went on to say that my success as a bookseller delighted her, that she'd made *Ethics from the Earth* required reading among her staff, and that Natalie must be 'a very smart lady if she decided to marry you'. Concerning the John Snow crisis, Londa claimed to be as much in the dark as I. 'How strange to think there's a fourth beaker freak in the world. Find your way to Themisopolis, Socrates, sooner rather than later, and we'll talk of life and its mysteries. Yolly will be thrilled to see you, Quetzie too, and once you're actually standing in my presence, I might even deign to give you a hug.'

I journeyed to Bel Air at a leisurely pace, sleeping in motels and prospecting for bibliographic gold in every thrift store between Boston and Philadelphia. By the time I'd crossed the Maryland border, the trunk of my Subaru wagon held some rare Willa Cathers, a couple of Theodore Dreiser first editions, and the obscure Thomas Bergin translation of *The Divine Comedy*. I checked into a bed-and-breakfast called Harriet's Hideaway, then switched on my cell phone and buzzed Londa's reedy-voiced secretary, who told me that tomorrow's password would be 'pitchfork'. I slept in Harriet's guest room, snatched a couple of warm bagels from the breakfast spread, and continued down Route 97.

No artist's brush, no photographer's lens, no digital Da Vinci's pixels could have captured the grandeur of Themisopolis in its glory days, though I could imagine Edmund Spenser's quill rising to the occasion. Book One of *The Faerie Queene* is not long under way when our hero, the Red Cross Knight, is obliged to enter 'a stately palace built of squared brick, which cunningly was without mortar laid'. Its turrets hold 'fair windows and delightful bowers', and the knight is especially entranced by the gleaming walls, 'golden foil all over them displayed, / That purest sky with brightness they dismayed'. Approaching the City of Justice for the first time, I gasped in astonishment at the flowering cherry trees flanking Avalon Lane, the billowing fountains of Hypatia Circle and, in the distance, the luminous marble walls of Themisopolis itself. Only when I reached the main entrance, its bronze gates flashing in the sun like the doors to God's private vault, did my awe turn to bewilderment. Here on the periphery of Quehannock State Park had arisen an institution consecrated to benevolence and the Beatitudes, yet it presented to the world a face as formidable as a maximum-security prison.

I deposited the Subaru in Visitor Parking and proceeded on foot, inhaling the candied scent of the cherry blossoms. Observing my approach, a wiry woman with a buzz cut sauntered out of the sentry box, her sturdy frame clothed in a black leather jacket studded with surly nodes of metal. From her shoulder holster poked the snoutish grip of an automatic pistol.

'Pitchfork,' I said.

'Name?'

'Mason Ambrose.'

The guard consulted her clipboard, handed me a map, and thumbed a button on her remote control. Slowly the mammoth gates opened, clanking and creaking to reveal a lavish panorama of spires, gables, clock towers, and groves of sycamores and maples.

It wasn't really a city, of course. As I strolled down Shambhala Avenue, surveying the sunny piazzas, neo-Bauhaus buildings, manicured quadrangles, and knots of passers by – scientists in lab coats, engineers in button-down denim shirts, graduate students in turtleneck sweaters – Themisopolis struck me more as a kind of genteel community college, or perhaps a retreat for Westernised Buddhists who saw no incompatibility between higher consciousness and creature comforts. Reaching the Boudicca Street intersection, I started across Alethia Square, a flagstone courtyard featuring a bronze statue of Themis herself, her famous balance scales connected to an electric motor, so that the two pans moved in a seesaw cycle, up, down, up, down, beneath the weight of invisible deliberations.

A woman came zooming towards me on a Vespa. She jammed on the brakes, dismounted, and pulled off her helmet, unfurling a banner of auburn hair.

'Londa!' I shouted.

She looked almost the same as on that long-ago night when she'd kissed me following Proserpine's immolation – older, of course, but not significantly older. Barely a day over twenty-five.

'Try again.'

I immediately guessed my mistake. 'Yolly!'

'Bull's-eye, Mason.'

We shook hands, our fingers entwining like Isla de Sangre vines. 'Nifty scooter,' I said.

'I still prefer horses.'

'Dear old Oyster.'

'Believe it or not, he's in the land of the living, collecting his pension on a farm in Wheeling. A touch of arthritis, but the cortisone keeps him on his feet.'

I told Yolly that, of all my Blood Island reveries, none enchanted me more than a girl mounted on a Chincoteague pony galloping across the scrub.

'Those were the days,' she said in a neutral tone, as if those days were neither good nor bad.

We proceeded to trade memories like two third-grade Sabacthanites swapping Dame Quixote trading cards on the school playground: Donya's little planetarium, Brock's weird paintings,

Charnock's uncanny chimeras, the red coral, psychedelic blossoms. Much to my surprise, Yolly had always thought of me not as some aloof intellectual but as 'that cool young philosopher guy who understood Londa better than Londa did'.

'Sometimes I thought I understood her, yes.'

'She's still the pick of the litter,' Yolly said. 'It's funny, we're supposed to be carbon copies of each other, but Londa got all the best traits – the brains, the drive, the looks.'

'Nonsense,' I said. 'If I weren't married, I'd ask you to the senior prom.'

'Hey, Mason, remember where you are,' she said breezily. 'In Themisopolis we know nothing of senior proms, double dating, June weddings, or any of that normalcy stuff.'

At which juncture, and as if to corroborate Yolly's claim, two women strolled by hand in hand wearing silver-studded black leather, one partner hulking, the other merely zaftig, automatic pistols rolling on their considerable hips.

'Our security force is second to none,' Yolly said, gesturing towards the passing daughters of Sappho. 'When Jordan first got a load of them, she said they should be wearing metal brassieres and winged helmets, so we started calling them the Valkyries, which is better than what Enoch Anthem's cyberflunkies call them – the Dyke Brigade. A misnomer, by the way. Anybody can sign up as long as she's a woman and can shoot straight. About a third of our Valkyries are suburban housewives who couldn't take it any more.'

I told Yolly I was gratified to learn that Jordan hadn't dropped out of her life. She replied that her legal guardian was, in fact, on the payroll, coordinating the lobbying efforts of the Elizabeth Cady Stanton Foundation from an office in DC.

'The boss said to give you two choices,' Yolly informed me. 'You can grab yourself some breakfast in the Vision Institute food court, or you can have coffee with her and Quetzie right now.'

'For thirteen light years I travelled across the vast emptiness of space, searching for the lost cult of the feathered lizard. Take me to your leader.'

In a gesture so blatantly allegorical it would have embarrassed even Edmund Spenser, Londa had sited her headquarters atop the tallest building in Themisopolis, a graceful fieldstone tower known as Caedmon Hall. Hera in her heavenly palace. Ishtar in her Sumerian aerie. Yolly and I ascended via a glass elevator, the glimmering car shooting skywards like the Eighth Avenue Express roaring through a vertical subway tunnel. We disembarked into a stylish reception area appointed with live ferns and dead post-impressionists, presided over by Londa's secretary, Gertrude Lingard of the reedy voice and, I now learned, the equally reedy physique. Beyond lay a labyrinth of offices, the largest of which belonged to the sloe-eyed Dagmar Röhrig, who had famously turned down a Hollywood contract to become Londa's manager. The beauteous Sabacthanite was too busy yelling at somebody over the phone to engage us in conversation, but she flashed us an efficient smile and waved towards the holy of holies. Yolly rolled back a frosted-glass door, and we proceeded across a semicircular space so thickly carpeted it was like walking on an immense sponge, the curved picture windows offering epic views of the surrounding farmland, until we reached a terrace crowded with flowering plants.

The first time I ever saw Londa she was emerging from the floral embrace of a tropical rainforest; now, once again, she appeared before me wreathed in blossoms – tulips, lilacs, orchids, plus several hybrids I couldn't identify. Quetzie was perched on one shoulder, her opposite hand gripping a transparent watering can shaped like an alchemist's alembic. Instead of a crown, she wore a telephone headset, and before acknowledging my presence she spoke into the spindly microphone, telling her listener – an annoying person, to judge from her tone, a politician or lawyer or Phyllistine – there was nothing more to discuss. She removed the headset and extended her hand. Our fingers connected, and the gesture instantly transmuted into a protracted hug.

'It's been an eternity,' she said.

'Much too long, at any rate,' I said.

'An eternity, and then some,' she added, breaking our embrace. Her attire evoked the False Florimell: white cotton slacks, white silk blouse, white linen jacket, white silk scarf. Time had largely exempted her from its passage: some creases around her mouth, a few wrinkles extending from her eyes, that was all. To my bookseller's sensibility she suggested a leather-bound volume so skilfully crafted that years of affectionate thumbing had left only the faintest traces.

'Believe me, dear,' I said, 'the last thing you needed during this past decade was a Darwinist Jiminy Cricket lodged in your ear.'

'As a matter of fact, that was the *first* thing I needed.'

Sensing a quarrel was brewing, Yolly stepped between us. She kissed my cheek, urged me to drop by more often, gave the iguana a pat on the head, and reminded her sister to call Senator Kitto by three o'clock. Londa relaxed, as did her auxiliary conscience.

'Quetzie is a handsome devil,' the iguana squawked.

Diplomatic mission accomplished, Yolly excused herself and trotted off to a meeting of the Wollstonecraft Fund.

'She sleeps with women,' Londa informed me. 'Men too. If there were a third sex, she'd sample that as well.'

'I had a feeling.'

'I tried the Sapphic option once, a ravenous save-the-whales lady named Loretta. It was pretty thrilling while it lasted, but I'm not really wired that way. Have you ever wanted to screw a man?'

'Only Oscar Wilde, and he's seeing somebody else.'

'Quetzie is a handsome devil,' the iguana repeated.

'I wish I could be more like Yolly,' Londa said. 'She finds time for – I believe it's called *fun*. Skiing in Vermont. Poker with the Valkyries. Follows her libido wherever it leads her. It's strange, my little sister is really my *big* sister, somebody I can look up to. For two years now she's been working on a fantasy novel about a mystical book nobody can understand.'

'If she needs a model, let me suggest anything by Heidegger.'

'I've read the first chapter. Wonderful stuff, very sensual.' She stroked her iguana's plumage. 'Guess what, Quetzie? On his way over here, Mason was wondering if I'll try leading him down to my secret beach.'

'The last thing on my mind,' I said, though it was actually the second thing on my mind, the first being John Snow.

She took my hand, massaging the palm, then guided me towards a coffee bar. 'Don't worry, we goody-goody altar girls aren't into adultery, though it happens that my bedroom' – she gestured vaguely towards a dark alcove – 'is only twenty feet away.'

'You sleep here in your office?'

'I sleep, eat, drink, scheme, and wrestle private demons here.'

'You should get out more.'

'Jordan tells me the same thing. You moralists all think alike.'

'*Cogito ergo sum*,' Quetzie noted.

'Until two weeks ago I was dating a computer geek,' Londa said. 'A sweet guy, very sincere, but he never understood the difference between a relationship and a flow chart. Before that I fell for a film professor at Georgetown. We broke up because I didn't cry at the end of *La Strada*. Somewhere along the line I had a wild affair with a tennis instructor from Owings Mills. Opposites attract. They attract, they stick together, then nothing else happens. The verdict is in, Mason. I'm not cut out for romance.'

Computer geek, Fellini scholar, tennis instructor: I loved every one of Londa's suitors, for without their attentions she would probably have tracked me down in person and thrown my life into disarray. I also hated them. How dare they presume to know my vatling's heart?

I lifted a glass carafe from the burner and filled a mug bearing the Themisopolis logo, Lady Justice on a galloping horse, balance scales held high. When the brew touched my tongue, I shuddered to experience the familiar flavour of rococonut milk.

'I detect a trace of Proserpine,' I said.

'Not enough to cause an opium dream, just your basic euphoria-inducing dosage.' Londa filled her own mug, a real collector's item decorated with Weill and Brecht's Pirate Jenny waving a cutlass and singing 'That'll Learn Ya'. 'The crop we harvested is still in the Faustino freezer. Henry sends us a shipment every now and then. The Hallucinogen-of-the-Month Club.'

I swallowed some nectar and said, 'Londa, I'm going to ask you this only once. Are you the source of my immaculoid?'

She fluted her lips, siphoning up a measure of well-being. 'We must approach this mystery rationally. Do I have a motive to torment you? Let me think. If it wasn't for those goddamn ethics tutorials, I might be leading an enviable existence by now. House in the suburbs, white picket fence, golden retriever, a couple of kids. But thanks to you, the house burned down, the fence collapsed, the dog ran away, and the kids are in jail.'

'I ruined your life, no doubt about it. But I still need to hear you had nothing—'

'I had nothing to do with your immaculoid.' She fixed me with her fiercest basilisk stare. 'Do you believe that?'

'Yes.' And I did.

'All you need is love,' Quetzie said.

'I imagine Mr Snow has put a strain on your marriage,' Londa said.

'We'll survive.'

'I must meet your fortunate bride.'

'She's one of your greatest admirers.'

'As you may have noticed, I have a regular fan club,' said Londa, smirking. 'I used to be a member, but then I outgrew the whole thing. There comes a time in every girl's life when she must throw away her *League of Londa* comics.'

Spontaneously we drifted towards a conference table that held an architect's model as intricate as Donya's toy amusement park. It was all there, Londa's riposte to the Phyllistines – the Vision Syndicate, the Artemis Clinic, Arcadia House, the Institute for Advanced Biological Investigations. The longer I contemplated this solar-powered El Dorado, the more it received my begrudging esteem. How far my pupil had come since her Faustino days of chain-smoking Dunhills and wondering how she might insert 'fuck' into her next sentence. God knows I wasn't about to acquire a Dame Quixote T-shirt, but perhaps I'd been wrong to turn my back on Themisopolis.

'Edwina would be proud of you,' I said.

'And what about my auxiliary conscience? Is he proud of me?'

'Your auxiliary conscience thinks he must've done something right.'

'There's a good chance Yolly and I will leave the world a better place than we found it,' she said in a corroborating tone. 'Don't tell anybody, but the Susan B. Anthony Trust is about to supply the UN with enough information to nail more than a hundred traffickers in female sexual slavery. Operation Velvet Fist. And we've got another miracle in the pipeline. You've never heard of a drug called Xelcepin, but after the Institute runs some clinical trials, we hope to announce a breakthrough in the treatment of ovarian cancer.'

For the first time in years a snippet from *The Egyptian* flashed through my brain – the courtesan disrobing before Sinuhe, showing him the malignancy that had deformed her beauty. No wonder drugs for Nefer. Only suffering and blood and futile prayers.

'In certain contexts, my difficulties with John Snow seem trivial,' I said.

Londa's next remark caught me by surprise. 'You know what's appalling about you, Socrates?' she said, passing a hand over the miniature city.

'Pray tell. What's appalling about me?'

'You think I had a choice about all this. You think Themisopolis was an act of free will.'

'Of course you had a choice.'

'I'm trapped, dearest Mason. I'm locked inside my own lousy comic book, Dame Quixote versus the whole goddamn Phyllistine world.' She grasped my shoulders, turning me until our eyes met. 'Don't you have *any* idea what you did to me? Are you completely clueless?'

'Not completely.'

'You carved a thousand facets on my face, so I'd never run out of cheeks to turn. You took the stone that never hit the adulteress and hung it around my neck.' She issued a cryptic laugh, then released her grip. 'All signs point to Charnock.'

'I had the same thought,' I said, pleased to realise she'd changed the subject. 'Unfortunately, he's dropped off the face of the Earth.'

'And landed in the armpit. Armpit, North Carolina, to be precise, otherwise known as Jacob's Notch, an insolvent little town on the Pasquotank River. He's become an aquatic hermit, living on a houseboat. Once a month I get a screed from his laptop, no punctuation, all lower case. Our species has lost its collective mind, modernity is a swindle, the future belongs to the ants.'

'Did he mention making another vatling?'

'Nope. Shall I have a Valkyrie ride down to Jacob's Notch and give the old man a scare? Major Powers would be good for the job. She'd crack him like a walnut.'

'Thanks. I'd like to try a simple conversation first.'

Not far from the Vision Syndicate replica lay an object resembling a hockey puck. In fact, it was a hockey puck. The label read, 'Circus of Atonement'. 'And what goes on here?' I asked, pointing to the thick disc. 'Gladiatorial combat?'

'Testosterone has no friends in Themisopolis.'

'Then what?'

'Our chief source of recreation.'

'What sort of recreation?'

'*Secret* recreation,' Londa replied in a tone clarifying that the topic would enjoy no further elaboration just then. Again she waved her hand over the model City of Justice. 'You'd be amazed at all the details the architects got into this thing.' She pointed towards the building in which our fractious encounter was now occurring. 'Pop the roof off Caedmon Hall here, and you'll see a tiny clockwork Londa trading barbs with her old morality teacher. Can you stay for lunch? I'll order Chinese, then we'll drop by the Circus.'

A tempting offer, as I was truly enjoying her company, but my obligation to Natalie came first. 'I have an appointment with the Mad Doctor of Blood Island,' I said, edging towards the rolling glass door. 'I'll let you know if I need you to set Major Powers on him.' I slid back the door and crossed the threshold. 'If there's a stone around your neck, it's because you put it there.'

'No, Socrates. You did it. I wonder if I'll ever forgive you?'

Noon found me embedded in a traffic jam on the DC Beltway, mired and miserable like the carp Londa had almost drowned on the Faustino patio. I called Natalie and told her I was bound for North Carolina, hot on the trail of Vincent Charnock. 'Assuming he's the culprit,' I asked, 'is there any message you want me to give him?'

'John Snow came to my Arthurian Romance class this morning,' Natalie said. 'He kept quiet for a whole hour, then started screaming, "She wouldn't take the risk!" Here's my message to Dr Charnock. "I hope you fucking rot in hell."'

I circumvented DC, heading south-east until I reached Norfolk, where I checked into a Wanderer's Lodge, flagship of a burgeoning hotel chain whose self-conscious name, postmodern décor, and popcult mystique catered to middle-class bohemian nomads who fancied themselves to be following in Kerouac's exhaust fumes. My sleep was fitful and dreamless – perhaps I never slept at all – and shortly after 9 a.m. I hit the road again, three Wanderer's Lodge cranberry muffins huddled in my stomach like scoops of cement. Soon I reached the Carolina border, where the essential sign appeared, JACOB'S NOTCH NEXT EXIT. Once I was within the town proper, getting a fix on Charnock proved simple. The scraggly young man who ran the bait shop, the wisecracking belle behind the 7-Eleven cash register, and the skinny kid skateboarding across the First Baptist Church parking lot all eagerly pointed the way. It was as if the locals knew that, one of these days, the crazy misanthrope living on the river would have a visitor – an IRS agent, a private detective, a hit man.

When I finally came upon my quarry, he was slumped in a captain's chair on the afterdeck of his houseboat, smoking a cigarette and staring at a stand of cat-tails, a depleted fifth of Old Kentucky bourbon snugged between his bare feet. He rubbed the bottle with his toes. A tattered straw hat sheltered him from the sun. I couldn't decide which was the greater wreck, Charnock's body or the dilapidated vessel he now called home. Moored to a floating dock, the *Ursula* was a conglomeration of warped planks, rusty nails, and a superstructure reminiscent of a derelict chicken coop. Of the paint job little remained but leprous scabs and burst blisters.

'Hello, Vincent.'

Evidently he recognised my voice, for without lifting his head he said, 'I figured you'd show up one day, Ambrose. Did you come to question me, kiss me, or kill me?'

I stepped from the wharf to the afterdeck. Strangely, the boards didn't crumble beneath my feet. 'Kiss you?'

'For inventing the machine that resurrected your son.'

'John Snow is not my son.'

'And Brutus was an honourable man,' Charnock said, winching himself to his feet. He tossed his cigarette into the water, picked up the Old Kentucky, and poured the few remaining swallows into a plastic tumbler embossed with the Creature from the Black Lagoon. Spiky whiskers speckled his jaw and neck. 'The bastards betrayed me, Ambrose. They promised to keep me in the loop. They lied.'

'What bastards?'

'The ones who hired me to teach them the art of ontogenesis. Their leader was in the news a couple of months ago, railing against Operation Redneck.'

'Enoch Anthem?'

'That's the bastard.'

'I've never even *met* Enoch Anthem. Why the hell would he single out Natalie and me?'

'It was the other bastard who singled you out. Anthem's *consigliere* – you know who I mean?'

'No.'

'That tough-as-nails postrationalist up in Boston. Felix Pielmeister. I gather you two have a history.'

'Pielmeister? Jesus.'

'I also gather that the professor and you and a glamorous literary lady used to hang around the same bookstore, and it wasn't long before he figured out you and she were an item, and then a pregnant item. When he realised you'd got an abortion, he decided your foetus should become the first of the mackies.'

I moaned and gripped the gunwale. Pielmeister. Horus help me. During the past week I'd driven nine hundred miles, travelled through eight different states, slept in five strange beds, and it turned out that the answer to the mystery lay on my doorstep – or, as Dorothy told Glinda at the end of Donya's favourite movie, 'If I ever go looking for my heart's desire again, I won't look any further than my own backyard, because if it isn't there, I never really lost it to begin with,' a sentiment whose breathtaking incoherence I'd never fully appreciated before.

'You have to realise, this project of Pielmeister's isn't really about him settling an old score with you,' Charnock continued. 'He and Anthem are out to get *everybody* who did what you did. I must admit, even though they stabbed me in the back, I'm damn impressed with those two. They have moral fibre. Think about it.

Six thousand foetuses stalking their unfeeling quasiparents. It's the greatest anti-abortion protest in history!'

'Six thousand? Thundering Christ!'

Charnock pressed the tumbler to his lips and let the bourbon trickle down his throat. 'Anthem's organisation paid me a fortune for the RXL-313 blueprints, and now they've got three onto-generators, maybe four. Your John Snow is actually John Snow 0001. Next will come John Snow 0002, followed by John Snow 0003, not to mention Jane Snow 0001 and all her sisters. I didn't want the three million dollars. I gave it to the Red Cross. All I wanted was to be in the loop.' He pulled off his straw hat and fanned his sweating face with the brim. 'There are wheels within wheels here, Ambrose. Everybody's heard of the Center for Stable Families, but nobody knows it's a beard for a subterranean network called CHALICE, the Christian Alliance of Immaculoids, Chiliasts, and Evangelicals. And here's the rub. The CHALICE biologists don't understand the RXLs. They miss the nuances. Did you know that if a newborn baby started listening to a recital of the human genome sequence, he'd still be hearing it when he turned fifty? The same damn base notes – guanine, thymine, cytosine, adenine, over and over in countless combinations? As a matter of fact, the song doesn't end until he's ready to die. No wonder CHALICE screwed it up. No wonder your son has an atrophied arm and a crooked spine, not to mention his limp – he's got a limp, right?'

'And a lazy eye. He says his days are numbered.'

'When the mackies start dying like flies, Anthem will realise what a blunder he made, taking me out of the loop. Thirsty?'

'Now that you mention it.'

In a gesture more affectionate than he might normally have accorded an unfeeling quasiparent, Charnock set his hand against my back and guided me toward the superstructure. We crossed a mildewed parlour, its fitted benches stacked with books, mostly Russian novels – I don't know whether, as per his gazebo conversation with Edwina, he'd got around to reading *War and Peace*, but at least he owned a copy – and proceeded to the galley. A diverse collection of half-empty wine and liquor bottles crowded the counter-top, obscuring the buckled Formica.

'What's your pleasure?'

'How about a rum and Coke? Hold the rum.'

Charnock opened his built-in refrigerator and removed a solitary Diet Pepsi. 'Don't you want me to hold the Coke instead?'

'I never consume alcohol before noon.'

'Neither do I.' He handed me the Pepsi, then screwed open a fresh bottle of Old Kentucky and splashed several ounces into his tumbler.

'It's eleven-thirty.'

'Not in Madrid.'

I ripped the tab off my Pepsi, then chugged down all twelve ounces in the same short interval that Charnock required to finish his bourbon.

'So tell me, what's the most fascinating thing about your son?' he asked. 'His bedrock nihilism? His bottomless contempt for his parents?'

'He's not my son,' I said.

'Sorry. Forgot.'

I realised I was staring at a box of Earl Grey wedged between a quart of brandy and a fifth of vodka. 'Might I have some tea?'

'Caffeine is bad for your digestion.' Charnock filled a small copper kettle with water and set it to boil atop his Primus stove. 'Let me tell you something. Even after I came to detest Edwina's project, I still admired her style. A decisive woman. She had a craving for total motherhood, so she made it happen.'

Two minutes later my host yanked the screaming kettle off the stove, filled a grimy ceramic mug, and began dipping a teabag up and down in the hot water as if he were making a candle. He presented me with my tea, then replenished his tumbler. We drank in silence, drifting through the superstructure and back on to the afterdeck. The sun beat down on the river, baking the sodden banks into aromatic loaves of mud.

'You obviously came to question me,' Charnock said at last. 'But what about kiss and kill?'

'Neither.'

'You signed off on your own son's murder, yet you baulk at shooting a useless old drunk? Philosophers are supposed to be rational.'

'The D and C was absolutely necessary,' I hissed. 'Natalie might have died of a blood clot.' A quick short leap brought me from the *Ursula* to the dock. 'Thanks for the tea. The conversation, too. My wife sends you a message. "I hope you fucking rot in hell."'

As I started up the hill towards town, I realised I was still holding Charnock's ceramic mug, a situation I immediately remedied by smashing it against a rock.

'They're coming, Ambrose, six thousand strong!' he called after me. 'The greatest political demonstration of all time! The whole world will tremble beneath their unborn feet!'

The immaculoids were coming. Lurid as it sounded, I had no reason to doubt Charnock's forecast, so upon returning to Norfolk I pulled into a Dunkin' Donuts, grabbed my phone and, after pleading my case to Gertrude Lingard, got Londa on the line. If Charnock could be believed, I told her, he'd sold his soul and his blueprints to a shadowy society whose members included not only Enoch Anthem but also the very professor with whom I'd sparred during my dissertation defence.

'They call themselves CHALICE,' I said. 'The Christian Alliance of Immaculoids, Chiliasts, and Evangelicals.'

'Beware of Phyllistines bearing acronyms,' Londa said.

'Charnock thinks they have at least three ontogenerators. They're planning to cook up an army of foetuses and set them loose on the world.'

'What an atrocious idea.'

'It was a dark day when Anthem and Pielmeister found each other.'

'Raiders of the Lost Christian Consensus. Keep me posted, Socrates.'

Next I called Natalie. The news of Pielmeister's involvement flabbergasted her, but she was cheerier than the last time we'd talked. Our foetus had not attended the most recent meetings of British Renaissance Poetry, Greek Drama, or Arthurian Romance.

'Listen, darling, this shitty thing we're going through, Charnock says it's about to happen to lots of couples.'

'How many is lots?'

'Thousands.'

'Is that supposed to comfort me?'

'I thought it might. Does it?'

'No. Maybe. I don't know. Hurry home. If I have to deal with that fucker again, I'm going to jump out of a window.'

I spent the next thirteen hours on the road, stopping only to empty my bladder and fill my gas tank. By 2 a.m., Natalie and I were lying in bed together, conjoined like jigsaw-puzzle pieces, drifting off to sleep.

A storm was raging when I awoke, alone, the thick grey rain clattering on the windows like scrabbling claws. My stomach seemed filled with electrified acid, as if I were digesting a flashlight battery. I glanced at the alarm clock – it was almost noon. Soon Natalie would be back from British Renaissance Poetry. I staggered to the kitchen and phoned Dexter, telling him about the rarities I'd scored en route to Maryland. He said we'd sold two copies of *Ethics from the Earth* while I was gone, and that the schizophrenic I'd taken under my wing had been asking for me.

Natalie and I entered the living room from opposite directions, our gaits identical, a despairing shuffle. Stark red veins encircled her eyes, their lids swollen with weeping.

'I don't hate him, not exactly,' she said. 'But I can't take much more of this.'

My anger was primal. I became my own sort of immaculoid, pure in wrath, pristine in fury, and it was this incarnation of Mason Ambrose who now grabbed an umbrella, rushed out into the storm, and drove nine blocks to the Silbersack Building, home of the Philosophy Department. I dashed down the second-floor hallway like a small but implacable cyclone, then blew uninvited into Pielmeister's office, an exquisite little sanctum, all oak wainscoting, teak moulding, and cedar beams. No doubt he had appointed it himself. Postrationalists knew their wood.

Pielmeister stood hunched over a cardboard box, filling it with books. He was doing it all wrong, jamming the corners of the covers against each other when he should have been laying the volumes spine to spine. The denuded shelves held only a few forlorn paperbacks, plus the half-dozen awards he'd won for his theological treatises. One such commendation depicted Hugh of

Saint Victor, another represented Thomas Aquinas. Spiritual bowling trophies.

'Good afternoon, Ambrose.' His supreme tranquillity sent a chill through my bones. 'Let me guess. You've been connecting the dots.'

'I'd like to connect a gila monster to your scrotum.'

He fiddled with the box flaps, and after several attempts managed to interlace them. 'Whatever inconvenience John Snow is causing you, it's nothing compared with the anguish you inflicted on him.'

'Fuck you.'

'Fuck me, indeed. But why confine ourselves to generalities? If we're going to have one of your nuanced secular discussions, let's fuck me in the ear or fuck me up the ass.'

He seized the box and bustled out of the room. I followed directly behind him like a mackie dogging its quasiparent.

'Changing offices?' I asked. 'Or were you fired for bullying one too many grad students?'

'I'm leaving this place.'

'Really? You're breaking my heart. I'll have to keep reminding myself that the Hawthorne community's loss is Enoch Anthem's gain. I'm right, aren't I? Anthem offered you a job?'

'Matter of fact, I'll be heading up his Bureau of Apologetics.'

'Congratulations,' I said, then added, hoping to unnerve him, 'Maybe you'll get to lead the great anti-abortion protest Charnock told me about.'

Pielmeister remained his usual granite self. 'You would do well to ignore half of what Charnock says and discount the other half. The man's delusional.'

For the next few minutes, I became Pielmeister's shadow, matching his steps as he exited the building and made his way across Parking Area C to his Ford SUV. The rain had stopped. Puddles dotted the macadam like shards of a shattered mirror. Pielmeister opened the boot, which was already stuffed with boxes, and attempted to insert the last box. He failed. He rotated the box about its horizontal axis. Again he failed. He tried the vertical axis. No luck. I'd always known that academics were people who got paid to problematise the putting of square pegs into square holes, but I'd never before seen such a vivid demonstration.

Pielmeister set the box on the passenger seat, slammed the door, and looked me in the eye. 'Wake up, Ambrose. History is happening right in front of your nose, and you're totally blind to it. Even as we speak, Protestantism and Anglicanism are melting back into their parent Catholicism, and soon that great insatiable body will suck up all the rest, Eastern Orthodox Mariolaters, American heartland Charismatics, Mormon polygamists, snake-handlers, scorpion-swallowers, until Christendom has once again been made whole, pole to pole, crust to core!'

'With liberty and justice for all blastocysts.'

'Go ahead, scoff, all you want. The paradigm shift is upon us, sweeping away the things of Caesar and Sabacthani. Nominalist and humanist, peacenik and Bolshevik – doomed and damned, every last one of you. Checkmate, sir. Secularism is dead, Christ has switched off the Enlightenment, and the ruby-throated Darwinist will soon be extinct as the dodo.'

'Charnock tells me you've got thousands of immaculoids in the works.'

'Give up, Ambrose,' Pielmeister said, smiling through his beard. 'Corporate Christi has arrived. We're putting the crucifixion back where it belongs, dead centre.'

'My wife is having a nervous breakdown,' I said.

'She has a conscience then?'

'You shit.'

'The amoeboid conscience of Natalie Novak.'

Deep within some sub-basement of my brain, a hideous id-thing cracked out of its egg. My gorge rose like lava fountaining from a volcano. I lunged at Pielmeister, closing my hands around his throat.

He broke my grip. I slapped his cheek. He stomped on my foot. I grabbed his beard and spat in his face. Is there anything quite so ludicrous as two intellectuals grappling in a philosophy department parking lot? Each of us wanted to pummel the other to a pulp, but neither knew how to go about it. We couldn't even name the blows, much less inflict them deliberately. Quite possibly we were landing uppercuts, roundhouses, sidewinders, haymakers, and bolo punches. There was no way of telling. Eyes turned black, knuckles acquired the look and texture of uncooked bacon, and lips burst open like blood packets exploding on a Sam Peckinpah set. Somehow Pielmeister scrambled behind the wheel of his SUV, started the engine, and pulled away, enveloping me in a stinking aura of greenhouse gases.

I yanked the phone from my jacket and called Natalie.

'I beat him up,' I told her.

'Beat who up?'

'Pielmeister. He did the same to me. We drew blood.'

'Can you get home by yourself?'

'There's more blood to come. The world is changing, Natalie. Corporate Christi has arrived, and soon we'll all be crushed – you, me and the Sisters Sabacthani. Well, maybe not Londa. No, never Londa. I made her out of steel. When this nightmare is finally over, my vatling will still be standing.'

CHAPTER 10

The march of the immaculoids began early in October, suffusing the normally genial ghoulishness of the Halloween season – the grinning rictus of the jack-o'-lantern, the clownish gyrations of the rubber skeleton, the cartoon malevolence of the cardboard witch – with authentic horror and genuine dread. No group was exempt from the plague. The walking unborn descended upon rich and poor alike – black and white, Jew and Gentile, Catholic and Protestant, atheist and evangelical. Hundreds of semifathers endured humiliation at the hands of their foetuses, but it was the semimothers who suffered the most, particularly those who'd kept their pregnancies and subsequent abortions a secret: teenagers who'd never told their parents, wives who'd been thinking of leaving their husbands, mistresses who'd decided things were already complicated enough.

While the immaculoids' coming was theoretically the sort of sensational event on which the television medium thrives, the networks simply couldn't get an angle on it. Convinced that the phenomenon was essentially an epic human-interest drama, CNN, Fox News, and their rivals initially broadcast a panoply of feature stories, all cleaving to the same maudlin plot. Act one, the mackie appears on his quasiparents' doorstep and is rebuffed. Act two, the quasiparents see the light. Act three, the foetus is welcomed into the family. The problem was that the story typically included a fourth act, and the network was now obliged to present a follow-up report that nobody wanted to see. How John Snow 0714 set his quasiparents' house on fire. How Jane Snow 2039 got her semifather arrested on a false charge of sexual abuse. How John Snow 1190 switched his semimother's birth-control pills for

186

placebos, with predictable consequences. How Jane Snow 1347 bankrupted her quasiparents by transferring all their savings to the South Dakota Pro-Life Coalition.

In some cases TV journalists were forced to file despatches from a realm they normally avoided at all costs: the low-ratings domain of acid irony and mirthless absurdity. One immediately thinks of John Snow 2047, crucifying himself on the lawn of the family's ranch house, a martyrdom made possible by the carpentry skills of his twin brother, John Snow 2048. Then there was Jane Snow 1264, summarily executing her quasiparents with a Colt .45, a case that the anti-abortion judge dismissed on grounds of retroactive self-defence. And John Snow 0339, brutally impregnating his sixteen-year-old semisister, who shortly thereafter announced that, having discussed the matter at length with Enoch Anthem, she would bring the baby to term.

Of course, the average immaculoid narrative was neither heartwarming nor horrifying, merely sad. The foetus came knocking, and the beleaguered semimother would subsequently find herself divorced, disowned, or both, end of story. 'We've never seen such a potent and dramatic pro-life demonstration, and we salute the anonymous activists who organised it,' enthused George Collander of BUBBA, Baptists United against Butchery, Bestiality, and Abomination. The therapeutic community was equally keen on the mackies, who'd triggered a bizarre variation on post-partum depression among the semimothers, 'reversed-abortion angst', as one psychiatrist termed it. Faced with the unprecedented epidemic, scores of previously underpatronised counsellors and analysts were blessed with more cases than they could handle.

Given the degree of public indignation over the immaculoids' excesses, Attorney General Monica Giroux made a perfunctory stab at locating their creators and enjoining these biological activists against further mischief. When the federal grand jury asked for my deposition, I revealed what Vincent Charnock had told me – that two of America's leading postrationalists, Enoch Anthem and Felix Pielmeister, were planning to unleash legions of aborted foetuses on their unsuspecting quasiparents. Naturally the jury sought to subpoena Charnock so he could corroborate my accusations, but he and his houseboat had vanished without a trace.

For reasons best known to himself, the father of the RXL-313 was presumably hiding in an obscure cove along the Intercoastal Waterway.

In defending his client, Anthem's lawyer cleverly cast my testimony as the fantasies of a man 'whose previous attempt to win an audience for his atheism took the form of a ludicrous Darwinist tract called *Ethics from the Earth*.' He went on to explain how, in my former capacity as Londa's tutor, I had 'gleefully filled her head with the materialist philosophy that underlies the Themisopolis lifestyle'. Pielmeister's lawyer had an even easier time impugning my motives. Bitter over the professor's disinclination to support my PhD candidacy, I now sought revenge by 'forging a spurious link between this controversial pro-life demonstration and one of America's most respected theologians'. After twenty minutes of deliberation, the grand jury declined to indict either man.

Today it is generally acknowledged that if Alexander Hornbeam, that most pious of FBI directors, had instructed his agents to monitor our nation's abortion clinics, sooner or later they would have caught an Anthem acolyte in the act of pilfering some D & C residue. By subpoenaing the hard drives and filing cabinets of the Centre for Stable Families, this same Hornbeam could have uncovered a trail leading to the penumbral organisation called CHALICE. Given the man's attitude towards all things foetal, however, this simply wasn't going to happen. As he told one CNN reporter, 'Naturally I'm concerned that so many women are being inconvenienced, but isn't it high time that a day of reckoning befell America's pro-death feminists?'

At first Natalie and I couldn't understand why we enjoyed a better relationship with John Snow 0001 than most quasiparents had with their foetuses, but eventually we figured out that CHALICE was programming its pawns with increasing levels of vindictiveness. As the primal immaculoid, ours was also the least hostile, endowed with sufficient free will to make Natalie and me not merely the focus of his scorn but also the object of his curiosity.

That year we decided to attempt a quiet Christmas at home. Natalie's parents had recently moved to São Paulo so that her father, a retired professor of political science, could research his book about globalisation. My own progenitors, meanwhile, were inhabiting their respective vales of self-delusion – Mom living with a Dallas real-estate agent who'd promised to make her rich, Dad writing a spec screenplay while holed up in a Los Angeles efficiency apartment down the street from my sister Delia who was currently enjoying celebrity status as Scarlet O'Horror, hostess of Frisson Theatre. Natalie and I agreed, however, that if the opportunity presented itself, we would ask John Snow 0001 to spend Christmas Eve with us – and the opportunity did indeed arise, one blustery December afternoon when we all converged by chance on the Pieces of Mind coffee bar. It was Natalie who made the pitch, interlacing her sentences with so much hemming, hawing, and verbal filigree that at first John Snow 0001 didn't realise what she was getting at. When he finally grasped the nature of her invitation, the immaculoid insisted he had other plans for that particular night. We were simultaneously saddened and relieved – saddened because he was, after all, our foetus, relieved because we had no desire to spend any night, and most especially Christmas Eve, answering accusations of homicide.

On the morning of 25 December, shortly after dawn, our barbaric door-buzzer shattered our sleep, catapulting us from our bed. Even before reaching the window, I'd guessed who the intruder must be. I glanced down at the street, and there he was, standing on the front stoop, clutching a large canvas tote bag and stomping the snow off his boots.

'If he tries to intimidate me,' Natalie said, 'I'll spit in his eye.'

'Scramble some eggs,' I told her.

'I think not.'

I descended to the ground floor and greeted our foetus with a tepid 'Merry Christmas, Mr Snow.'

'Merry Christmas, Father,' he replied in a splintery whisper, stepping into the foyer. He wore a down-filled orange parka and a ragged woollen scarf. 'Christmas is the birthday of Jesus Christ, a fact you doubtless knew.'

'And of Isaac Newton.'

'Jesus Christ is the Saviour of mankind,' John Snow 0001 said. 'Have no fear – this visit won't last more than twenty minutes.' He set down the tote bag and rubbed his chest with his functional hand, apparently to warm himself. 'I don't really mind the cold. An unpleasant feeling is better than none.'

As we mounted the stairs, the immaculoid explained that his nervous system had finally started delivering sensations. Stimuli were getting through. Qualia no longer eluded him. Biting wind, burning matches, stirring marches, soothing lullabies, anchovies, chocolate bars, creosote, thorns.

'Last night I had a bad headache,' he said, 'which means I had a *good* headache – do you follow my reasoning, Father?'

'I believe I do.'

Natalie was waiting for us in her threadbare red bathrobe. Briefly I took satisfaction from my knowledge that the blue velvet caftan I'd got her would soon supplant this pathetic rag. She extended her hand. Our foetus grasped it firmly, then leaned forward and kissed her cheek. She clenched her teeth, the skin along her jaw growing tight as a drum.

'I'm not a monster, Mother,' he told her.

'Neither am I,' she replied.

'Let me take your coat,' I offered.

John Snow 0001 popped the line of brass buttons on his parka, but instead of shedding it he shuffled towards our gaudily decorated Christmas tree, a portly Scotch pine rising from an atoll of presents wrapped in recycled Sunday cartoons. 'I've brought gifts,' he announced proudly, lifting his tote bag high.

'How thoughtful,' Natalie said evenly. Now a softness entered her voice, plaintive to a degree that probably surprised her. 'We didn't get you anything. I'm sorry, Mr Snow.'

With supreme logic our netherson replied, 'You didn't know I was coming.'

He proceeded to distribute our gifts. Natalie received a pendant he'd made by braiding bits of aluminium foil into a long crinkled snake, then bending it into a heart shape. She slipped the twine loop around her neck, aligning the pendant between the lapels of her robe. The red terrycloth showed the silver foil to good advantage. I received a necktie made of nylon swatches cut from a discarded umbrella. The third gift was for both of us, a goldfish bowl containing two grasshoppers that John Snow 0001 had caught the previous summer and, against the odds, managed to keep alive for six months. He'd outfitted their habitat with grass and twigs. Amory and Claudius were orphans, he explained, and they wanted Natalie and me to adopt them.

I set the bowl on our favourite piece of furniture, a squat glass-doored bookcase from Ikea. The top shelf held six copies of *Ethics from the Earth* flanked by *The Phenomenology of Spirit* and *Tractatus-Logico Philosophicus*. In the outside world, Hegel and Wittgenstein kept company only with other geniuses, but here they had to associate with me.

'Would you like to stay for breakfast?' I asked the immaculoid, then immediately thought better of the idea. I turned to Natalie, soliciting forgiveness. Her eyes released daggers and other pointed objects.

'This has been a good visit,' John Snow 0001 replied, 'but I should get home before my rage boils up again.'

'Where is home?' I asked.

Strangely enough, his answer was straightforward. 'They've put us up in all sorts of places. Flophouses, church basements, college dorms, the YMCA. At the moment I'm living in a tower.'

'Which tower?' Natalie asked.

With his functional hand John Snow 0001 caressed the star atop our Christmas tree. 'It's a good place. Plenty of room. I did nothing to deserve that trip to the abortionist.'

'The Prudential tower?' I asked. 'The Hancock building? A clock tower? A bell tower?'

Bending low, our netherson pressed his face into the pine branches. The needles brushed his newly sensate cheeks. He inhaled deeply and declared, 'This is surely how a pleasant fragrance smells.' He took a step backward. 'And the visual appearance – for a person who came from a womb, such a sight would be entirely lovely. I, too, find it agreeable.'

'Do you need anything in your tower?' Natalie asked. 'A blanket? A mattress?'

A barking laugh spilled from the immaculoid's lips. He aligned the flaps of his parka, snapping each brass button into its shell, then yanked open the door. 'You shouldn't have scraped me away.'

Rummaging around in her shoulder bag, Natalie retrieved her madras wallet. She removed her ATM card and pressed it into our netherson's good hand. 'Withdraw as much cash as you want. The PIN is one-eight-one-eight, the year of Emily Brontë's birth.'

'Eighteen eighteen,' he echoed tonelessly. 'Thank you. I believe I'll purchase a heating device. I'm told the weather will get colder before it gets warmer.' He turned abruptly and bolted down the stairs. 'It was not necessary to exterminate me.'

'God bless you, Mr Snow,' my wife called from the doorway.

'I've started reading Heidegger,' he said, his voice fading like steam on a fogged mirror. 'You robbed me of my *Dasein*, Mother. The hottest places in hell are reserved for women like you.'

Natalie and I didn't know what to make of our Christmas presents from John Snow 0001. Should I start wearing my umbrella necktie, Natalie her foil pendant, as tributes to the loving son we'd almost brought into the world? Or should we toss these trinkets into the trash as the reproachful tokens he'd almost certainly intended them to be? On Boxing Day, before setting out for lunch at the Tasty Triffid, Natalie dutifully adorned herself with the pendant, while I put on the necktie. The instant our food arrived, we removed our accessories without exchanging a word and stashed them in Natalie's shoulder bag.

The new year was not long under way when Amory and Claudius died. I glanced at the bookcase and there they lay, two dry and delicate corpses, recumbent in the bottom of the fishbowl. Their passing perplexed me. Hadn't I given them plenty of water to drink? A surfeit of leaves to nibble? Evidently their little orthopterous clocks had simply stopped. I wrapped the insects in a white handkerchief, bore them to the rooftop garden and buried them beneath the philodendron.

Shortly after 5 p.m., we heard from our foetus again. He'd left a message on Natalie's voicemail, explaining that he'd used the ATM card for several purchases, including a cell phone and a kerosene heater. He wanted us to visit him. His home was an abandoned switch tower in the freight yards adjacent to South Station.

'Please come,' he said. 'It's quite important.' A long pause. 'I believe I'm very sick.'

Possessed by some raw Darwinian instinct, we sprinted to the parking garage, scrambled into the Subaru, and set out in quest of John Snow 0001. Reaching South Station at the height of rush hour, we exploited the hurly-burly and the gathering gloom to climb unseen off the platform and make our way across six parallel sets of tracks. My heart pounded frantically, though I couldn't say how much of this internal percussion was due to my fear of being arrested, how much to my anxiety over our foetus's health. At some undefined point we crossed from Amtrak's realm into the freight yard. Tank cars, hopper cars, boxcars, reefers, and gondolas loomed out of the darkness like prehistoric beasts straining to escape a tar pit.

Thanks to our heavy-duty flashlight supplemented by a full moon, we had no trouble spotting the deserted switch tower, a warped and weathered structure reminiscent of Charnock's houseboat. I knocked on the door, half-expecting to be greeted by a skeleton in the ectoplasmic employ of the long defunct Boston & Maine Railroad, but no one answered. A rickety exterior staircase led to the upper level, where a faint light seeped through the sooty windows. Natalie and I ascended to the observation platform, one wobbly step at a time, and nudged open the door at the top.

Strewn with scraps of wood, chunks of plaster, and bits of broken glass, the room was dimly illuminated by an electric lantern whose battery was almost dead. The back wall displayed a faded but elaborate chart depicting the freight yard, each switch circled and numbered, below which our netherson lay shivering on a stained bare mattress. A down comforter enswathed his body. His newly purchased kerosene heater, an upright thrumming cylinder, released ineffectual gasps of humidity. Discarded wrappers and empty packages littered the floor. In recent weeks our foetus had treated himself to Ring Dings, Twinkies, Tootsie Rolls, Triscuits, Slim Jims, Wise potato chips, and Keebler Toll House cookies.

'Thank you for coming,' he said.

I extended my hand, cupped his brow. His fever warmed my palm. 'Where's the nearest emergency room?' I asked Natalie.

'Mass General.'

'Listen, Mother,' John Snow 0001 said. 'Hear me, Father. I can feel the whole world now. Not just a few things. *Everything*. Isn't that remarkable?'

'We're taking you to the hospital,' I told him.

'Right now,' Natalie added.

The icy air made spectres of our breath.

'The twitchings in my stomach, I *know* that's hunger,' the immaculoid said. 'And the fire inside my body, it must be a fever.'

Natalie asked, 'Can you walk? Should we carry you?'

John Snow 0001 seized my wrist. 'Here's something even stranger. All these words coming out of my mouth – they're the ones I want to be speaking.' He relaxed his grip. 'A week ago, I would have said, "You're taking me to the hospital? Sure you don't want to get out your curette and slaughter me all over again?"'

Acting in unspoken but complete accord, my wife and I crouched over our foetus and peeled back the comforter. As Natalie slid her arms under his back, I took hold of his legs, and together we lifted him several inches off the mattress.

'No!' he screamed. 'It hurts too much!'

We set him back down.

'What hurts?' Natalie asked.

'Everything.'

'We would never hurt you on purpose,' Natalie said.

'I know, Mother. Before, I would've said, "You certainly hurt me on purpose when you lanced me like a boil."'

Natalie stifled a groan.

'The paramedics have painkillers,' I told our foetus, slipping the phone from my jacket pocket. 'They'll give you a shot of Demerol, then rush you to the hospital in their ambulance.'

With the suddenness of a frog catching a dragonfly, John Snow 0001 snatched the phone away and hugged it to his chest. 'I can picture it all in my mind. Sharp and clear, like a leaf floating on still water.'

'Picture what?'

'My entire race. The mackies. Moving against the city.'

'What city?' I asked. 'Boston?'

Before he could answer, a coughing fit seized him, the gouts of breath bursting from his windpipe along with a sprinkle of saliva. Natalie reached into the rubble and retrieved a half-litre 7-Up bottle. She gave our foetus a foamy gulp of warm soda. He coughed again, bathing us in carbonated spray, then took a second gulp.

Sucking in a deep breath, he squeezed my hand and looked me in the eye. 'Themisopolis,' he said. 'The place where they perform the abortions.'

'The immaculoids will attack Themisopolis?' I asked.

'And you know something?' he said, nodding. 'I'm not . . . what's the word? I'm not *jealous*.' He coughed. 'The other mackies will get to join the crusade, but I'll be too sick to go' – cough – 'and I don't care. What they're planning to do'– cough – 'it's wrong. Gasoline and firebrands, that's simply wrong.'

'Gasoline?' I said.

'And firebrands,' our foetus said.

'When does the crusade start?' Natalie asked.

'Soon, they told us,' our foetus replied.

'Who told you?' I asked. 'Enoch Anthem? Felix Pielmeister?'

'What I really want to know is how Amory and Claudius are doing.'

'They're both doing fine,' Natalie said.

'We love them very much,' I said.

A tremor passed through his body, and then came a series of overlapping vibrations, a seismic dying for our netherson. Natalie and I threw ourselves atop the creature, massaging his muscles with taut nervous fingers, as if we were making John Snow 0001 all over again, sculpting him from an immense lump of clay.

'Can I' – cough – 'ask you a question?'

Natalie's tears glistened in the lantern's sallow glow. 'Of course.'

'What is it like' – cough – 'to be alive?'

I winced. Tenured philosophers have a taste for grandiose questions, and failed philosophers relish them even more. What is it like to be a bat? What if our senses disclose only the shadows of reality? What if our language prevents us from thinking the most important thoughts of all? But my skull was empty just then, a grail devoid of wine, water, or any other useful fluid. I could not have said what it was like to scratch an itch, much less to be alive.

'City on fire!' our foetus cried. 'Jehovah's holy torch!'

Even as Natalie and I tightened our grip on John Snow 0001,

we felt his heat leak away in all its forms, first his acute fever, then his mammalian warmth, and finally the spark of life, leaving behind only his cold confected flesh. Natalie pulled her Christmas gift out from beneath her sweatshirt, lifted the twine loop over her head, and placed the foil heart atop our foetus's chest. Evidently she'd grabbed the thing as we were rushing out of the door.

'I meant for him to see I had it on,' she said.

'He probably knew we were lying about Amory and Claudius,' I said.

Natalie set her palm on the pendant. 'I should've showed it to him and said, "I've never stopped wearing it."'

We stayed in the tower throughout the night, inhaling the fumes of the kerosene heater and talking about John Snow 0001's short, unhappy incarnation. For Natalie his essential tragedy lay in 'his knowledge that he was living an unlived life'. He could never escape his realisation that his memories were contrived, his opinions programmed, his soul an epiphenomenon of his software. What truly impressed me, by contrast, was his brave and seemingly successful fight against his congenital disconnection from pleasure, so that his final days, miserable though they were by most indices, had included the savour of Ring Dings, the splendour of Twinkies, and the bliss of Triscuits.

'If he'd lived, I wonder, would he have remained sentient?' I asked Natalie.

'We'll never know,' she said, combing her netherson's hair.

With the coming of dawn we sneaked across the freight yard and started down Atlantic Avenue, Natalie leading the way, John Snow 0001 wrapped in the comforter, his sorry husk slung across our shoulders. Our fellow Bostonians took little interest in this strange procession. We must have looked harmless, certainly not miscreants disposing of an inconvenient corpse: perhaps rug merchants delivering a Persian carpet to a Beacon Street penthouse, or archaeologists bearing an ancient sceptre to the Boston Museum of Art. We reached the car, opened the trunk, transferred the clutter to the back seat – jumper cables, a bag of potting soil, four empty motor-oil cans – and, after working John Snow 0001's stiffening flesh into a foetal position, snugged him into the compartment.

For the next half-hour we fled the rising sun, driving aimlessly west, then eased the Subaru into the drive-through lane at a Brookline Burger King. I requested a couple of Egg Croissandwiches and some coffee, but when the order arrived neither Natalie nor I could eat a bite. God knows we were hungry. The problem was that the Croissandwiches were so damn tasty, emanating delights that John Snow 0001 had largely been denied.

We slurped down our coffee and resumed our wanderings. Buoyed by the caffeine, we talked about our netherson's vision of a foetal army firebombing Londa's city. An implausible narrative, we decided, but no more implausible than the immaculoids themselves.

'Pielmeister is capable of anything,' I said.

'You really think he would burn Themisopolis?' Natalie said.

'If that's what the paradigm shift requires.'

We visited a Starbucks, consumed more coffee, and changed drivers. Logic said the mortuaries would now be open, and so while Natalie piloted us down Beacon Street, I pulled out the phone and called the West Newton Funeral Home. No sooner had I said the word 'immaculoid' than the smarmy proprietor, an r-dropping Boston aborigine named Stephen Hammond, assured me that he understood our situation. We were the fourth couple this month to approach him concerning the disposition of such a creature.

'Your predecessors opted for cremation,' he said.

'I see.'

'Simply place the remains in your trunk.'

'We've done that already.'

'There's no shame in this, Mr Ambrose,' Hammond said. 'Nobody invited the mackies here.'

The instant we pulled into the mortuary driveway, two pale but sprightly young men came bustling on to the veranda, wearing black serge suits and exuding soft grey sympathy. The undertakers acted with exemplary speed. The last I saw of John Snow 0001 was a glimpse of his mouldering sneakers as the sombre men bore him across a vacant lot towards a squat brick building. A round tapered chimney rose from the roof like a candle on a one-year-old's birthday cake.

With a mournful tread Natalie and I mounted the veranda steps and entered the parlour. The place was a reified lie, all ferns and perfumes and uplifting synthesised harp music. The funeral director materialised from behind a red velvet curtain, introducing himself in the unctuous tones his profession had perfected down through the generations. He conformed surprisingly well to the mental image I'd assembled over the phone: a balding, roly-poly man with a small white moustache like the bristles on a toothbrush.

'Most of our immaculoid families prefer to leave the ashes here,' Stephen Hammond said.

Without consulting me, Natalie said, 'We'll take them home.'

'No, we won't,' I said.

For a full minute my wife and I exchanged annoyed glances. Hammond looked away and took a discreet step backwards: doubtless he'd witnessed many such communication breakdowns between quasiparents. It was Natalie who ended the stalemate, taking my hand, drawing it towards her, and pressing my fingers against her sternum.

'I don't ask for many favours, Archimago.'

Fixing my gaze on Hammond, I said, 'The ashes will come with us.'

The funeral director returned to our sphere, flashing a major smile. Humming in counterpoint to the ecclesiastical muzak, he guided us to a display case featuring ceramic urns. Natalie selected one bearing an enamelled image of wildflowers. They reminded her, she explained of the habitat our netherson had created for Amory and Claudius.

'The procedure takes ninety minutes,' Hammond said.

About as long as a D & C, I mused. Later I learned that the same thought had occurred to Natalie.

Under Hammond's guidance we staggered into a small room lined with leather-bound books, reminiscent of the children's alcove back in Pieces of Mind. Rummaging among the magazines on the coffee table, Natalie extracted a recent issue of *Time* featuring the annual circulation-boosting 'So What's the Big Deal about this Jesus Person?' cover story. I selected the complete works of W. H.

Auden, then joined my wife on the Naugahyde sofa. I attempted to read, but the poems kept dissolving into typographic jetsam adrift on a white sea. Eventually we put our printed matter aside and held hands. It was like waiting for an exhaust-pipe to be installed, only with harps instead of Johnny Cash.

Hammond appeared right on time, bearing the urn. While Natalie cradled our foetus's remains, I took care of the bill – $530.75 including tax – charging it to our Visa card.

We immediately agreed that John Snow 0001 must not be consigned to the trunk again. This time he would ride up front on Natalie's lap. By noon we were back in our apartment, setting the ceramic vessel atop the same bookcase where our grasshoppers had once resided.

'You were right all along,' I told Natalie. 'I'm glad we brought him home.'

'It's the least we can do for him'.

I stroked the vessel. 'I wonder if he's the only child we'll ever have.'

'He was not our child.'

'He was not our child,' I agreed.

Gasoline and firebrands, John Snow 0001 had said. City on fire. Jehovah's holy torch. As I entered the kitchen to call Londa's office, my imagination showed me Cinemascope images of siege towers grinding towards Themisopolis, their turrets crammed with vengeful immaculoids. Gertrude Lingard answered. Her boss, she said, was in Miami evaluating the effectiveness of the Wollstonecraft Fund in helping Cuban and Haitian immigrants find jobs. I tried Londa's cell phone and got her on the first ring.

Yes, ladies and gentlemen, you may be sure that I was reluctant to tell my vatling that John Snow 0001 had died. Her annoyance with her ponderous conscience, that philosopher who'd inflicted so many facets on her face and hung that uncast stone around her neck, would surely preclude any genuine expression of sympathy. So imagine my surprise when, on learning that the creature was no more, Londa became choked up – I don't think she was faking it – and then went on to assure me that Natalie and I had lost not a son, but a cruelly exploited anti-abortion icon who was probably better off dead.

It was only after I changed the subject, describing John Snow 0001's forecast of an imminent attack on the city, that the conversation began to unnerve me, Londa's voice becoming incongruously calm, as if I'd said the immaculoids would be spray-painting the walls with graffiti rather than burning them down. She proposed that on Monday we make our separate ways to Themisopolis, where we could analyse my netherson's last words over a leisurely dinner.

Like many an obsessive, Londa never stopped working, and so predictably enough our meal occurred in her executive suite atop Caedmon Hall. We ate at the conference table, adjacent to the model City of Justice, as Quetzie roosted on the Vision Institute. When not discussing the possibility of foetal violence, Londa and I shared vegetarian delicacies – 'my homage to little Donya', she explained, 'everybody's favourite animal-rights advocate' – prepared by the Artemis Clinic's live-in cooking staff, each tureen covered by a silver dome suggestive of a DUNCE cap. Since our phone conversation, Londa had, if anything, become more cavalier towards the presumed menace. With each new course I grew increasingly emphatic, averring that a dying immaculoid would not cry 'City on fire!' or 'Jehovah's holy torch!' without good reason, but only after we'd broached the desserts did Londa deign to explain her nonchalance. She crowned her pecan pie with a globe of vanilla ice cream, ambled towards a filing cabinet, and slid out the upper drawer.

'The cornerstone of Themisopolis was barely laid when the threats began,' she said. 'Each morning's email includes a dozen hate letters, most of them promising to gun down Yolly and me on sight. When it comes to sending us anthrax and explosives, of course, the Internet doesn't work very well, so the Phyllistines have to use a courier company instead. At first I was freaked, but then – you'd be proud of me, Socrates – I became philosophical. We've got a smart bomb squad in the mail room, and their dog is even smarter.' She brushed her fingers across the files and grabbed a random document. '"Your days are numbered, you sick twisted weirdoes,"' she read. She made a second arbitrary choice. '"You know you're the Antichrist, and I know it, and soon the whole world will know it."' She slid the drawer home. 'Junk mail from Jeremiah. Cassandra learns to spam. Forgive me if I don't take your immaculoid's warning more seriously than the ten thousand others that came before it.'

'Pielmeister,' I said.

'What?'

'Felix Pielmeister.'

She asked me to elaborate, and I attempted to paraphrase the Augustinian's rant in the Hawthorne parking lot. I told her how he'd screamed about geysers of blood, and how before long Corporate Christi would engulf the globe with godly profiteering and eschatological lava.

'He absolutely fucking terrified me,' I said.

'Quetzie is a handsome devil,' the iguana said.

'And how do you suggest we react to this crisis?' Londa asked drily.

I couldn't tell whether she wanted my opinion or merely sought to befuddle me into silence. 'You're the only superheroine in the room. I'm just another bookseller who never got his PhD. I suppose you should post some Valkyries along Avalon Lane and double the watch on the ramparts.'

'Here's my idea,' Londa said brightly. 'Let's spend the rest of the week making merry in the Circus of Atonement. That way we'll be in a good mood when the mackies come and put us out of business.'

'Blessed are the facetious.'

'But before we hit the Circus, we have to drop by the cemetery.'

'Cemetery?'

'White Marsh Cemetery.'

'I spent Wednesday morning in a funeral home. I have no wish to visit a cemetery.'

'When a gumbo girl goes bad, sweetie, she goes very, very bad. It's possible my case is hopeless. You'll have to judge for yourself.'

Londa was the most reckless person into whose hands I had ever commended my flesh, a driver for whom the Baltimore Beltway was a latter-day Hippodrome where any sufficiently foolhardy charioteer might garner laurels and a sack of sesterces. While her passenger scrunched down in the adjacent seat, staring at the recessed letters spelling out AIR BAG, she intimidated sedans, and bullied SUVs, all the while treating the 65 m.p.h. speed limit as nothing more than a baseline for measuring the calibre of her nerve. By the time we reached the cemetery, the sun had set, the moon had risen, my heart had entered my mouth, and my stomach had migrated upwards.

We stopped outside the main entrance, an austere post-and-lintel affair surmounted by a puffy-cheeked angel blowing a trumpet. A heavy black chain was slung between the wrought-iron gates like an immense watch fob. Someone, a Valkyrie presumably, had hacksawed open the padlock. In a matter of seconds we broke into the graveyard, a procedure rather easier than peeling the cellophane off a CD, then got back into the Volvo. As the moon brightened and Jupiter bejewelled its portion of the night, we cruised at a respectful velocity past the brooding tombstones, vaults, and naked winter trees.

'Cemeteries are the most philosophical of places,' I told Londa.

'Whatever you say.'

'As Heidegger would have it, by fully facing the fact of death and deliberately engaging the Nothing, a person can learn to live authentically.'

'I'm afraid I don't need a Heideggerian right now, not even one who can deconstruct cemeteries.' She reached past me and un-latched the glove compartment. 'What I need is a navigator.' Two folding maps and a tube of lip balm tumbled into my lap. 'Get us to the corner of Hyperion Avenue and Chancery Way.'

I spread the map across my knees, edging it into the pool of light cast by the glove compartment's reading lamp, but before I could locate the intersection on paper Londa found the real thing, thanks to a parked truck emblazoned with Lady Justice at full gallop. A half-dozen shadowy figures stood around the adjacent grave like mourners, though their picks and shovels suggested a more controversial agenda. We abandoned the Volvo and joined the leather-clad gang. Upon learning I was the ethicist who'd presided over their leader's legendary youth, the Valkyries presented me with a complex array of facial expressions conveying both their admiration of my success in giving her a moral compass and their wish that I'd made this particular instrument a bit less complex.

Londa now introduced me to Major Carmen Powers, a short, perky woman with chipmunk cheeks and a page-boy haircut parted laterally by the metal strap connecting her earmuffs 'the second-highest ranking member of the Themisopolis security force'. The Valkyries' highest-ranking member evidently had better things to do that night than creep around a freezing graveyard.

I fixed on the tombstone, which shimmered in the full moon like a radioactive menhir. Two bas-relief cherubs protruded from the granite, their pudgy bodies framing an inscription: IN LOVING MEMORY OF ETHAN AND AMELIA PEPPERHILL.

'Ethan Pepperhill,' I said. '*The* Ethan Pepperhill?'

Londa grunted in the affirmative.

Of all the congressmen who'd laboured to shield the American tobacco industry from the unpatriotic lawsuits of lung-cancer victims, none had been more successful than Ethan Pepperhill of North Carolina. 'What's he doing here?'

'Naturally he wanted to be buried in his home state,' Londa explained, 'but he wanted to share the sod with Mrs Pepperhill even more, and she'd already joined her parents in this neck of the netherworld.'

A few errant snowflakes sifted down from the sky, the swirling crystals turning bright as fireflies in the moonlight. I zipped up my bomber jacket. The Valkyries set to work, breaking the hard January earth with their steel tools. It took them only twenty minutes to penetrate the frost line and begin shovelling away the pliant dirt below. They excavated the glossy oblong box, lifted it free of the hole and, like newlyweds installing their first refrigerator, set it upright on the mound of freshly turned soil. Major Carmen Powers smashed the clasps with her shovel, and the lid fell away, tumbling into the open grave. Like a gust from a blast furnace the stench swept over us, and we reached for our scarves, and handkerchiefs, pressing them against our faces. My eyes teared up. I wiped away the salt water and there they were, limned by the lunar glow, the erect remains of the Winston-Salem Corporation's greatest benefactor, still dressed in a crumbling tuxedo. Being dead, he looked understandably peaky, though still prepared to wage one more battle against the enemies of free enterprise and spiked tobacco.

A fleeting but bizarre episode followed, grisly even by the norms of this night. Carmen Powers took out her Swiss Army knife, waded through the ghastly fumes, and sawed off Senator Pepperhill's little finger. An unexpected gesture, yet I managed to apprehend its significance.

I turned to Londa and said, 'You've got your own ontogenerator.'

'The next big consumer item,' she replied, accepting the detached finger from the Major.

'This carnival of yours – the performers are all beaker freaks?'

Londa offered me a corroborative smirk, then slid a baggie from her coat pocket and sealed the finger in plastic. 'We'll have Pepperhill on the playbill in a month or two. I picture him walking into a cancer ward with an ice-chest containing his recently extracted lungs, offering them free of charge to whoever speaks up first.'

I gestured towards the corpse and scowled. 'A reverent person – not myself, certainly – but a reverent person would call this desecration.'

'No, Socrates, *this* is desecration,' Londa said, drawing out a pack of her customary Dunhills. She approached the senator and inserted a cigarette between his lips.

'I thought you'd given up smoking.'

'I use these for political purposes only,' she explained, then turned to Carmen. 'It would be fun to read about this in tomorrow's paper. Send an anonymous tip to the night desk at the *Sun*.'

'Christ, Londa, aren't you going to rebury him?' I gasped.

'Thanks to Jordan's efforts, the American Brotherhood of Grave-diggers has secured a fair wage for its members. Whoever puts him in the ground tomorrow will be whistling while he works.'

'Fuck.'

'Lighten up, sweetie.' Londa provided the senator with a second cigarette, so that he now seemed to possess the elongated canine teeth of a vampire. 'We're off to watch the Circus troupers play their parts. It's the most popular way to pass a Saturday night in Themisopolis. You're only young once, Socrates. *Carpe diem*.'

204

Depressed by recent events in White Marsh Cemetery, and certain that I would derive no delight from the Circus of Atonement, I spent most of our return trip telling Londa, truthfully, that I was bone-tired and could feel a cold coming on, if not the flu, so would she please take me to the Themisopolis guest house or, better still, a motel? My vatling would hear none of it. What I needed, she insisted, was a rococonut julep followed by a circus act or two, and within the space of an hour I found myself in her lofty office.

The canopic jar in which she kept her mumquats – authentic Eighth Dynasty, she insisted – evoked for me the most vivid shot in *The Egyptian*: Sinuhe performing his penance in the House of the Dead as a lowly embalmer's apprentice, stirring a stinking vat of natron. Londa made me the promised julep, serving it in a crystal goblet. The nectar did not so much relieve my symptoms as decontextualise them. Once you've been abstracted from your body, the discomfort of an upper-respiratory infection loses all claim on your attention.

Bathed in Proserpine's manufactured serenity, I allowed Londa to guide me out of Caedmon Hall and across the flagstone plaza. Soon the Circus of Atonement rose before us, a squat rotunda: black, smooth and featureless – hence the ease with which the architects had represented it using a hockey puck. We passed through an unmarked entryway and entered a dimly lit foyer appointed only with a coat rack, a water fountain, and a vending machine dispensing fruit juice and granola bars. Londa flashed me a cryptic Sabacthanite smile, a sure sign of heavy weather and sizeable ironies ahead, then led me into the darkness beyond.

As we moved along the central corridor, following the curve of the hockey puck, compact prosceniums emerged on both sides, each featuring a live actor earnestly performing a minimalist drama. Nearly every play seemed to be well attended, only one or two empty seats per theatre, but according to Londa the vatling thespians took no pleasure in their popularity, as their DUNCE cap programs precluded any such sensation. They were zombies to the core – beyond delight, outside despair.

Intrigued by the lurid poster, I suggested that we sample *Mother-hood Comes to the Holy Father*. We slipped into the theatre, taking care not to annoy the actor or disturb the other audience members, and quietly assumed our seats. I quickly became absorbed in a situation of transcendent tastelessness. Through the machinations of a Wiccan sisterhood, Pope John Paul II had awoken one morning to find himself burdened with an unsolicited uterus and a concomitant unplanned pregnancy. Happily for the Supreme Pontiff, his silk robe billowed so broadly that his condition, like the Fifteen Rosary Mysteries, remained obscure. I could not imagine how Londa had obtained the tissue sample, and I did not want to know. The present scene was set in a Vatican clinic. Having dropped beseechingly to his knees, the Pontiff was begging an audio-animatronic doctor to give him an abortion. A queasiness spread through me – political theatre was one thing, feminist Grand Guignol with reincarnated ecclesiastics quite another – and I politely told Londa that I wished to see no more. As we exited the theatre, the Vatican physician presented the Pope with a brochure touting the virtues of adoption.

'Do not begrudge us our diversions,' Londa said defensively. 'The circus is essential to our mental health.'

We continued along the corridor, patronising each play only long enough for the plot to manifest itself. Even as I recoiled at the sheer charnel pornography of it all, Londa's deranged museum brought out the critic in me, and I began evaluating the scripts, performances, and directorial flourishes. Perhaps the mumquat nectar had lowered my standards, but I was deeply moved by *The Martyrs of Modernity*, CEO Warren Anderson's abject apology for the 1984 methyl-isocyanate leak at the Union Carbide factory in Bhopal, India – eight thousand dead in a week, fifteen thousand by the end of the decade, countless mothers yielding toxic breast milk well into the next century – a disaster for which neither he nor his corporation had taken any responsibility at the time, instead sending each victim a paltry $500. By contrast, I found little to admire in *The Art of Atrocity*, Henry Kissinger's lachrymose lament over the lagniappes he'd added to America's catastrophic involvement in the Vietnam War, including the secret invasion of Cambodia and the Christmas bombings of Hanoi and Haiphong. Far more satisfying was *Searching for My Soul*, in which Ronald Reagan denounced himself not only for supporting Central American death squads, but also for curtailing heating-fuel assistance to the elderly, declining to speak out against apartheid, refusing to acknowledge the AIDS epidemic until he had no choice, and appointing a Secretary of the Interior who believed that the imminent Second Coming rendered environmental stewardship irrelevant.

'Could you give us a publicity quote?' Londa asked me as we slipped away. 'We're always looking for endorsements from celebrity ethicists.'

I assumed she was joking, but replied with a blurb reflecting my genuine enthusiasm for the piece in question. 'In real life Ronald Reagan neither received nor deserved an Oscar, but having seen *Searching for My Soul*, I'm ready to give him one.'

We moved on. Davy Crockett's confession, a tour de force called *Moon over Bexar*, took as its theme the dubious ideals of the Alamo defenders: how they were ultimately seeking to found a republic in which they could own West African slaves, the Mexican government in its wisdom having outlawed that controversial institution. While the beaker freak's bucolic locutions seemed completely natural, he inevitably evoked scores of post-Crockett scoundrels who'd attained office by affecting such folksiness, their talent for faking the common touch matched only by their aptitude for screwing the common man. After sampling the Crockett soliloquy we dropped by *Jesus Winced*, in which Mary Baker Eddy sought forgiveness from the on-stage ghosts of a dozen deceased children whose parents had sacrificed them on the altar of Christian Science. Londa assured me that the youthful spectres were audio-animatronic simulacra. No children had been disinterred for this production. Next we joined the audience for what proved to be the evening's most disturbing presentation, *Mega Culpa*, in which the brilliant physicist Edward Teller bemoaned the ebullience with which he'd fathered the hydrogen bomb. At first his anguish captivated me, but then the *fusionfamilias* tore off his shirt and started biting into his mortified flesh with a flagellant's whip, and I left in a huff, repulsed by the gratuitous violence.

'Major Powers wrote that script,' Londa muttered as we returned to the corridor. 'You're right – it's over the top.'

Before I could elaborate on my dismay, my hostess hustled me into the vicinity of two recently deceased and copiously mourned clerics. Prior to his death in an auto accident, Percival Sarnac had been Enoch Anthem's right-hand man, tirelessly transmitting God's views on homosexuality via WXPF-AM in Chicago, 'your station for salvation'. Before succumbing to leukaemia, Leopold Ransom had hosted the talk show *Countdown to Jesus* on the Rapture Channel. And now here they were in the circus, acting out a love story titled *The Semen on the Mount*. I had to admit I'd never witnessed a more moving courtship. The fleeting caresses, the furtive kisses, the tender embraces, the candlelit dinner, the passionate grapplings on Ransom's waterbed – it was all impeccably programmed and poignantly performed, and by the time the men had exchanged their wedding vows, most of the attending Valkyries were weeping.

'I have a treat for you,' Londa said, ushering me towards a velvet curtain, red and heavy as a coronation robe, 'the dress rehearsal of an epic set in the fifteenth century.' The adjacent poster identified the show as *Clone of Arc*. 'Tonight our youngest malefactor runs through my latest script. We bribed about thirty functionaries and broke a dozen international laws, but at long last Saint Joan's charred femur came into our possession.'

'A malefactor? Joan of Arc?'

'I must concede, your admiration for the Maid of Orléans is practically universal. Even the toughest-minded thinker will melt before our dear Joan. Mark Twain devoted his worst novel to her. Bernard Shaw put her at the centre of an extraordinarily tedious play – a feat later duplicated by both Jean Anouilh and Maxwell Anderson. She's waiting, Socrates. A private performance. If you liked *Searching for My Soul*, you'll love *Clone of Arc*.'

I stepped behind the red curtain and entered a theatre far smaller than the others, barely a dozen seats, all empty. Assuming the best possible vantage point, front row centre, I fixed on the proscenium, expecting to see the resurrected Joan wearing a prison smock and chained to her notorious stake – or perhaps she would be in full armour, mounted on a charger, holding the French standard high as she urged her troops into battle. Instead she stood beside a fir tree rooted in a mound of earth carpeted in lush grass and golden buttercups. She was blindingly beautiful, her raven hair secured in a bun, her voluptuous form wrapped in a muslin shift, her blue feline eyes darting in all directions. A gleaming broadsword – Joan's, no doubt – protruded from the hillock like Excalibur rising from its anvil.

'Yes, my achievement was astonishing, *pas de question*,' she began. 'I saved a nation. *Vive la France!* But there is still a difficulty, *un grand problème*.'

In an unbroken and balletic gesture, she untied her sash and laid it along her outstretched forearm. The accessory slithered across her skin and floated to the grass, and suddenly I knew how this untried and untested commander had rallied an entire army to her side. In some lubricious sector of his soul, every French infantryman had imagined himself embracing this divine peasant.

'It's an old story, perhaps the oldest on earth,' Joan said. 'The sky rumbles. The clouds congeal. Is that a saint I see on high? An angel? The Lord God Jehovah himself? Now a holy voice booms down, instructing the poor prophet to grab a sword and thrust it into a fellow human, or perhaps a hundred fellow humans, or even a million if the cause is sufficiently sacred. The prophet never talks back. The tradition flourishes to this day. The sword, the blood, the freshly created corpses littering the battlefield, exuding the stink of epiphany.'

She issued a merry programmed laugh, then hiked up her shift and cast it aside. Her flesh elicited appreciation from all my senses. I could smell her lovely pheromones, hear the whisper of her limbs, feel the softness of her hands, taste her salty thighs.

'I wish I had it to do over again,' Joan said. 'I would have tried bargaining with my voices.' She unfastened her hair. Her tresses spilled on to her bare shoulders and cascaded downwards, swirling around her eminent breasts like an incoming tide. 'I wish I'd said, "Why must so many lose their lives, dear God? Why not turn the English swords to glass and their pikes to aspic, so our enemies will capitulate without a fight? Whence cometh thine appetite for carnage, O my Father? Why this thirst for blood? *Pourquoi le sang?*"' She looked me in the eye. 'Come hither, knave.'

I obeyed, joining the maid on stage. She made a circuit of the fir tree, then approached me in all her mind-boggling nubility. I had consumed too much rococonut milk. Deftly she removed my clothes, then guided me to the hillock and bade me lie with her. Her lovely fingers sculpted me into the rigid amoretto her appetite required. The mumquat juice saturated my neurons. She climbed on top, and soon her moist quoit found its object – no resistance from Mason the morality teacher: too much nectar. Synaesthesia overcame me, everything melting together, the warmth of her skin, its fine rural fragrance, the blue of her eyes, the eddies of her hair, the surrounding meadow.

'On the day we broke the siege,' she said, 'I disembowelled twenty men.'

In the dream that now suffused my sleeping mind, my netherson was still alive. The two of us were standing beside an Isla de Sangre swamp, tossing gobbets of raw meat to the alligators like a couple of Boston Common bench-sitters feeding the pigeons.

I awoke in time to catch the end of Joan's soliloquy. 'There are no just wars,' she said. 'There are no greater goods.'

Evidently I'd wept during my ethereal reunion with John Snow 0001 – my cheeks were wet: the dew of my mourning. The maid sprawled beside me, tickling my nose with the stem of a buttercup.

'Four days ago I lost a foetus,' I told her. 'A miserable and misbegotten creature, but I'm still very sad.'

'I wish I had it to do over again,' Joan said, echoing herself. 'I would ask God a question or two.'

CHAPTER 11

Many are the consolations of literature, and not the least such solace occurs when an annoyingly virtuous hero succumbs to carnal temptation. Case in point: the Red Cross Knight who dominates Book One of *The Faerie Queene*, as pious a protagonist as you can imagine, a man whose life's ambition is to enter orthodoxy's dictionary – 'see also *holiness*, *probity*, and *Saint George*. So how does this chainmail messiah behave when the degenerate witch Duessa throws herself at him in the guise of the fair maiden Fidessa? We might expect Sir Red Cross to resist. But no. The enchantress has only to wiggle her wiles, and soon our randy *chevalier* has 'poured out in looseness on the grassy ground', which means exactly what you think it does.

I was staring up at the starry winter sky, drained and sated and vaguely enjoying the sensation of being carried away from the Circus of Atonement on a stretcher borne by Major Powers and another Valkyrie, when it occurred to me that, just as Spenser exonerated his knight, so might Natalie eventually pardon my dalliance with Joan of Arc. Or if my wife failed to forgive me, then perhaps I would in time gain absolution from the readers of the self-serving memoir I was certain to write one day. Maybe Joan herself would let me off the hook, coming to me and saying, 'Your lack of chivalry appals me, monsieur, but I must allow for certain extenuating circumstances and tumescent conditions.'

In keeping with Londa's egalitarian principles, all visiting dignitaries to Themisopolis stayed at Arcadia House, the same neo-Tudor building that sheltered the outcasts and indigents who routinely sought refuge within the city's walls. As she tucked me into bed that night, Major Powers reported that the present population of this heartbreak hotel included seventeen orphans, eleven pregnant adolescents, ten battered wives, five abused girl-friends, and fourteen general pariahs who, until recently, had been eating out of restaurant garbage pails. Lolling on the mattress, I imagined that I could hear my fellow residents' sobs, whimpers, and moans seeping through the walls. Strangely enough I was glad to be among these wretches, whose phantom lamentations served to deepen my admiration for Londa. Yes, the woman was out of whack, unbalanced by her profligate conscience – how else to interpret the Circus of Atonement? – and yet here was the harvest of that disharmony: a place for those with no place to go.

The following morning, surfacing into consciousness, I imme-diately wished that I was still asleep. My skull had become an accordian operated by an ape. My throat and stomach were joined by an oesophagus once owned by a sword swallower. By punching a bedside button labelled 'NURSE', I prompted a lovely young paramedic to flutter into the room, and presently she confirmed my diagnosis: I had the flu, complete with a 102-degree fever. My angel prescribed water, electrolytes, aspirin, and bed rest. I decided to start with the last, wrapping the pillow around my head and snuggling beneath the patchwork quilt.

Several hours later the telephone wrenched me from my dream – Donya and I were wandering the beaches of Isla de Sangre, rescuing stranded sea urchins – and dumped me back into my febrile body. The caller was Londa, inquiring after my health.

'I expect to be on my feet in a day or so,' I told her. I wondered if she'd written the *Clone of Arc* script solely with her old tutor in mind: a kinky recapitulation of her seduction attempt back on the island, though with a different climax. 'Tell me honestly, Londa, did you get a vicarious thrill from my misbehaviour last night?'

'What misbehaviour might that be?'

I grunted indignantly.

'I'm not a voyeur,' Londa said. 'I have no idea what happened between you and Joan.'

'You designed the damn program.'

'And you chose to *follow* it?' she replied with fake dismay. 'Am I to infer that you ravished that poor dead gamine? I'm shocked.'

'Oh, come off it. Your troupers are all zombies. You said so yourself.'

'Hey, Mason, I would love to spend the afternoon discussing the inner lives of beaker freaks, but have a million things on my plate right now. It seems you were right about Pielmeister and CHALICE having grand ideas. Get well, sir. And don't worry about our Joan. She's one tough gumbo girl.'

'Grand ideas? What's going on?'

'Gotta run. Drink plenty of fluids. Ciao.'

I didn't want to stick Themisopolis for a long-distance call, so I hauled myself out of bed and slipped the cell phone from my bomber jacket, which Major Powers had thoughtfully draped across the solitary chair. My efforts were rewarded not with Natalie's dulcet tones but with a computerised voice urging me to leave a message. What to say? Reached Maryland safely, caught the flu, had wild illicit sex with a bioengineered Joan of Arc, miss you, will call again tomorrow? When the beep sounded, I told Natalie I was sick and hoped to be home in two days.

Briefly I surveyed my quarters. Somebody had retrieved my overnight bag from Caedmon Hall and set it on the dresser, a sturdy antique with a pristine mirror, adjacent to which hung a paint-by-numbers canvas depicting the Gospel narrative of the woman taken in adultery. At the centre of the tableau stood a seraphic Jesus who looked about as Semitic as Peter O'Toole. 'Let him among you who is without sin cast the first stone,' ran the superfluous caption, rendered in an Old English font. As I climbed back into bed, it occurred to me that, from CHALICE's viewpoint, Londa and her colleagues had already cast many such stones, and it was high time they got their own geologic comeuppance.

A tribal chant – basso, growling, ominous. A frenzied drumming, as if rival marching bands had assembled outside my window, rehearsing half-time routines for the Bedlam-Charenton all-lunatic gridiron match. I blinked myself awake. Morning, or so I guessed. Day four of my Arcadia House sojourn. Throat healed, sinuses drained, fever broken.

'Feeling better?'

A grain of sand had nestled in my eye, bringing a tear, so that

Londa seemed encapsulated, a bouillababy in a bubble. 'Much better,' I said, wiping the grit away. The chant and drumming continued, threatening to revive my headache. 'What's that damn racket?'

Instead of answering, she made a circuit of the room, gathering up my socks, underwear, and street clothes like a suburban mom on laundry day. She tossed the pile on to the bed.

'The barbarians are at the gates,' she said, and it was then that I noticed her face, as pale and stiff as Senator Pepperhill's. 'Get dressed.'

I did as instructed, then grabbed my phone, intending to contact Natalie. Before I could key in the number, Londa told me not to bother. The immaculoids were jamming all transmissions from Themisopolis.

'I don't get it,' I said.

'You will,' she said.

We left the building and hurried down Shambhala Avenue, the raucous voices and unruly percussion growing louder by the minute. Reaching the main entrance, we stepped into Londa's private elevator, all plush Victorian velvet – 'My vertical limousine,' she explained – and ascended to the top of the rampart. Apprehension throbbing in my chest, I crossed the windy causeway and, accepting Londa's offer of binoculars, set about absorbing the coming of Corporate Christi in all its lurid spectacle.

An army was bivouacked outside the city, a seething foetal sea, roiling, churning: three thousand pock-faced, silver-haired immaculoids deployed amidst rows of canvas tents and nylon pavilions, plus another three thousand arrayed in protest along Avalon Lane, their legions spilling into the snow-covered cherry orchard beyond. Dozens of bazookas, assault rifles, and grenade-launchers glistened beneath the gelid eye of the January sun. Scores of placards trembled in the wind, rank upon rank of epigrammatic anger. EVERY CONDOM IS A NOOSE. SPOTLESS AS THE LAMB. NEVER TO SAVOUR THE ROSE. D & C = DESTRUCTION & CRUELTY. Dressed in identical orange jumpsuits, the foetuses banged lug wrenches against trash can lids and beat 55-gallon drums with claw hammers, chanting all the while like insti-tutionalised Gregorian monks.

'They've had us sealed in since Monday afternoon,' Londa said, 'commuters and residents alike.' She explained that upon their arrival the foetuses had employed an electromagnetic pulse to disable the city's cell phones, satellite dishes, and wireless modems, and shortly thereafter they'd severed all phone lines and coaxial cables. 'Yolly and I were watching the TV coverage of the siege when the screen turned to static.'

'TV coverage?' I said. 'Good, great, *that* should put a crimp in Pielmeister's paradigm shift.'

'Don't count on it. Two days ago the news helicopters were as thick as mosquitoes, but the pilots got jittery when the bazookas appeared. Whatever the mackies pull next, the viewing public won't see it.'

The sun glinted off the snow, lancing through my irises. I yanked the Ray-Bans from my bomber jacket and slid them into place. 'Is Pielmeister down there? Anthem?'

'Our favourite Phyllistines are keeping their distance. When CNN interviewed Anthem, he said he had no idea who'd encouraged the immaculoids to bring their complaint to our door.'

Although nearly half of Londa's staff commuted to work, the parking lot outside the city was barren of the usual sedans, station wagons, and SUVs. Instead the macadam held more than a hundred Greyhound buses, plus ten Mayflower moving vans and seven semi-rigs sporting the Mountain Dew logo: not a surprising sight, really – how else could CHALICE have got so many mackies and their camping gear on to the scene? Far more disturbing was the battery of howitzers, ideal for pulverising our gates, not to mention the thirty-odd Caterpillar hydraulic lifts, perfect for sending waves of foetuses over our walls, and the forty or so diesel tractors pulling tankers filled with gasoline.

'City on fire,' I muttered. 'Jehovah's holy torch.'

'That appears to be their intention,' Londa said, each syllable dipped in venom.

'The Maryland Governor, what's his name – Winthrop – he'll have to call in the National Guard, right?'

'Tucker Winthrop? Are you kidding? A major Phyllistine.' Londa slipped on her mirrorshades. 'The last thing Yolly and I saw on CNN was Winthrop's press conference. Quote: "These poor innocent foetuses are exercising their right of peaceable assembly, and my office has no reason to thwart them."'

I heaved a sigh. 'Not to mention their right of peaceable arson.'

Londa strode back and forth across the causeway, like Davy Crockett sizing up Santa Ana's army as it paraded past the Alamo. 'I'm supposed to join Yolly and our security chief at noon for a meeting with the mackie general. I'd like my conscience to come along.'

'Your conscience has nothing better to do.'

'I appreciate that.'

Again I heaved a sigh. 'Suppose they gave a paradigm shift and nobody came?'

We entered the Victorian elevator and returned to the ground. Yolly was pacing around by the main entrance, accompanied by Dagmar Röhrig and a leather-jacketed Valkyrie who introduced herself as Colonel Vetruvia Fox. She was an astonishingly intense woman, small but fearsome, a lark of prey. An instant later the gates pivoted open with the ponderous force of a hippopotamus shifting in its wallow of mud. Remote control in hand, our escort stepped forward, Captain John Snow 0851 according to the embroidery on his jumpsuit – a cadaverous mackie with hair the texture of a Brillo pad. He asked Colonel Fox for her side arm. She surrendered her Glock 19 with a resentful snort. The foetal army had stopped chanting and drumming, but we still endured a barrage of bitter grunts and toxic glances as Captain Snow, limping, led us through the encampment. Angry words appeared wherever we turned. BURN, BABY-KILLER, BURN. OUR PORTION WAS ABORTION. NEVER TO FEEL A PUPPY'S TONGUE. ABLATED LIKE A TUMOUR.

Our destination proved to be a prefabricated tin shanty, cold as an igloo, drafty as a crypt. Apparently these immaculoids were all still strangers to sensation. Captain Snow seated us at a collapsible aluminium picnic table, directly across from a short scowling foetus labelled Major John Snow 3227 and his commanding officer, the squint-eyed, simian-shouldered General John Snow 4099. Wrapped in shadows, a dozen mackies of indeterminate rank stirred in the background.

'The evacuation begins at dawn,' General Snow announced, his exhalations turning visible in the frigid air.

'We expect you all to show up promptly,' Major Snow said. More palpable breaths. Everyone seemed to be speaking in *League of Londa* dialogue balloons.

'Evacuation?' snarled Colonel Fox.

'What?' gasped Dagmar.

For some reason Captain Snow preferred to remain erect, strutting back and forth across the dirt floor. 'We'll march the lot of you to Quehannock State Park, where your commuters will find their missing cars and vans,' he said. 'Next we'll issue cell phones to your residents, so they can commission private transportation and thereby continue the exodus.'

Colonel Fox fixed her eyes on the vaulted ceiling and muttered, 'Fuck this.' The tin walls replayed her words, turning her throw-away epithet into a malediction.

General Snow glowered at the Valkyrie and said, 'In other words, your people will be at a safe distance when the conflagration starts.'

'Conflagration?' said Yolly, who'd evidently not spent much time mulling over the implications of the gasoline trucks parked outside the city.

'Conflagration,' General Snow repeated, rolling the word around on his tongue like a cherry stone.

A hush descended. The stillness held dominion for two full minutes.

'What makes you think we won't stand our ground?' Londa asked, digging the nail of her index finger into her thumb.

Major Snow issued a toothy immaculoid smirk. His teeth suggested an encounter between a piano keyboard and a sledge-hammer. 'If it's a fight you want, Dr Sabacthani, we'll gladly give you one. But remember that every mackie will be dead of his infirmities within the week. You'll be battling the very legions of despair.'

'We have guns,' Colonel Fox noted.

'We have more guns,' countered General Snow.

'We have the high ground,' Colonel Fox asserted.

'We have the howitzers,' General Snow replied.

'We have the wisdom of experience.'

'We have the lethality of innocence.'

'We have *esprit de corps*.'

'We have nothing to lose.'

A second silence came, during which I contemplated General John Snow 4099. Beyond his programmed frown, lazy eye, and immaculoid pocks, I caught glimpses of the handsome face he might have owned had his godfather been Charnock and not some incompetent CHALICE technician. His heritage, I decided, was heterogeneous. Several months earlier, a comely Asian soul had connected with an attractive human of Caucasian descent. I imagined that the two of them had truly loved each other, and might eventually bring forth several splendid children who would make a sincere effort to forgive their pyromaniacal semibrother.

'We suggest that, between now and sunrise, you gather together all possessions of sentimental value,' said Captain Snow.

'Unlike our parents, we are not heartless,' said Major Snow. 'We shall permit you to retain whatever photographs and trinkets you keep in your offices.'

'No weapons, of course' – General Snow threw Colonel Fox a gloating glance – 'no pistols, no rifles, those all stay behind. Likewise your laptops, cell phones, PDAs, iPods, hard drives, and storage media. You'll be strip-searched and X-rayed, so there's no point trying to smuggle any computer chips past our guard.'

Londa was trembling now, and not from the cold.

'If you won't allow us any CD-Rs,' Colonel Fox said, training her laser gaze on General Snow, 'then shut off your electromagnetic pulse for a couple of hours so we can send our files over the Web.'

'You don't seem to understand,' the immaculoid commander replied. 'When the city burns down, all of your unscriptural initiatives will burn down with it.'

'Unscriptural initiatives?' Dagmar gestured wildly in the direction of Themisopolis. 'Do you have any idea what sort of data we've got back there?'

For the next few minutes she expounded upon two enterprises Londa had mentioned during my first visit to the city: Project Xelcepin, aimed at producing a treatment for ovarian cancer, and Operation Velvet Fist, a full-bore assault on the international sexual-slave trade. Both of these breakthroughs were girded by digital information. Apropos of Xelcepin: the complex protocols for administering the drug and the recent results of a double-blind trial. Concerning the prostitution rings: the secret identities and hidden lairs of more than one hundred slave traffickers, plus the location of several dozen churches and private homes where the exploited women could seek sanctuary before the UN made its move. Precious data, priceless facts, all of it still awaiting export-ation beyond the walls of Themisopolis.

'We're OK with wiping out ovarian cancer, and on the whole your anti-prostitution campaign sounds like a good thing,' General Snow said. 'What worries us is the other data you'd like to carry out of here.'

'What other data?' Dagmar demanded.

'Don't be coy,' General Snow said. 'We know that Project Xelcepin is a front for the scheme that *really* matters to you, the development of ... what's it called?'

'Nildeum,' Major Snow said.

'Nildeum,' echoed General Snow. 'The breakfast-cereal additive that makes children stop believing in God.'

'Oh, for Christ's sake,' Dagmar said.

'It's time we took leave of these clowns,' Colonel Fox observed, squeezing her boss's arm.

Londa said nothing. She simply regarded the far wall with the sort of glassy stare Henry's young audiences had doubtless accorded *Professor Oolong's Oompah-pah Zoo.*

'And we also know what you're *really* designing at the Vision Syndicate,' Captain Snow said.

'The fuel whose secret ingredients are corn oil and menstrual blood,' Major Snow said.

'We've worked out the implications,' General Snow said.

'We're no dummies,' Captain Snow said.

'Once women realise they can sell their menstrual blood, they'll try to produce as much of the stuff as possible,' Major Snow said.

'We're talking about de facto infertility,' Captain Snow said. 'Diaphragms, IUDs, condoms – whatever it takes.'

'Enough of this shit,' Dagmar growled.

'We're out of here,' Yolly said.

'You people won't rest until every oil company in America has gone out of business,' General Snow said, 'and pregnancy has become a thing of the past.'

A heavy snow was falling when we left the mackie headquarters and started back towards the city, though I doubted that the flakes would be large, wet, or plentiful enough to insulate Themisopolis from the coming inferno. Midway through our return journey, Londa stopped walking, as if she'd acquired the plaster flesh and steel bones of Alonso the Conquistador. She managed to communicate her immediate wishes through clipped phrases and spasmodic gestures. We carried her, literally carried her, to my room in Arcadia House. At first she simply sat on the mattress, grinding her molars and wringing her hands, but finally she spoke, telling her manager to have the city's administrators and division heads gather in one hour at the Institute for Advanced Biological Investigations.

Not long after Dagmar's departure, the immaculoids' chanting and drumming started up again. Londa cast her livid gaze first on Colonel Fox, then on Yolly, and finally on me.

'The strategy session that matters isn't the one I just arranged,' she said. 'It's the one that's going to happen right now.'

By scouring the paramedics' station, Yolly managed to scare up everything we needed for a tea party – Earl Grey, chai, lemon, sugar, biscotti. As the tea bags steeped, Colonel Fox took out her PDA and began working the keyboard with her pen, the point striking the membrane with the precise pistoning action of a sewing-machine needle as she summoned crucial statistics to the matchbox-size screen.

'Monday afternoon, as soon as I saw those swarms of mackies, I started running the numbers,' she said. 'Our present civilian population is three thousand and seventeen. I immediately subtracted the orphans and pregnant teens, also the zombie troupers – there's no time to reprogram them for patriotism – which gave me a hypothetical fighting force of two thousand and fifty-eight, including professional staff and maintenance workers. Next I conducted an informal survey and learned that about a third of those potential defenders, six hundred and eighty-five, are prepared to take up arms and hold the fort. Naturally we can count on total commitment from my Valkyries.'

'That's maybe nine hundred against six thousand,' Yolly concluded, aghast.

Colonel Fox lifted a biscotti and set it between her teeth like a cigar stub. 'Not great odds, I grant you. But we can still win. The minute the foetuses draw blood, they'll lose public support. Even Governor Winthrop won't dare to say it's just another anti-abortion demonstration. He'll have to send the National Guard to our rescue.'

'Unless the immaculoids have already massacred us,' Yolly observed.

'And here's another factor in our favour.' Colonel Fox flipped an insouciant hand in the general direction of the mackie encampment. 'Those are pretty unhealthy creatures out there. I doubt that they can shoot straight.'

'You heard General Snow,' Yolly protested. 'Their despair makes them abnormally dangerous.'

'With all due respect, Yolly,' Colonel Fox said, 'never use the enemy's propaganda in assessing the enemy's strength.'

Londa arced her thumb and middle finger into the shape of calipers, employing the instrument to massage her temples. She lifted her head and fixed her gaze on the Valkyrie commander. 'You make a compelling case for manning the walls.' She climbed off the mattress and presented me with a meandering grin. 'Nevertheless, I've decided to follow the advice of my ethical advisor. Go ahead, Mason. Tell me what to do.'

'You're dumping the decision in *my* lap?' I said.

'I'm confident you can rise to the occasion.'

'This isn't fair.'

'Sorry, Socrates,' Londa said. 'I'm responsible for Themisopolis, and you're responsible for me. You knew it might come to this. Take a posh job tutoring a gumbo girl for a hundred dollars an hour, and eventually there'll be hell to pay.'

I felt as if my body had become fused with some sinister machine, its gyroscopes spinning in my aorta, its meshed gears nibbling at my stomach. I swallowed some tea and studied the paint-by-numbers tableau over my dresser: Jesus holding up a potential projectile, the famous unthrown first stone, inviting the vigilantes to contemplate its fearsome solidity, even as they took stock of their soggy souls.

'I've always liked that story.' I gestured towards the painting. 'It cuts through a lot of nonsense.'

'Mason used to have us act it out,' Londa told Colonel Fox. 'He played the mob leader. My friend Brittany was the adulteress, and I was—'

'Let me guess,' Colonel Fox said scornfully. 'You were the rock.'

'It's not generally known that Jesus had encountered a similar situation the week before – same adulteress, different mob,' I said, improvising wildly. 'Only he didn't intervene. He just stood and watched as a passing Pharisee told the vigilantes, "Let all the sinners gathered here start stoning the woman, while the flawless among you undertake to defend her." So the mob broke into two groups, pelters and protectors, and soon the stones were flying every which way. When the dust settled, all the pelters lay dead, but no protector had received so much as a lump on the head. And the Pharisee said, "What a glorious outcome – the defeat of the vengeful." And Jesus asked him, "What if the protectors had been slaughtered instead?" And the Pharisee replied, "That too would have been glorious – the martyrdom of the righteous." And Jesus said, "We can do better than that."'

'Listen to your conscience,' Yolly implored her sister. 'We have to make a strategic retreat.'

'If we don't fight, we'll lose the data,' Colonel Fox said with equal urgency.

'Remember how you programmed Joan of Arc?' I asked Londa. '"There are no just wars. There are no greater goods."'

'No just wars,' Yolly echoed.

'A miracle drug for ovarian cancer,' Colonel Fox said. 'The end of sexual slavery.'

Londa approached the dresser and stared into the mirror. Whether by serendipity or intention, her reflected eyes lay along the same horizon as the lush blue Protestant orbs of the Jewish rabbi.

'There's really no contest, is there?' she said.

'None at all,' I replied.

'Mason, you earned every penny of that hundred dollars an hour,' Yolly stated.

'You have a coward for a conscience,' Colonel Fox told her boss.

'By this time tomorrow,' Londa said, 'we'll all be out of here. No massacre, no martyrs, not one life squandered, and I'll be wishing I were dead.'

I lay awake for many hours, perhaps the entire night – certainly no dream came, no alligator feedings with John Snow 0001, no sea-urchin rescues with Donya. Dawn found me thrashing around beneath my blankets like the reanimated Lazarus struggling against his winding-sheet. I summoned my remaining strength and staggered to the dresser, where I studied the play of the morning sunbeams on the Gospel canvas. In this light the adulteress and her Nazarene advocate seemed positively beatific, painted not by numbers but by numinosity.

I scrambled into my clothes and packed my overnight bag, whereupon the Sisters Sabacthani appeared, Yolly looking haggard and jumpy, Londa maintaining an uneasy détente among her warring selves. Each woman had brought along a small valise, and Londa also carried a bird cage. Its outraged occupant, Quetzie, repeatedly poked his indignant snout through the bars.

'Tell me this isn't happening,' Yolly said. 'Tell me it's all a mumquat dream.'

'It's happening,' I said.

The instant the mackies issued us a cell phone, Londa explained, we would call Jordan and have her retrieve us from the state park. Apparently Londa's decision to surrender Themisopolis, which she'd represented as 'my former morality teacher's decision to surrender Themisopolis', had been well received by the medical and research personnel, who'd hastened to point out that they'd been signed on to practise healing and pursue knowledge, not to cross swords with foetuses. Several Valkyries, custodians, and groundskeepers had volunteered to stay behind and wage guerrilla war against the arsonists, but Londa had told them, 'I don't want your blood on my conscience, or my conscience's conscience either.' Of all the creatures in our care, only the zombie troupers would not be joining the retreat. They were mere machines, after all, insensate as sock puppets, and by Londa's account they had opted to remain in the city and allow the mackie flames to end their meaningless programmed lives.

I grabbed my overnight bag, and then the three of us left Arcadia House, marched across the quadrangle, and headed down Boudicca Street past the leafless, brainless ranks of trees, each elm and sycamore oblivious to its imminent incineration.

The mood at the main entrance was sombre, almost funereal. Knapsacks on their backs, suitcases by their sides, the city's entire population had collected in silent clusters of twenty and thirty. I spotted several terrariums and pet carriers – gecko, ferret, parakeet, chihuahua, tortoiseshell cat: Londa wasn't the only person who'd be saving an animal from the conflagration. Everyone spoke in whispers. To judge from their empty holsters and disgruntled deportments, the Valkyries had complied with the directive to leave their guns behind. I was pleased to note a team of paramedics ministering to our orphans and pregnant teens, making sure they all had their mittens, scarves, and medicines.

For twenty minutes we huddled in the raw morning air, stomping our feet and rubbing our hands, and then the gates opened to admit a company of three hundred heavily armed immaculoids, Lieutenant Colonel Jane Snow 3221 in command. With rude shoves, loutish punches, and the occasional coercive boot, the foetuses herded us through the portal and into a kind of open-air rat maze improvised from saw horses and quivering ribbons of barricade tape. An additional immaculoid regiment appeared, breaking us into groups of ten and forcing us to negotiate the labyrinth, until eventually we stood before a line of nylon pavilions, eight labelled 'WOMEN', four 'MEN'. Lieutenant Colonel Snow then explained that we were about to be 'processed' – checked for smuggled goods – and anyone who resisted would be 'treated as callously as our parents treated us'.

More waiting, a full hour this time, an interval during which I beheld the immaculoids climb into the forty gasoline trucks and drive them, engines gasping with diesel flatulence, through the gates towards the city's combustible heart. Goaded by the butt of an assault rifle, I followed my nine fellow evacuees into pavilion number 12, where Sergeant John Snow 0875 required us to strip down to our goose pimples. A squad of enlisted immaculoids X-rayed our innards with portable radiology gear, searching for ingested computer chips and microfilm capsules. A second squad commandeered our wristwatches, credit cards, and loose change, any of which might have been storage media in disguise. Squad number three examined our clothing, probing pockets, turning gloves inside out, inspecting every seam and cuff. A fourth cadre took out utility knives and peeled away the linings of our valises and suitcases like fur trappers skinning beavers. My overnight bag came back to me in tatters, but at least I'd passed the test, as had the rest of my group – not a single piece of contraband among us.

At long last the sergeant issued the blessed command. 'Get dressed, and no stalling!'

As the next band of ten entered the pavilion, the mackies' gun muzzles nudged us through the rear flaps. An instant later the Sisters Sabacthani emerged from pavilion 3, Londa still holding Quetzie's cage. Stupefied by the cold and grateful for the restoration of our clothes, we became putty in the hands of Lieutenant Colonel Snow and her regiment, and nobody raised the feeblest protest during our subsequent ordeal, which had us first standing around Hypatia Circle for two hours while the remaining Themisopolians were processed, then tramping four miles across frozen fields, until at last we spied a line of snow-dusted evergreens marking the eastern edge of Quehannock State Park.

The foetuses and their rifle butts continued to treat us harshly, pressing us towards our destination at a rapid clip. Upon reaching the parking lot, the Themisopolis commuters rebonded with their cars and vans, then took off, while Lieutenant Colonel Snow and her subordinates moved among the rest of us, passing out the promised technology. When Londa received her cell phone, she made a point of sidling away from the mackies, subsequently ringing up Jordan and speaking to her in a whisper. At the end of the conversation she offered Yolly a freighted nod the significance of which eluded me. I took the phone and called Natalie, but she didn't answer, so I left a message assuring her I was out of harm's way and would probably spend the night in Jordan Frazier's Georgetown apartment.

Within a half-hour the evacuation vehicles started arriving – sedans, station wagons, hatchbacks, SUVs, pickup trucks, limousines, taxis. Particularly conspicuous were the shuttles bearing the logos of various Maryland hotels and motor inns, Londa's medical staff having arranged for our orphans and outcasts to enjoy commercial lodgings until more permanent accommodation could be secured. I took comfort in the thought of our paramedics tucking these wretches in for the night, assuring them that a second City of Justice would one day rise from the ashes.

Jordan was among the last chauffeurs to appear, vaulting athletically from the cab of her Plymouth Carmilla minivan. I wanted to tell her she looked fabulous – her buoyant brown eyes and lavish smile had ceded little to the years – and how much I admired her lobbying efforts on behalf of Sabacthanite ideals. But I was so frazzled I could only give her a doleful hug and thank her for being the one bright spot in an otherwise wretched morning.

Under the immaculoids' watchful gaze, we climbed into the minivan, Yolly settling beside Jordan while Londa, Quetzie, and I assumed the back seat.

'On track with Plan Omega?' Londa asked Jordan as we cruised out of the park. 'Materiel in hand?'

'Lady Justice is looking out for us,' Jordan replied cheerfully.

Plan Omega? Materiel? The terminology of the moment made me nervous. Evidently my companions had a scheme up their collective sleeve.

'I'm confused,' I said.

'Have patience,' Londa replied.

Yolly inserted *Linda Ronstadt: Greatest Hits* into the dashboard music centre. As the Carmilla resounded with 'You're No Good' followed by 'Silver Threads and Golden Needles', Jordan piloted US to I-95, gunned the engine and sidled into the fast lane, everybody except me singing along with the tunes. By the time we reached the Havre de Grace turnoff, Ronstadt and her backup trio were belting out 'That'll Be the Day'.

Jordan followed the exit ramp to a Burrito Junction, where she parked and switched off the engine.

'Can't we do better than this?' I pleaded. God knows I was

hungry, but I wasn't in the mood for fatty ground beef enshrouded in a soggy tortilla.

'We aren't here to eat,' Londa explained. 'We're here to use the restrooms. Let's say we get into our disguises in ten minutes max – OK, gang?'

'Disguises?' I said.

Londa squeezed my knee. 'On her way to pick us up, Jordan bought everything we'll need to turn ourselves into immaculoids. Orange jumpsuits, silver wigs, greasepaint.'

'I could find only three suits,' Jordan said, 'but as your getaway driver, I don't really need one.'

'Getaway driver?' I said.

'Last night we burned three hundred gigabytes on to sixty CD-Rs and hid them inside our statue of Themis,' Londa explained. 'Not the first place the mackies will think of looking, but not the last either, so the sooner we three go fetch the data the better.'

'Including me?' I said.

'The plan turns on us having as many Sabacthanites as possible inside the city,' Jordan said.

'Sounds dangerous,' I noted.

'Only if we do something amazingly stupid,' Londa said.

'We can count on you, right, Mason?' Yolly asked.

Of course they couldn't count on me. Who did they think I was, Anthony Quinn in *The Guns of Navarone*? 'I would say we need *two* getaway drivers,' I suggested.

'Sheesh,' Jordan exclaimed.

'I'm a philosopher,' I said, 'not a fucking commando.'

Londa unsnapped her seatbelt, curling one arm around Quetzie's cage, the other around my shoulder. 'Hey, Socrates, don't you recognise a second chance when you see one? Help us get those CD-Rs, and the world will forgive you for cooking up Dame Quixote.'

It wasn't merely the carrot of redemption that sent me to the Burrito Junction men's room that afternoon. The ovarian-cancer drug also figured in my reasoning, as did the slave traffickers. Initially I did a lousy job, applying the greasepaint so liberally I looked like a leper, but by rubbing the stuff away with paper towels I eventually acquired the pocked complexion Plan Omega required. Before returning to the minivan, I donned my silver wig and studied my face in the mirror. An ageing mackie stared back at me – not a generic ageing mackie, but the one whose features I knew best, the former inhabitant of an abandoned Boston switch tower. If I could believe his dying words, John Snow 0001 would have refused to join the imminent burning of Themisopolis. He was a highly principled foetus, a fact of which his semifather would always be proud.

CHAPTER 12

To sneak into the occupied city on a mission whose unmasking would surely occasion our deaths; to lay hold of the treasure without drawing the attention of six thousand watchful foetuses; to spirit the data away the instant the immaculoids turned their backs, was a foolhardy plan indeed, bound to spark tension and discord within our ad hoc commando unit, and so I was hardly surprised when a heated argument erupted between the Sisters Sabacthani. Londa, the reckless rationalist, wanted Jordan to drive right up to the city gates, on the theory that the mackies would be too distracted to note the incursion. Yolly, the sensible sybarite, insisted that we park at least a mile from the ramparts. Better safe than sorry. Just when it seemed the women might come to blows, Jordan resolved the controversy by stopping the van at a spot she insisted was the precise Pythagorean midpoint between Londa's impetuosity and Yolly's prudence.

At three o'clock, eight hours after our captors had marched us through the police-tape labyrinth, Jordan presented Londa with a Phillips screwdriver, Yolly with a cell phone, and me with a knapsack full of Gatorade and cereal bars. Itching beneath our foetal patinas, we dashed down Avalon Lane past the dormant cherry trees until we reached the mackie encampment. Now Londa increased the pace, leading us through the grid of tents and pavilions to the parking lot. Running faster still, we swerved among the moving vans, buses, and semi-rigs, the air growing ever thicker with the aggressive aroma of gasoline. At last the great portal loomed up, its bronze gates hanging open, doubtless so the foetuses could make a quick retreat if the conflagration got out of hand. The noxious fumes became sharper yet, scoring our tonsils, and scouring our lungs.

A final sprint, and we were inside the city. The scene I beheld was so appalling that for a moment I simply stood and stared, frozen in begrudging awe of CHALICE and its foetal minions. Having attached auxiliary pumps, hoses, and nozzles to the forty gasoline trucks, the immaculoids were busily siphoning this liquid munificence and releasing it in wild ejaculatory spurts. Whatever one thought of Enoch Anthem and Felix Pielmeister, they were consummate apocalypticians, men who could envision a Judgement Day of surpassing surrealism and render it in fossil fuel.

Normally the city's sewer system would have channelled the deluge underground, but the mackies had stoppered all the gratings so that slowly, inexorably, the gasoline collected in the streets, the puddles fringed by iridescent rainbows. My brain seemed to float free of my body, a neural balloon. Despite the urgency of our situation, or perhaps because of it, the women started squabbling again, Yolly insisting that we proceed at the immaculoids' characteristically crippled gait, Londa arguing that we should run like mad. The right tactic soon become apparent: we needn't limp at all, the mackies were far too busy constructing their holocaust to notice impostors in their midst.

We charged down Shambhala Avenue, weaving among the ever expanding petroleum pools, and a few minutes later arrived in Alethia Square. Resolute as ever, bronze heart throbbing with her undying devotion to fairness, Themis held her motorised balance scales aloft. The fumes pursued us like vengeful ghosts. Londa dropped to her knees before the statue like a pagan supplicant worshipping an idol, then took out the screwdriver and fitted it into a screw holding the access plate to the pedestal. She rotated her wrist. The screw resisted. She cursed and increased the torque. The screw surrendered. My headache spread through its bony enclosure, colonising every sinus. Londa loosened all four screws and the access plate hit the flagstones. She thrust the screwdriver into the hollow, triggering the emergency shut-off mechanism. The balance scales ceased oscillating, as if, after all these years, Lady Justice, had finally reached an equitable decision. From the depths of the pedestal Londa retrieved a crumpled Kevlar satchel, hugging it to her breast.

The blocked sewers were turning the city into a nightmare Venice, the canals swollen with dark seething torrents of Regular, Plus, and Supreme. From these ghastly waterways there now arose a shimmering gallery of hydrocarbon mirages. I pulled out a Gatorade bottle and took a big gulp, seeking to wash the cretaceous taste from my mouth. My eyes swam with tears and my dizziness increased. A blackout seemed imminent, but I fought to forestall it, chewing the insides of my cheeks and slapping my brow with the flat of my hand.

Yolly yanked the cell phone from her jumpsuit. Evidently the immaculoids had shut off the EMP, for she reached Jordan without difficulty, telling her to expect us back shortly. 'The data's in hand,' she informed her guardian, at which instant the foetuses, having set their torches ablaze, thrust them into the gasoline.

In a blinding flash the canals caught fire, then flowed together in a confluence of infernos that soon erected a wall of roaring flame between the city gates and ourselves. A great swell of scalding air rolled towards us like a boiling tsunami. We dropped to the flagstones. For a full minute we lay prone in the courtyard, gasping and coughing, while Londa explained that we had only one option. We must make our way to the Circus of Atonement and hide in the basement ontogenerator until the firestorm passed.

'The vat's lined with ceramic tiles,' she noted. 'Heat resistant as hell's hinges.'

Clutching the satchel fiercely, Londa lurched to her feet and led us on a frantic dash down Boudicca Street. Billows of smoke filled the sky, vast and black as the clouds whose cache had scrubbed Noah's contemporaries from the earth. Cinders flew everywhere like squalls of demonic snow. Insectile sparks stung our cheeks and brows.

As we drew within sight of the Circus, Yolly called Jordan again, informing her of the obvious fact that Themisopolis was burning, and the equally obvious fact that thus far we'd avoided incineration – a circumstance we intended to prolong by taking refuge in the ontogenerator. Next Londa got on the phone, telling Jordan to move to the nearest hotel and stand ready to retrieve us at a moment's notice.

The plaza outside the rotunda was unexpectedly crowded. Galvanised by whatever survival instinct had leaked into their algorithms, the circus troupers had armed themselves and fled the building – a sensible step, but insufficient, for their path was blocked by a foetal battalion, one hundred strong. Clearly a massacre was in the offing, the immaculoids' assault rifles being considerably more powerful than the troupers' theatrical props. Joan of Arc wielded her sword, Pope John Paul II his crozier, Davy Crockett his Kentucky rifle, Edward Teller his flagellant's whip. Mary Baker Eddy had emerged into daylight accompanied by her band of audio-animatronic victims, all of whom had evidently forgiven her, for they pressed protectively around her like a bodyguard of midgets. Fresh from their church wedding, Percival Sarnac and Leopold Ransom brandished gold altar crosses, which they evidently intended to use as cudgels. The most poorly outfitted performers were Warren Anderson, Henry Kissinger, and Ronald Reagan, their only weapons being spindly aluminium stands stolen from the circus's lighting system.

Sensing her authority and perhaps also remembering her victories, the troupers rallied to Joan of Arc's side. For a fleeting instant the maid and I exchanged glances of mutual recognition, acknowledging our moment of choreographed passion.

'There are no just wars!' she exclaimed in obedience to her DUNCE cap programming. 'There are no greater goods!'

So intense was the immaculoids' delight in having an entire theatre company to annihilate, they simply ignored Londa, Yolly, and myself as we slipped behind the Maid of Orléans's rag-tag army. Reaching the rotunda entrance, we paused to survey the battle. It was predictably quick and entirely brutal. Anderson, Kissinger, and Reagan were the first to fall, blasted to pieces as they attempted to poke out their assailants' eyes. The foetuses fired again, killing Sarnac and Ransom, and then came the third volley, raining down on my poor Joan and leaving her as perforated as Saint Sebastian after the archers had martyred him. More bullets flew. Before succumbing to their wounds, the Pope managed to cosh a foetus with his crozier, Crockett shot one between the eyes, and Mrs Eddy issued a piercing battle cry, ordering her entourage into the fray. The audio-animatronic children fought bravely, collectively dragging a mackie to the ground before salvos of lead separated them from their electric intestines.

Throughout the slaughter I occasionally glanced at Londa, who seemed proud that her troupers were displaying such fortitude in the face of the mackie host. Even before the butchery ended, I realised that, while she still detested the primal Ronald Reagan, the original Warren Anderson, and all their Phyllistine kind, their repentant reincarnations had emerged in her eyes as brave and even noble beings. As we slipped into the Circus, Londa looked over her shoulder, eager to glimpse her slain creations one last time before their bodies turned to ash.

Many are the conditions under which a man might relish intimate confinement with a comely heterosexual woman and her polymorphous-perverse sister, but I soon realised that my interval in the Themisopolis ontogenerator would not be one of them. Londa and Yolly hated the situation no less than I. True, they had experienced these sweltering diving bells before, not so much from their prenatal immersions as from the deliberate descent they'd made with Donya in Torre de la Carne several months after their mother's funeral, an episode they now proceeded to relate in detail. Nothing in their previous experience, however, had prepared them for this premature burial with its benumbing boredom, unrelieved claustrophobia, and requirement that we twist ourselves into poses suggesting some sadistic school of yoga.

But for our battery-operated fan, its feeble plastic vanes plying the glutinous air like spatulas stirring mud, languidly expelling the vat's stale atmosphere through the vent in the hatch, we might well have suffocated. Hour after hour we sat on our haunches, simmering like meatballs in a crock pot, as the billowing flames consumed the city. Yolly tried contacting Jordan again, but the call did not go through. Even as it saved our skins, the ontogenerator blocked all communication with the outside world.

We slaked our thirst courtesy of Gatorade, assuaged our hunger with the cereal bars, and preserved our sanity by telling stories. For my own contribution I drew upon Edmund Spenser's epic, recounting the Red Cross Knight's three-day battle with the great dragon, scourge of Faerie Land. When Londa's turn came, she elaborated the misdeeds of the Phyllistines she'd been intending to put in the Circus: Ethan Pepperhill, of course, as well as Pol Pot, Idi Amin, Slobodan Milosevic, and Joseph Stalin, assuming the necessary grave-robbing arrangements could be made. Our stellar performer, predictably, was Yolly, who told us the plot of her evolving fantasy novel. Set in Ondoluria, a feudal world where books were living creatures, 'The Citadel of Paradox' followed a band of adventurers – three men and four women, ever eager to enter into various carnal configurations with one another – who'd undertaken a long, perilous, continent-spanning quest to heal the sole and sickly copy of the *Epistemologia*, a protoplasmic encyclopedia containing the whole of human and divine knowledge.

'So what do you think?' Yolly said upon finishing her presentation. 'Am I on the right track?'

'A very Yolly sort of epic,' Londa said approvingly, and indeed it was, full of horses and eros and the juices of life.

'Maybe the quest should be part of a larger narrative,' I suggested. 'Once your adventurers have restored the book to health, they attempt to decipher it, and just when they're about to give up, a cosmic Rosetta Stone falls into their laps.'

'I like that,' Yolly said.

'What sort of knowledge does the book contain?' Londa asked. 'The periodic table of the elements? Maxwell's equations? The Beatitudes?'

'All of the above, I should imagine,' Yolly said, stroking the green satchel. 'Not to mention a cure for ovarian cancer and a map disclosing the whereabouts of every sexual-slave trade in the galaxy.'

On the morning of the third day, we decided to take the risk and test the air beyond the ontogenerator. The instant we popped the hatch, an agile breeze wafted into the vat, cooling our cheeks and brows. A gust from the gods, I decided – a breath from noble Horus. The inferno, it seemed, had burned itself out.

As we ascended to street level, Yolly called Jordan on the cell phone, telling her to jump in the van and drive like a maniac. Before us lay a lunar plain, bleak, shattered, sterile. Emerging from our titanium womb we had entered a void. We had been born into death. The fire had gutted the buildings, blasted the trees, and turned the gasoline trucks into amorphous lumps of metal. Galaxies of particulate matter swirled everywhere, their motes dancing like cathode-ray static. An unnamable sensation screwed through my nasal passages, a stench compound of evil resins, depraved plastics and polymers.

Like survivors shambling away from a crashed jetliner, we stepped uncertainly across the Circus plaza, moving past the charred bodies of the zombie troupers. Poor Joan of Orléans – twice born, twice burned. We headed down Boudicca Street, Londa hunched protectively over the Kevlar satchel like a mother shielding her infant from a rainstorm. Caedmon Hall, Arcadia House, the Vision Syndicate, the Artemis Clinic, and the Institute for Advanced Biological Investigations had all been reduced to naked matrices of blackened beams and melted girders. Waves of ash rolled across the scorched terrain in a vast unnavigable sea.

Gradually we became aware of the immaculoids, most of them now corpses, having variously succumbed to asphyxiation, dehydration, and the defects bequeathed them by incompetent CHALICE technicians. Of the remaining mackies barely fifty were still standing, wandering amidst the cinders like extras in a cinematic collaboration between George Romero and Martin Heidegger: *Dasein of the Dead*. The other survivors floated upon the ocean of ash, gagging and thrashing as the grey pools sucked them down.

In time our fitful journey brought us to Alethia Square. Themis had fallen, her bronze knees turned to butter by the heat. The blindfolded goddess lay supine in the courtyard, staring up at the winter sky. Curious, I touched her sword – still warm – whereupon a series of sharp reports reached my ears, pop, pop, pop, pop.

At first I thought it was an automobile backfiring – could Jordan be here already? – or perhaps a metallic echo caused by the cooling of Themis's hollow innards. Then I glanced at Yolly. For an instant she simply stood there, jerking like a gaffed fish. A sound of primal dismay, more animal than human, broke from Londa's throat. Yolly pitched forward and collapsed on the flagstones beside the statue's massive head.

I spun, glancing in all directions, but no sniper caught my eye. Londa tossed the satchel aside, sprinted to the statue and, falling to her knees, cradled her spasming sister.

'Get it out!' Yolly cried.

Lurching forward, I melded with the pietà. Just below Yolly's left shoulder a ragged wound blossomed like a carnation, petals of blood spreading outward from the axis. Her complexion grew white as alabaster.

'Jordan's coming!' I insisted, squeezing Yolly's hand. 'We're taking you to the hospital!' – the very words I'd spoken to my netherson five days earlier.

'It burns!' Blood dribbled from Yolly's mouth like the effluence of a punctured scream. 'Get it out!'

'We'll get it out!' Londa shouted.

'It burns!'

Yolly's fingers turned to ice and her eyes rolled upwards.

Foetal snorts filled the air. Pivoting away from Yolly's lifeless face, I glanced once again across the square. As smoke poured from the muzzle of his assault rifle, General John Snow 4099 came gimping down Shambhala Avenue, the last of the immaculoids, manifestly pleased that he'd recognised us beneath our disintegrating disguises. I estimated I had fifteen seconds to live. No philosophical truths flitted through my brain. I did not learn the veracity or falsity of Platonic idealism. I did not see God. I merely let out a yelp of despair and vomited on to the flagstones.

Were it not for Londa's next action – grabbing the satchel and hurling it towards the approaching foetus – we would surely have died then and there, joining Yolly and the circus troupers on Corporate Christi's roster of victims. General Snow fell instantly upon the green bag, tearing it to pieces. Soon sixty shining CD-

Rs lay strewn around the courtyard like wafers baked for a post-industrial Eucharist. Next the mackie went to work with his rifle butt, an assiduous alchemist grinding pestle against mortar, so that the disks became a thousand glittering shards.

Acting on raw instinct, Londa and I pulled Yolly's body to a standing position and laid it athwart our shoulders. We began our retreat, hurrying along Shambhala Avenue as the satisfied snarls of the dying foetus grew fainter. Passing through the city gates, we staggered across the parking lot and entered the mackie encampment, except there was no parking lot, no encampment, only my Heideggerian hallucination, a bottomless abyss swallowing the tents, pavilions, howitzers, hydraulic lifts, moving vans, buses, semi-rigs, cherry trees, and fountains. One instant Jordan was there, standing beside her minivan, staring at Londa and me and Yolly's corpse, and the next she was gone, consumed along with Avalon Lane and Hypatia Circle and Patuxent State Park. As the illusory vortex ingested me, I briefly wondered what precise portion of the universe would satisfy its appetite. The answer, of course, lay somewhere in the *Epistemologia*, that omniscient anthology with its recipes for ambrosia, spells for raising the dead, and compendium of methods by which a philosopher might commit suicide without effort or pain. I merely had to crack the spine and read.

These days many historians and social commentators perceive a tragic grandeur in the fall of Themisopolis. According to this theory, Londa and Yolly Sabacthani were too spiritually advanced to prosper in the mundane world, their vision too noble to survive the slings and arrows of Corporate Christi. The destruction of the city, the loss of the data, the murder of Yolly: these disasters were inevitable given the rarefied plane on which the sisters' souls resided.

While I would award this interpretation high marks for romanticism, I personally favour a more prosaic argument. In my view, Londa and Yolly made the banal and common mistake of underestimating the opposition. The vatlings' tragedy lay not in their presumed surfeit of purity, but in their failure to appreciate the enemy's surplus ruthlessness.

237

Unlike her superstar twin, Yolly had never been accorded her own action figure, trading cards, board game, or comic-book series, and yet she was a celebrity in her own right, and I was not surprised when her death made the front page of the *Bel Air Gazette*, the *Baltimore Sun*, and the *Washington Post*, plus several hundred other papers. Predictably, Maryland's Governor Winthrop told the reporters that Yolly had 'died accidentally when a legitimate anti-abortion protest went awry', and at the time Londa, Jordan, and I were too dazed and depleted to offer a rebuttal. Instead we simply huddled in Jordan's Georgetown apartment, trying to reweave the unravelled threads of our lives.

Throughout this wretched period the emotional atmosphere among us was, to say the least, tempestuous. Jordan blamed Londa for talking her into Plan Omega, and me for not talking Londa out of it. Londa reviled her former tutor for giving her such a malignantly idealistic psyche, even as she faulted Jordan for making Yolly only slightly less obsessed. As for me, I alternately heaped scorn on Londa for thinking up the whole crazy Omega scheme and abuse on Jordan for facilitating it.

When not trading accusations with my roommates, I instinctively sought solace in Natalie, telephoning her every morning and afternoon, but I never caught her at home. The one time she called back, leaving a message expressing her sorrow over Yolly's death and her frustration that we weren't getting hold of each other, I was down the street buying whole-wheat bread and red wine, the staples of our unhappy community.

In deference to Yolly, we all agreed to suspend our mutual antipathy long enough to select a burial site – an easy task, as it happened. Two years earlier, on a pellucid October afternoon, Yolly and Jordan had gone hiking together around Parnassus Acres, the West Virginia horse farm where Oyster was spending his dotage. When they reached the cherry grove, Yolly had casually mentioned that in the world of her novel, an Ondolurian normally arranged to be buried in an orchard, so that his remains might nourish the trees, and his descendants continue to know him in the succulent person of apples, pears, peaches, figs, or plums.

Parnassus Acres belonged to a divorcee named Sally Quattrone, a middle-aged neo-hippie who practised yoga, meditation, and other disciplines that, in her neighbours' eyes, verged on sexual perversion. When we approached Sally with the idea of interring Yolly among the cherry trees, she was understandably nonplussed, but then we gave her the extant pages of 'The Citadel of Paradox' – Jordan had kept a printout in her apartment, reading it with an eye to one day offering Yolly a critique – and a single perusal was sufficient to win Sally over. She would happily facilitate our scheme, providing we didn't harm any roots, a point she underscored with a quotation from the novel celebrating 'those fleshy fibrous anchors binding Tolvaganum the Oak to Goncelia the Earth, and Goncelia the Earth to Tolvaganum the Oak'.

Two burly Valkyries helped us dig the grave, a familiar enough task for them: six days earlier they'd driven their shovels into the frozen ground of White Marsh Cemetery in prelude to disinterring Ethan Pepperhill. After wrapping Yolly's remains in a shroud, Jordan, Londa, and I lowered the corpse into the cavity, threading it through the tangle of roots. The task proved emotionally draining for both women, and they immediately fled the scene, leaving the Valkyries and myself to restore the dirt.

Twenty-four hours before the scheduled memorial service, Henry, Brock, and Donya flew from Key West to DC and checked into the Mayflower Hotel. I could hardly imagine a sadder set of circumstances under which the Hubris Academy faculty might hold a reunion, and yet the arrival of the Isla de Sangre contingent had an immediate and salutary effect. Simply knowing that the youngest Sister Sabacthani was in town inspired Londa, Jordan, and me to stop quarrelling and cultivate a more seemly grief.

On the morning of the funeral, we all met for breakfast at an art-deco café near Jordan's apartment. My male colleagues had come through the decade unspoiled. Far from diminishing his good looks, Brock's wrinkles actually augmented his aura of bohemian rascality. Henry's billowing paunch struck me less as a sign of laxity than as a deliberately acquired enhancement. He arrived bearing good news. After years of being strung along by various Nickelodeon executives, he'd just learned that the current regime had loved, absolutely loved, his concept for *Uncle Rumpus's Magic Island*, and they were equally enamoured of his sample scripts. As soon as Donya was safely installed in the freshman class at Yale, her guardians would head to New York City, Henry to attend a series of pre-production meetings, Brock to start designing Plessey the Plesiosaur, Siegfried the Snapping Turtle, Basso Profundo the Bullfrog, and the rest of Uncle Rumpus's friends.

The instant I laid eyes on Donya, I realised I'd been wrong to stay away from Isla de Sangre all these years. In maturing from a freckled preschooler to a feline eighteen-year-old, she'd become the spitting image of the adolescent Londa – lithe, graceful, tall as a sunflower – but the resemblance, thank heaven, was confined to the physical. She had none of Londa's scary intensity, none of the fervour that had raised and then razed Themisopolis. It was hard to believe that the self-possessed young woman now sitting before me eating a vegetarian omelette had once threatened to sever her little finger in protest against the outcome of a croquet game.

We finished our breakfast, climbed into Jordan's van, and drove to Parnassus Acres, where Dagmar Röhrig and Vetruvia Fox joined our mournful company. Somehow Londa's disciples had got wind of the imminent ritual, and about three hundred were waiting for us, wearing Weltanschauung Woman sweatshirts and Dame Quixote baseball caps. Patiently but firmly, Colonel Fox explained to the acolytes that gate-crashing the service would be a poor way to honour either sister, and so the Sabacthanites retreated to the adjacent dairy farm, where they milled around smoking dope, strumming guitars, and singing songs from Pischel and Ploog's Tony Award-winning rock opera about Londa, *Doctor Madonna*.

For several minutes the six of us stood in the orchard and said nothing, the communal aphasia of the bereaved, and then the ceremony officially began with Jordan reading a passage from 'The Citadel of Paradox' in which a vain prince suddenly grasps the inner beauty of the hideous toads of Nobdagob Bog, 'who asked nothing of the world save mud and methane, swamp and solitude'. Henry came forward next, setting a bouquet of amaranth on the grave, after which Londa recited Emily Dickinson's 'Because I Could Not Stop for Death'. In turn I offered up my favourite

240

stanza of all time, Lord Byron's '"She walks in beauty like the night / Of cloudless climes and starry skies; / And all that's best of dark and bright / Meet in her aspect and her eyes ...'

The instant he'd heard the news, Brock had sculpted a piece of Blood Island driftwood into a little horse, and now he used Sally Quattrone's trowel to plant this elegant eohippus several inches down, beneath a rock that marked the spot – I could guide his hand with confidence – where Yolly's heart lay.

Shivering in her windbreaker, tears trickling down her face like meltwater from an icicle, Donya delivered an oration she'd composed the night before, a verbal collage assembled from email exchanges with her elder sister. Repeatedly, with great patience, Yolly had explained to Donya why there was no shame in being a gumbo girl, and she'd also helped her little sister undertake an Internet search for Edwina's mother and father – that is to say, Donya's mother and father, and Yolly's too, and Londa's. Before they died, Francine Sabacthani, née Miller, and her husband, Arthur Sabacthani, had been high-school biology teachers, dedicated to their profession, beloved by their students, and bewildered that their only child had turned out to be a genius.

Not long after Donya's tribute ended, Londa slipped away without explanation. Although Dagmar insisted that Londa simply needed to be alone for a while, Donya soon grew fretful. Perhaps her remaining sister was going to shoot herself, she speculated, or maybe she intended to jump into quicksand.

My search took nearly an hour, and by the time it ended the sun was setting, gilding the trees and thickening the shadows. I found Londa sitting by a brook whose sparkling course marked the border between Parnassus Acres and the neighbouring dairy farm. Having constructed a cairn on the bank, she was now systematically disassembling the pile and throwing the stones into the water.

'I love Donya,' she said without looking up. 'And I love Jordan too, and Henry and Brock, and when you're not being a jerk, I even love you. But I loved Yolly most of all.'

'Of course.'

'Tell me I didn't kill her.'

'You didn't kill her.'

'I killed her.' She hurled a stone. It bounced off a drifting log and plopped into the brook.

'No. It was the mackie.' I glanced towards the far shore. A scarecrow stood guard over a barren field – not a gaunt Ray Bolger off to see the Wizard, but a joyless sentry stuffed with corncobs. 'You probably feel like murdering Pielmeister right now.'

'If I'm an honest woman, then I must look my morality teacher in the eye and say, "You're right, sir. I want to see Pielmeister dead, buried and eaten by maggots. Likewise Anthem, Governor Winthrop, and the rest."' Our gazes met. 'You'll be happy to hear I'm planning a different destiny for the Phyllistines. It's fine to love your enemies, but it's even better to *cure* them, wouldn't you say?'

'Not necessarily.'

'Curing is better than loving.'

'Maybe. I don't know. Let's go back to the funeral.'

Seizing the handiest rock, she wound up her arm like a gaucho preparing to unleash a bolas. 'Watch me, Socrates. Watch me take a lump of enlightenment and plant it in that scarecrow's brain.'

'Donya's worried sick about you.'

She released the rock, and it flew across the brook, coming to rest exactly where she'd predicted, north of the scarecrow's nose, south of his dome, like David's missile lodging in Goliath's brow.

'Bull's-eye, Socrates. I knocked out his pineal gland and replaced it with a vastly superior one. The pineal gland is a divine organ, the locus of the human soul. Your friend Descartes revealed that to the world.'

'Not his finest hour. The man was no neurologist.'

'I just did to that scarecrow what you did to me. I gave him a soul. Now he's cured.'

I made no reply, but took Londa's hand and led her away from the brook. The closer we drew to the orchard, the more certain I became that no seer or sibyl would ever step forward to bless Londa's plan to rehabilitate the Phyllistines. Unfavourable stars hung over the enterprise, disapproving runes. And yet, when Donya ran across the field and threw her arms around both of us, I suddenly became convinced that, for her surviving sister's sake, my vatling would reject this nascent scheme, and all such demented projects to come. Before the year was out, I told myself, any visitor to Londa's abode would hear a biblical verse that she'd inadvertently added to Quetzie's repertoire.

'Let us reason together,' the feathered reptile would say. '*Cogito ergo sum*, and all you need is love, and Mason is a genius, and let us reason together.'

PART THREE

Prometheus Wept

CHAPTER 13

I know what you're thinking, ladies and gentlemen. The instant I heard Londa speak of transplanting superior pineal glands into the Phyllistines' brains, I should have realised that the loss of Yolly, Themisopolis, and the omnibenevolent data had warped her in ways that went well beyond mere bereavement or simple rage. Were I not close to madness myself in those days, I would have contacted some avatar of the law and explained that the most benign of Londa's selves, the rational and circumspect Scarlet Darwinist, had evidently perished along with her younger sister. Keep an eye on Dr Sabacthani, I would have pleaded. Observe her night and day. She has ceded her psyche to the sinister Crimson Kantian. But instead of alerting the agents of justice, I limped back home to Boston and attempted to get on with my life.

Perceptive readers that you are, you may already have deduced why Natalie made only a perfunctory effort to contact me during my sojourn in Jordan's Georgetown apartment. But I remained clueless. It never occurred to me that my wife had better – that is to say, worse – things to do with her time.

His name was Castorp Muller, his parents having suffered from an unfortunate preoccupation with *The Magic Mountain*, and he was both a Hawthorne MFA candidate in fiction, endlessly noodling with his half-written, half-assed, wholly autobiographical novel, and a member of the Tuesday night reading group Natalie had organised several months after the abortion. The sea change in their relationship traced to the club's decision to read *Ship of Fools*: an incendiary choice, as it happened, splitting the membership into a postmodern contingent obsessed with Katherine Anne Porter's gender, and a humanist faction who believed that refracting the novel through a feminist lens trivialised the author's larger artistic accomplishment. Eventually these exchanges became so heated that, following each formal meeting at the Caffeine Fiend, everyone would head for the Shepherd's Pie to cool down with lager and stout. At first this drinking society comprised all nine *Ship of Fools* enthusiasts, but in time the demands of academic life reduced their number to five, then three, until finally the party comprised a volatile total of two.

Already a hero in Natalie's eyes for having taken the feminist side in the Katherine Anne Porter controversy, Castorp Muller boasted the additional virtue of seeming to enjoy her conversation unreservedly. On only one occasion was I privileged to observe the man in action, but the memory remains vivid. Natalie and I had run into him, looking spiffily world-weary in his goatee, red bandana, and black fisherman's sweater, at the Coolidge Cinema's weekly midnight revival of *The Adventures of Buckaroo Banzai*. After the show the three of us retired to a nearby bistro, where I soon apprehended the fellow's talent for ostensibly hanging on to Natalie's every word, his uncanny ability to interrupt her so subtly that she never even noticed. I should have thrown in the towel immediately. Here was a man who could bring a woman to orgasm simply by listening to her.

As their Tuesday night ritual progressed from a pleasant diversion to the week's most passionately anticipated event, the conversation between Castorp and Natalie inevitably focused on John Snow's presence in her life. Apparently Castorp's self-centred empathy enabled Natalie to get through each new phase of the crisis – our netherson's sudden advent, his increasingly abusive behaviour, his unexpected Christmas visit, his final disposition in a ceramic urn atop our bookcase. But Castorp the fiction-writer began to conceive a broader narrative. By way of helping Natalie discover her heart's own truth, he encouraged her to free-associate like a neurotic on Freud's couch, and before long they had collaboratively constructed a story in which I was the villain and she the victim.

According to the Muller–Novak version of her tribulations, she had wanted to bring the baby to term, but she knew I would never forgive myself if anything bad happened to her during the pregnancy. In other words, her decision to abort was a submission to my will. But for my paranoid attitude towards her blood clots, she would now be enjoying unequivocal motherhood. Instead she'd become the object of her unborn child's infinite scorn.

At some point during the siege of Themisopolis, this cute couple began savouring illicit afternoons in Castorp's apartment, a situation that Natalie successfully – and, I'm chagrined to report, effortlessly – kept under wraps for two whole months following my return. Ever looking for a way to break the bad news, she finally got an opportunity courtesy of the same reading group that had blessed her with Castorp. Arriving home one evening after drumming Victorian Poetry into several dozen pairs of indifferent undergraduate ears, she noticed that idle curiosity had prompted me to remove the seminar's current selection, Harry Mulisch's *The Procedure*, from the coffee table. Years ago at Villanova I'd been assigned this neglected but beguiling moral fable, in which Mulisch takes a twelfth-century Kabbalist's ambition to create a clay golem and cleverly counterpoints it with a contemporary Dutch biologist's success in wringing organic molecules from the same substance. Natalie immediately plucked the book from my hands and recited a passage concerning Rabbi Löw's attempt to enlist his son-in-law, Isaac, in the momentous project.

'"Isaac's hair and beard are red as a blazing fire,"' she read, '"which seems to point to an ecstatic character, but the opposite is the case. Esther, Löw's daughter, also found that out too late; but that's nothing out of the ordinary, since virtually everyone marries the wrong person."'

She closed *The Procedure* and said, 'Is Mulisch right? Does virtually everyone marry the wrong person?'

'I recently saw a statistic suggesting that mutually satisfying marriages are not the norm,' I said.

'There's something I've been meaning to tell you. I believe I married the wrong person.'

I chuckled in amusement. She laughed in distress.

'In fact, I *know* I married the wrong person,' Natalie continued, whereupon I began to feel sick, and then it all spilled out, the trysts with Castorp, the joys of having a friend who would rather talk to her than read Kierkegaard, my determination to manoeuvre her into the abortion clinic, my failure to comfort her adequately when John Snow 0001 was calling her a murderer, my initial resistance to bringing the immaculoid's ashes home.

I freely admitted that these accusations were not without merit, which of course did me no good, since this wasn't about my shortcomings – it was about Natalie being in love with Castorp. We wandered into the living room and took up positions on opposite sides of the couch, goalies in that most ancient of sports, domestic discord. For the next four hours we vilified one another as our marriage burned down all around us. At the dismal hour of 2 a.m. my desperation peaked, and I declared that I would seek out Dr Charnock and convince him to fashion an infant from John Snow 0001's bottled ashes so that we would have our son again. Natalie reminded me that we'd never regarded the immaculoid as our son, and this was no time to start pretending otherwise.

'You're taking this much harder than I'd imagined,' she said. 'Look at it this way. Now you're free to go chasing after Londa. You've always been half in love with her.'

'Londa is a deeply disturbed person. You're the one I love.'

'Mason, I'm willing to sit here and talk till dawn, but we'll just keep covering the same ground.'

'You want to be with Castorp right now, don't you?' I said.

'More than you can imagine.'

'At least you're being truthful. Philosophers appreciate the truth. Please lie to me. Please tell me I have a chance.'

'It's over, Mason. Sorry. I'm so crazy about Castorp, I can hardly stop singing.'

At the methodical pace of a pallbearer I rose from the couch, walked to the bookcase, and with both hands took hold of our foetus's brittle sarcophagus.

'Don't do something you'll regret later,' she said.

'Fuck you.'

I raised the urn high above my head and sent it on a collision course with the hardwood floor. The moment of impact was gratifyingly spectacular, ten thousand glittery splinters radiating outwards from the impact point. I thought of bombs exploding, universes expanding, paradigms shifting. With a demented cackle

I dropped to my knees and, reaching into the rubble, closed my fist around a scraggly carbon nodule.

'I hope you and Castorp have lots of children.' Rising, I assumed the posture of a catapult. 'I hope you have so many goddamn children the *Catholic Worker* names you Baby Factory of the Year.'

'Mason, don't,' she said between gritted teeth.

'Heads up, Natalie! John is coming to get you!'

I laughed and launched the projectile. The lumpish remains found their target, splattering across Natalie's chest. She screamed and called me a piece of shit, a not inaccurate evaluation under the circumstances, then stormed out of the apartment. There could be no doubt concerning her destination.

It took us a mere five weeks to legalise our enmity. The Commonwealth of Massachusetts had long ago recognised the pragmatic concept of no-fault divorce, which during the course of our negotiations I started calling recursive-blame divorce, and because our mutual assets were few and our children non-existent, the whole process set us back only three hundred dollars each. When it was over, we shook hands on the steps of the Massachusetts State House, wished one another well, returned to our separate domiciles – Natalie and Castorp had just bought a condo on Beacon Hill – and set about the business of never seeing each other again.

The rest of my winter passed in three unrelated activities: feeling sorry for myself, presiding perfunctorily over Pieces of Mind, and appearing before Virgil Harkness's Congressional Commission on Foetal Activism. Although his heart wasn't in it, Senator Harkness had hastily convened his panel upon realising that for most Americans the immaculoid phenomenon had proved impossibly distressing, and these shaken citizens wanted the government to protect them from any future invasions. The initial sessions were televised, but C-Span viewers soon found them unpalatable (too much talk about mackies driving their quasiparents to suicide), and so the network began broadcasting the far livelier Chaffey Hearings into allegations that certain gratuitously compassionate physicians in Pennsylvania were systematically violating the Mother Teresa Anti-Euthanasia Laws. Somewhere in my disorganised cache of DVDs is the C-Span coverage of a bitter Londa, a shattered Jordan, and a depressed Mason presenting their testimony to Harkness and his colleagues. Among the highlights of this colloquy is a sound bite of Londa admitting that her now defunct Institute for Advanced Biological Investigations had 'acquired an RXL-313 ontogenerator with an eye to conducting human-duplication experiments' and forthwith urging the committee to 'excavate this treacherous device from the ashes of Themisopolis and oversee its destruction'. The C-span video also includes a brief image of Jordan imploring Harkness to hunt down the 'self-righteous criminals' who, through their foetal proxy General John Snow 4099, had 'murdered Yolly Sabacthani in cold blood'. But my favourite clip shows me assuming a gesture of *j'accuse*, explaining that, if only I knew their exact location, I would point my indignant digit directly at Enoch Anthem and Felix Pielmeister, 'who almost certainly convinced General John Snow 4099 that it was open season on the Sisters Sabacthani'.

As unimaginative sycophants go, Harkness was a fairly decent chap, and he took my indictment of Anthem and Pielmeister seriously enough to despatch a team of FBI agents to the Centre for Stable Families. In giving their depositions to the G-men, Anthem and Pielmeister vociferously denied any connection to the mackies beyond, as Pielmeister put it, 'an unashamed sympathy for their pro-life agenda'. Eventually it became obvious that the two suspects and the Harkness Commission had struck a deal, for a week later the FBI invaded an abandoned limestone-processing plant near Bellefonte, Pennsylvania, and found a clandestine bio-engineering laboratory. The prize of the haul was three onto-generators, and the following day Harkness, in keeping with Londa's recommendation, convinced Governor Winthrop to send a Maryland National Guard unit to Themisopolis and recover the machine through which she'd populated the Circus. Before the month was out, the Harkness Commission had arranged for the effective extinction of this technology, contracting with the US Merchant Marine to load all four ontogenerators on to a container ship, bear them twenty leagues due east of Cape Hatteras, and there consign them to a watery grave.

Even though the chances of another grand-scale immaculoid

protest were virtually non-existent, there being no more RXL-313s in the world save the mouldering remains of the prototype back on Isla de Sangre, I suspect that for the likes of Felix Pielmeister, Enoch Anthem and Tucker Winthrop, this was a golden age. Recent biblical exegesis by Anthem's newest organisation, Hermeneutics Unlimited, had established beyond doubt that Jesus Christ was adamantly opposed to universal health-care insurance, handgun control, and corporate whistleblowers. Several prominent postrationalist theologians had successfully exposed public education for the misguided Marxist boondoggle it was, while a majority in Congress now advocated replacing the secular school system with private academies committed to sparing children the bad news that Charles Darwin had brought back from the Galápagos Islands. As for the dubious projects nurtured by the so-called City of Justice, it would be years, perhaps a decade, before the data pulverised in Alethia Square could be replicated by the scattered staff of the Susan B. Anthony Trust and the tattered remains of the Institute for Advanced Biological Investigations.

One particularly telling sign of the times was the consummation of Ralph Gittikac's campaign to rebuild the RMS *Titanic*. Much to my amazement, our primal Phyllistine had managed to get the luxury liner's doppelgänger off the drawing board and into the water. Gittikac Getaway Adventures was now taking reservations for the 'Great Cathartic Voyage of the *Titanic Redux*', scheduled to sail from Southampton, England, on the first of July and arrive in New York City on Independence Day.

From the Phyllistine perspective, of course, one felicitous development eclipsed all the others. According to a confluence of rumour, gossip, and paparazzi espionage, Londa Sabacthani was no longer a force to be reckoned with. Evidently she'd been checking herself into one Manhattan mental institution after another, while her press secretary, the faithful Pauline Chilton, proceeded to frost her client's fruitcake condition with obfuscation and euphemism.

With my marriage a void, my vatling an inmate, and Corporate Christi poised to conquer the world, I found it increasingly difficult to get up in the morning. Day by day I retreated ever further into the deepest reaches of myself: Mason Ambrose, shipwreck victim, washed up on the deserted shores of his own *Dasein*, a condition that he perversely compounded by disconnecting his phone, selling his computer, and instructing the post office to hold his mail. No man is an island, John Donne had famously insisted – true enough, but I had certainly become whatever land mass entailed an equal measure of estrangement: a tidal peninsula, perhaps, joined to my fellow beings by the narrowest of shoals.

My condition worsened, from isolation to desolation. Acting on impulse – if a man gripped by stupefying malaise may be said to act on impulse – I appointed Dexter Padula the sole manager of Pieces of Mind and sold him the bulk of my shares, using the ready cash to pay the rent three months in advance, send anticipatory cheques to the gas company, and provision my rooms with certain essentials: a case of canned salmon, the Erlanger House *Collected Works of Friedrich Nietzsche*, twenty bottles of red wine, a stack of Vaughan Williams CDs. I closed the door, turned off the lights, and waited for Godot. The days elapsed at the velocity of molasses. Camus, I decided, had got it right – there is only one important philosophical question: why not suicide? My apartment was an embarrassment of possibilities. A set of stainless-steel steak knifes. A heavy-duty extension cord, easily fashioned into a noose. A fire-escape platform offering a thirty-foot plunge to a concrete alley.

To this day I'm not certain how I survived my long, dark fortnights of the soul. Through some felicitous synergy of Nietzschean fortitude, Cabernet Sauvignon, and 'The Lark Ascending', I continued to elude the abyss. And then came my deliverance. I was sitting beside my bedroom window, staring across the alley into the parlour of my closest neighbour, Thomas Cochran, a professor of Medieval Studies so ancient of days that his colleagues joked how he'd joined the department back when it was called Contemporary Theology. At some point during my twelve-week immurement, Dr Cochran had acquired an enormous plasma television set, and to my astonishment the screen now shimmered with a familiar Cinemascope longshot. There he was, my old mentor Sinuhe, walking the banks of the Nile. Half in jest and half in desperation, I told myself that this was a sign, and the meaning was unequivocal: my philosophy career had not yet run its course. Rather than become a corpse, I must follow up *Ethics from the Earth* with additional impertinent tomes that nobody wanted to read. Isis expected it, Horus would settle for nothing less, and who was I to defy the gods?

Twenty-four hours after the Egyptian deities made their wishes known, I enjoyed an equally welcome visitation when young Donya came knocking at my door. I was ill prepared to receive her. Unsightly stubble covered my chin, uncivilised aromas wafted off my skin, and my apartment looked like a rutting ground favoured by oxen. She didn't seem to notice – a spontaneous Platonist, that girl, unconcerned with the immediate world's superficial splotches and smudges.

She revealed that she now lived a mere two hours from Boston, her email correspondence with several renowned marine biologists having netted her a summer internship at the Woods Hole Oceano-graphic Institute. Apparently everybody was concerned about dear old Mason – Donya, Henry, Brock, Jordan, especially Londa – so Henry had persuaded the youngest Sister Sabacthani, the only Massachusetts member of our fellowship, to track me down. I related how the collapse of my marriage had landed me in Spenser's Cave of Despair, but I had more or less recovered, having found a provisional answer to Camus's notorious question. Any day now, I told Donya, I would start writing a new treatise on evolutionary ethics.

'To be honest, I wasn't terribly anxious about you,' she said. 'Those who can kill themselves do, and those who can't, teach philosophy. It's weird big sister who's got me worried. Did you know her iguana died?'

I shook my head. 'You're worried about Londa because her iguana died?'

'I'm worried about Londa because she's Londa.'

'Poor old Quetzie. What happened?'

'Nothing. A bad case of mortality. At least she has a clear conscience on that score.'

Forty minutes later, having disinfected myself, put on a clean shirt, and located a viable credit card, I accompanied Donya to the Tao of Sprouts in Copley Square. The best local vegetarian restaurant was still the Tasty Triffid, but returning there without Natalie on my arm would have been excruciating. While the chef heated our ratatouille, Donya reminisced about her childhood, breezily recounting a Yolly anecdote I'd never heard before – how she'd once made a hilarious home video by taking her documentary footage of Blood Island fiddler crabs and altering the soundtrack, so that the creatures appeared to be playing a Beethoven string quartet. Throughout Donya's narrative my eyes rarely left her face. How strange to be sitting across from this willowy adult version of the diminutive six-year-old who'd once served me peanut-butter sandwiches and chocolate-chip cookies in a tree house. Strange, and also a little sad, because the preschool Donya was gone for ever now, as irretrievable as Edwina or Yolly or John Snow 0001.

Our ratatouille arrived. We consumed several morsels, then broached the evening's unhappy topic.

'Apparently Londas's plotting something – a weird-big-sister sort of something, ingenious and dangerous and likely to end badly,' Donya said.

'The last I heard, she was on a grand tour of New York's loony bins.'

'A subterfuge.'

From her shoulder bag Donya produced a sheaf of computer printouts, crumpled like the treasure maps Brock used to create for her cartography lessons. Emails from Londa, she explained, then read me a series of quotations. I soon concluded that Donya was correct concerning her sister's sanity. These weren't the ravings of a madwoman, but something even more disturbing – the effusions of a frighteningly rational person systematically setting a trap for her enemies.

Call me an egotist, dear Donya, but I believe I've devised a way to cure the Phyllistines.

I won't deny it: certain aspects of Operation PG are morally ambiguous. I'd better secure Mason's services the instant he surfaces.

The pieces are falling into place. At first the Phyllistines will denounce me, but in time they'll realise I've delivered them from their own evil.

Matthew logically locates the Sermon on the Mount on a hill, but Luke places the same speech on a plain. I have planned Operation PG for the middle of the Atlantic Ocean. Future historians will probably stick it in the Gobi Desert.

'What do you suppose the PG stands for?' Donya asked. 'Parental guidance?'

'Pineal gland,' I groaned. 'Londa's into Cartesian physiology.'

'I've memorised her last message. "Zero hour is barely a week away, so please make every effort to locate Mason. The plan requires his input."'

'Zero hour. Christ.'

Donya pulled a phone from her jacket, plunking it down on the table with the weary air of a jaded Russian-roulette referee preparing to adjudicate a game. 'Every time I call, she chatters merrily until the subject turns to Operation PG, and then she clams up. You'll probably have better luck.'

Londa answererd immediately. After insisting how wonderful it was to hear my voice, she suddenly turned sombre and proceeded, characteristically, to take charge of my life. I was to catch the 6.45 a.m. Amtrak out of South Station and get off four hours later in Manhattan. She would meet me in Pennsylvania Station near the Seventh Avenue exit, right by Hudson News.

'I hope your wife can spare you for a while,' Londa said. 'I'm in dire need of an ethics tutorial.'

'Three months ago Natalie ran off with a failed novelist who found fucking easier than plotting. I'm free as a bird.'

'Oh, my poor Socrates, you didn't deserve that. Was Joan of Arc part of the problem?'

'Not as much as Katherine Anne Porter.'

'Are you on the mend?'

'Healthy as a horse. Speaking of health, Donya tells me you've found a way to rehabilitate the Phyllistines. Operation PG. Let me guess: pineal gland.'

257

'Details at eleven.'

Throughout the rest of our meal Donya brought me up to date on the Hubris Academy faculty. Traumatised by the Themisopolis catastrophe and despondent over the loss of Yolly, Jordan had disavowed political activism and was now pursuing her PhD at the University of Toronto. Henry had begun his rule as the host of *Uncle Rumpus's Magic Island* on Nickelodeon, and initial ratings suggested that America's four-year-olds had found a new idol. The Rumpus franchise had also proved a boon to Brock, whose agent had arranged for him to receive a portion of the licensing fees generated by the characters he'd created for the show. Thanks to Plessey the Plesiosaur and friends, Brock was in danger of becoming embarrassingly rich.

Later, as Donya and I strolled down Beacon Street, she rhapsodised about the Oceanographic Institute – by her account a truly utopian community, its scientists ever eager to pour their molten obsessions into the crucible of her curiosity. Her immediate guru was a cephalopod expert, whose explorations of the giant squid's singularly accessible nervous system bid fair to revolutionise the field of neurophysiology. The resident arthropod aficionado had likewise taken an interest in Donya, initiating her into the cult of the primitive horseshoe crab. Somehow we managed to get all the way to her car without mentioning Londa again, a fact on which Donya remarked as she slid behind the wheel.

'To tell you the truth,' she said, 'even when I was talking about squids, I was thinking about you-know-who.'

'Me too.'

'Watch over her, will you, Mason?' Donya snapped her seatbelt into place, then twisted the ignition key. The engine coughed to life. 'Back on the island she needed a morality teacher. Now she needs a guardian angel.'

Although the Amtrak timetable had promised a noon arrival, my train didn't pull into Pennsylvania Station until 12.13 p.m., which meant that by the corporation's amoeboid clock, ever beholden to the whims of the freight lines, we'd actually hit New York ahead of schedule. We were nevertheless objectively late, and I was not surprised when, approaching the Seventh Avenue exit, suitcase in

258

hand, I came upon Londa pacing in circles and checking her watch. Still very much a celebrity and hence vulnerable to unwanted attention, she had affected a disguise: dark sunglasses, scarf across her mouth, hair stuffed beneath a black beret. Only when we were secluded in a Yellow Cab, moving uptown in fits and starts, did I get a good look at her face. I hadn't seen her since Yolly's funeral, an afternoon on which grief had bloated her features. Today I was sharing a taxi with the most attractive woman in Manhattan, a svelte enchantress with high cheekbones and opalescent eyes.

'Donya told me about Quetzie,' I said. 'Please accept my condolences.'

'It's all right,' she said wistfully. 'He didn't know he was supposed to live any longer. Maybe he wasn't.'

'That lizard had a more complicated relationship with language than Wittgenstein. I've never seen you looking better.'

'That's hard to believe. I've been working around the clock.'

'On curing the Phyllistines?'

'I even worked on my birthday. We beaker freaks do have birthdays – you knew that, didn't you?'

'Of course.'

Later that afternoon, surveying Londa's claustrophobic living room on the second floor of 58 West 82nd Street, I tried to decide whether or not she was a tidy housekeeper. The place was awash with clutter, but on closer inspection I realised that most of the detritus traced to a single source: her preoccupation with both the maiden voyage of the original *Titanic* and the imminent cruise of Ralph Gittikac's *Titanic Redux*. Her apartment would probably seem quite neat if she were to jettison the myriad books, news clippings, brochures, bills, and blueprints concerning the primal Ship of Dreams and its decadent descendant.

'Want my advice?' I wedged my denim jacket into a hall closet crammed with jeans, blouses, skirts, and sweatshirts. 'Stop brooding about the *Redux*. Rich people get to go on luxury cruises, poor people don't, and there's nothing you, I or Thoth on his throne can do about it.'

'I *always* want your advice, Socrates,' Londa replied, 'and in the case of Operation PG, I'm positively *lusting* for it. I'd happily put you up at the Essex House, but I'm hoping you'll reconcile yourself to my futon. My next deontological crisis could strike anytime, day or night.'

'The futon's fine. Shall we begin the tutorial now?'

'First lunch, then philosophy.'

We dined on reheated fried rice and sesame scallops from the previous evening's Chinese dinner. Throughout the meal we chatted superficially, Londa deflecting my questions about Operation PG, but then events took a surprise turn when she dropped a manila envelope into my lap and announced that it contained 'the single most libidinous object in New York'. Instead of explaining herself, she suggested that I investigate her claim while she took a shower.

Londa trotted off to the bathroom, and an instant later came the rubbery percussion of the spray hitting the plastic curtain. I shovelled some *Titanic* memorabilia off the futon, sat down, and separated the envelope from its contents – a charged artefact indeed – the twelve-page manuscript of her old one-act play, 'Coral Idolatry'.

'A sea nymph lives with one purpose in her heart!' she called from the bathroom, projecting her first line over the water's drumming. And suddenly I was back on Isla de Sangre, watching her portray the undine Sythia climbing on to the shore. 'She seeks a mortal who will love her, betroth her, and lavish his body upon her, for in this manner alone might she acquire a soul!'

Londa glided into the room wearing nothing but her facial expression. A smile. The residue of her shower spilled from her drenched auburn hair and sluiced down her limbs.

My throat constricted. My blood rolled in all directions. Nothing about the moment failed to astonish me. There she stood, the unhorsed Dame Quixote, the deposed empress of Themisopolis, glistening as if newly emerged from Charnock's broth – 'Her birth was of the womb of morning dew' – and I knew that despite everything, despite her plots and zombies and titanic machinations, I was still in love with this person and always would be.

'Two hundred days have I followed the submarine currents, seeking the legendary Isle of Sérifos, whose pleasure-loving hedonists never hesitate to avail themselves of succulent sprites and willing sylphs,' she continued. 'Could it be that my search is finally ended? Will the man I see before me grant my wish?'

I peeled off my turtleneck. The undershirt came with it, accompanied by the crackle of static electricity. 'No problem with lavishing my body, Miss Nymph, but the betrothal will have to wait.'

'Stick to the script, Mason. Your line is, "Forgive me for gaping, but I'm astonished to find myself a mere stone's throw from a creature of your kind."'

'Forgive me for gaping, but I'm astonished to find myself but a stone's throw from a creature of your kind.' I subtracted my jeans, jockey shorts, and socks from the situation, then scrambled to my feet, clutching my script in one hand and touching Londa's cheek with the other. 'Until now I've observed undines only from afar. Whenever I take ship, I stand on the deck and stare out to sea, hoping to glimpse a nymph sporting with the dolphins.'

'My name is Sythia. Are you a hedonist?'

'Call me Thales, disciple of Epicurus.'

She wrapped a damp hand around my wrist and led me down the hall and into her boudoir. There was no bed in sight, simply a queen-size mattress strewn with quilts. 'Epicurus? Then I must surmise that for you the essence of pleasure is the removal of pain.'

'True, fair Sythia. Once pain is gone, pleasure admits of variation but not of increase—'

'If we made love until the sun comes up, you might decide that ecstasy comes in gradations,' she said.

'I thought we were sticking to the script.'

'Poetic improvisation is encouraged,' she said.

'Then I suggest we improvise an elision and jump to page four. Stage direction: "Sythia kisses Thales squarely on the lips. Thales reciprocates."'

Sythia did as the text required, according Thales a protracted kiss. Fingers scurried across bodies not their own. Blood vessels swelled. Words were exchanged concerning the sea nymph's fertility, as neither party desired a foetal outcome to their frolic, and they agreed to meet this contingency with a selection from Sythia's collection of condoms from around the world.

She liquefied, my passionate vatling, and inevitably I thought of those colourful enzymes, crimson, purple, gold, turquoise, in which Charnock had braised her nascent frame. We sat on a floral quilt

261

and connected face to face. She told me I made a fine supplementary superego but an even better subsidiary id. I replied that I'd nearly forgotten what a splendid thing was the mammalian mode of descent.

'A miracle, really,' I said. 'No dreary anthropomorphic deity could have thought it up in a million years.'

'True enough,' Londa said. 'And yet the most erotic sentence I've ever heard doesn't come from *Fanny Hill* or *Justine* or *Lady Chatterly's Lover*. It comes from the Anglican Book of Common Prayer.'

'The most erotic sentence?'

'With my body I thee worship.'

No pillow talk for my undine, no basking in the afterglow, no lolling about on the shores of Sérifos. This was Londa, after all, the driven Crimson Kantian, the edgy Purple Pietist. She slid free of my embrace, grabbed her cell phone, and slipped away, leaving me to contemplate the afternoon's remarkable events in private. A few minutes later, her urgent mutterings wafted into the room. I heard an occasional 'Dagmar'. She was talking to her manager, doubtless about their plan to fix the Phyllistines.

My mind raced like a machine shorn of its flywheel. Was it possible that Londa's reasons for staging this off-off-Broadway performance of 'Coral Idolatry' were less romantic than I'd imagined? Had she merely sought to win my approval of Operation PG? I brushed my palm along the quilted cavity from which she'd emerged. The fabric was still warm. No profit in pessimism, I decided. For the immediate future, I would refrain from thinking the worst of my undine. Gradually my anxiety faded, and I drifted off to sleep, lulled by the comforting rumble of the rush-hour traffic rolling up Amsterdam Avenue.

It was dark when I awoke – 8.17 p.m. by the gimlet gaze of the digital alarm. Slowly I slid free of my dream, an expressionist extravaganza that found Charnock and me sailing his houseboat across a nameless sea, pursued by pirates, menaced by sharks, and engulfed by a maelstrom. Londa brought me her restive flesh and a crystalline goblet of mumquat nectar. For the next two hours we lay together, entwined like strands of DNA, my vatling

262

demonstrating an uncanny talent for combining recitative and fellatio, her morality teacher reciprocating with *a cappella* cunnilingus. Finally Londa asserted that I would do well to get a good night's sleep, as tomorrow we were leaving on a long journey.

'I just got here,' I protested.

'We're hitting the road, first thing in the morning, Thales and Sythia, off on another adventure. We'll be away for at least three months, maybe four.'

'Four months? You're not making much sense, darling.'

'Don't worry if you didn't bring enough underwear. Where we're headed, consumer goods grow on trees.' She presented me with her cell phone. 'Call your landlord. Tell him to sublet your apartment.'

'This is crazy.'

'No, it's your gumbo girl. Trust her.'

A wave of fatalism washed through me, a not entirely unpleasant sensation. Trust her? Why not? What did I have to lose?

I pestered Verizon for Fred Packer's number, punched in the digits, and caught him in a good mood, the Sox having just vanquished the Yankees on a ninth-inning grand slam. He said he'd try to find a substitute tenant for one semester, though naturally it would be easier to lease the apartment for the whole year. Either way works, I told him, figuring that once Operation PG had run its course, Londa and I would start playing house in Manhattan.

Next I called Dexter Padula, telling him he could have my remaining shares in Pieces of Mind if he would hire a van, drop by my apartment, remove all possessions of value, and stick them in a storage shed. He agreed without batting an eyelid, no doubt delighted that his increasingly unreliable business partner was getting out of the game entirely.

'So what happens after we cure the Phyllistines?' I asked Londa. 'Your disciples will expect something even grander from you. They'll want you to become a deity.'

She snickered and said, 'I'm not ruling out that possibility.'

'What sort of deity? Plato's demiurge? The Creator God of Judaeo-Christian revelation?'

'That job's already taken,' she said.

'But you could do it better,' I said.

'When it comes to the physics, no, but in other areas – you're right.'

Londa's voice fell, her eyelids drooped, and her mouth opened in a cavernous yawn revealing all thirty-two of her mother's straight white teeth.

The digital alarm roused us at eight o'clock. Londa served me coffee and a toasted-poppy-seed bagel. Naturally I'd imagined that our departure from Manhattan would occur by car, taxi, bus, train, or some other horizontal means, so I was taken aback when she announced that we'd be travelling by helicopter.

'Travelling where?' I asked, harbouring not the remotest expectation of a straight answer.

'To the radiant crux of justice.'

As a mellifluous July morning flowed over the city, Londa and I stepped into the hallway gripping our respective suitcases. We lowered the fire ladder from the ceiling and climbed to the roof, where a helicopter stood ready to receive us, rotor blades churning, cockpit enclosed by a dirty Plexiglas blister – a hydrocephalic dragonfly. Dagmar Röhrig sat behind the controls. We fought our way through the prop-wash, climbed into the cab, and secured our luggage. Londa seated herself in the co-pilot's chair, and so I joined my suitcase in the storage compartment, involuntarily assuming a painful and unnatural posture. I wondered if all trips to the radiant crux of justice required such contortions of their pilgrims.

'Did we make the *Times*?' Londa asked.

'The front page,' Dagmar replied. 'Also the last three minutes of *Coffee Klatch* and the news banner on the Flatiron Building.'

We flew south along the Hudson River docks, soared across Upper New York Bay, and swung so close to the Statue of Liberty that I could see the startled faces of the tourists clustered in her crown. After skirting the western lobe of Brooklyn we veered away from the rising sun and entered the vast foaming tracts of the North Atlantic. Each time I posed a question to Londa or Dagmar, they declined to answer, insisting that the present mission was too complicated to be summarised in a few sentences shouted over the roar of our engine – a feeble excuse, since the women were perfectly happy to speak with one another. From the snatches I caught of their conversation, I gathered that our destination was the *Titanic Redux*, currently somewhere on the high seas, steaming towards New York.

As we zoomed across the white-capped ocean, I resolved to inhabit the moment as fully as I could. Here I was rambling around with a goddess whose body I'd recently worshipped in the best High Church style, beginning an exploit that, whatever its hazards, would most likely include intervals of canal bliss aboard a luxury liner. Apart from certain disconcerting mysteries, my situation had much to recommend it.

After perhaps an hour, I once again attempted to make Londa tell me more.

'Let me guess,' I said. 'You've bought the *Titanic Redux*, and you and Dagmar plan to spend the summer cruising from port to port.'

'We haven't bought her,' Londa explained. 'We've hijacked her.'

'*Hijacked* her? No, Londa, no! Bad idea!'

'Even as we speak,' Dagmar said, 'Colonel Fox's commandos are parading around the decks, keeping everybody in line.'

'This is madness!'

'True, but it's a very *efficient* madness,' Londa said. 'In a single toss of the net we've caught three hundred of America's top Phyllistines, all ripe for enlightenment. Enoch Anthem is part of the haul, and your old nemesis Felix Pielmeister.'

'I can't believe I'm hearing this!'

'God knows I wanted to discuss the project with you ahead of time, but you'd disappeared down your spider-hole,' Londa said. 'Try withholding your judgement till you've grasped the broader picture.'

'Screw the broader picture! We're going to have that ethics tutorial, *right now*!'

'Shut up, Mason!' Dagmar screamed. 'You're making me nervous! Can't you see I'm trying to fly a goddamn helicopter?'

At noon we sighted the *Titanic Redux*, her stern cutting a billowing furrow in the endless blue field. With the sun almost directly overhead I couldn't be certain of her bearing, but a glance at the chopper's compass confirmed my intuition that, though we were still flying east, the ship was now on an aberrant course, south by south-west. I decided to forego the ethics tutorial, demanding instead that Londa just answer two questions. Why wasn't the sea swarming with Coast Guard cutters, and why wasn't the sky dark with CNN helicopters?

By way of reply, she produced from her shoulder bag an object that looked something akin to a DVD remote control, its numbered keys encircling a small red button, ominous as a smallpox pustule. Thanks to the Valkyries' derring-do, she explained, the *Titanic*'s foreward hold was filled with plastic explosives of her own design.

'A momentous instrument, wouldn't you agree?' she said. 'A Godgadget if ever there was one. Colonel Fox and her Valkyries have eight more just like it. The outside world is appropriately impressed. The instant the Coast Guard or a SWAT team or a news organisation appears on the scene, ka-boom, the Ship of Dreams is blown to kingdom come.'

'Fuck this!' I shouted, a hundred times more furious than on the day I learned she'd burned her palm in homage to Stoicism. 'You'd kill three hundred Phyllistines, not to mention the other passengers, the officers, the crew, the Valkyries, Dagmar, yourself, and me?'

'Of course not,' Londa replied. 'First we'll evacuate the innocent, and then we'll blow up the ship. That's the whole point of a radio-controlled detonator.' She stroked the metallic casing of her Godgadget. 'Now, there's always a possibility, and I mean a distinct possibility, that this thing is a fake, no more lethal than a water pistol.'

Her cryptic disavowal soothed me. Not much, but a little. 'I want the truth,' I told her. 'Is that thing wired to the detonator or not?'

'Sorry, Mason, my lips are sealed. It's the only way I can keep *your* lips sealed too.'

'Until I have more data,' I said, 'I'll assume the best of you.'

'You're a peach, Socrates. Believe me, we'll have that ethics tutorial at my earliest possible convenience.'

Now the mighty vessel loomed up, her magnificence multiplying with each passing instant, she of the noble prow, majestic decks, soaring masts, and raked funnels exhaling cottony puffs of smoke.

A seagoing skyscraper, tilted ninety degrees, plying the waves under full steam. Londa grabbed the radio mike and contacted the bridge, instructing the skipper to hold steady. The man's reply reverberated through the Plexiglas blister. In a tone wavering between defiance and bewilderment, Captain Drew Pittinger said that, while he would do as instructed, he was still master of *Titanic Redux*.

'You are indeed her master,' Londa replied. 'And I am her queen.'

For a full minute we followed the frothy wake, and then Dagmar increased our speed and circled the stern mast. Anticipating our descent, the assembled voyagers – sunbathers, fishermen, noonday strollers – dispersed in all directions. We dropped from the sky like a slain duck landing on the poop deck.

As Dagmar shut off the engine, Londa explained that the people we'd just sent scurrying inhabited the plebeian confines of F and G decks. On the *Titanic Redux*, as on her ill-starred predecessor, social stratification was the norm. At the moment these third-class passengers were more likely to receive engraved invitations to the White House than admittance to the boat-deck promenade.

'But that's all about to change,' Londa insisted. 'By the time the sun rises tomorrow, the last shall be first, and the first shall be last. Just like in heaven.'

CHAPTER 14

Go ahead, adopt an ape, it sounds like fun, a chimpanzee or maybe even an orang-utan, but be prepared to justify your decision when he eats your neighbour's begonias. By all means, have a baby, you deserve a descendant, but stand ready to defend your parenting skills when he grows up to become a serial killer. *Mais oui*, acquire a belief in God, theism is a popular and comforting lifestyle, but first do your homework. Learn how the world's great minds have explained the Creator's seeming indifference to human suffering, lest you waste your time fretting about tsunamis and cystic fibrosis.

How might I rationalise my initial acquiescence in Operation Pineal Gland? Why did I make no immediate effort to thwart this manifestly criminal escapade? In retrospect, I realise that my infatuation with Londa kept me from seeing that her scheme was irredeemable. Then, too, I must confess that my contempt for Ralph Gittikac and his fellow Phyllistines made me believe that, at some level, they deserved whatever they got. Eventually I started thinking like a moral philosopher again, but throughout my first day aboard the *Titanic Redux* I was in thrall to a mixture of love and disgust, that poisonous compound with which the Devil's apothecary is always so well stocked.

No sooner had I retrieved my suitcase and stepped free of the helicopter, than Colonel Fox came striding across the poop deck. She acknowledged her leader with a crisp salute, her leader's manager with a respectful nod, and her leader's conscience with a bruising scowl. Obviously she'd not forgiven me for convincing her boss to abandon Themisopolis to the mackies. Londa returned the salute, then hustled me through the nearest hatchway, explaining that I could best serve the cause of justice by lying low for the next twenty-four hours. I replied that the cause of justice and Operation Pineal Gland were evidently two different things, but before I could elaborate, a sprightly apple-cheeked lieutenant appeared, outfitted in the standard Valkyrie black leather jacket, an AK-47 slung over her shoulder. She introduced herself as Marnie Kristowski, 'your faithful aide-de-camp', though my instincts told me she was expected to function more as my custodian. Londa promptly fobbed me off on this vivacious daughter of Odin, asserting that in time 'the *Redux* hijacking will make complete sense to the entire world, you included, Socrates'.

'Been a security officer long?' I asked Lieutenant Kristowski as she grabbed my suitcase and directed me towards the companionway.

'Barely a month, sir. I was one of those kids who grew up reading *League of Londa* comics. Did you know you're in number forty-six?'

What a ghastly thought. 'No kidding.'

'It's not *literally* you, but you were clearly the inspiration. Dr Sabacthani goes back to her birthplace, somewhere in Indonesia, and meets Masai Ambooloy, the kung-fu alchemist-philosopher who taught her the way of the Splanx.'

'The Splanx?'

'An occult mental discipline. The Splanxist can send out psychic waves that scramble her enemies' brains. Masai Ambooloy, Mason Ambrose – get it?'

'Number forty-six? I'll have to track it down.'

'My all-time favourite is the lead story in issue thirty-two. A gang of South American drug lords has imprisoned Dr Sabacthani in a concentration camp, so the Valkyries engineer a flock of giant condors and ride them to the rescue. Those condors are probably the main reason I'm wearing this uniform.'

We descended to D deck and entered a commodious second-class cabin that, though lacking a porthole, was chock-a-block with other amenities: a private bath, a writing desk, a refrigerator, a room-service intercom, and – in a break with the period purism that characterised the *Redux* – a home-entertainment centre crammed with classical CDs, including, appropriately enough,

Wagner's *Ring des Nibelungen* with its stirring 'Ride of the Val-kyries'. The kitchen staff knew of my special status, Lieutenant Kristowski explained, so whenever I felt hungry I should simply get on the horn and order any items that tickled my fancy.

She saluted and slipped away, leaving me to spend the next fourteen hours in idyllic circumstances. In the refrigerator lay two dozens cans of Guinness, the bookshelves held a fiction collection ranging from J. R. R. Tolkien's melancholy optimism to Ernest Hemingway's nuanced fatalism, the reading chair was a scholar's wallow, and the D-deck stewards delivered broiled lobster tails to my door as casually as a mailman bringing the day's credit-card offers. Even the bed was luxurious – down blankets, silk sheets, satin pillows – though not quite luxurious enough to quiet my mind and calm my nerves. Londa has not gone insane, I kept telling myself. In time her capsized soul will right itself, and she will be restored to me. But still I could not sleep.

Contemplating Operation Pineal Gland through the pellucid lens of hindsight, I realise that it comprised a dozen distinct though interconnected strategies, one of which continues to elicit my awe. I speak of Londa's decision to have Colonel Fox and her thirty bravest soldiers purchase second-class tickets on the maiden voyage of the *Titanic Redux*. Shortly after coming aboard in Cherbourg, these stalwart commandos had pooled the contents of their steamer trunks, each jammed with ostensibly innocuous materials that, cleverly combined, became a score of automatic weapons and a panoply of explosive devices. The Uzis and the AK-47s had proved every bit as philosophically persuasive as Londa and Colonel Fox had hoped and the Valkyries had had little difficulty filling forehold number 3 with plastique, winning the crew's allegiance, convincing the service personnel to join the insurrection, and coercing Captain Pittinger into informing the outside world that any attempt to foil the hijacking would trigger a horrendous but not unprecedented maritime catastrophe. The *coup de grâce* had occurred twelve hours before our helicopter landed on the poop deck. With wry smiles on their lips and taut fingers on their triggers, Colonel Fox's commandos had rounded up all the first-class passengers and ordered them to hunker down in their staterooms until further notice.

Indulging in her affection for the theatrical, Londa waited until exactly 12.18 a.m. before addressing our captive Phyllistines, for that was when the first-class passengers aboard the original *Titanic* had been roused from their quarters on 15 April 1912. She even insisted that the hostages dress exactly as their twentieth-century counterparts had, in pyjamas and life jackets. Although the majority of her audience – an elite group of two hundred and twenty-five corporation presidents, congressmen, lawyers, judges, arms dealers, government advisors, and political operatives – was predictably male, our catch also included three female CEOs and a woman lobbyist for the petroleum industry. Using their rifle butts like cattle prods, the Valkyries herded the prisoners down the C-deck passageways and into the reception room outside the Grand Dining Saloon, leaving the Phyllistines' ancillary spouses and children to brood in their cabins. Dressed in a glossy black microfibre suit, Londa strode past the murmuring crowd with a stateliness appropriate to her status as queen of the ship. Her decision to include her conscience had evidently been an afterthought – my invitation had arrived at the stroke of midnight, delivered in person by Lieutenant Kristowski – and yet she seemed pleased to have me by her side. As we ascended the great marble staircase she squeezed my hand and whispered, 'She seeks a mortal who will love her, betroth her, and lavish his body upon her . . .'

Colonel Fox and Major Powers awaited us on the first landing. The Valkyries exchanged conspiratorial nods with Londa, who then faced the highborn mob like Mark Antony preparing to turn Rome's citizens against Caesar's assassins.

'Masters of the universe!' she shouted over the hubbub. 'Mistresses of creation! Your attention please. I have astonishing news!'

The multi-millionaires ceased their disgruntled muttering.

'My name is Londa Sabacthani, and I'm here to inform you that, like her legendary ancestor, the *Titanic Redux* has struck an iceberg.'

Instantly the muttering resumed, now seasoned with outrage. Ralph Gittikac stood up straight, dropped his Hapsburg jaw, and shouted, 'I know who *you* are, but do you know who *I* am? You're talking to Ralph Winston Gittikac, CEO of Gittikac's Getaway Adventures and director of Project *Titanic* Ascendant, and when this ridiculous caper is over, I'm going to jam your sorry ass in jail!'

Apparently Gittikac didn't recall meeting the adolescent Londa twelve years earlier in the Bahía de Flores, and I figured she had no particular reason to remind him of the encounter.

'Where's Captain Pittinger?' demanded a lithe Phyllistine whose matinee-idol features were probably not unrelated to his personal fortune. 'What have you done with him?'

'Are you aware that I'm a United States senator?' snarled a ruddy man wearing a silk bathrobe over his pyjamas. 'Have you any idea how much trouble you're in?'

'Let's get something straight!' Colonel Fox snapped, lifting her Uzi high above her head – the Statue of Liberty's glamorous anarchist sister. Her fellow Valkyries also brandished their weapons. 'There are worse things than listening respectfully to Dr Sabacthani, like getting blown into such tiny pieces the sharks will use you for spare change, which is exactly what's going to happen if you don't shut the fuck up!'

Silence enshrouded the reception room like snow blanketing a meadow. Surveying the chastened plutocrats, I traded stares of reciprocal contempt with Felix Pielmeister, who appeared dignified despite his pyjamas, and of mutual recognition with Ralph Gittikac, who would have looked like a humourless boor even in a Brooks Brothers suit.

'As I was saying, the *Redux* has struck an iceberg,' Londa continued. 'Not an ordinary iceberg, but a malignant mass composed of your own frigid vanity and frozen gall.'

The crowd indulged in various snorts and huffs but stayed on the circumspect side of articulation.

'That's the bad news,' Londa continued. 'The good news is that the ship will not founder. As your damaged souls begin to mend, the gash in our hull will also heal. In short, masters of the universe, think of us not as your captors but as your teachers.'

Jowls flapping, nostrils flaring, Enoch Anthem stepped free of the mob and, folding his arms across his barrel chest, addressed Londa in a bravely stentorian voice. 'Teachers?! *Teachers?!* What you are is a bunch of sicko lesbian pirates, and I hope I'm there to see the fireworks when Jesus gets his hands on you!'

Colonel Fox responded to Anthem's outburst by aiming her rifle vertically and squeezing off a round. Squalls of plaster sifted down from the shattered ceiling. A dozen arms reached out and pulled Anthem back into the collective Phyllistine body.

'Allow me to introduce your other benefactors.' Londa leaned towards me and, in a gesture more condescending than affectionate, pinched my cheek between her thumb and index finger. 'This is Mr Ambrose, my ethical advisor. The woman who fired at the ceiling is Colonel Fox, our chief of security. Beside her stands Major Powers, second in command.' Beaming a smile that would have looked equally at home on Anthem's sanctimonious face, she abruptly pulled the Godgadget from her jacket. 'And yes, the rumours are true. Our hold *is* packed with explosives, a fact that has so far kept your would-be liberators at bay. Make no mistake. Should we get word that a Coast Guard cutter or a SWAT team helicopter is chasing us, we'll lock you up, man the lifeboats, and detonate the plastique.'

She extended her index finger and allowed it to hover menacingly near the red button. The plutocrats engaged in a synchronous cringe.

'Even as I speak, many of you are imagining you might pave the way for a rescue operation by wresting the transmitter from me. Such a gesture would be futile – am I right, Colonel Fox? Major Powers?'

The officers flashed their own Godgadgets, holding them up like touts hawking Super Bowl tickets. 'Three of our subordinates have transmitters as well,' Colonel Fox said, 'and there are three more hidden around the ship.'

'But for now let's drop this depressing talk of bombs and address a happier topic – your ethical growth,' Londa said, repocketing her transmitter. 'At dawn we reach our first port of call, Brigantine, New Jersey, where we shall unburden ourselves of your spouses, your children, and our second-class passengers. After the evacuation, you and the third-class passengers will trade places, the latter taking over your staterooms while you move into the spartan cabins on G deck. It occurs to me that the mere experience of living so close to the waterline might even effect your cure. What do you think, Colonel?'

'I've never seen a smarter bunch of capitalists,' Vetruvia Fox said.

'And you, Major?' Londa asked.

'We've caught ourselves some real sharp cookies, and that's the truth,' Carmen Powers said. 'When I think of how deeply they comprehend the stock market, I know they'll have no trouble with the Beatitudes.'

'Tell me, Mr Ambrose, do you share the prevailing optimism?' Londa asked me.

'Oh, yes,' I hissed between clenched teeth. What else was I supposed to say?

Londa scanned the mob with a piercing eye, fixing first on Ralph Gittikac, then on Enoch Anthem, and finally on Felix Pielmeister. 'Could it be that your teachers are right?' she said, her voice dripping with derision. 'A few days of tender loving privation, and you'll all acquire a moral compass? I'd like to think so. In any event, it's time we returned you to your quarters. Enjoy your staterooms whilst ye may, for there are no Persian rugs on G deck, nor damask curtains, nor flutes of champagne – in fact, it's rather like a darkling plain down there, where ignorant armies clash by night.'

Socialist in worldview and cynical in sensibility, Colonel Fox predicted that the third-class passengers would leap at the opportunity to trade stations with the Phyllistines. What she didn't understand was that the cheapest *Titanic Redux* tickets had been purchased not by oppressed Old World wage slaves eager to inaugurate a dictatorship of the proletariat, but by unionised European factory workers and civil servants who had no particular problem with the prevailing economic order and whose presence on the ship reflected a simple desire to cross the Atlantic at a bargain rate. When the Valkyries explained to these thrifty British, Irish, Scottish, French, Swiss, Belgian, Dutch, Italian, and German voyagers that, rather than spending the rest of their vacations in the United States, they could remain on the *Redux* and be treated like royalty, only three dozen out of five hundred and fourteen accepted the offer – a number sufficient for Londa to claim that she'd turned the status quo on its head, though hardly the Marxist revolution forecast by Colonel Fox. I could not fault the vacationers' wariness. Given a choice between putting to shore right now and spending three weeks in the company of thirty Uzi-armed harpies on a floating munitions dump, I likewise would have erred on the side of caution.

At first light I staggered from my cabin and ascended the companionways, arriving on the boat deck just before we dropped anchor off the Jersey coast. A dozen seamen and all four junior officers hovered near the lifeboats, removing the canvas tarps, plugging the drainage holes, unlocking the davits. Soon the second-class passengers appeared, most wearing expressions of blasé resignation, as if they'd endured many such instances of monumental inconvenience throughout their second-class lives. Next came the plutocrats' families – two hundred and eight angry wives, three befuddled husbands, and several dozen confused children – followed by the scores of third-class passengers who'd been rational enough to turn down Londa's offer of an all-expenses-paid cruise to the heart of her darkness. Last to arrive was the *Redux*'s twenty-one-piece orchestra, along with thirty or so stewards, waiters, and scullerymen who'd decided to jump ship while they could.

Perched on the wheelhouse roof, amplifying her authority by way of a battery-powered megaphone, Londa directed the evacuation with the zeal of an impresario barking outside a carnival tent. She assured everyone that the bay was only slightly choppy this morning, 'which means you'll have no trouble rowing to Brigantine', then added that there were still plenty of unreserved first-class staterooms for any third-class passengers who wanted to 'stick around and be waited on hand and foot by CEOs who earn upwards of two million dollars a year'.

As Londa made her pitch, I retreated to the bridge and continued observing the spectacle from the starboard wing, where I was soon joined by my aide-de-camp, gripping a pair of binoculars. It happened that Lieutenant Kristowski was a native of these shores, having grown up in the Atlantic City suburb of Absecon. 'The state flower of New Jersey is the common violet,' she explained, smirking, 'the state bird is the eastern goldfinch, and the state fragrance is unrefined petroleum.'

I scanned the lifeboats, each hovering two feet above the deck on its davits. Londa announced that before taking their seat, each departing voyager must present his passport to a junior officer and demonstrate that he'd not exceeded the luggage quota: a single valise or sack jammed with cash, jewellery, medicines, laptop – whatever items the passenger deemed indispensable. Many evacuees refused to climb aboard until they'd received an officer's personal assurance that their remaining worldly goods would be stowed away and ultimately returned. In lieu of conventional baggage, three plutocrat wives had brought along their dogs – pug, basset hound, cairn terrier – and because each pet was secured in a plastic carrier nobody raised any objections.

Once Londa was satisfied that the loading operation was proceeding apace, she permitted the captive Phyllistines to leave the staterooms and come on deck. As per Colonel Fox's orders, they arrived still dressed in their pyjamas. Searching for their families, our hostages surveyed the crowded lifeboats with eyes that betrayed variously rage, bewilderment, shock, and longing. A succession of farewells followed, some quite poignant, though probably none as wrenching as the partings that had occurred a thousand leagues to the north-east on the morning of 15 April 1912. Reaching over the gunwale of her lifeboat, Enoch Anthem accorded his chubby, whey-faced bride a protracted embrace. Ralph Gittikac was obliged to perform an especially elaborate adieu, as he'd embarked with an entourage that included his wife, their four daughters, and his divorced sister's grumpy adolescent son. Felix Pielmeister did not appear on the boat deck that morning, so I assumed he'd left Southampton unaccompanied.

On Londa's orders, the junior officers swung the lifeboats out over the water – a frightening experience for the evacuees, judging from their howls and shrieks – then further employed the davits to send these voyagers on a brief but bumpy downward ride. Throughout the lowering process the Brigantine harbour police, tooling around in their patrol boats, worked diligently to keep the local fishing boats and pleasure craft out of the *Redux*'s vicinity.

For the moment, at least, our plastique was having the effect Londa desired.

Within half an hour, all the evacuees were bobbing about on the foam-flecked bay. Their attempts to work the lifeboat oars proved unintentionally comic, but their incompetence hardly mattered, as the tide was rolling landward. Assuming no boat sprang a leak, our superfluous passengers would reach Brigantine in time for lunch.

Borrowing the binoculars from Lieutenant Kristowski, I studied the crowded shore. It seemed that half the population of New Jersey was milling around on the beach, and I wondered what had inspired them to get up so early on a Saturday morning. While some onlookers had probably come to glimpse the fabled ship, others doubtless hoped to witness a rescue attempt by the Coast Guard or a SWAT team, still others to express their solidarity with the abducted plutocrats. And surely our audience included scores of Sabacthanites: youthful idealists who owned complete runs of *The League of Londa*, and spent their free time mastering the way of the Splanx.

Even as the evacuees headed for Brigantine, a flotilla came cruising towards us: two tugs hauling a barge bearing the additional coal required by this unforeseen amendment to the maiden voyage plus three bumboats loaded with food, sundries, and prescription-drug refills, Major Powers having researched the hostages' medical histories as part of the general strategising for Operation PG.

'So what's our next port of call?' I asked my aide-de-camp.

'There isn't one, sir. We're going to steam around in circles until our hostages are cured or the Coast Guard shows up.'

'And what happens if the Coast Guard shows up?'

'We can count on Dr Sabacthani to exercise restraint,' Lieutenant Kristowski said, pulling out her Godgadget. The metallic casing glinted in the morning sun. 'Samson didn't slay those four thousand Philistines until his back was against the wall.'

Shortly before nine o'clock, the *Titanic Redux* weighed anchor, the bumboat supplies having been stowed away, the coal barge lashed to our stern, and the demoted plutocrats exiled – sans clothing, laptops, cell phones, radios, money, and other such

277

earthly possessions – to their draconian digs in the bowels of the ship. As the great voyage to nowhere began, I bade Lieutenant Kristowski adieu and retired to the Café Parisien, a swanky first-class eatery on B deck featuring bilingual menus and international cuisine. The cooks were happy to whip me up an extravagant breakfast: cheese omelette, Belgian waffles, croissants, fruit salad. I carried the feast to the table myself, as the former first-class passengers hadn't been assigned their duties yet. No sooner had I taken my first bite, than the stirring 'Gonna Fly Now' theme Bill Conti had composed for *Rocky* filled the air, borne through the café – and the rest of the ship, too, I assumed – by the public-address system.

'Good morning one and all!' boomed Londa's disembodied voice over the brass-heavy melody. The music diminished in volume, and she proceeded to lecture the hostages in the tone of a Devil's Island commandant intimidating new arrivals. 'This is Dame Quixote, welcoming you to the premiere of *The Last Shall Be First*, the one and only radio programme originating aboard the *Titanic Redux* – local in its coverage, planetary in its reach, universal in its message!' The music swelled, then dropped away as Londa resumed talking. 'Before long, dozens of stations will be broadcasting *The Last Shall Be First* to every corner of the globe. Doubtless your friends and relatives will tune in to each episode, eager to know about life aboard the Ship of Dreams.'

A tremulous anticipation seized the recently promoted first-class passengers in the Café Parisien. They set down their utensils and cocked their ears towards the loudspeaker, a fluted cone mounted on an art-nouveau pillar.

'Many of you are familiar with the Revelation to Saint John – hardly the noblest book in the Bible, though certainly the most garish. I'm sure you will remember the spectacular onslaught in chapter six, the thrilling cavalry charge of War, Famine, Pestilence, and Death. Look inward, masters of the universe, and you will each realise that the horseman called War has already arrived. I speak now of the conflict raging within your heart, the battle between your inflated self and atrophied soul. As for Famine, Pestilence, and Death, they are not far behind.'

After this pompous prelude Londa shifted to more pragmatic

matters. A new monetary system had been instituted aboard the *Redux*, she explained, predicated on a medium of exchange called the lucre. Thanks to the bumboats, seven thousand freshly printed lucres in several denominations now filled the bank vault. For the duration of the voyage, the former first-class passengers would toil at 'monotonous but spiritually rewarding jobs', receiving a wage of five lucres per day.

'Would you like my advice? Practise frugality, and you'll be able to make all sorts of impulse purchases, such as, for example, food.'

She went on to assure the Phyllistines that, although their private health-insurance policies were invalid under the new regime, their physical well-being would not suffer. The ship's pharmacy was brimming with the drugs they took for their assorted ailments – diabetes, kidney disease, congestive heart failure, depression – and every pill would be distributed free of charge.

'In other words, simply by booking passage on the *Redux*, you've become beneficiaries of our socialised health-care system. I can't help pointing out that two of your fellow voyagers, Senator Frank Endicott of Iowa and Senator Rupert Marbury of Alabama, have worked unstintingly to keep America's citizens from enjoying affordable medical insurance. You can thank whatever gods may be that Endicott and Marbury are not in charge of political arrangements aboard this ship.'

For the next twenty minutes the plutocrats learned of the scrubbing, scouring, waxing, polishing, scraping, painting, swabbing, lifting, loading, fetching and ferrying they would be required to perform in the days to come.

'And so, masters of the universe' – the audio engineer snuck in the *Rocky* theme – 'until the next exciting episode of *The Last Shall Be First*, this is Dame Quixote wishing you a memorable and enlightening voyage!'

The music swelled in a crescendo. I took a final sip of coffee, sopped up a dribble of egg with a waffle, and considered what to do next. My greatest urge was to seek out Londa and tell her that, in my opinion, this crude approach to curing the Phyllistines was certain to fail, but I figured she hadn't slept in the last twenty-four hours, so it would be prudent to postpone my visit. With a confused heart and an ambivalent gait I returned to my D-deck cabin, where I spent the rest of the day revisiting Middle Earth while glutting myself on room-service lobster tails, delivered in person by Senator Endicott. I thanked him for his trouble. He told me to go crack a walnut in my ass.

At 9 a.m. the next morning, episode two of *The Last Shall Be First* came pouring from the ceiling speaker and gushed uninvited into my brain. As the *Rocky* theme faded, Londa began gleefully enumerating the menial tasks the plutocrats had completed during their first day under the new regime. I looked around for a way of silencing the broadcast. Eventually I resorted to repositioning my writing desk under the speaker, stacking books on top, and capping the pile with a pillow pressed tightly between Londa Sabacthani's sardonic recitation and *A Farewell to Arms*.

I passed the afternoon putting Hemingway's novel to a different use, immersing myself in Frederic Henry's problems in order to escape my own, most especially my anxiety over being in love with a person whose aptitude for malice seemed to increase every day. Shortly after six o'clock Lieutenant Kristowski appeared at my door with an invitation from on high. If it would not be inconvenient, might I come to OPG headquarters for some 'mumquat and moral discourse'?

'Lead the way,' I told my aide-de-camp.

'Did you hear this morning's broadcast, sir? Sounds like those folks on G deck are going to get their improved pineal glands sooner rather than later.'

Although the B-deck corridor presided over by Dagmar Röhrig had been designated the reception area, anyone seeking an audience with Dr Sabacthani was in fact received by two Valkyries who regarded most supplicants with the same calibre of suspicion that Omar the Dobermann had accorded all visitors to Casa de los Huesos. They were a redoubtable pair, the imposing corporal evoking the bronze Themis who'd once graced the fallen city, the lithe sergeant suggesting Alonso the Conquistador following a sex-change operation. A simple nod from Lieutenant Kristowski was sufficient to make the guards step aside – she outranked them both – whereupon Dagmar abandoned her desk, guided us along a glass-walled promenade offering spectacular views of a calm

North Atlantic sea, and ushered us into the Louis XIV parlour suite that now functioned as Londa's command-and-control centre.

True to her solidarity with the downtrodden, Londa had peeled away the suite's opulent trappings, so it was up to my imagination to supply the brocade curtains, Persian carpets, gilt-framed mirrors, and Fragonard reproductions that had doubtless once appointed the place. Although her surroundings were spare, Londa herself had opted for elegance that evening, her lips dabbed with magenta, her exquisite skin wrapped in a strapless green taffeta evening gown. After sending Dagmar and Lieutenant Kristowski away, she gave me the sort of deep aqueous kiss at which undines are adept, then sidled towards a serving table where a samovar was heating over an open flame.

'Ever drunk your nectar warm, darling?' she asked, indicating the great silver urn. 'Dagmar recommends the experience, so I thought we should try it.' She worked the stopcock, filling a black ceramic mug with a steaming measure of Proserpine. 'Naturally I hoped we'd get together before now, but it's been pure madness around here.'

'I heard your first two broadcasts. I guess you think you're being unbelievably brilliant inflicting your justice on the Phyllistines—'

'Not brilliant necessarily. Clever, I suppose. Droll.'

'But paying them starvation wages, that's *cruel*.'

She presented me with eight savoury ounces of equanimity. 'At the risk of sounding too forward, I would like to formalise our bond.'

My heart seemed to rotate on its axis. Formalise our bond? What was she suggesting? That we march straight into Captain Pittinger's cabin and demand that he marry us? A bizarre tableau flashed through my mind: Londa and myself standing before the master of the *Redux*, the vatling in her evening gown, her groom wearing a three-piece Italian suit that had once belonged to a local plutocrat, Dagmar and the Lieutenant getting ready to pelt us with rice. Did such a union make sense at any level? Would marrying Londa give me some sort of psychological leverage, a Splanx-like power by which I might convince her to shut down Operation PG?

'My most precious and impossible undine,' I sighed. 'My infinitely exasperating nymph.'

Londa stared at me as if I'd started speaking Chinese. 'I'm wild about you too, Mason, but that's another day's conversation. Right now we have to fix the Phyllistines.'

'You said this was about our bond.'

'Correct. Ambrose and Sabacthani, united against the misogynists and theocrats.' She turned the stopcock and filled a second mug. 'Ah, *now* I get it – you're referring to another sort of bond: Sythia and Thales rolling around on their secret beach.' Her tone was wistful, as if our lovemaking had occurred in some mythic realm beyond space and time. 'Believe me, Mason, I get goosebumps just thinking about that day, and if it gave you further proof of my good intentions, so much the better.'

My overwhelming impulse was to bounce the ceramic mug off her skull. 'Are you saying that because you fucked me, I'm now supposed to go along with this hijacking crap?'

'I suggest we not dwell on those aspects of Operation PG you find objectionable. Let's focus on the greater good.'

'May I once again quote you to yourself? "There are no greater goods."'

'That's Joan of Arc's line.'

'Written by Londa Sabacthani.'

'Your nectar will have cooled by now. Try some. You'll feel much better.'

I took a protracted swallow. 'Shall I tell you the truth? For a minute there I imagined you wanted Captain Pittinger to marry us.'

The perplexity that came to Londa's face was even deeper than before. She sipped some nectar, then marched to the writing desk: a typical piece of *Redux* furniture, so graceful it seemed intended solely for penning sestinas and would turn to sawdust the instant anybody used it for anything as prosaic as paying a bill. Sliding open the top drawer, she removed her fanciful account of her non-existent pre-adolescence. 'I saved only two mementos from Faustino – 'Coral Idolatry', and this quaint and curious volume.' She deposited 'The Book of Londa' in my hands, its brown leather binding scuffed like an old shoe. 'I've been using it to scribble down anecdotes from my life. At some point in the story, fiction turns into fact. Note the most recent entry.'

As the mumquat molecules navigated my bloodstream, I did as Londa instructed. The specified page contained a mere sixty words, rendered in a script so ragged I wondered if she'd composed it under Proserpine's influence.

Today my auxiliary conscience and I shared mugs of nectar in my office. We weren't far into our conversation when he told me he fully supports the grand experiment in social justice now unfolding aboard the Redux. *He even offered to sign this entry as a testament to his blessing, hence the 'Mason Ambrose' at the bottom of the page.*

She reached into the drawer again and retrieved a fountain pen: a genuine Mont Blanc. 'I need your blessing,' she said, pressing the pen into my palm. 'It would make all the difference.'

The nectar bathed my brain, bestowing a certain serenity, but I was too distressed to enjoy it. 'I can't.'

'Of course you can.'

'No,' I said, regarding the fancy pen as I would a rattlesnake.

'Always the philosopher. Always the contrarian. Very well, Socrates – think it over. Think it over a whole fucking bunch. The evening's young.'

'I've already thought it over.'

'All I want is your goddamn signature.'

I threw the pen across the room.

'Am I supposed to *beg* you – is that it?' she asked.

'No, you're supposed to bring the ship about, steam back to Brigantine, and set the hostages free. If Donya were here, she'd tell you the same thing. Yolly, too. Even Edwina.'

Londa's eyes became dark and narrow, like visor slots in a medieval helmet. She snatched her journal away and unleashed a diatribe of vast scope and epic proportions. Left to their own devices, she insisted, Ralph Gittikac and his compatriots would turn the planet into a toxic dump. If Enoch Anthem and his brethren retained their stranglehold on the zeitgeist, life would become even more wretched for those Americans who'd made the mistake of being born poor, unhealthy, gay, pigmented, or female. Once Pielmeister and his kind finished bringing Corporate Christi into being, a dark age would descend upon the human spirit.

'I forget, Londa, what sort of weapons did the disciples bring to the Sermon on the Mount? As I recall, Mark says Browning machine guns, but Matthew reports AK-47s.'

'Don't make yourself my enemy, Mason. I have enemies enough.'

In a quick unbroken gesture I tore the last page from 'The Book of Londa' and jammed it into the flame beneath the samovar. Londa shuddered but did not move. I pulled my hand away and released the burning page. Buoyed by a draft, it turned into a lamina of ash, then floated to the floor and consumed itself.

'According to Saint John,' I said, 'the Good Samaritan acquired his legendary benevolence only after Jesus handcuffed him to a fig tree under the scorching sun.'

'Have it your own way. We won't be lovers. We won't be friends. We won't be fellow warriors in the great crusade.'

'In Luke's version, the conversion takes a bit longer.'

'Kindly leave my office before I count to ten. One ... two ...'

I strode towards the door. 'First Jesus locks the Samaritan in a dungeon for six months, then lays into him with a horsewhip.'

'Three ... four ...'

'Until finally the Samaritan becomes a man of compassion.'

'Five ... six ...'

I was gone before she got to seven.

Now that the great schism had occurred – as wrenching for me as it was doubtless inevitable from the plenary perspective enjoyed by Isis, Horus, Thoth, and the rest of my antique pantheon – I assumed that Londa would exact a swift revenge. I imagined her cancelling my room-service privileges and requiring me to join the Phyllistines in waiting on our first-class passengers. And yet I retained my pampered status – though apparently Londa did tell the security force I was no longer to be trusted.

'It's none of my business, sir, but I gather that you and Dr Sabacthani had a falling-out,' Lieutenant Kristowski said.

'True,' I said.

'What did you do to offend her?'

'I quoted her to herself.'

'I used to do that to my boyfriend,' Lieutenant Kristowski said. 'It's why we broke up. I'm sure Dr Sabacthani doesn't hate you. Do you hate her?'

'No.'

'If I had to take a guess, sir, I'd say that you're in love with her.'

'That may be the case.'

'You philosophers do like to make things complicated, don't you? If you ever need a break from your brain, drop by our shooting range on C deck. I'll teach you how to fire a Galil.'

Throughout the second week of the voyage, as the ship oscillated aimlessly between the thirty-third and thirty-fifth parallels, I undertook a kind of anthropological study, systematically analysing the behaviour of victims and oppressors alike as they played out their parts within the privileged precincts of A and B decks. Besides the three dozen former third-class passengers, our local elite included nineteen stewards, twenty-one scullerymen, and – when they weren't on duty shovelling coal in the boiler rooms – fifteen stokers. As far as I could tell, our entire population of parvenus had already got the hang of arrogance. Before making a particular demand, the first-class passenger usually invoked the captive plutocrat's name: an easily obtained datum since, pursuant to a directive from Major Powers, the Phyllistines had all signed their pyjama pockets with indelible pens.

'Albert, old sport, at four o'clock I shall require a repast of oysters and beer on the first-class promenade.'

'Enoch, this Martini glass appears to be empty, a situation I expect you to remedy without delay.'

'Quentin, would you kindly visit the library and scare me up a Tom Clancy novel?'

'Donald, be a dear and retrieve your wife's cardigan from my stateroom.'

'Felix, my man, it has come to our attention that fresh croissants are now available in the Café Parisien. Bring me a dozen in five minutes flat, and I'll reward you with a lucre.'

I wondered what a devout Fabian like George Bernard Shaw

would have made of Londa's deranged experiment. He probably would not have approved. It was one thing to argue, as Shaw did in *Pygmalion*, that the class system was arbitrary and unnatural; quite another to demonstrate that, given the opportunity, the working poor would happily turn themselves into callous egomaniacs every bit as tyrannical as Henry Higgins.

Owing both to my personal investigations and to my daily conversations with Marnie Kristowski, I had a pretty good idea of what was going on in the Phyllistines' heads. As in their previous lives, the subject of money rarely left their thoughts, but the focus of the obsession had changed, from piling up mountains of wealth to figuring out whether they had enough ready cash to buy toothpaste from the pharmacy and toilet paper from the commissary. For the brutal truth was that five lucres a day – thirty-five lucres a week – did not go very far on the luxury liner. In accordance with Londa's latest fiat, a loaf of bread now cost thirty lucres, a quart of milk forty, and a box of raisins eighty. I shuddered to imagine what would happen if she repealed universal health insurance aboard the *Redux*. No doubt she would start charging the same outrageous prices as the pharmacist in a certain famous moral dilemma.

It was alternately painful and amusing to watch our hostages labouring in the Grand Saloon and its adjacent kitchen, where their duties included arranging the place settings, taking the orders, serving the food, clearing the tables, and doing the dishes. Our first-class passengers showed their inferiors no mercy. They addressed the plutocrats as 'garçon' and 'Jeeves', required them to memorise long wine lists, sent back half the entrées, and left worthless tips in the form of dollars, pounds, and euros. At the end of each meal, the more spiteful parvenus heated their plates over the dinner candles, thus guaranteeing that the Phyllistines would have to spend hours scraping away baked-on bits of poached salmon and kidney pie.

When it came to maintaining their staterooms, our first-class passengers held their servants to the highest standards. Every day, whether the task needed doing or not, the plutocrat responsible for a given suite was expected to vacuum the carpet, dust the furniture, disinfect the toilet, launder the linen, wash the portholes, clean the curtains, make the beds and, after stripping the wardrobe of its jackets and pants – most of which had once belonged to the plutocrats themselves – brush each garment with a lint remover. Our parvenus soon became sticklers for detail, and God help the G-deck passenger who neglected to turn down the sheets or leave a chocolate on the pillow.

Londa took particular delight in publicising the astonishing monetary harvest the Phyllistines had been reaping prior to their departure from Southampton. Third-class passenger Gary Pons, the whiz kid behind the Macro-Mart phenomenon, pulled down a cool five million a year, more than three hundred times the take-home pay of his average employee. Sheila Portman, CEO of several fast-food empires, enjoyed an annual salary equal to two hundred times the income of those who scrubbed the floors of her Grab-a-Crab restaurants. Morris Hampton, owner of the supernaturally profitable Prester Pharmaceutical Laboratory, had in recent years accumulated sufficient wealth to purchase private yachts for all four of his ne'er-do-well brothers.

'You wouldn't know it to look at him since he's a physically diminutive chap,' Londa said, wrapping up an especially caustic instalment of *The Last Shall Be First*, 'but it turns out that Frank Diffring, the guiding light behind Blue Château hotels, is nine hundred times worthier than the women he hires to change the bedding in his exemplary inns.'

Thirty-five lucres a week – and if that wasn't pathetic enough, Londa soon arranged for inflation to plague our unhappy community, so that the plutocrats' newfound ability to budget judiciously for toothpaste and toilet paper suddenly ceased to matter. Now the big challenge was to get through the day on your meagre allotment of plain tofu and rice, supplementing these rations with string beans gleaned from the Grand Saloon floor, bread crumbs scavenged from the parvenus' plates, and apple cores retrieved from the garbage pails. In short, a low-grade Famine had come to the *Redux*, the second horseman of Londa's aquatic apocalypse, though whether that wasted rider would trample the Phyllistines completely or reunite them with their souls, I could not begin to say.

*

Like many brilliant philosophers – and, closer to home, like many middling philosophers who never managed to get their PhDs – I have always been susceptible to insomnia. Throughout the voyage of the *Redux* this condition visited me with alarming frequency. Typically I would awaken at 5 a.m. and, knowing that my restlessness was certain to persist, make my way to the weather deck. For the next ninety minutes I would pace in circles around the foremast, head tilted back, meditating on Orion and Ursa Major. I shall never cease to marvel at the clarity of stars when viewed from mid-ocean, each as sharp and bright as the laser pointer God uses when lecturing the angels on evolution. At length the constellations would fade, and I would greet the rising sun with an awe verging on adoration – I was no longer Sinuhe just then but another character from *The Egyptian*, the monotheistic pharaoh, Amenhotep IV, prostrating himself before a graven image of his divine and shining Aton – after which a delicious drowsiness would overcome me, and I would return to my cabin for a long nap before Londa's nine o'clock broadcast roused me from my dreams.

On the morning of my thirtieth day aboard the *Redux*, my post-devotional sleep was terminated by an especially distressing episode of *The Last Shall Be First*. Londa began by expressing her 'profound disappointment' in the hostages' performance to date. Her office had received myriad complaints: spots on the crystal, stains on the tablecloths, socks inadequately mended, shoes not sufficiently shined, toilets neither spick nor span. But incompetence was not the primary reason that fifty per cent of our G-deck passengers were about to lose their jobs. Sheer economic necessity had proved the deciding factor. The fewer superfluous workers we employed in servicing the staterooms and the Grand Saloon, the more likely the voyage was to turn a profit.

'Downsizing is an imperative with which certain of my listeners are well acquainted, especially you, Corbin Thorndike, president of Aries Athletic Wear, and you, Barry Nelligan, founder of Beyond Style, and you, Wilbur Conant, CEO of Ultra Office, and you, Alexander Lerner, board chairman of General Heuristics. In your former careers, you collectively outsourced 132,000 manufacturing jobs to atrociously run factories in Asia and Latin America. But hear me now, masters of the universe. The *Redux* is a generous ship. Of the one hundred G-deck residents we're about to drop from the payroll, none will become destitute, for in our compassion we've decided to retire all our stokers and offer you their jobs at four lucres a day. True, the boiler rooms are an austere environment – quite similar, in fact, to the sweatshops that figure so crucially in your corporations' prosperity: long hours, foul air, hazardous working conditions, infrequent bathroom breaks. The temperature is one hundred and ten degrees Fahrenheit in the shade. But at least you'll be gainfully employed.'

She went on to assure our former third-class passengers that those plutocrats not assigned to the boiler rooms would be working double shifts. To wit, the parvenus needn't fear a decline in the stateroom service, and the Grand Saloon would remain a place where one might enjoy a transcendently gracious dining experience.

'For many of you, I imagine the thought of your imminent demotion is distressing,' Londa said. 'But here's a late-breaking story to cheer you. Despite frenzied efforts by well-funded lobbyists, we shall continue to bless all G-deck residents with free health insurance. In other words, your pill bottles will remain full, and should you perchance fall sick, the *Redux* will cover your medical bills.'

The new economic order was in place barely a week when a combination of curiosity and boredom persuaded me to venture into the bowels of the ship. My Virgil for this Dantesque descent was Lieutenant Kristowski, who gladly accepted my offer to assist in her daily task of bringing tepid water to the patrician stokers, along with cold beer for their guardian Valkyries. Prior to our departure, we loaded our backpacks with plastic pints of Poland Spring and crammed twelve Thermoses of Tadcaster ale into a canvas duffel bag. We shouldered the water and set off, the duffel bag swinging between us like a hammock as we clambered down a series of aft companionways. Throughout our journey, we discussed that most fascinating and confounding of topics, Londa Sabacthani. In a tone more equivocal than she probably intended, Lieutenant Kristowski announced that she'd decided to give her employer the benefit of the doubt concerning the boiler-room scheme, and I replied that thus far I could discern no doubt on which to predicate a benefit.

As we reached the lowest deck, a stifling gust of heat blew towards us, and our conversation tapered into silence, as if the blistering air had melted our words away. A huge iron slab, embroidered with rivets, blocked our progress. The presiding sentry, a statuesque Valkyrie sergeant whose name-patch read SKEGGS, thanked us so extravagantly for her Thermos that, had a video camera caught her reaction, the result would've been a singularly persuasive commercial for Tadcaster ale.

'It's a real honour having you visit us, Mr Ambrose,' said Sergeant Skeggs, draining the Thermos. 'May I ask you a question? My boyfriend could use some ethical fine-tuning himself, so I was wondering – how did you make Dr Sabacthani the way she is?'

'Londa was a blank slate when she became my student,' I said. 'I doubt that her case is relevant to your problem.'

'You don't know Douglas.'

'He's not a *tabula rasa* – I can tell you that.'

'Maybe,' said Sergeant Skeggs. 'In any case, what did you *do*?'

'We started with role-playing exercises,' I said. 'Get your search engine to track down "Lawrence Kohlberg" and "moral dilemmas".'

'I'll give it a try.'

'Eventually we did Jesus. Be careful with the Sermon on the Mount. It's not for amateurs.'

'Thanks. It all sounds a lot easier than hijacking a fucking ocean liner.'

The guard threw a switch on the wall, whereupon the watertight door squealed its way upwards like a portcullis. Lieutenant Kristowski and I crossed the threshold. Swathed in tendrils of sallow steam, eight enormous horizontal cylinders dominated boiler room I, each demanding ceaseless attention from a team of Phyllistines, the first member responsible for opening the furnace door and feeding the fire with shovelfuls of coal, the second for stirring the burning fuel with an iron lance inserted through the stokeholes, and the third for keeping the adjacent bin filled with wheelbarrow-loads of anthracite drawn from a communal heap. The spectacle transfixed me. For a full minute I simply stood and stared, my eyes dazzled by the glare, my ears throbbing with the roar of the furnaces, the horrific scarlet heat casting my mind back to Themisopolis's fiery demise. Now the Lieutenant and I started working the room, moving among the stokers like a couple of minor angels ministering to Ben-Hur and his fellow galley slaves. My first customer was chubby Wilbur Conant, his soft features and stern expression suggesting a teddy bear in touch with his dark side. Upon receiving his pint, the CEO of Ultra Office set down his shovel, removed the cap with a single twist of the wrist, and consumed the entire portion in one prolonged gulp.

'I remember you from that first night, when those dyke bitches gathered everybody together outside the Grand Saloon.' Conant ran his tongue across his lips in search of stray drops. Medallions of soot speckled his chest. 'Tell me, Mr Ethical Advisor, where's the goddamn *ethics* in condemning us to this stinking place?'

'Dr Sabacthani wants you to start thinking about your life in new ways,' I replied.

'Yeah? Well, I'll tell you something. Most of the time I'm exhausted and hungry, and until you showed up I was dying of thirst. Under conditions like that, how am I supposed to do any goddamn *thinking*?'

'I can see your point.'

'I'm not a monster, Mr Ambrose. I've sponsored orphans in India. I give to the United Way. You don't know me, and neither does Dr Sabacthani.'

I assured Wilbur Conant that Dr Sabacthani did not think him a monster, merely an avaricious miscreant who trafficked in sweatshop labour. While this characterisation obviously displeased him, he offered no rejoinder beyond ratcheting up his scowl and asserting that 'sweatshop labour' was an exaggeration.

My next thirsty plutocrat was Beyond Style's dynamic manager, Barry Nelligan, whose face had graced the cover of *Fortune* on three different occasions. A trim, athletic man who bore a startling resemblance to the young Robert Redford, he seemed to take a certain pride in artfully jabbing his lance through the stokeholes. After thanking me for the water, Nelligan wiped the sweat from his forehead and said, 'I've got a message for Londa Sabacthani.

Tell your client I forgive her, for she knows not what she does. You understand what I'm getting at?'

'I believe I grasp your allusion.'

'The crucifixion, right?'

'I'm afraid Dr Sabacthani wants nothing to do with me these days.'

'Oh, really? Well, if you ever bury the hatchet, let her know she can torture me all she wants, and I'll still forgive her.'

For the next half-hour Lieutenant Kristowski and I moistened dry mouths and cooled blistered brows, until at last we'd serviced all twenty-four amateur stokers. In most cases the Phyllistine's understandable bitterness was leavened by a less predictable reaction: a show of stoicism, a declaration of innocence, an outburst of contrition, a recitation of philanthropic acts, and in a few instances – the sentiment I'd first encountered in Barry Nelligan – a short speech absolving Londa of her sins. For better or worse, it appeared that Operation PG was an experiment of greater psychological complexity than I'd allowed.

Upon reaching the far end of the compartment, Lieutenant Kristowski approached a tall Valkyrie whose grey blouse matched the oiled metal of her rifle, making the weapon seem less a gun than a fashion accessory. The guard swilled down the contents of her Thermos, then opened the watertight door.

We crossed over and began bringing our charity to boiler room 2. Halfway through my toils, the formidable figure of Felix Pielmeister emerged from the steam, naked to the waist, huffing and grunting as he filled his wheelbarrow with coal. Sensing my presence, he leaned his shovel against the barrow and fixed me with a brutish stare.

'I knew we'd meet again one day,' I told him, 'though I didn't think the location would be hell itself.'

'Your antics before the Harkness Commission were despicable,' Pielmeister rasped. Sweat sparkled on his chest. Burns and blisters peppered his skin: evidently he was slow to dodge the errant embers forever spewing from the furnaces. 'How irresponsible of you to blame me and Reverend Anthem for that Sabacthani woman's death.'

'Irresponsible. Yes. Also reckless and rash. So tell me, what did you and Anthem say to the mackies when you gave them their marching orders? "Remember, my precious vigilantes, Themisopolis is the abortion capital of the world. The Sisters Sabacthani deserve to die."'

Pielmeister glowered, grabbed his shovel, and added another measure of coal to the barrow. His thirst, I figured, must be intolerable, and I was not surprised when he gestured towards my backpack and said, 'Got any more water in there?'

'Lots of water. Too proud to ask me for a drink?'

'Hardly. Pride is a sin. So is withholding water from a thirsty man.'

'What's your preference?' I set my backpack on the floor, unzipping it to reveal my seven remaining pints of Poland Spring. 'Today's choices are perfect for a man of your persuasion. This one holds the joyful tears Mary shed after the Annunciation. This one comes from the basin in which Pilate washed his hands. And here we have the wine that Satan turned back into water following the Wedding at Cana.'

'You're loving this, aren't you, Ambrose?' Pielmeister laid his shovel across the barrow. 'You're having the time of your life.'

'Please satisfy my curiosity,' I said, tearing a bottle from its plastic tether. 'Am I the first person you ever screwed out of a degree?'

'Are you going to give me that water, or aren't you?'

'I'd like to think I was the first. That would be quite a distinction.'

'You've cast your lot with a lunatic – I hope you realise that. Your protégée is out of her mind, and one way or another she's going to destroy us all.'

I tossed the bottle to Pielmeister, who caught it in one hand. He wrenched off the cap and began guzzling. I did not stay to watch him finish but returned to my Kantian duties, irrigating the arid throat of Senator Rupert Marbury, soothing the desiccated tongue of Macro-Mart wizard Gary Pons, salving the parched tonsils of Aries Athletic Wear CEO Corbin Thorndike, while all around me the furnaces seethed and bellowed, spewing sparks like those burning braziers in which the priestesses of Isis – not the least of the deities to whom Sinuhe had bent his body while withholding his devotion – would glimpse the future.

How good a prophet was Pielmeister? What was the calibre of his brazier? I hated to admit it, but I feared he'd seen our collective fate. Sooner or later, Londa would bring the *Titanic Redux* to the edge of the world, and then with both eyes open and both hands on the helm, she would contact the engine room, order them to crank up the turbines, and sail us into the void, full steam ahead.

CHAPTER 15

On the first Sunday in August, while the equatorial sea raged with Charybdian fury and the *Titanic Redux* entered her fourth week of functioning as Londa's empire and toy, the most disturbing instalment yet of *The Last Shall Be First* resounded through the ship. I was sitting in my cabin, sipping room-service coffee, oblivious to the storm, when the broadcast started spilling down from the ceiling like acid rain sterilising a lake. Once again I resolved to muffle the programme with my pillow, but then I became transfixed by Londa's mordant account of what the Phyllistines could expect from the next phase of their treatment.

'Yes, masters of the universe, we finally see the light. We now accept the arguments by which certain clear thinkers among you convinced the US Congress to gut and geld so many pieces of environmental legislation. I'm speaking of you, Clarence Garmond, enterprising chairperson of the White House Council on Air and Water Quality, and you, Robert Arnold, tireless lobbyist on behalf of the Greater Pacific Electric Company, and you, Senator Chad Wintergreen, assiduous pimp for the petroleum industry.'

A tawdry trumpet melody underscored the word 'pimp', though the Phyllistines were probably too hungry and tired to appreciate the audio engineer's wit.

'And so we've decided to banish environmental extremism from the *Redux*,' Londa continued as the trumpet faded, 'systematically rescinding those regulations that until now have forbidden us to collect the fumes from our smokestacks and vent them on to G deck.'

A wave of nausea rolled through me. I leaned back in my reading chair, grasping the armrests for support.

'We're confident that Messrs Garmond, Arnold, and Wintergreen will not baulk at the introduction of lead, mercury, sulphur dioxide, carbon dioxide and carbon monoxide into their living spaces,' Londa continued. 'After all, in their various campaigns against eco-fetishism, they managed to assemble mounds of solid right-wing scientific evidence proving that heavy metals and hydrocarbons pose no long-lasting threat to human health. Of course, those of you already suffering from lung ailments may find that your symptoms are aggravated, but I'm sure you're prepared to endure such discomforts in the name of a profitable voyage.'

I jerked free of my chair and stood staring at the speaker.

'Of one thing we may be certain. As news of the venting initiative spreads around the globe, scores of self-righteous physicians will raise their voices in alarm, glibly predicting that the third horseman, Pestilence, is about to go galloping through the *Redux*.'

Thanks to the dexterity of her audio engineer, the sound of thundering hooves counterpointed Londa's image of equestrian contagion.

'But even if those smug doctors are right, you needn't fret, as you can still avail yourselves of our free medical services. True, we *have* started reviewing the position papers that G-deck citizens Endicott and Marbury once wrote with the aim of persuading their fellow senators to torpedo universal health insurance. But if I were you, I wouldn't worry. God will provide.'

The engineer eased in the *Rocky* theme.

Blood boiling, dudgeon rising, I bolted from my cabin and charged through the maze of D-deck corridors like a maiden in flight from the Minotaur. I scrambled up the companionways and, arriving on the boat deck, dashed across the wheelhouse, much to the sputtering dismay of the officer on duty. A Valkyrie with the proportions and demeanour of a New Jersey nightclub bouncer interposed her body between myself and the communications shack.

'Dr Sabacthani thought you might show up,' she said, waving her Uzi in my face.

'Listen to me, Londa!' I yelled towards the shack. 'Cease and desist! No toxic fumes on G deck!'

The Jersey bouncer wrapped her thick intractable fingers around my upper arm.

'No fumes, Londa!' I persisted. 'The whole world will turn against you!'

Chuckling at the low comedy of the situation – a gangly neo-Darwinist philosopher struggling to break a musclebound Valkyrie's iron grip – the bouncer rudely escorted me back to my cabin. She forced me into the reading chair, fixed me with the burning gaze of the believing Sabacthanite, and wafted out one of those reverential banalities so characteristic of Londa's security force.

'What you have to understand,' she said, 'is that there's a good reason for everything Dame Quixote does.'

The bouncer stalked out of the room, leaving me to spend an ethically indefensible afternoon getting drunk on Guinness while consuming plate after plate of broiled lobster tails.

No less chilling was the next instalment of Londa's radio show, a roll call of those G-deck residents who'd experienced asthma attacks during the first day of the venting initiative. Once again I sprinted to the communications shack and screamed my outrage in Londa's direction until the bouncer whisked me away. Twenty-four hours later I endured another broadcast, Dame Quixote's report on how the emphysema rate was climbing under the deregulation regime, and so for the third time that week I ascended to the wheelhouse and shouted my impotent objections.

Shortly after the bouncer deposited me in my quarters yet again, I realised that a day might soon dawn when I would be called upon to testify against Londa in a court of law. Would I leap at this opportunity? Greet it with fear and trembling? Whatever the case, my Kantian duty was clear. I must obtain an oxygen rig and inspect the venting initiative first-hand.

As usual, Lieutenant Kristowski proved willing to help – I didn't tell her the real reason I wanted to visit the hostages' quarters, claiming instead a morbid interest in their latest ordeal – and the following morning she appeared at my door bearing a face mask, regulator, and scuba tank. I thanked my aide-de-camp, strapped on the gear, and descended to G deck. Entering the plutocrats' domain, I immediately found myself negotiating a web of heating ducts, PVC pipes, vacuum-cleaner tubes, and firehoses, all carefully configured to foul the corridors with the ship's effluvium. A half-dozen Valkyries, likewise equipped with oxygen rigs, presided over this jerry-built torture device. The air was visibly gritty, sallow as an October moon, a jaundiced miasma. There was no need to take notes – for how could I ever forget the misery of the Phyllistines now wandering the corridors, their eyes streaming, bronchial tubes wheezing, diaphragms racked by coughing fits?

I deposited the oxygen rig in my cabin, then found my way to the C-deck infirmary and marched uninvited through a door marked 'HOWARD FLETCHER, MD'. A gangly man with skin the colour of goat cheese, Dr Fletcher stood before a vertically mounted light table to which was secured a chest X-ray, its subject's lungs and ribs rendered in electromagnetic chiaroscuro. I introduced myself as 'a former member of Dr Sabacthani's inner circle, now a defector'.

Dr Fletcher revealed that he recognised me from the television coverage of the Harkness hearings. 'As I recall, you once tutored her in moral philosophy.'

'That was ages ago. Believe me, when they put her on trial, I'll gladly denounce her from the witness stand.'

'Christ, Ambrose, you should be denouncing her *right now*. You should be denouncing her to her *fucking face*.'

I told him that Londa had exiled me from her sphere – not exactly a momentous event, I hastened to add, because these days she took the advice of no one but herself, and there were doubtless times when she ignored that counsel as well.

In the ensuing conversation, the doctor disclosed that, owing to the venting initiative, his staff was now obligated to obtain daily blood samples from the hostages. If any third-class aristocrats exhibited signs of lead contamination or mercury poisoning, he was prepared to offer them chelation therapy, but so far they all seemed free of heavy metals.

'Which is not to say I'm remotely happy about what's happening down there,' Fletcher said. 'Almost everybody who came aboard with a pre-existing lung condition is doing badly. Yesterday I treated five asthma patients. This morning it was four emphysema cases, plus something that looks suspiciously like pneumonoconiosis.'

I thanked the man for his time. He said he hoped my testimony would 'land that bitch in prison for the rest of her life', then added, lest I imagine that he thought me heroic, 'So tell me, who were your other morality students? Richard Nixon? Osama bin Laden?'

I clenched my jaw hard enough to induce tinnitus, then returned to D deck, where the day's second great humiliation awaited. Major Powers stood in the corridor, her waist girded by a utility belt that evoked the holstered arsenal of a Dodge City marshal, and I soon apprehended that she'd just finished converting my cabin into a jail cell. Steel rods and 2 x 4 studs reinforced the door, and instead of a knob there was now an outside latch equipped with a padlock.

'Fuck this,' I said.

The Major opened the door and, gesturing with her screwdriver, directed me across the threshold. 'Perhaps you'd prefer one of those smoggy hovels on G deck?'

'Tell Londa she's making a big mistake.'

'What a coincidence – that's her message to you. "Tell Mason he's making a big mistake, condemning the deregulation regime before it's had a chance to prove itself."' The Major followed me into the cabin, then pointed to the six-inch slot she'd jigsawed into the bottom of the door. 'That's right, Mr Ambrose, you'll still get your beer and lobster.'

'I was just talking with Dr Fletcher. He thinks you're all a bunch of thugs.'

Major Powers made no reply, but reached into her jacket pocket and produced a cardboard sleeve holding a compact disc. 'Londa had me troll the Internet and download a bunch of low-end Frankenstein movies for your amusement and edification,' she explained, setting the disc atop my DVD player. '*I Was a Teenage Frankenstein*, that sort of thing.'

'It's nice to know she still loves me.'

'She said you'd find them, quote, "relevant to solving the riddle of Edwina Sabacthani".'

The Major made a snappy about-face and returned to the corridor.

'One final message from headquarters,' she said before locking me in. '"Tell Mason that at some point in their relationship, an undine and an Epicurean will set out to change one another. The results are always disastrous."'

Thus did I find myself living under house arrest aboard the *Titanic Redux*. In retrospect, I realise I was enduring the sort of cushy incarceration our Phyllistine captives would have enjoyed had they been convicted of their various crimes against the planet and its life forms. But at the time I found no irony in my imprisonment, only infinite frustration, for I was evidently missing the most significant events of the voyage.

The first thunderbolt struck during Londa's regular nine o'clock broadcast. 'Good news, masters of the universe! My staff reports a virtual orgy of self-reflection on G deck, and Colonel Fox believes that many of you are now on the road to recovery, so we've decided to put your rehabilitation on hold. Even as I speak, we're shutting down the venting initiative, and in a matter of hours the ship's regular staff and stokers will come out of retirement and take over those character-building jobs that have absorbed you of late.'

She spent the rest of the programme telling her captives what to expect in the days to come. One by one, they would be brought up to OPG headquarters for an interview 'not unlike those that routinely occur between felons and parole officers'. As the evaluation progressed, Londa would assay the hostage's soul, and if she deemed him cured he would be put ashore when the *Redux* reached the Florida Keys on 17 September. Anyone who failed the examination would remain on the ship 'under the regrettable but necessary plastique regime', until he too became fluent in the Beatitudes.

'How many G-deck residents have thus far acquired a moral compass?' Londa wondered aloud. 'Some? Most? All? None? Be sure to tune in to our next exciting episode!'

Prompted by a combination of inquisitiveness and fear, I did indeed tune in to the next exciting episode – that is, I decided not to censor it with my pillow – and a half-dozen subsequent episodes. What I heard astonished me. For if Londa were to be believed, Operation PG was a glorious success, with nearly every Phyllistine lamenting his former indifference to the downtrodden and his past offences against Lady Justice.

'Tomorrow we drop anchor off Key Largo,' she said over the swelling *Rocky* theme, 'whereupon two hundred and eighty-eight of you will be ferried to the mainland. Those dozen voyagers who still require treatment will remain on board until they are ready to join the fellowship of the gentle.'

As the music reached its climax, I muttered an acid paraphrase of Londa's final sentence – 'Those dozen voyagers who refused to tell me what I wanted to hear will remain on board until I broker a deal with the FBI' – for such was the depth of my hostility towards Operation PG, my cynicism regarding the Phyllistines' redemption, and my disgust with Dame Quixote and her poisonous dreams.

Hostility, cynicism, disgust: and yet – wonder of wonders – these sentiments were evidently misplaced. Although Londa did not permit me a shortwave radio or an Internet connection, she did allow Lieutenant Kristowski to drop by D deck once a day and shout the latest news through my barricaded door, and each such bulletin proved more heartening than the last. Against all odds, defying every rational expectation, our recently released Phyllistine legislators were sponsoring Beatitudinous measures around the clock, aimed variously at sparing the planet the ravages of industrialisation, curbing the theocratic agenda of the Centre for Stable Families, undermining Corporate Christi, and raising the republic's foreign-aid budget to levels commensurate with Jesus of Nazareth's reported enthusiasm for generosity. Our liberated CEOs, meanwhile, ashamed of their former complicity in sweat-shops and global poverty, were arranging for the planet's toys, running shoes, designer clothing, household appliances, and cybernetic consumer goods to be assembled in convivial environments by reasonably contented workers who received fair wages. As for our rehabilitated lobbyists, they were switching allegiances with an alacrity to tax the vocabulary of even the most articulate neo-Nazi radio host – for after you've labelled them traitors, quislings, and agents of Lucifer, what *else* can you call them? In nearly every case, the reformed influence peddler announced that his new cause, whether it was educating pre-schoolers, protecting rainforests, or securing affordable daycare for single mothers, had blessed him with an unaccustomed quantity of self-respect.

Concerning our immediate circumstances, Lieutenant Kristowski reported that after leaving Key Largo, the *Redux* had steamed to Isla de Sangre, and presently lay at anchor in the Bahía de Colón. Captain Pittinger and his officers, as well as the deck hands, stokers, stewards, galley staff, and medical personnel, had all been sent home, and in a goodwill gesture Londa had transferred the twelve unrepentant Phyllistines – a group that, predictably enough, included Enoch Anthem, Felix Pielmeister, and Ralph Gittikac – to second-class cabins on E deck. Throughout the luxury liner, the Lieutenant told me, an eerie quietude reigned: not surprising, really, since the guards now outnumbered the prisoners. Plenty of food remained in the pantries, and the Valkyries were amusing themselves by preparing gourmet meals for one another. Owing to our explosive cargo, the outside world was still disinclined to harass us, though it wasn't clear how much longer the standoff would prevail before somebody blinked, baulked or blew up the ship.

Hour by hour, the glad tidings poured in. The civilised world watched in awe as drug companies voluntarily lowered their prices, cigarette manufacturers launched class-action lawsuits against themselves, and automobile manufacturers burned the midnight oil seeking ways for future generations to burn innocuous fuels instead. But you know more about these halcyon days than I, ladies and gentlemen. After all, you were sitting in front of your television screens every night, witnessing heaven come to earth, while I languished in my boring windowless cabin, watching grade-Z Frankenstein movies.

When not contemplating Mary Shelley's cinematic descendants, clearing away the resultant cranial cobwebs with the aid of J. R. R. Tolkien and Guinness, or sending impotent messages to Londa imploring her to let me out of the clink, I talked through the door with Lieutenant Kristowski. Despite her inveterate faith in Dame Quixote, my aide-de-camp was having as much trouble as I believing that the miracle had occurred. 'To be truthful, I wasn't always sure she'd pull it off,' the Lieutenant said. 'There's a moment in *The League of Londa* number twenty-four when her followers lose faith. Dame Quixote has resolved to talk the world's leaders into destroying all their nuclear weapons, and of course her disciples think she's gone off the deep end, but then she actually makes it happen: universal disarmament. You must be proud of yourself, giving her such an ironclad conscience.'

'Proud? Right, Lieutenant. You bet. I taught her everything she knows. Love your enemies, and if that doesn't work, grind them into the dirt. Turn the other cheek, and if the bastard slaps you again, imprison him on a polluted luxury liner. Next time you meet a rich man, try dragging him through the eye of a needle, and if the experience leaves him a bloody pulp, well, you've certainly shattered his complacency.'

'Really, sir, I don't think this is a time for negativity,' Lieutenant Kristowski said.

'Londa would agree with you. That's why she keeps me in jail.'

'You never told her to grind her enemies into the dirt.'

'Back when we were mentor and mentee, I told her that at least once a day. Obviously she learned her lesson. I'm a better teacher than I know.'

In these sneering, jeering, jaded times we tend to forget how close my vatling came to redeeming Western civilisation through Operation Pineal Gland. For a full seven weeks following the release of the cured plutocrats, an epidemic of decency raged through the corridors of power and the citadels of privilege. Sometimes the blessing in question traced directly to the activism of a former *Redux* hostage, sometimes to a mover and shaker who'd been moved and shaken by a rehabilitated Phyllistine's example. It seemed not only that the meek stood a plausible chance of inheriting the Earth, but that the concomitant taxes would be paid by, of all people, the rich. Within the walls of corporations once shamelessly engaged in gangbanging the biosphere, moderation was now the watchword, even as a previously unthinkable distinction, that between an honest profit and a profit beyond cupidity's wettest dream, was now openly discussed in boardrooms everywhere. Behind the ramparts of America's gated communities, a discourse had arisen whereby the promiscuous accumulation of wealth was regarded less as a mark of genius than as an index of sin.

The bubble, I am told, did not so much burst as implode. Apparently one could practically hear the sluggish suck of unearned income returning to plutocrat pockets, the plaintive peal of progressive legislation falling into procedural purgatory, the agonised cries of Lady Justice squirming and writhing in the jaws of alleged necessity. It was as if the rehabilitated Phyllistines and their acolytes had all awoken one morning and said to themselves, 'Wait a minute. What's going on here? This is the United States of America, not fucking Camelot. What were we *thinking*?'

Believe me, ladies and gentlemen, I understand why many of you recall the golden age of Operation PG with fondness. If the Beatitudes broke the bank once, the argument goes, the same thing could happen again, so let us celebrate the dream. For what it's worth, though, I have come to regard Londa's transient success as an unequivocal tragedy. Far better for the merciful, the gentle, the just, and the spat-upon if they'd remained permanently in the shadows and never endured the fate that actually befell them: a day in the sun followed by the cruellest imaginable eclipse.

Though filtered through several layers of pine and oak, Lieutenant Kristowski's sobs clawed at my soul. Numb with sorrow, paralysed with despair, my aide-de-camp could barely bring herself to relate the depressing despatches now arriving from every corner of the globe. Sweatshops once again running at a pace to wreck their employees' health and rack their spirits. Logging companies chewing their way through the world's forests as if there were no tomorrow. Legislators cutting nutritional programmes for the urban poor even as these same elected representatives rigged the tax code to guarantee that no CEO need suffer ever-empty-yacht-berth syndrome again.

'Back to square one,' I moaned.

'Dr Sabacthani will think of something,' my aide-de-camp asserted in the bravest voice she could muster. 'She always does.'

Lieutenant Kristowski's instinct was doubtless correct. Dr Sabacthani would think of something. And at that particular moment, sitting in my prison as *Lady Frankenstein* played across my plasma television monitor, I could not imagine a more disturbing prediction.

While the unravelling of Operation Pineal Gland broke my heart, it also hardened my resolve, convincing me to do everything within my power to prevent the circumstances through which Londa Sabacthani had come into the world – her vatling birth, her DUNCE cap infancy, her scattershot moral education at the hands of a dubious philosopher – from ever converging again. How I longed to break free of my prison and appear on Londa's doorstep: not in my persona as her ethical advisor, of course, a sympathetic Jiminy Cricket nudging her back on to the straight and narrow. Her caller would be an insect of Gregor Samsa pedigree, bent and grotesque, graphically reflecting her own misshapen soul, or perhaps an anthropod more monstrous yet, a chittering, chitinous mutation out of a 1950s science-fiction movie, *It Came From Beneath the Family Hearth*. You may fancy yourself a semidivine genius, I would tell her, but in truth you're just another autocratic narcissist whose followers have guns.

As the days slogged by, I came to wish that my DVD library actually included some of those 1950s giant-insect thrillers. In my experience such spectacles were marginally diverting, which is more than I could say for my digitalised Frankenstein omnibus. Despite their promising titles, none of these films could be rehabilitated through hermeneutics. There was no compelling discourse on gender occurring between the frames of *Lady Frankenstein*, no postmodern insouciance afoot in *Jesse James Meets Frankenstein's Daughter*, no tacit political subtext crying out for deconstruction in *Frankenstein Conquers the World*. There was only tedium, and turgidity, and my gradual realisation that Londa was severely mistaken if she imagined that these cinematic catastrophes could provide insights into her mother's mind.

Month three of my imprisonment was not long under way when, early one morning, Major Powers popped the padlock, marched into my cabin, and, after hauling my semi-conscious self out of bed, explained that Londa wanted to see me. I dressed frantically – linen slacks and a silk shirt that in fact belonged to one of our twelve on-board Phyllistines, Clarence Garmond of the White House Council on Air and Water Quality – and soon we were on B deck, marching towards Londa's headquarters. Although I'd never doubted Lieutenant Kristowski's report that the *Redux* lay moored in the Bahía de Colón, I was startled to look beyond the glassed-in promenade and see not the usual expanse of ocean but a range of forested hills wreathed in clouds. It was a typical Isla de Sangre dawn, pure travel brochure, the rising sun fruiting the trees with emeralds and filling the bay with diamonds.

Major Powers and I arrived in time to observe the changing of the guard, two steely-eyed Valkyries stepping away as their day-shift counterparts – the avatar of Themis and the transsexual conquistador – came on deck. A shroud of melancholy enswathed all four sentries. Dagmar Röhrig sat slumped behind her desk, staring despondently into space. Saying nothing, she waved us into the parlour suite.

Londa, wrapped in shadows, lay sprawled across a green velvet divan, a raven cloaked by its own wings. Major Powers made a discreet exit. A calculated cough escaped my throat. My vatling struggled to her feet and stepped into a shaft of sunlight streaming through the porthole. Her flesh looked battered and swollen, as if she'd been swallowed by Spenser's allegorical Error, judged indigestible, and vomited out.

'Guess what, Socrates?' she muttered. 'You've been replaced. Like a worn-out fan belt. I've got a new conscience now.'

Although rococonut milk was Londa's anaesthetic of choice, today she'd opted for rum. She approached her antique desk and, taking hold of a half-empty Captain Morgan bottle, slopped a measure into a cracked white coffee mug.

'Is this development supposed to make me jealous?' I asked.

'Yes.'

'It doesn't.' Actually it did.

She swallowed some rum, then moved her hands with the staccato awkwardness of a stymied player of charades, eventually directing my gaze towards the porthole and the island it disclosed. 'The Wild Woman of the Jungle.'

'What?'

'My new ethical advisor. The Wild Woman of the Jungle. The feisty lady has blessed every aspect of Operation PG – past, present, and future. She even signed 'The Book of Londa'. Our relationship is not ideal, but she understands me better than you do.'

'That rum bottle understands you better than I do.'

She took another gulp of Captain Morgan. 'Be honest, Mason. You think I've lost. Lousy position, down a rook, and my opponent's about to queen a pawn. But as we all know, sweetie, the winner's not the one with great position, an extra rook, and a pawn storming the back row – it's the one who can flash the other player a smirk and say, "Checkmate." The whole world will be listening to tomorrow's broadcast, but my message will hold particular interest for our recently released Phyllistines. They have one last chance to get it right.'

'And what if they *don't* get it right?'

'You always ask such penetrating questions, Mason. I swear, the day you die, Aristotle and Plato will petition God to have you transferred south. If you can't liven up limbo, nobody can.'

'Limbo doesn't exist any more.'

'Nor does God. Been enjoying your Frankenstein films?'

'They're garbage. What if the released Phyllistines ignore you?'

Londa sipped some rum and removed a Jerusalem Bible from her desk drawer. 'Major Powers tells me there's a great speech in *I Was a Teenage Frankenstein*. "Come, come, my boy, say good morning to your creator. Speak! You've got a civil tongue in your head – I know you have, because I sewed it back myself."' She flipped open the book and made a beeline for the Gospels. 'This Jew you think is such a splendid moral philosopher – you know what he *really* is? He's Victor Frankenstein's monster. Go digging through the New Testament, and eventually you'll unearth enough material to stitch together any sort of Jesus you want. When you neo-Darwinist sentimentalists go about it, you naturally assemble the brother-loving, mother-loving, other-loving, love-loving rabbi of your cuddliest fantasies. But suppose we want to build ourselves a different kind of Christ – say, the lock-and-load Messiah of the Rapture mongers? No problem. Take the Gospel According to Matthew. Chapter eleven, verse twenty-three, Jesus blithely condemning an entire city to hell – men, women, children, and foetuses. Chapter thirteen, verse forty-two, the Messiah merrily throwing sinners into a blazing furnace. Chapter eighteen, verse thirty-five, the Prince of Peace threatening his followers with torture if they fail to accord their estranged relatives sufficient forgiveness.' She snapped the book closed. 'What if the Phyllistines ignore me? Simple, Socrates. Colonel Fox brings Enoch Anthem on to the weather deck, and the first thing he notices is the dozen nooses dangling from the foremast shrouds.'

'Nooses?'

'The apocalypse, Anthem now realises, is about to become complete. War, Famine, and Pestilence have already visited the ship, which leaves only the pale rider on his pale horse.'

'No, Londa! Forget it! Absolutely not!'

'I see your point of view. I really do.'

In a gesture so cartoonish it was doubtless prefigured in some *League of Londa* splash panel, I strode towards her with arms raised, my fingers curled into talons. To this day, I'm not sure what I had in mind. Did I intend to close my hands around her throat and threaten to strangle her if she didn't surrender to the FBI?

She foiled the attack with her Godgadget, pulling it from her hip pocket and pointing it in my face. I froze, arrested by my vision of a rather different sort of splash panel: the *Redux* exploding, bright orange flames roiling outwards from ground zero.

'Back off, Socrates.'

I retreated two steps.

'Have you any idea how empowering this device is?' Her index finger danced above the transmitter. 'At the press of a button, I can change the channel of reality itself.' She brought the remote to her lips and kissed it. 'By my calculation, the threat of Enoch

Anthem's execution will inspire thousands of his followers to find their inner Samaritan. But perhaps my prediction will fail, in which case I'll have to lynch Anthem and play the game all over again with a second hostage – Corbin Thorndike, say, or Ralph Gittakac, or your friend Pielmeister.' Circling back to her desk, she threw a switch on the intercom and delivered an order to Dagmar. 'My lame-duck conscience has become impossibly annoying. Kindly instruct Major Powers to remove him from my vicinity.'

'Imagine you've borrowed my axe,' I said. 'When I come to claim it, I'm obviously in a lather, and so you—'

'And so I defend myself by splitting your head open,' Londa said.

'And so you refuse to give it back.'

'Ah, yes, I forgot that step. The Wild Woman would be ashamed of me. I refuse to give it back, and *then* I split your head open.'

I cursed Londa to her face, specifying the precise ratio between her corporeal contents and shit, whereupon Major Powers appeared and casually imprisoned me in a half nelson.

'Your husband is dying of cancer, but a radium extract might save him,' I told Londa as the Valkyrie dragged me away. 'You can't afford the druggist's outrageous price, so here's the question: should you break into the pharmacy and steal an ampoule?'

'Of course I should steal it,' Londa said. 'And the next morning I'll return to the store with my borrowed axe, and I'll hack the pharmacist to pieces for being such a greedy Phyllistine.'

Shortly after Major Powers brought me back down to D deck and locked me in my cabin, I managed to prevent *The Last Shall Be First* from ever intruding on my awareness again. The procedure was surprisingly simple, a mere matter of transforming a coat hanger into a metal rod and thrusting it repeatedly through the perforated ceiling plate. Each time my rapier pierced the paper speaker, I experienced a small thrill. To cleanse my cabin of Londa's voice wasn't the same as thwarting the vatling herself, but it was a start.

At the end of the week I suffered two minor misfortunes when my wristwatch and my travel alarm both ceased to function. My immediate impulse was to ask Lieutenant Kristowski for replacement batteries, but she no longer came down to D deck – evidently Londa had decided to deprive me of all human contact. And so it happened that, with no clock at my disposal, no sun within view, and my food appearing at random intervals, I lost track of time. My dawns, mornings, afternoons and dusks forsook their normal boundaries, melting into one another, even as my Wagner recordings and cheapjack monster movies coalesced into a surrealist German opera whose cast had been exhumed and reanimated by Victor Frankenstein himself. When at last a fellow being darkened my door, I could not say for certain if a week had passed, or a fortnight, or an entire month.

My visitor was Major Powers, crashing unannounced into my cabin and brandishing a pair of steel handcuffs whose intended destination was brutally apparent.

'You're going ashore,' she told me. 'Londa has arranged for you to meet with her new ethical advisor.'

'I'd rather see if *I Was a Teenage Frankenstein* gets better the tenth time around.'

'The Wild Woman is expecting you,' Major Powers insisted, yoking my wrists together. 'Sorry about the bracelets, but Londa says you've been acting strange.'

'Could I ask you a stupid question? Is it morning, noon, or night?'

'Morning in New Delhi, night in London, noon aboard the *Redux*.'

Now Lieutenant Kristowski appeared, according the handcuffs a quick scowl and an unhappy sigh. Evidently it pained her to see Masai Ambooloy's prototype being treated so harshly, but then her face softened, as if she'd just told herself, for the thousandth time, that Dr Sabacthani worked in mysterious ways.

My reluctant wardens guided me out of my cabin and down the D-deck corridor towards the companionway. Although neither woman was in a talkative mood, I managed to elicit a few provocative facts concerning Londa. By Major Powers' account, she'd recently vacated the ship and moved back into Faustino, relaying her commands to Colonel Fox via her cell phone. Despite the 'ostensible failure of Operation PG', Londa had triumphed over her despair and was now brimming with 'new ideas for curing the Phyllistines', which was exactly what I didn't want to hear.

The natural music of Isla de Sangre greeted our arrival on the boat deck, a polyphony of breaking waves, screeching parrots, and gibbering monkeys. Colonel Fox awaited us near one of the *Redux*'s three remaining lifeboats, hanging from its davits like a baby's cradle. As Major Powers and Lieutenant Kristowski prepared the vessel for launch, Colonel Fox made an ominous announcement: 'Before you go ashore, Londa wants you to see something.' She then propelled me through the deserted wheelhouse to the lookout booth on the starboard wing, a vantage point that gave me an unobstructed view of the weather deck.

The rigging now featured a dozen nooses, each dangling from its own ratline. Was I surprised that Londa had gone ahead with her plan to turn the foremast into a gallows? Not really. What shocked me was the bodies, one suspended from the starboard shroud, the other from the port, both twisting in the noonday sun like exhibits in a butcher's window. Vultures and seagulls made languid circles around the dead men, periodically swooping down and partaking of the feast their carrion god had spread before them. Judging from the pitted condition of his flesh, Enoch Anthem had probably been lynched several days before Corbin Thorndike – unless it happened that, for a bird of prey, a cleric is tastier than a CEO.

Seconds after my mind absorbed the grisly scene, my stomach registered it as well and, leaning out of the landward window, I vomited my breakfast into the Bahía de Colón.

'We're not yet sure how many such executions the future holds,' Vetruvia Fox said, noting my distress, 'but Londa is confident that the meek will inherit the Earth long before we run out of hostages.'

The Colonel took my hand and propelled me towards Major Powers and Lieutenant Kristowski, who in our absence had managed to ready the lifeboat for lowering, its elliptical form casting a sharklike shadow on the water. I must confess, ladies and gentlemen, that my first rational remark concerning the fate of Anthem and Thorndike was informed less by moral outrage, humanist sympathy, or even simple sorrow than by mere flippancy. Am I more of a cynic – and less of a Cynic – than I would like to believe?

'Those decaying corpses will look terrific on the cover of *The League of Londa*,' I told Lieutenant Kristowski. 'Even at the height of its glory, *Tales from the Crypt* never had a grabber like that.'

CHAPTER 16

In recent years I have managed to acquire, against the odds and despite my bank account, a complete set of *The League of Londa*. Number 46, which I purchased on eBay, arrived in the mail only yesterday, and it indeed features a story about Londa's inscrutable mentor, the philosopher-alchemist Dr Masai Ambooloy. I even appear on the lurid full-colour cover: superheroine and mentor standing shoulder to shoulder amidst a fretwork of film-noir shadows, cooking up a homunculus in a subterranean laboratory. The resemblance between Dr Ambooloy and myself is so precise that, were I a litigious man, I might sue the artist for appropriating my face.

But if I am to enjoy an exalted status in your eyes, ladies and gentlemen, let it not be as Dr Ambooloy. Rather, let my mythic alter ego be Prometheus that eternal friend of the human race. Does this mean I fancy myself a Titan, a son of Gaea, a ruler of the universe? Hardly. My point is simply that I was among those who gifted Edwina's vatlings with the ambiguous boon of scruples. Like Prometheus, we acted out of compassion for our charges. You must believe that. We loved those children. If I had to do it over again, I would surely have spared Londa the Beatitudes and shielded her from the Good Samaritan. But I would still have brought her the fire.

As Major Powers, Lieutenant Kristowski and I took leave of that hubristic ship to which the Titan race had leant its name, the late Enoch Anthem continued to haunt me, and Corbin Thorndike proved equally pitiless. Their suspended remains broached my skull, split my brain, seared my visual cortex. Throughout our trip to Isla de Sangre, I sat in the bow of the lifeboat and moaned.

The two Valkyries ignored their wretched passenger, concentrating instead on rowing us safely past the reef. It occurred to me that during our earliest lessons I might have fruitfully presented Londa with a role-playing exercise spun from the sinking of the original *Titanic*. 'Imagine this scenario, young woman. You've made it into lifeboat number five, which like most of the others is not filled to capacity. The great ship has gone down, and you can hear the screams of the less fortunate passengers, bobbing about in their lifejackets as they freeze to death. The quartermaster commanding boat five calls for everyone's attention. "Raise your hand", he tells his forty-one charges, "if you believe we should go back and pull some of those screaming souls from the water." Now here's the question, Londa. Do you endorse the quartermaster's plan? Or are you swayed by the argument that scores of panicky survivors will try scrambling into the lifeboat, capsizing it in the process?'

We came to rest in a palm-sheltered cove that, despite various overland explorations during my Blood Island sojourn, I'd never seen before. While Lieutenant Kristowski remained behind on the beach, guarding the boat, Major Powers led me along a labyrinthine path winding past mammoth flowering plants. On all sides fat vines formed graceful parabolas, macaws swooped from tree to tree, and dragonflies darted about like remote-control syringes inoculating the air against Phyllistine pollution. During the journey I repeatedly explained to Carmen Powers that, while I was quite willing to speak with the Wild Woman of the Jungle, I would not listen to any glib rationalisations about the dead men on the foremast. The Major had no reaction to this high-minded sentiment, but at one point she told me in a surprising spasm of candour, 'As long as *you* were her conscience, there was hope.'

Our hike ended before a vast expanse of inland water, not the pristine Laguna Zafira on which I'd once lived but rather its aquatic opposite – dark, bleak, silent and tide-fed, its shores fringed with mottled masses of algae. A decrepit and perforated wooden dock, free lunch for myriad marine invertebrates, extended six feet from shore. My immediate obligation, the Major explained, was to stay here and wait for the Wild Woman. If the meeting between

314

her ethical advisors went well, Londa would see fit to remove my handcuffs.

Carmen Powers slipped away, leaving me to sit on the dock and brood. The afternoon stretched into an orchid-scented dusk that soon became a shimmering tropical night bathed in amber lunar hues. A dozen jellyfish rode the tidal currents, their umbrella bodies glowing an iridescent blue. At length a female human figure appeared on the water, limned by moonbeams, standing erect in the stern of a skiff as she poled her way towards the ruined pier. She was blessed with Londa's commanding height, athletic build, and imperial poise. As this lithesome Charon drew nearer, my vatling's lovely features emerged from the gloom, her green eyes piercing the fog like beacons.

'I've seen the bodies on the foremast, Londa,' I said in the most venomous voice I could summon. 'The vultures have done their worst.'

Charon stood up straighter still, exuding a pale presence: white shirt, white slacks, white face – a vision that suggested alternately a June bride and a shrouded cadaver. 'I'm not Londa,' she rasped.

'OK, fine, and I'm not Mason, and those two corpses are Gilbert and Sullivan.'

'Step aboard, Mr Ambrose. Take a seat. My shack is on the far side of the lagoon. I'm not Londa.'

'Take these damn handcuffs off me.'

'Only Londa can do that. The key is with her at Faustino. Step aboard. My name is Edwina 0004. Londa made me. The child is the mother of the woman. We're having steamed crabs for dinner. I caught and cooked them myself.'

Ah, the brilliance, the audacity, the sheer recklessness of my vatling. The wanton genius. The transcendent cheek. So your original conscience isn't willing to rubber-stamp your sins? Have no fear. Simply drop by Torre de la Carne, reactivate the onto-generator, reprogram the DUNCE cap, and bring your faux mother back to life. After all, the *Übermom* was always your greatest friend and supporter.

Slowly she poled us away from the dock, guiding the skiff through the alien jellyfish nation. I hunched in the prow and stared at Edwina 0004, studying the moonlit elegance of her cheekbones, the graceful sweep of her jaw. The resemblance to Londa was at once disturbing and inevitable: the primal Edwina had been Londa's present age when she died, so it followed that the Wild Woman and my vatling would mirror one another – indeed, Edwina 0004 lacked only her creator's faint wrinkles and incipient eye pouches. A thirty-eight-year-old who'd yet to celebrate her first birthday, the present beaker freak displayed no marks of the life she'd never lived.

Much to my surprise, she was prepared to discourse upon her *Dasein*, and by the time we reached the far shore, all my most burning questions had been answered. Unlike the species from which she'd arisen, an animal that in accounting for itself faced an unhappy choice between a groundless theism and a groundling Darwinism, Edwina 0004 knew how she'd come into the world. She fully grasped her ontological status – doppelgänger of a deceased biologist, puppet of the DUNCE cap's algorithms, mother and mentor to the notorious Dame Quixote – and she radiated a sense of mission. The original Edwina had devoted herself to her triune daughter's welfare, and Edwina 0004, if I could believe her, was equally determined to secure Londa's happiness.

'At one time her happiness mattered to *you* too,' the Wild Woman admonished me. 'A golden age, Londa calls it. She hopes it will return.'

'Golden ages rarely return,' I said, 'especially if they never existed.'

A coughing fit seized the Wild Woman, the guttural convulsions ringing across the open water, and I wondered whether this particular Edwina, like her predecessor, might be cursed with poor health. 'Technically I'm as sociopathic as any newborn vatling, but so far I've committed no crimes,' she said. 'I haven't burned down Faustino, or pulled the wings off a butterfly, or sneaked on to the ship and slit Felix Pielmeister's throat. This morning I came up with a theory. Want to hear it? My psyche or soul or whatever you call it – my program – it's bursting with love for Londa, and this affection keeps my depravity at bay.'

'Entirely plausible,' I said, though I doubted that a DUNCE cap program could provide its recipient with anything but the most schematic beneficence. Her depravity, I suspected, was merely biding its time.

Although the Wild Woman had called her dwelling a shack, it had obviously once been the most picturesque of lakeside cottages, a virtue it might still have boasted had the jungle not laid claim to the exterior. Flowering vines enswathed the walls like veins coursing through aged skin, dark roots emerged between the porch planks like ebony piano keys, and the roof had become a Swinburnian garden of bougainvillea and Spanish moss.

'Back when I was the primal Edwina, this place was my secret world,' said the Wild Woman, leading me through a tidy kitchenette into a cosy living space dominated by a table spread with the promised feast of freshly caught crabs. 'Here and only here could I escape the commotion of myself.'

'Speaking of escape ...' I cast an indignant eye on my shackles.

'Even if I had the key, Londa wouldn't want me to use it. She loves you, but she doesn't trust you.'

I sat down and, through a series of gestures made oafish by the handcuffs, slowly dismantled a crab. We ate in silence. Evidently Londa had stencilled some first-rate recipes on to Edwina 0004's *tabula rasa*, because the meal left nothing to be desired. Even the wine was admirable, a Chablis drawn from a rack in the kitchenette, though we had to consume it at room temperature.

'Last night, while you and I were sleeping, thirty thousand children died of malnutrition,' Edwina 0004 suddenly declared, using a grapefruit spoon to extract a final titbit from her crab shell. 'We're all guilty bystanders to that tragedy, but certain bystanders are more guilty than others. Some, in fact, are accessories to the crime.'

'I quite agree,' I said. 'But that hardly gives Londa the right to *murder* those accessories.'

'Believe it or not,' the Wild Woman said, swallowing a morsel, 'just hearing another person say my daughter's name gives me a thrill. "But that hardly gives Londa the right to *murder* those accessories." Please, Mr Ambrose, let me hear you say "Londa" again. Any sort of sentence will do, as long as it includes her name.'

'Sure. How's this? It would be my guess that Londa has gone completely insane.'

Edwina 0004 sipped her Chablis. 'It's such a privilege being a mother. I'm relishing every minute. "It would be my guess that Londa has gone completely insane." Marvellous. As I'm sure you know, if western Europe and the United States committed seven billion dollars annually to the cause of clean drinking water worldwide, that investment would save four thousand lives a day. Might I convince you to say it again? "It would be my guess that Londa has gone completely insane." I pity any woman who isn't a mother.'

I dabbed the corners of my mouth with a tattered but spotless napkin. 'How about we change the subject, OK?'

'Seven billion dollars. That's less than Europeans spend each year on perfume and Americans on cosmetic surgery. Before he went to the gallows, Enoch Anthem spoke often about Christ turning water into wine, but he never once implored Christendom to turn perfume into water. God, I do love it – I love being a mother. Annual global expenditure to fight AIDS, a disease that kills millions each year, amounts to three days of military appropriations. Londa, Yolly, Donya. I love them all. Three children in one. One child in three. My dearest, sweetest Yolonda.'

Our encounter continued in this vein for another hour, Edwina indicting the geopolitical status quo by piling gruesome fact upon gruesome fact, until at last she fixed me with Londa's most piercing gaze and said, 'My daughter was right. She predicted you would join our side once I made my presentation.'

'"All mimsy were the borogoves,"' I said, '"and the mome raths outgrabe."'

'That too.' She smiled seraphically. 'Remember our first meeting? Mason and the primal Edwina, sitting on wicker chairs in the geodesic dome? I gave you a mumquat from Proserpine. The mattress in the sleeping loft is a bit lumpy, but the one in my bedroom is soft as a cloud. Shall we draw straws?'

'The loft is fine,' I said, moving my fettered hands in a circumscribed gesture of nonchalance. 'But I must ask you something. After Londa decided to create you, did she take the trouble to—'

'To dig up the primal Edwina? Or did she simply use a specimen of her own DNA?'

'That's my question, yes.'

'What do you think?' she asked.

'I have no idea.'

'Yes, you do,' the Wild Woman said.

'Knowing Londa, I would imagine she did it the hard way.'

My hostess nodded and pressed both hands against her brow, as if to assuage a headache. 'According to my program, she exhumed and then reburied her mother with the greatest care. A wayfarer happening upon the grave would never know it had been disturbed. That's the sort of person my daughter is – respectful of the dead. She does us both proud, wouldn't you say?'

I couldn't sleep that night, though the problem was neither the lumpy mattress, the despicable handcuffs, nor the Wild Woman's ghoulish origins, but the far more vexing issue of Londa's madness. The problem was the corpses on the foremast. To quiet my mind I meditated on Zeno's paradox, recited Aristotle's taxonomy of causes, and tabulated leaping sheep. Nothing worked – not even the additional glass of Chablis I obtained through a furtive visit to the kitchenette.

Shortly after dawn, I descended from the loft. The Wild Woman was up and about, dressed now in khaki pants and a safari shirt. Insomnia had lately plagued her as well – such was the testimony of her face, so haggard she looked more like Londa than ever. Silently we breakfasted on raw oysters washed down with freeze-dried coffee. The caffeine proved sufficient to open our eyes and get us talking past each other again, with my hostess attempting to convince me that her daughter was a libelled saint, while I countered her arguments with unassailable mountains of unequivocal evidence, not one particle of which successfully completed the arduous trek from Edwina 0004's ears to the rational portions of her brain. Throughout this vaporous exchange – this nonversation, if you will – she filled her knapsack with bananas and cashews: snacks for our hike to Faustino, she explained.

'Londa is eager to see you again. Now that I've entered her life, she's prepared to forgive you your trespasses, a majority of them at least, maybe even your unwillingness to bless Operation PG.'

'And who's going to forgive Londa *her* trespasses?'

The Wild Woman scowled impatiently. 'Who do you think?'

No dirt road, no jungle trail, no thoroughfare of any sort lay between the lagoon and Faustino, and so we spent the better part of the morning hacking our way through the undergrowth. The heat was relentless, the mosquitoes gave us no quarter, and Edwina 0004's incessant chatter – another depressing and pointless catalogue of Phyllistine transgressions – drove me crazy. At long last we reached the valley of acacia groves and, passing beneath the dysfunctional crossing gate, its arm raised in an eternal *Sieg heil*, headed down the dirt road towards the mansion.

Against my expectations, my first glimpse of Londa that afternoon aroused in me neither rage, revulsion, nor righteous indignation. There she was, dressed absurdly in a saffron silk muumuu and a Florida Panthers baseball cap, humming off-key as she stood on the veranda casually whipping up a jug of sangria, and this utterly banal tableau filled me with longing for the virtuous vatling I'd once known and also – I make my confession with great reluctance – for the fanatical vatling she'd become.

Whooping with joy, the women raced towards each other, Londa travelling from the veranda to the ground in a single balletic leap. Their embrace was spontaneous and passionate, and for a brief instant I fancied that the primal Edwina was actually walking the Earth again, revelling in motherhood. Threaded on a gold chain, the Godgadget hung from Londa's neck like a crucifix, and I cringed at the thought that in hugging so tightly these two beaker freaks might inadvertently detonate the explosives in forehold 3. At last Londa pulled free of her – her what? – her mother? daughter? sister? student? conscience? – then returned to the veranda, where she poured a round of sangria for all.

'Cheers,' she said, clinking glasses with Edwina 0004. 'Tell me, *Maman*, what sort of philosopher have you brought me today?'

'The former master has become the humble disciple. He bows to your wisdom, and he loves you more than ever.'

I needed the whole of my cerebrum to process these words, my analytical left hemisphere rejecting Edwina 0004's ridiculous assertion that I was now a Sabacthanite, even as my irrational right hemisphere contemplated the strange truth that, yes, I still adored my vatling.

'As I was leaving the *Redux*, I thought of an ethical dilemma,' I told her, gulping some sangria.

'The good old days,' said Londa with only a modicum of sarcasm.

'Imagine you're in lifeboat number five, rowing away from the wreck. Screams fill the air – the abandoned passengers, afloat in their lifejackets, freezing to death. There are twenty-four extra spaces left. Do you vote to go back, or do you—'

'Or do I decide that a mob of survivors will arrive en masse and sink the boat? Difficult question, Socrates. Give me till sundown.'

'In the meantime, kindly unshackle me.'

'Sorry. Can't. As Mother says, you love me, but there's something you love even more. You love the idea of hogtieing your homicidal gumbo girl and bringing her to justice.'

A protest formed on my lips – No, Londa, I just want to be rid of the damn handcuffs – even as I admitted to myself that Mason unbound might try to do exactly what she imagined. But before I could make my complaint, Londa took Edwina 0004 by the arm and escorted her into the mansion.

Throughout the rest of the day, the women focused their physical and emotional energies on each other, gleefully pursuing those mother–daughter activities that had so gratified the primal Edwina during her final months. They erected a badminton net on the lawn and played a series of three games, all of which Londa won. They took tea and biscuits on the veranda, simultaneously pursuing a conversation whose levels of rapport and intimacy were doubtless off the charts. As the sun descended, arraying the tropical sky with sashes of gold and turquoise, they slipped into identical yellow spandex bathing suits and went down to the beach, intent on frolicking in the surf.

Having nothing better to do, I prowled through the library where Londa and I had first enacted the Riddle of the Borrowed Axe and the Fable of the Stolen Radium. In time I gravitated towards the philosophy section, spontaneously unshelving a key influence on *Ethics from the Earth*: John Caputo's *Against Ethics*, with its wry argument that lofty theories of virtue have done the world a grand total of no good. Briefly I traded stares with Alonso the Conquistador and, intuiting that he approved of my choice, I ferried it to the reading table and set about revisiting the various passages spun from Heidegger's *Es gibt* – 'There is' – which for the author meant 'There is obligation,' savouring them as I might a rococonut julep.

'"Obligations happen, bonds are formed, tables are set, and the earth is covered in cold white snow, while the surf roars, while the stars dance their nightly dance, while worms inch their way towards forgotten graves."'

At seven o'clock my stomach began rumbling. As if cued by this gastric clamour, Londa suddenly appeared, dressed once again in her saffron silk muumuu and holding a silver salver heaped with lobster canapés, caviar-smeared crackers, salmon croquettes, and oysters Rockefeller, all of which she'd pilfered from the *Redux* shortly before taking up residence at Faustino. She'd also brought a local delicacy, a blue ceramic flagon filled with mumquat nectar. I set the book on the reading table, splayed and spine up so that it suggested a capital A. A is for *Against Ethics*. Adam's fall, Augustine's confessions, Anthem's broken neck. Londa pulled up a chair. The Godgadget was no longer slung about her neck – hardly a cause for celebration: with eight duplicates on board, she could permanently mislay her own, or deliberately destroy it, or wrap it up in ribbons and give it to me for my birthday.

We fed ourselves uncouthly, wolfing down one dainty after another, sluicing them into our stomachs with large swallows of serenity. Then Londa gestured towards *Against Ethics* and asked, 'What's that one about?'

'Obligation,' I said. 'The Loch Necessity Monster.'

'Caputo's a Kantian then?'

'More of a Kierkegaardian.'

'Are we still friends?'

'No.'

'Enemies?'

'That's quite likely the case.'

'Lovers?' she asked tentatively.

'Perhaps that's how history will remember us.'

She ate the last of the lobster canapés. 'I would vote to go back.'

'What?'

'I'm in boat number five, remember? I would vote to go back and rescue as many passengers as possible. They're exhausted and weak and half frozen. It's preposterous to imagine they would swamp us.'

'Good answer,' I said, consuming the last oyster Rockefeller.

From her pocket Londa produced a toothed steel rod, pressing it into my palm like a queen setting her seal on a decree. The key, she explained. I immediately attempted to free myself, but thanks to the handcuffs this ambition proved paradoxical, like trying to write on a pen using the pen with which you're writing. Londa came to my aid, popping both shackles open in a matter of seconds.

I swung my arms in joyous circles. 'What did I do to deserve this?'

'You haven't done it yet, but you will. Listen, darling. I just got off the phone with Colonel Fox. Our liberated hostages are still behaving badly. It would appear that their new and improved pineal glands have atrophied.'

'You expected otherwise?'

She pointedly ignored my question. 'In keeping with Dame Quixote's ultimatum, I should call Colonel Fox back and arrange for Pielmeister to join his fellow incorrigibles on the foremast – unless you think Gittikac or Wintergreen would be a better choice.'

'The hell with Dame Quixote. The hell with her ultimatum.'

'A worthy sentiment, Mason. I quite agree. The hell with them. Hear my proposition. I'm assigning you to Mother's old bedchamber, second floor, the suite with the grandfather clock outside the door. The Wild Woman will sleep in my room. I'll come to you at midnight. We'll drink nectar together, and kiss our pain away, and for a few glorious hours we'll become the same person. At dawn we'll start talking again, a full-blown philosophical conversation, Socrates and his gumbo girl, all morning and maybe all afternoon, however long it takes us to figure out what my next move should be.'

'I already know what your next move should be. Surrender to the FBI, and convince the Valkyries to do the same.'

323

'Such high expectations you have for your student,' she said.

'The mark of a caring teacher.'

She brought a hand to her mouth, her thin fingers set across her lips like sutures, then used the opposite hand to silence me. 'No words,' she whispered. 'From now until the sun comes up, no words.'

I nodded. She dropped her hands, brushed my cheek and, shifting softly within her muumuu, slipped out of the room.

With its driving rain, explosive thunder, and brilliant bursts of lightning, each discharge flashing through the black sky like an aneurysm bursting in God's brain, the tempest now raging across Isla de Sangre inevitably evoked the stormy night Henry and I crept into Torre de la Carne and observed Yolly's advent. In a matter of hours, the island would, Isis assenting, Thoth willing, witness the birth and maturation of a rather different creature. If I played my part well, wielding my philosopher's scalpel with consummate skill, by noon tomorrow I would give the world a rehabilitated Londa Sabacthani, moral agent extraordinaire, committed to shutting down Operation PG before it spilled more blood.

True to my expectations, the primal Edwina's former boudoir was a paragon of opulence, shaming even the most extravagant stateroom aboard the *Titanic Redux*. The canopy bed was especially splendid, a hushed bower girded by green velvet curtains fastened to the posts by silken cords. As the wind rattled the casements, hurling barrages of rain against the panes, I set about increasing the ambient eroticism – lighting candles, igniting a stick of patchouli incense, equipping the CD player with Castelnuovo-Tedesco's Guitar Concerto No. 1 in D major, arraying the night-stand with the mumquat flagon flanked by two crystal goblets – then took a quick shower and, returning to the bedchamber, put on a black satin caftan, the sole garment hanging in the closet.

Midnight arrived, heralded by the grandfather clock in the hall, and as the twelfth chime died within its depths Londa appeared before me, wearing only a white silk dressing gown. We embraced. No words. I untied her sash and parted the halves of her gown, portals to her beauteous estate. Grasping my caftan by the shoulders, she slipped it smoothly over my head. No words. We climbed on to the mattress and, like Tristan and Isolde hoisting the sails of their love barge, pulled the silk cords loose from the bedposts, so that the curtains glided noiselessly into place.

In a matter of minutes, the wind and the tide carried us far from shore. And still no words, though of course we didn't need them, being absorbed in the discourse of our skin. How abundantly I loved my creature that night. I loved her confabulated flesh and ontogenerated smile, her synthetic psyche and labyrinthine mind. I loved each cell in her marrow, every synapse in her brain. Occasionally we procured the flagon and filled our goblets, and at one point we broke our vow of silence and recited Shakespeare to one another – 'So long as men can breathe or eyes can see, / So long lives this, and this gives life to thee' – the nectar all the while heating our blood, until at last our private orgy ended, and our love barge came to rest, and we descended into a delicious and unfathomable sleep.

The concert began with warbling finches, and soon the squawks of the parrots arose, followed by the cries of herons and flamingoes. Golden shafts of sunlight slanted through the gaps in the bed curtains, and I knew that the storm had blown out to sea. I yawned, stretched, and with a slow downward stroke propelled myself into wakefulness. Time to beguile Londa with all my powers of reason. Time to make the Scarlet Darwinist once again sovereign over her soul.

But she was gone, my errant undine, absconded from our love barge. I drew a slow breath. No need to fret, I told myself. She was merely taking a shower, or once again sharing tea with her mother on the veranda. Or perhaps Londa had acquired the primal Edwina's habit of spending Saturday morning in the conservatory, though I imagined that the place must be more Swinburnian than ever, all canker and rot and wilt.

I slipped into my clothes and began the search, repeatedly calling Londa's name as I checked the bathrooms on all three floors, then descended to the foyer and headed for the veranda. Suddenly Edwina 0004 stood in my path, dressed in her safari jacket and demanding that I join her for coffee in the geodesic dome. She claimed to know Londa's whereabouts. Our forthcoming conversation would be of epochal significance, she said, keyed to matters of life and death.

'Londa's life, to be specific,' she insisted as we arrived among the languishing orchids and expiring ferns. 'Londa's death.'

The coffee urn held a potent mocha java. I filled my mug to the brim and, settling opposite Edwina 0004 at a small wrought-iron table, ventured a small electric sip.

'Let me summarise the situation as baldly as I can. My daughter is now my prisoner.' With unnerving sang-froid the Wild Woman poured a fragrant cup of hazelnut from a glass carafe. 'Earlier this morning I put your handcuffs on her, then locked her in Dr Charnock's old laboratory.'

It took me a moment to absorb this unlikely but not unwelcome piece of news. I reached across the table and squeezed the Wild Woman's wrist. 'Believe me, Edwina, you did the right thing.'

'My action knew nothing of virtue. Four hours ago, an especially aggressive component of my program kicked in.'

'The next step, I assume, is to contact the authorities.'

For a brief dreamy interval Edwina 0004 ignored me, casting a weary gaze around the dome. 'I think this is where I died,' she rasped. 'Yes, I'm sure of it. How strange. I passed away in this very room, under a mutant mangrove.' She looked me in the eye. 'The authorities? If you had the full picture, you would never say that. So here it is, Mr Ambrose. Full disclosure. Bless me, Father, for I have trafficked in moral ambiguity.'

A ball of lead congealed in my stomach like a failed alchemy experiment. How foolish of me to have forgotten that we were living on Isla de Sangre, illogic's own atoll. 'I'm listening,' I said apprehensively.

Edwina 0004 seized a bread knife and bisected a raisin bagel. 'I'll start with a question. Why do you suppose Londa created me?'

As would any self-respecting philosopher at this juncture, I frowned pensively and drank more coffee. 'She wanted to get her mother back, simultaneously replacing me with a more permissive advisor.'

'Correct. Go on.'

'And apparently she thought your advent would somehow allow the primal Edwina to continue enjoying the pleasures of motherhood.'

'True, every bit of it, but you've barely scratched the surface.'

'The story of my life.'

'The *real* reason I was brought into the world . . . I have difficulty saying this.'

'Yes?' I took a measure of coffee into my mouth, allowing it to trickle slowly down my throat.

'Londa created me for the purpose of murdering her.'

I aborted the swallow, spraying coffee into the air. 'What?'

'I'm a homicide machine,' the Wild Woman continued. 'Or, if you prefer, a suicide implement. I detest this situation, but there's nothing I can do about it. Londa is far more complex than you realise. You can't begin to imagine the intensity of her distress over Enoch Anthem's death. The instant the man stopped kicking, she suffered excruciating pangs of remorse.'

My hands trembled, setting the coffee awhirl in its mug. Was I in fact sitting three feet from Londa's designated assassin? I wished I had an auxiliary conscience of my own just then, somebody who would tell me exactly what to do – such as dragging Edwina 0004 into the jungle and roping her to a tree.

'Excruciating pangs,' I echoed. 'Though not quite excruciating enough' – an unbidden sarcasm entered my voice – 'to stop her from killing Corbin Thorndike, too.'

'That second hanging tortured her even more than the first. Her pineal gland began to bleed.' The Wild Woman mortared the halves of her bagel together with cream cheese. 'The Londa who stood on the weather deck, watching those two Phyllistines twist in the wind, was she a creature out of control? Of course. But here's the thing, Mr Ambrose. She *knew* that she was out of control, and in time she saw the answer, or thought she did, and so she cooked me up: Edwina 0004, Anthem and Thorndike's personal avenger, and that's why she's locked away in Charnock's lab right now, listening for my footsteps.'

'But you *love* Londa. You're her mother.'

'I'm her mother, yes. But I'm also my algorithms.'

'No, Edwina. This is crazy.'

'Are you appealing to my conscience, Mr Ambrose? I don't have one. There was no convenient ethicist around when I was growing up.'

I slammed my coffee mug on to the table. 'Listen, Edwina, there's no need to *murder* her. Here's the plan. We'll go to Charnock's lab, take her into custody, turn her over to the G-men – and then we'll try our damnedest to make sure she gets a fair trial.'

'Perhaps some hypothetical Edwina could do that,' the Wild Woman said, voraciously consuming her bagel. 'Edwina 0005 maybe, or Edwina 0006, or conceivably even the primal Edwina. But not I. My program won't permit it. I shall execute Londa, or I shall set her free. Either, or – that's me. Utterly binary. Totally digital. But there's *another* reason we won't be turning her over to the G-men. The symptoms should arrive any second now.'

'Symptoms?'

'First a tingling in your hands and feet, then a throbbing behind your eyes, and finally a loss of gross motor functions.'

My heart began racing, not only in reaction to the Wild Woman's revelation but also, no doubt, from the chemical contents of her treachery. 'You drugged me? You goddamn fucking drugged me?'

'More of Londa's ingenuity, a mixture of nectar and curare. It attacks the midbrain and spinal cord only. You needn't worry about blindness, aphasia, or respiratory complications.'

My best course, I decided, would be to find an emetic and cleanse myself of the contaminated coffee. I bolted from my chair, started for the dome entrance – and then it happened: not the predicted tingling, not the throbbing behind my eyes, but something considerably more frightening, a sharp blow, whack, as if Socrates' borrowed axe had made contact with my cranium. My knees went rubbery, my spine became jelly, and I collapsed on to the dirt floor.

'If Londa has calculated correctly, you won't black out.' The Wild Woman stood over me, devouring the last of her bagel. 'The paralysis, however, should last at least two hours, and by then she'll be beyond all medical and philosophical intervention.'

I languished on my back and stared at the glass ceiling, wheeling my limbs like a beetle pinned to an entomologist's corkboard. The curare colonised still more of my nervous system, so that the same tragedy that had befallen Proserpine now visited me. I was a basket case, stranded in my cortex. 'Edwina – please – you don't have to *kill* her.'

'That statement is more accurate than you imagine.' She crouched beside me like a mother helping her toddler build a tower from alphabet blocks. 'Permit me to describe my program's most provocative feature. If you were to look me in the eye right now and forbid me to destroy Londa – you and only you, Mr Ambrose – my need to murder her would vanish. Isn't that remarkable. Six words from you, "Thou shalt not murder thy daughter," and the death sentence is lifted. But then, of course, she'll start doing those things we've come to expect of the world's most famous vatling. Calling up the Valkyries, for example, and instructing them to lynch Felix Pielmeister.'

'Shit.'

'I'm not sure *why* she placed her fate in your hands. My guess is that she's never forgiven you for refusing to sign "The Book of Londa". Go ahead, Mr Ambrose. Say it. Say, "Thou shalt not murder thy daughter," and I'll set her free.'

'Set her free to murder Pielmeister.'

'Most likely. But maybe not. We all know how unpredictable she can be. She'll probably hang a second hostage into the bargain. Gittikac, Wintergreen, North – there are nine Phyllistines left in the queue. Give me your answer.'

'I *can't*.'

'I know, but give it to me anyway. Come on, Mr Ambrose. You're fond of ethical dilemmas. What's the lesser evil here? What's the greater good? Make your choice. Pick the door that leads to the lady, because the tiger is ravenous this morning.'

My decision to walk out on my dissertation defence – that had been a choice. My resolve to continue tutoring Londa after learning her true heritage – that had been a choice, too. My insistence that she abandon Themisopolis and allow the immaculoids to burn it – once again, a choice. But this wasn't a choice. This was something else. This was the death of a thousand cuts.

I boxed the compass with my eyes, north, north-north-east, north-east, east-north-east, east, east-south-east, south-east, all the

329

way to north-north-west, until at last my gaze came to rest on the Wild Woman. 'I'm going insane.'

'You'd be well within your rights to do that, but first you must flip the coin. On the count of ten. One ... two ... three ...'

'I need more time.'

'Four ... five ... six ...'

'*You're* the one who should die,' I protested.

'I don't disagree. Seven ... eight ... nine ... do I hear it? Do I hear, "Thou shalt not murder thy daughter"?'

Like my tongue, lips, larynx, and ocular muscles, my salivary glands remained in working order. I did my best to spit in Edwina 0004's face, but the projectile fell short and landed on her safari jacket.

'Know something, Mr Ambrose? In your shoes, I would've answered that way too.' She stood up, straight and tall as when she'd first come towards me in the skiff. 'But I'm not in your shoes. I'm in my own shoes, a mother's shoes, so naturally I've decided to use those shoes to kick you in the teeth.'

It was not a shoe, however, but the pointed tip of a hard leather boot that collided with my mouth. Thanks to the curare, I didn't feel a thing. Apparently she struck me pretty hard. There was much blood.

'If you wish to bury the body, come down to the beach,' said the Wild Woman, striding away. 'She hopes to draw her last breath in sight of the Red Witch.'

The blood continued pouring from my mouth and streaming on to the floor. Had my nervous system been more functional, I could have shifted to a prone position and, extending my index finger, used the spilled blood to draw a stick figure on the flagstone path, or scrawl a hieroglyph, or write my name. But instead I simply lay there, glued in place and transfixed by an astonishing thought. I had just saved the life of my worst enemy, while arranging the annihilation of the person I loved best.

CHAPTER 17

To hobble the body, a good Cartesian dualist would say, is not necessarily to impede its complementary opposite, the mind. A Hegelian idealist might take the argument even further, asserting that a physical handicap may under certain circumstances increase a person's mental prowess. By this theory Charles Darwin's chronic exhaustion became a lens focusing his intellectual energies on the origin of species, Friedrich Nietzsche's racking ailments sponsored the composition of his wrenching aphorisms, and Stephen Hawking's amyotrophic lateral sclerosis subsidised his explorations of the astronomical abysses he called black holes.

The longer I lay paralysed in the geodesic dome, however, the more sceptical I grew regarding any attempts to correlate suffering with wisdom. Stuck on my back like an inverted turtle, I reviewed the shocks of the past forty-eight hours. The corpses on the foremast, the Wild Woman's lineage, Londa's suicide scheme, the curare in my coffee. In declining to shut down Edwina 0004's assassination program, had I committed a terrible sin? Prevented the execution of ten innocent Phyllistines? Become party to a murder? A hero to the angels? I contemplated the ceiling, and pondered my questions, and arrived at the nexus of nowhere.

It seemed that my material self had fallen prey to a kind of neuromuscular postmodernism. My brain disclaimed any absolute duties. My tissues disavowed any universal mission. But after two hours of such discourse, the very interval predicted by the Wild Woman, my body transcended its chemically induced indifference and regained a sense of purpose. Joint by joint, ligament by ligament, I struggled to my feet, then spent a minute reacquainting my flesh with my spirit. I wriggled my toes, splayed my fingers, clapped my hands, massaged my neck. As my pain receptors came back on line, my gums started smarting from the damage inflicted by the Wild Woman's boot.

Chimes filled the air, the ominous bongs of the grandfather clock on the second floor, tolling the hour. Noon. Each brassy reverberation energised me. 'She hopes to draw her last breath in sight of the Red Witch,' the Wild Woman had said. *Draw her last breath*, a locution that suggested a gradual passage, not the abrupt obliteration of 'drop dead' or 'keel over'.

I raced to the primal Edwina's bedchamber and retrieved the mumquat flagon, and before the twelfth chime sounded, I had dashed across the veranda, raced down the steps, and hurled myself into the forest.

In the twenty years that had elapsed since Londa attempted to stage 'Coral Idolatry' on her secret beach, the crimson invertebrates had continued to add their exoskeletons to the Red Witch, so that her once conical hat now resembled a jester's cap and bells. Otherwise the place hadn't changed much. Conch shells, glistery pebbles, tufts of seaweed, a few dead starfish. Even the piece of Cretan-bull driftwood remained intact. The tide advanced in thick staccato whispers, like incantations sprung from the witch's brittle lips.

Londa sat on the sand beside a tide pool, head bobbing, legs splayed, back pressed against a boulder. Firming my grip on the flagon, I vaulted the bull and ran towards her. My vatling's eyes were closed, her cheeks pale, lips pulled back in a grimace. A low liquid moan soughed through her clenched teeth.

The Wild Woman had pursued her program with a vengeance. A rivulet of dark frothy blood streamed from the midriff of Londa's white cotton blouse. It rolled down her white denim shorts, spilled across her thighs, bubbled on to the sand, and flowed along the beach like a freshet bound for the sea.

Londa pressed her manacled hands against the wound, but the blood kept coming, coating her fingers like potter's slip. She shivered as if she were packed in ice. For an indeterminate interval my thoughts stopped dead, as if some residual curare had found its way to my brain, and then the questions came, flooding my cranium like the gasoline the mackies had unleashed on Londa's city. Should I tear off my shirt and bind her wound on the spot? Carry her back to the mansion? Would the act of moving her reverse whatever clotting process had already begun?

I planted a foot in the tide pool, got down on one knee. The scent of iron filled my nostrils. Londa's eyes flickered open. Her tongue thrust forward, accompanied by two dribbles of blood that scored her jaw with crisp red lines, giving her the appearance of a ventriloquist's puppet. I expected a scream of pain to follow, but instead she winced and said, with typical *Weltanschauung* Woman bravado, 'Present evidence suggests that the curare did not kill you.'

'Christ. What happened?'

'She stabbed me.'

'With a knife?'

'Sword. My idea. It came from our conquistador.'

'Alonso?'

'Yes. Don Quixote's first name – did you know that? Alonso Quixano.'

'I brought you some nectar.'

'Great. Lay it on me, Socrates. It turns out I'm not much of a Stoic after all.'

She tried to speak again, but the words lodged in her throat. I brought the flagon to her lips. She drank greedily, sputtering and gagging like my netherson perishing in his tumbledown tower.

'Get out your notebook,' she said at last. 'It's not every day a philosopher is privileged to watch somebody die. I might say something profound.'

'I'm taking you to Faustino,' I told her. 'We'll call in a medevac chopper.'

'I was expecting a razor-sharp pain. Instead it's more like somebody's punching me in the stomach, again and again and again.'

I gave her a second swallow of nectar, then slid one arm beneath her legs, another around her shoulders. Her face relaxed, and her teeth stopped chattering. She smiled, awash in the nectar's counterfeit serenity.

333

'Brace yourself,' I said. 'On the count of three, I'm going to pick you up.'

'No, Socrates. Sorry. I've lost too much blood. The sand soaked it up. Imagine the castle we could build. Take your arms away.'

'Faustino, that's the plan. Faustino, then a chopper.'

The nectar continued to bless her. 'What's eating you, Socrates? Ashamed of your complicity in all this? Cheer up. You made the best of a bad situation: kill one beaker freak, save ten Phyllistines. Very Utilitarian. Let me go. I mean it.'

I relaxed my muscles but kept my arms in place. 'They won't convict you, I promise. We'll hire the best lawyers money can buy.'

'Praise the humble mumquat. Glory be to rococonuts everywhere. I don't feel a thing. Raw existential terror, yes, but otherwise nothing.' And still she bled, growing paler with each passing instant. 'Your arms are really bothering me.'

'And once your trial is over, you can go back to work. Londa Sabacthani, bane of Phyllistines, bulwark against Corporate Christi.'

'Sorry. No. This doesn't end happily. Get that through your thick philosopher's skull. I won't be dragged in chains to Rome. Cleopatra had the right idea. She opted for the asp.'

Isis forgive me, Thoth absolve me, I did as Londa wished, withdrawing my arms and jamming my hands into my pockets.

'"When I am dead, my dearest" – do you know Christina Rossetti's poem?' she said. 'Henry taught it to Donya, and Donya taught it to her sisters. "When I am dead, my dearest, / Sing no sad songs for me. / Plant thou no roses at my head, / Nor shady cypress tree."' A sudden spasm contorted her features. 'I wrote you a letter. A confession, actually. Like it or not, your gumbo girl gets the last word. You can't contradict a corpse.'

'What sort of confession?'

'Go to the library. Darker and darker. Look inside the obligation book.'

'*Against Ethics*?'

I think I'm going blind. Kiss me.'

I pressed my lips to hers. 'This is all my fault.' I kissed her mouth, brow, cheeks, and eyes. I kissed her bloody jaw.

'"Be the green grass above me / With showers and dewdrops wet. / And if thou wilt, remember. / And if thou wilt, forget."'

'Of course I'll remember,' I said.

'Hold me,' she said.

Obligation. Mine was entirely clear, and now I proceeded to enact it, bestowing what comforts I could as the *Dasein* leaked out of her. I wrapped my arms around her torso, easing her face against my chest.

'Are you holding me? I can't tell. I'm numb as a brick.'

'I'm holding you.'

'I love you, Mason Ambrose. Make sure Donya finds out about this place. I can picture her standing on the shore, befriending the Red Witch, telling her what to do. "The next time any Phyllistines come sailing by here, counting their gold and spilling their garbage, how about casting a spell on them?"'

She twitched and trembled in my embrace.

'I'm holding you,' I said again.

'Killed by a Spanish sword. That almost happened to Don Quixote. Lots of times. But he always walked away. He got to die in bed.'

'I love you, Londa Sabacthani.'

He got to die in bed. Londa's last words. A few seconds of soft gurgling, and then she grew utterly silent, and her quivering ceased. But of course this was still Mr Darwin's planet. In the midst of death we were in life. Macaws screeched. Howler monkeys cried. A pelican flapped across the sky and landed atop the witch. And now came a fiddler crab, pressing against my heel as if it were the portal to some crustacean heaven, an empyrean to which he might gain admittance by rattling the gates with all his invertebrate resolve.

I hugged Londa's vacant frame, the tears falling from my cheeks and giving their substance to the tide pool. Water to water, salt to salt. Human tears, that unique precipitation, their salinity looming large among those facts suggesting that we once belonged to the sea.

When at last my weeping had run its course, I took hold of her body – she was horribly cold but still supple – and carried her beyond the reach of the tide. I set her prone on the white sand, carefully arranging her head and limbs in the posture of one asleep, then entered the forest and harvested a dozen fronds. They covered her completely, head to toe, a green shroud for my beloved.

I returned to the jungle, soon picking up the trail to the Bahía de Flores, in thrall now to a different obligation, political and perhaps even apocalyptic. Throughout my hike I kept an eye peeled for the Wild Woman, but I didn't expect to see her. Most likely she'd gone into hiding – perhaps in the mansion, perhaps in her cottage – or else she'd left the island entirely and was now heading for Key West in Captain López's cabin cruiser.

Reaching the water, I broke into a jog, following the horseshoe curve of the beach. My obligation assailed me. It fell from the sky, burst from the jungle, breached the churning bay. I quickened my pace, soon arriving at the dock that Nick, the most ambitious of the primal Edwina's imported adolescents, had built during Londa's first summer on earth. Lashed to the piles were four decrepit vessels, a fleet that various Isla de Sangre squatters had evidently collected over the years and then abandoned, including an ancient rowboat with two oars, a battered kayak and paddle, a swamped catamaran, and a dilapidated outrigger canoe. After studying each option and imagining the particular way it might fail me, I settled on the rowboat. I scrambled aboard, cast off, and pulled free of the dock. The boat leaked, but not disastrously. Unless I hit an iceberg, I would reach the *Titanic Redux* before dusk.

Stroke by stroke, breath by breath, I made my way along the shoreline, carefully avoiding the surf on one side and the crimson reef on the other, as I navigated the island's southern hump. And, yes, ladies and gentlemen, you may be sure I felt a strong impulse to reverse course, make my way back to Faustino, enter the kitchen, and obtain the required implement. A paring knife would do, likewise a pizza cutter, corkscrew, or French peeler. And once I'd returned to her secret beach and snipped away some portion of Londa, a fleck of her splendid neck, perhaps, or a bit of perfect thumb, I would bear the specimen to Vincent Charnock in his hidden cove on the Intercoastal Waterway, and together we would visit the island and enter Torre de la Carne with blasphemous intent.

But instead I stuck to my plan, rowing into the Bahía de Colón as the setting sun was coronating the mangrove trees with a blazing scarlet aura. By the time I sighted the *Redux*, my whole body felt pummelled. From muscles I hadn't even realised I owned came every variety of pain and protest. Glancing upward, I beheld a bizarre drama unfolding on the weather deck. Galil pressed against her shoulder, Lieutenant Kristowski fired round after round at the gulls and vultures circling the corpses on the foremast. I couldn't tell if she meant to kill the birds or merely to scare them off, but in either case she evoked Coleridge's Ancient Mariner carrying out his ill-conceived design against the albatross.

'Ahoy, Lieutenant Kristowski! Ahoy! Ahoy!'

She fired again, and this time her bullet found a gull. The feathery white corpse plummeted to the weather deck. Its fellow scavengers took note of the event and flapped away.

'Lieutenant Kristowski!'

She leaned over the rail and, assessing my predicament, began outfitting a davit with a breeches buoy. I lashed the rowboat to the anchor chain, climbed into the harness, and placed my fate in the Lieutenant's hands. Methodically she turned the crank, reeling me free of the rowboat and drawing me skywards like a ripe bouillababy rising from its enzyme bath.

'Are you hurt?' she asked me after I was safely on deck. 'You're covered in blood.'

'It's not all mine. I must see Colonel Fox. Major Powers too, and Dagmar Röhrig. There's no gentle way of saying this. Dr Sabacthani is dead.'

'Dead, sir? Jesus. *Dead?*'

'Dead.'

'How?'

'Suicide. She stabbed herself.'

'With a knife?'

'A conquistador's sword.'

'Dead. That's awful.'

'Not entirely awful.'

'I know what you mean,' Lieutenant Kristowski said.

Two hours later, having taken a shower and changed my clothes, I entered Londa's denuded suite and, gesticulating wildly, repeated for Vetruvia Fox, Carmen Powers, and Dagmar Röhrig my various conversations with Edwina 0004. Her ontogenerated origins were not news to my listeners, as both Colonel Fox and Major Powers had attended her birth, firing up the machine on Londa's instructions, then lowering the foetus into the maturation chamber. My narrative of their leader's ultimate purpose in bringing forth the Wild Woman, by contrast, took all three hijackers by surprise. As the women fixed me with ever widening gazes, I revealed that Edwina 0004 was in essence the child of her creator's death wish, that the murderous component of her DUNCE cap program had started functioning about ten hours earlier, and that Londa's body now lay on an obscure Blood Island beach. I confessed that I could have saved her with a single glance and a six-word sentence, but had instead allowed the Wild Woman to carry out the assassination.

'What a horrible choice,' Colonel Fox said in a voice as flat as glass. I could not tell whether she meant to express sympathy for my plight or disgust with my decision.

'Londa insisted that this new Edwina was merely her second conscience,' Major Powers said, 'but we suspected there was more to the story.'

'Something crazy and pathological and perverse,' Dagmar said. 'Something quintessentially Londa.'

I studied the weary hijackers, their moist eyes, trembling jaws and quivering lips, each face conveying its own distinctive mixture of anguish and relief. Not for an instant did they imagine that lynching Felix Pielmeister or Corbin Thorndike or Ralph Gittikac would bequeath the earth to the meek – and now, suddenly, here I was among them, revealing that Londa would never again demand such ferocity of her apostles. Even as they grieved, their gratitude washed over me like a wave of warm rococonut milk.

Slowly, piece by piece, the women constructed a plan. Its essence was capitulation. Its particulars included removing the corpses from the foremast, putting them on ice, convincing the enlisted Valkyries that surrender made sense, and telling the world that Operation PG had been terminated. But the first order of business, Colonel Fox insisted, was for Major Powers and Lieutenant Kristowski to go down to the beach and retrieve Londa's body, without which the FBI might never regard the case as closed. When the G-men arrived, Colonel Fox would explain that, tortured by guilt and unable to abide captivity, Londa had stabbed herself to death, a story that in its own way was absolutely true.

'I've been honest with you,' I told the hijackers, 'and now I'd like some candour in return.'

I didn't have to say another word. Moving synchronously, the women took out their Godgadgets and pushed the red buttons in tandem. I steeled myself. No detonation reached my ears. No blast wave shook the hull. The *Redux* remained at anchor in the tranquil bay.

Major Powers pushed her button a second time. She merely wanted to emphasise the point, but still I flinched. 'You see, Mason?' she said. 'You were a better conscience than you knew. Londa wasn't really putting us at risk – not through our Godgadgets anyway.'

'Are the explosives themselves also a lie,' I asked, 'or just the part about them being wired to the transmitters?'

'Take a trip to forehold three,' Colonel Fox said. 'You'll find a long serpent of plastique weaving through the champagne cases and sardine crates.'

'I believe you,' I said.

'Londa liked to bluff, no doubt about it,' Dagmar said. 'But she liked holding aces even more.'

I shall not dwell on the denouement of the *Titanic Redux*'s maiden voyage, a succession of episodes that found the fifth horseman of the Apocalypse, Expediency, galloping along her corridors and promenades. The television coverage was both exhaustive and exhausting, and most of the key events were later hashed over ad nauseam by Sabacthani obsessives everywhere. Read their books, visit their websites, and you'll discover that, when it comes to recounting the raw historical data, there's a surprising harmony between the faction that regards Londa as a latter-day Joan of Arc and those who believe that she and Judas Iscariot were separated at birth. The dissolution of Operation PG is open to myriad interpretations, but the facts themselves are not in dispute. How Vetruvia Fox broadcast a special edition of *The Last Shall Be First* disclosing that Dr Sabacthani was dead and the Valkyries were hoisting the white flag. How the US Coast Guard decided to believe Colonel Fox and forthwith dispatched a cutter to the Ship of Dreams, whereupon the cutter's officers and crew purged forehold 3 of the plastique, collected the Valkyries' weapons, and ferried the surviving Phyllistines to Miami along with Londa's remains and the frozen bodies of Anthem and Thorndike. How the FBI, after accepting the Coast Guard's assurances that the liner was no longer booby-trapped, landed a succession of helicopters on the poop deck, evacuating the entire Valkyrie brigade within an hour and flying them to a government detention facility in Fort Lauderdale. How the American system of jurisprudence placed the captured women on trial for hijacking, kidnapping, piracy, torture, and premeditated murder. How the Valkyries' canny and, thanks to Donya's donations, well-funded attorneys succeeded in casting Londa as the one true villain in the narrative, their clients as mere accessories, with the result that every Valkyrie was spared life imprisonment, receiving instead a sentence of ten to twenty years, a penalty that in most cases transmuted into less than five years behind bars followed by a laissez-faire probation. And, finally, how Ralph Gittikac, reviving his impudent project, sailed the *Titanic Redux* from Southampton to New York City without incident, so that his original quarry, 'those imps, devils, and angels of catastrophe who haunted the North Atlantic on the fateful night of 15 April 1912', were finally vanquished.

There is one occurrence, however, that you didn't see on TV or read about in any Sabacthanite's blog. I speak of the conversation I had with Felix Pielmeister shortly before he departed the Bahía de Colón for points north. Different ambitions had brought us to the weather deck. The postrationalist merely wanted to get the hell off the ship, the Coast Guard having told him and the other former hostages to gather around the foremast until the evacuation craft was ready to receive them. As for me, I simply needed to survey the rigging and tell myself, over and over, that ten more Phyllistines would have died on these shrouds if I'd terminated the Wild Woman's mission.

'It appears that your protégée didn't sink the ship after all,' Pielmeister said. An ellipsis of white scars arced across his brow, a stark testament to his days down among the furnaces. 'My powers of prediction failed me on that one, didn't they?'

'Don't worry about it,' I said. 'Jesus was a poor prophet, too. He said his apostles would live to see the Kingdom come to Earth. Matthew 16: 28. Mark 9: 1.'

A grin broke through Pielmeister's scraggly beard. 'You atheists are such fundamentalists, always quoting Scripture. May I ask you a question?'

'As long as it's not about Charles Darwin.'

'Is it true what I heard? You played a role in the lunatic's death?'

'I won't deny it.'

'Here's what else I heard,' he said. 'You did it so she wouldn't order my execution.'

'I did it so she wouldn't order *anybody's* execution.'

'But she told you I was next in line.'

'Maybe. Don't take it personally. I just wanted her tawdry little reign of terror to end.'

'Nevertheless, you saved my life.'

'That's one way of looking at it.'

'Thank you,' Pielmeister said humbly.

'You're welcome,' I replied icily.

'No, I mean it. Thank you. If I can ever do you a favour, simply ask.'

'How about calling off the paradigm shift?'

He gave me a look of consummate perplexity. Could it be that Pielmeister no longer believed in Corporate Christi? Was it possible that, during his sweltering days in boiler room 2 and polluted nights on G deck, he'd forgotten about the twilight of the iconoclasts? With any luck, I figured, this theological giant would continue thinking small for the rest of his life.

A Coast Guard midshipman approached, a pimply youngster with an Adam's apple as large as his nose and, tapping Pielmeister's shoulder, requested that he go down to E deck. Pielmeister nodded, then faced me squarely and said, 'Goodbye, Ambrose. You're really not such a bad philosopher. Forsake your foolish scientism' – he stretched out his arm, his fingers soliciting contact with mine – 'and you might even get your PhD.'

'Know what you can do with that hand of yours?' I asked.

'What?'

'You can shove it up thy neighbour's ass,' I said, an answer I imagined would have pleased Yolly almost as much as if I'd thrown Pielmeister into the bay.

Saying nothing, he slid the rejected hand into his pocket. He strode past the foremast and joined the other released hostages, and then the lot of them were swallowed by the sun's noontime glare. Inevitably I thought of Amenhotep IV's lyrical hymn to his shining divinity, the Aton. 'Whatever flies and alights, they live when thou hast risen for them,' ran the panegyric. 'The fish in the river dart before thy face. Thy rays are in the midst of the great green sea.' Even Darwin, I decided, could not have said it better.

In theory it would be easy convincing the FBI that I'd played no part in the Valkyries' assault on the *Titanic Redux*. For one thing, I was not a woman. For another, Colonel Fox and Major Powers would vouch for me. Nevertheless, I decided to err on the side of paranoia, and so I secluded myself inside a furnace in boiler room 3, crouching amidst the carbon detritus and remaining there until the G-men had got all their prisoners off the ship.

Smeared with soot and ash, I climbed free of the furnace and with feline stealth ascended the aft companionways. It seemed entirely possible that I now had the *Redux* to myself, though my desire to sit alone in the Café Parisien was non-existent, likewise my wish to savour a solitary respite in the Turkish bath or enjoy a private screening of *Touched by an Angel: The Complete First Season* in the ship's cosy movie theatre. I had but one ruling passion just then – to return to the island and extinguish the last vestige of a technology that my species would be better off without.

Upon reaching E deck I entered the maze of corridors and found myself staring at an axe: not the morally charged prop from Plato's famous parable, but a fire axe of no symbolic significance whatsoever, sealed behind a pane of glass stencilled with the words 'EMERGENCY USE ONLY'. I detached the ball-peen hammer from the wall, broke the glass, and retrieved the axe. EXISTENTIAL USE ONLY, I mused, hurrying away, INCLUDING PERSONAL VENDETTAS AGAINST INFERNAL MACHINES. At last I reached the hatch through which the hostages had been evacuated. I turned the lock-wheel. The great steel door swung open, revealing a twenty-foot drop to the Bahía de Colón. I inflated my lungs, gritted my teeth, closed my eyes, and jumped. Surfacing, I employed a crude approximation of a sidestroke to bear the axe towards the bow of the ship. Warm and smooth and briny, the tropical waters washed the carbon from my skin. Soon I reached my rowboat, still moored to the anchor chain and miraculously afloat, the keelson inundated by several gallons of the Gulf of Mexico.

For the rest of the afternoon the Aton continued to smile upon my mission. Despite a choppy sea, an obstinate breeze, and the weight of my unwanted water, I rowed myself into the Bahía de Matecumba without any serious mishaps: blistered palms, strained muscles, nothing more. I made landfall near the great keep. Axe in hand, I strode across the drawbridge, then climbed the spiral staircase and immediately got to work, wielding my weapon against the RXL-313. I shattered the enzyme tanks, smashed the chamber ports, toppled the gantry, crushed the DUNCE cap, pulverised the plasma monitors, eviscerated the control console. Rampage accomplished, I stood back and surveyed the former laboratory, exhausted but unconscionably pleased with myself. Even Daedalus, I decided, could sustain no wonders here. Even God would strain to wring from this wreck any creature more substantial than a tick.

The jungle paths leading away from Torre de la Carne were soaked in shadows, but the westering sun shone brightly, guiding me safely past the treacherous roots and perilous bogs, until I arrived, famished, at Faustino, eager to consume whatever *Redux* delicacies I could find. I sat at the kitchen table and worked my way through a wheel of Gouda, a quarter-pound of caviar, and a half-empty bottle of Cabernet, until I felt both sated and insensate and therefore prepared to deal with Londa's letter. Abandoning the feast, I marched into the library, my apprehension growing with each step.

Alonso occupied his usual post, preventing visitors from choosing corrupting texts. Someone, Edwina 0004 presumably, had returned his sword to its scabbard. What thoughts had gone flitting through her head at the moment she'd sheathed her bloody implement? Did she see herself as a child-killer – Medea's doppelgänger – or simply as a machine like the RXL-313 from which she'd come, beyond good and evil? I half-expected to find her in the philosophy section, reviling the conquistador for supplying the murder weapon, but the only living entities around were a hairy black spider, a scattering of ants, and a grieving Darwinist from Boston.

Handwritten but legible, the letter was in its promised place: an 8 ½" x 11" sheet marking the Caputo chapter called 'Several Lyrical-Philosophical Discourses on Various Jewgreek Parables and Paradigms with Constant Reference to Obligation'.

My Dear Mason,

I must write quickly. Any minute now the Wild Woman will be here. Assuming you decline to suspend her destiny, I'll be dead by the time you read this.

Here's what I have to tell you. Two weeks ago my mother's hunger came upon me. I speak now of the primal Edwina, and of her all-consuming desire to have a child. Fashioning Edwina 0004 did not satisfy my craving to procreate – how could it? – and so I devised a different scheme.

The person you took to your bed last night was the Wild Woman. The whole arrangement appalled her, but she agreed to play her part out of love for me. There's reason to believe that a conception occurred. If our child is a boy, I hope you will name him Arthur, after the primal Edwina's father. If it's a girl, let me suggest Sofia, wisdom.

I can hear my mother's footsteps in the hall. She'll lock me up in Charnock's hut, long enough for you to make your decision, and then she'll take Alonso's sword and bring me down to the beach. My plan is to hide this letter inside Caputo, hoping you'll have cause to visit his pages again.

My sins are many. I failed to cure the Phyllistines. I murdered two men. I forced you to decide between two evils of which neither was the lesser: kill the gumbo girl, kill her not. Forgive me. She is coming. I love you, Mason. You're not a very good philosopher, and you're not really much of a conscience, but you're a great teacher.

Your difficult student,

Londa

Consider this thought problem. Imagine a technology that lets a person remove all trace of some terrible experience from his brain. Under what conditions, if any, would you use it? What might it be like to go through life knowing you'd once suffered an ordeal so dreadful that it demanded radical excision? How long could you endure this strange affirmative ignorance, this lost access to the unspeakable, without becoming neurotic, or even slightly mad? In the long run, might you not decide that such circumscribed amnesia was worse than whatever memory you'd felt compelled to erase?

The instant I finished Londa's letter, I decided that if an amnesia machine existed, I would avail myself of it immediately. Lacking such a device, I compensated as best I could, returning to the kitchen, lighting a gas burner and, with steely determination, edging the message towards the flame.

My flesh still throbbed with the exertion of destroying the ontogenerator. My head reeled from the effort of forgetting Londa's confession. I trod the stairs to the primal Edwina's bedchamber, that bower in which her fourth iteration and I had never made love, then lowered the curtains and surrendered to my dreams.

For the next six weeks I pursued an Uncle Rumpus sort of existence, combing the shore of my magic isle. I alternated my residency between Faustino and the primal Edwina's cottage, all the while keeping an eye out for the Wild Woman – she with whom I'd not slept, that person I did not impregnate – but I saw no trace of her, and eventually I decided she'd gone to the mainland. My scavenging skills were sufficient to keep me nourished, and the lack of distractions boded well for my new project, a sequel to *Ethics from the Earth* that I intended to call 'The Serpent Was More Subtle'. The real reason Charles Darwin distresses people, I would argue, is not that he stumbled on an argument against theism. No, the problem was that he *replaced* theism – replaced it with a construct more beautiful and majestic than any account of the Supreme Being outside of the Book of Job, a construct that invites us to see every variety of life, from aphids and archbishops, to zygotes and zoologists, as vibrant threads in an epic tapestry, its warp and woof stretching across the aeons back to the

Precambrian ooze, the primordial clay-pits, or wherever it all began. An astonishing construct, a mind-boggling construct, a construct of which Jehovah is understandably and insanely jealous.

Despite my tranquil surroundings and my enthusiasm for its theme, 'The Serpent Was More Subtle' did not flow easily from my pen. Each sentence was a tribulation, every paragraph an ordeal. The problem, I decided, traced to a combination of writer's block and procrastinator's malaise. And the remedy? I couldn't be sure, but it seemed likely that a return to Boston would do my book more good than harm.

True to his prediction, my landlord had failed to find a one-semester tenant for my Sherborn Street apartment. Instead he'd granted a full-year lease to, of all people, a Hawthorne philosophy PhD candidate who'd loved, absolutely loved, *Ethics from the Earth*, her zeal for my opus eclipsing even Natalie's enthusiasm of five years earlier. A spunky, thirtyish, divorced Spinoza enthusiast with an elfin face and a sensual overbite, Leslie Rosenzweig and I were not long into our first conversation before two noteworthy facts emerged: she found Boston as appealingly exotic as I'd found her native Los Angeles on those occasions when I'd visited my sister – Beantown's buskers and scrod versus La-La Land's surfers and palm trees – and she'd be delighted to let me crash on the living-room futon until I located more convivial digs. Leslie even offered me the master bedroom, citing the satisfaction she would feel in 'doing a mitzvah for the inventor of Darwinian deontology'. Such a sacrifice, I insisted, was unnecessary: I had no wish to exercise some presumed elitist prerogative over her – as far as I was concerned, all middle-class urban intellectuals were created equal.

Not only did I now have a place to sleep, I soon acquired a social life as well. It turned out that my original vision for Pieces of Mind – here would flower the headiest philosophical discourse to be found west of ancient Athens – was not so silly after all. If an unrepentant neo-Darwinist and a vivacious Jewish Spinozist decided to institute such a dream, then by God it would happen.

Our core group met on Tuesday and Thursday nights, gathering in the science fiction and fantasy section around a low circular table barely large enough to accommodate our books, coffee mugs, tea presses, and occasional slammed fists. Leslie and I had peopled the seminar the way the young Orson Welles had mounted his idiosyncratic Shakespeare productions, with an affection for flamboyance. We drew our requisite eccentrics and scenery-chewers from the Religious Studies programme, the William James Center, the Lewis Mumford Institute, and the congregation of bookstore barflies who passed their leisure hours at Pieces of Mind. I even allowed certain select members of the Hawthorne Philosophy Department to join our fellowship. We called ourselves the Whores of Reason, and our conversation was of sufficient general interest to eventually attract a regular audience. Week after week, our fans would appear, cheering us on as we spelunked in Plato's cave, settled Heidegger's hash, confessed to our guilty admiration for Nietzsche, forged a compromise with pragmatism, relativised relativism, categorically rejected absolutism, and presumed to know Spinoza's unknowable God.

Although I'd never regarded my recent sojourn on Blood Island as an attempt to elude the elastic arm of the law, the FBI didn't quite see it that way. Pleased to realise that I now had a known and fixed address, two agents from the Boston office began paying me regular visits. I told them more than they wanted to know, but nothing they didn't deserve to hear, and in the end they declined to indict me. When one of my interrogators, a grim and intelligent Russian expatriate named Bolkonsky, said I should thank my 'plucky stars' I hadn't ended up in prison along with Fox, Powers, Kristowski, and the rest, I informed him that at dawn I would sing my gratitude to the Aton.

Our philosophy group's prestige eventually reached such proportions that the average Boston intellectual crackpot, of which there are many, took pride in being invited to favour us with an informal talk. Although it wasn't my idea to have Vincent Charnock contribute to the Londa Sabacthani Memorial Lecture Series – the suggestion came from Dr Cochran, the professor whose high-definition television had saved my life by displaying *The Egyptian* at a crucial moment – I did not protest, for the man had clearly turned over a new leaf, several new leaves in fact. Truth to tell, Charnock had rewritten the entire 'Book of Vincent', not only climbing free of his self-constructed abyss (with a boost from

Alcoholics Anonymous), but also funding and administering the Charnock Consortium, a Cambridge-based enterprise that in its devotion to avant-garde cancer research was generally perceived as the stepchild of the incinerated Institute for Advanced Biological Investigations. Having supplied Anthem and Pielmeister with the means for spawning the immaculoids, Charnock would always seem to me an accessory to Yolly's murder, and yet he'd also become the bearer of Yolly's hope.

There was one way in which Charnock had not changed. This moralist who'd so adamantly opposed Edwina's removal of Proserpine's brain, and who would doubtless have voted against our proposal to uproot the sentient mangrove had he been around at the time, remained a steadfast foe of physician-assisted suicide. In his talk that evening, 'From Mercy to Mengele', he made a coherent philosophical case against euthanasia. He began by recapitulating Kant's claim that if the practice ever became commonplace, the effect would be to cheapen the intrinsic value of human life, then proceeded to demonstrate that John Stuart Mill's defence of euthanasia suffered from the same fallacy as other Utilitarian positions – namely, an assumption that to mathematise a dilemma was to resolve it. For his *coup de grâce*, Charnock explained why in his view the institutionalised destruction of individuals facing a life without quality lay on the same continuum as the Third Reich's eradication of those who supposedly had nothing to offer the Fatherland.

Although nobody agreed with Charnock's conclusions – as Leslie later put it, 'You could float the *Titanic Redux* through the holes in his argument' – it was an astute and heartfelt performance, drawing applause from the audience, myself included, and our guest was in good spirits when we adjourned to the Shepherd's Pie. We were celebrating two events that evening: Charnock's successful appearance before our group, and my recent contract with Prima Facie Press for 'The Serpent Was More Subtle', based on two sample chapters and an outline. Most of us ordered beer. Our speaker opted for a Cherry Coke and nachos. As the conversation heated up, Charnock confessed that he'd begun investigating the problem of physician-assisted suicide because the abortion controversy had proved too much for him, requiring that he search his soul more deeply than was compatible with his sanity.

'I came to feel that if I really cared about those seven embryos I poured into the bay, I should adopt seven unwanted children in their place. Or six, at least. Or five.'

'Or four unwanted children,' Leslie said.

'Or three or two,' I said.

'The truth is that I've never felt an urge to nurture,' Charnock said.

'Or one unwanted child,' Leslie said.

'Edwina certainly felt it,' he continued. 'She ached for motherhood. She needed it like oxygen.'

'So did Londa,' I said. 'Not at first. But sometime during the hijacking, the impulse kicked in.'

'I didn't know that,' Charnock said. 'I'm not surprised. Like mother, like daughter. This drive to rear the next generation, it's essentially a female instinct, wouldn't you say?'

'Nonsense,' Leslie replied.

'Nonsense,' I agreed, though I had nothing on which to base this assertion, my parenting experiences being limited to John Snow 0001, who hadn't exactly brought out my inner Geppetto.

'To the next generation,' Leslie said, raising her Pilsner high, and we all followed her lead, clinking our glasses together and giving posterity our permission to come forth.

On a chill, rainy evening in October, three days before Halloween, the Whores of Reason sat down to epistemology as usual. Our reading that autumn had been Hegel's preternaturally dense *Phenomenology of Spirit*, with its audacious account of the individual soul's journey from consciousness to self-consciousness to reason to spirit to religion to perfect knowledge. Although I'd always found this Byzantine ascent annoying in its obscurity, I figured that the fault lay with me, and as the evening progressed Leslie and I began playing 'good cop, bad cop' with Hegel's system, your narrator defending the man's attempt to privilege pure thought, Leslie arguing that we shouldn't hesitate to label metaphysical drivel as such. To clinch her case, she related how Hegel had in 1800 written a dissertation proving that, while the definition of a 'planet' had varied over the centuries, there could still be, philosophically, only seven planets. 'And then, in January of 1801, an eighth planet – the asteroid Ceres – was discovered by a non-Hegelian astronomer named Giuseppe Piazzi,' Leslie said. 'And so, once again, we see why the real world has always been such an embarrassment to German idealism.'

On that epigrammatic note, the clock struck nine, and the meeting broke up – or almost did. What kept everyone in place was the appearance of a stooped figure, wheezing and arthritic, her face obscured by the cowl of a rain-spattered poncho. She was toting, of all things, a wicker bassinet, and before she reached our inner circle several bystanders remarked that the conveyance held a baby.

Shuffling into my vicinity, our visitor set the bassinet on the table. Thanks to the auxiliary plastic hood and an abundance of blankets, the infant had been spared the wretched weather. Indeed, it was sleeping peacefully, eyes closed, nostrils emitting a pianissimo snore, a tiny sphere of saliva poised atop its delicate lips.

'The hospital insisted that I put something on the birth certificate, so I said her name is Jane,' our visitor told me. 'That won't do, of course. I'll leave the christening to you.'

I surveyed Edwina 0004. Evidently Londa and the Valkyries had assembled her so hastily that they'd introduced a flaw into her genotype. Her skin was as yellow as an ancient newspaper, her eyes had receded into her balding skull, and she had fewer teeth than fingers. The world at large would never recognise this broken crone as the late Dame Quixote's doppelgänger.

'The delivery occurred two months ago at Mass General.' From the lining of her poncho Edwina 0004 retrieved a glass baby bottle, pressing it into my hands. 'My milk has dried up. I use Similac instead. You make it from powder and water. Her pediatrician is Dr Ankers in Brighton. The sooner you assume your proper role, the better. If she remains in my care any longer, she'll languish.'

I thought of the newborn Sinuhe, cast adrift in a reed boat – 'Thus the city of Thebes was accustomed to dispose of its unwanted children' – coursing down the Nile before being rescued by the good-hearted couple who then adopted him. And now this unexpected infant had likewise floated into my life.

'Languish?' I tried returning the Similac to Edwina 0004, but she refused me with raised palms. 'No, you're doing a splendid job,' I told her. 'It's raining cats and dogs, but you kept her dry as a bone.'

'I'm a vatling,' she replied. 'No conscience. Receive your daughter, Mr Ambrose, before I harm her.'

'Harm her? She's your *child*.'

'So was Londa. Name the baby as you will. Goodbye.'

With an agility that belied her decrepitude, Edwina 0004 spun on her heel and hurried out the door. My impulse was to chase her down and beg her to relieve me of this burden, but just then the baby woke up and started crying.

'Mason, I don't understand,' Leslie said, bending over the bassinet. 'Are you the father?'

'That appears to be the case.'

An astonishing circumstance, but not without precedent. For it was here at Pieces of Mind that my netherson had made himself known to me.

Gently, Leslie unwrapped the woollen blanket and, inserting her hands under the baby's armpits, lifted the squalling bundle free of the bassinet. The Wild Woman had dressed her in a fluffy pink jumper. Her eyes, like mine, were a dark shade of brown.

'Give me the bottle,' Leslie said, snugging the infant into the crook of her arm.

'Do you know what you're doing?' I asked.

'I have a black belt in babysitting. Give me the goddamn bottle.'

I presented Leslie with the Similac. Edwina 0004's return, her terminal condition, the abandoned infant, my newfound fatherhood: it was all so abrupt, so absurdly sudden, like Ceres appearing before Giuseppe Piazzi. But beyond my confusion I felt exhilarated, and when my daughter stopped fussing and started feeding, thus prompting the crowd to break into spontaneous applause, my happiness grew greater still. My ignorance was endless – Did they sell Similac at the Whole Foods Market? Diapers? Did a baby need injections, like a puppy? – and yet I felt equal to the challenge. She was a normal person, after all, of conventional genesis. Ovulation, oocyte, orgasm, obstetrics. We humans had been tackling parenthood, often with impressive results, ever since *Homo erectus* had emerged from *Homo habilis*. When it came to the catastrophe in the bassinet, history was on my side.

This began with a butterfly, and it ends with one, too. We were a party of five that mellow April afternoon, eager patrons of the Hawthorne University Great Insect Carnival, organised annually by the Zoology Department. Besides myself, our fellowship included Leslie, with whom I'd been exchanging romantic protestations and sharing a Back Bay apartment for the past three months, plus Donya, Donya's charming boyfriend Raúl, and of course little Sofie Ambrose.

Now fifteen months old, my daughter could walk after a fashion. She could also sort her stuffed animals from her alphabet blocks, babble eloquently in a language of her own devising, play Level 5 Peek-a-Boo, and derive considerable amusement from the daily Nickelodeon broadcasts of *Uncle Rumpus's Magic Island*, starring Henry Cushing. What Sofie did not do was talk. Not a single word of recognisable English so far. The situation had me worried, but Dr Ankers was confident that the child would utter a Da-da or a bye-bye any day now.

Clinging to the southern face of the Environmental Sciences Building like a piece of avant-garde scaffolding, the Von Humboldt Butterfly Conservatory was a spindly marvel of glass and steel, a kind of secular cathedral dedicated to the adoration of the most exquisite invertebrates Mr Darwin's algorithms had ever brought forth. Several additions to the permanent collection had arrived in time for the Great Insect Carnival, including a colony of Nabokov's South American Blues, so named because the author of *Lolita*, a first-rate lepidopterist as well as a literary genius, had bestowed on *Lycaenidae* an innovative and valuable classification system. As our group wandered awestruck among the Nabokov's Blues, Donya and Raúl described their efforts to protect those unique Mexican forests where most of the planet's Monarch butterflies passed their winters. It was largely a matter of gauging one's audience. Sometimes Donya and Raúl would attempt to rehabilitate a given land speculator or industrial developer by appealing to his personal moral code, more often by enlarging his private bank account, but regardless of the tactic they usually managed to turn the clueless entrepreneur into a staunch butterfly advocate.

As you might imagine, habitat restoration was just one of the endeavours into which Donya had channelled her trust fund. Beyond her dedication to the welfare of beasts and butterflies, her munificence extended to the human realm; the call of the wild moved her, but so did the cries of the bewildered. I think especially of her invention called the Urban Igloo, an inflatable shelter for homeless people constructed from heavy-duty garbage bags and packing tape. Cheap and portable, every Urban Igloo boasted an ingenious feature – a heating device consisting of a plastic tube terminating in a simple gasket. After installing his igloo on the sidewalk outside an apartment complex, retail store, or corporate headquarters, the occupant would fit the gasket over the exhaust vent of the building's heating system. Thus an otherwise wasted resource, the litres of warm air expelled by HVAC ducts, was put to sensible use. So far Donya had distributed four hundred Urban Igloos up and down the eastern seaboard, and she hoped to give away a thousand before the year was out.

There was a mystery here. How did Donya manage to keep subverting the Phyllistines while eschewing the thorny forest of grandiosity into which her elder sisters had wandered? Why would she never even imagine initiating a project like Themisopolis or Operation Pineal Gland or Edwina 0004? Perhaps Henry and Brock had been more circumspect mentors than Jordan and I. Or perhaps Donya's sanity traced simply to her having enjoyed something resembling a childhood. Whatever the answer, one fact seemed clear. The last of the Sabacthanis was also the wisest.

If I am to believe my dear Leslie, your narrator has himself attained a certain sagacity. She claims that Mason Ambrose is 'no longer his skull's only tenant', but pays attention to his daughter and even his girlfriend 'with touching regularity'. And here's something else, ladies and gentlemen. Make of it what you will. In recent months I have shed my reflexive dislike of *The Faerie Queene*. There are passages in Spenser that now move me to tears, and I've come to regard that hidebound dogmatist as some sort of great poet.

Lovely though they were, the Nabokov's Blues did not captivate

Leslie and me for long, and we wandered off in search of gaudier *Lepidoptera*. Our quest took us to the cathedral's core, dense with ferns and blossoms, little Sofie waddling between us like a penguin. Eventually a Central Asian peacock butterfly caught our attention, a magnificent *Nymphalisio* perched on a yellow orchid, each wing stamped with an image suggesting a mask of comedy. I scooped up Sofie and brought her within view of the creature.

'See, sweetheart?' I said. 'See the beautiful butterfly?'

The child selected that moment to acquire the gift of language. No baby talk for Sofie. She didn't say, 'Bootiful.' She said, 'Beautiful.'

Joy rushed through my veins. My cup overflowed.

'Did you hear that? She said, "Beautiful."'

'*Mazel tov*,' Leslie told Sofie. 'No doubt about it' – she flashed me a wry smile – 'the kid'll grow up to become a philosopher, with a special interest in aesthetics.'

Beau-ti-ful. If Sofie's late mother Edwina 0004 could have heard her little girl articulate those syllables, she would have been immensely pleased. Sofie's departed mother the primal Edwina would have been equally delighted. But her deceased mother Londa would have been proudest of all. And so it was that, conjuring up the face and form of my impossible vatling, I bent low and inhaled the orchid's scent, happy in my knowledge that sometime tomorrow, or perhaps even later today, our daughter would move her tongue and part her lips and say her second word.

ACKNOWLEDGEMENTS

I am blessed with a circle of friends, relatives, and colleagues who have better things to do with their time than critique my novels in manuscript, but who perform this service nonetheless. In the case of *The Philosopher's Apprentice*, I owe a particular debt to Joe Adamson, Shira Daemon, Sean Develin, Margaret Duda, Justin Fielding, Peter G. Hayes, Michael Kandel, Reggie Lutz, Marlin May, Christopher Morrow, Glenn Morrow, Kathleen Morrow, Emmet O'Brien, Elisabeth Rose, Vincent Singleton, James Stevens-Arce, Michael Svobada and Paul Youngquist.

My gratitude also goes to Jennifer Brehl and Kirsty Dunseath for their editorial acuity, to Wendy Weil and Bruce Hunter for their agenting skills, to the Peter Gould Memorial Philosophy Seminar for nurturing my perplexity, and to my wife, Kathryn Smith Morrow, for in-house research and development.

When my narrator, in defending his doctoral dissertation, wonders why God procrastinated for aeons before bringing forth humankind, he is presenting an argument articulated by several estimable evolutionary thinkers, among them Frederick Crews in his remarkable *New York Review of Books* essay, 'Saving Us from Darwin'. The Urban Igloos of chapter 17 are derived from similar devices described in *The Interventionists: Users' Manual for the Creative Disruption of Everyday Life*, edited by Nato Thompson and Gregory Sholette. Other non-fiction influences on this novel include *Against Ethics* by John Caputo, *A Theory of Justice* by John Rawls, *Truth: A Guide* by Simon Blackburn, *Education and Mind in the Knowledge Age* by Carl Bereiter, *Cracking the Genome* by Kevin Davies, and *Darwin's Dangerous Idea* by Daniel C. Dennett. The land mass called Isla de Sangre is entirely a product of my imagination. I could not even begin to specify the conditions under which even the most fecund and far-flung Florida Key might come to resemble the extravagant ecosystem depicted in these pages. But fiction is, and always will be, stranger than truth.